of France and looking for a place to settle in Somerset, the county she grew up in. A journalist and travel writer for many publications, she has worked as an agony aunt and a restaurant critic. She was a teacher at a girls' school in Northern Kenya and has also written a weekly column from Los Angeles about her attempts to become a Hollywood scriptwriter. She is married to film producer Peter La Terrière and they have two children. This is her fourth novel.

For automatic updates on Daisy Waugh, visit HarperCollins.co.uk and register for AuthorTracker.

Also by Daisy Waugh:

A Small Town in Africa
The New You Survival Kit
Ten Steps to Happiness

DAISY WAUGH

Bed of Roses

HarperCollins*Publishers*

HarperCollins*Publishers*
77–85 Fulham Palace Road,
Hammersmith, London W6 8JB

www.harpercollins.co.uk

A Paperback Original 2005
1

A catalogue record for this book
is available from the British Library

ISBN 0 00 716819 5

Set in Sabon by Palimpsest Book Production Limited,
Polmont, Stirlingshire

Printed and bound in Great Britain by
Clays Ltd, St Ives plc

ACKNOWLEDGEMENTS

Many thanks to Anthea Donald. Thanks to Sarah Waters and all the staff at Kingston St Mary Primary School; Judith Furseland and all the staff at Lydeard St Lawrence Primary School; Jill Hodson and Father Donald Reece at St Stephen's Primary School. For the sake of moving the story along I have taken liberties with some of the drier information I was given, and I certainly apologise for any irritation that might cause. Thanks also to Sarah MacHattie, Fiona McIntosh, Helen Johnstone, Jenny Wilson, Honey Thomas, Eliza Waugh, Teresa Waugh and Nick Holmes.

Special thanks to Clare Alexander, Lynne Drew and Maxine Hitchcock.

Extra special thanks to Imogen, the best chatter in Britain.

Extra, extra special thanks to Peter, Panda and zuperzonic Zebedee.

Stretchy Matilda/Miss Marple/Mata Hari/
Lady Marchmain/Fatso-Crasher/
Retina Sputnik/Beauty/Mega-Dud/Genius/

. . . Panda Sarah de Sales La Terrière,

This one's for you. With all my love.

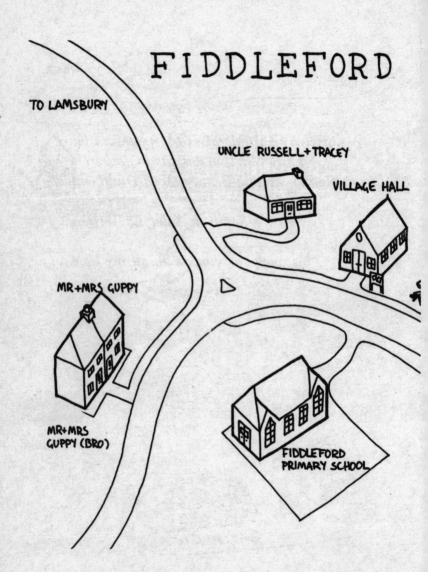

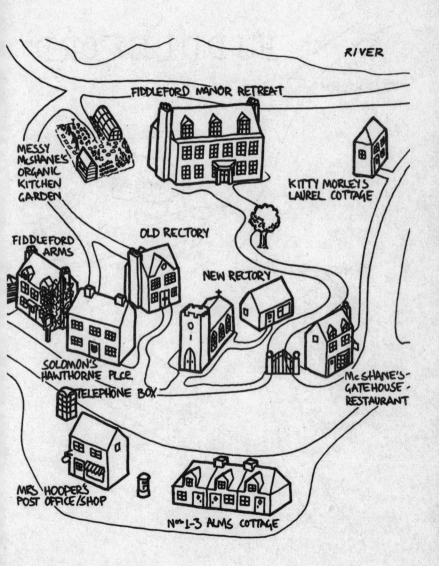

RIVER

FIDDLEFORD MANOR RETREAT

MESSY McSHANE'S ORGANIC KITCHEN GARDEN

KITTY MORLEY'S LAUREL COTTAGE

OLD RECTORY

FIDDLEFORD ARMS

NEW RECTORY

SOLOMON'S HAWTHORNE PLCE.

TELEPHONE BOX

McSHANE'S GATEHOUSE RESTAURANT

MRS HOOPER'S POST OFFICE/SHOP

Nos 1-3 ALMS COTTAGE

PART ONE

1

So. That's where the story begins. With Fanny Flynn and
her ghosts, and Brute the dog, and an ancient Morris Minor
half-filled with all their belongings, pulling up outside
number 2 Old Alms Cottages, in the village of Fiddleford,
near the market town of Lamsbury, deep in the heart of
England's south-west.

Fanny's new home is in the centre of the village, beside
the post office/shop and opposite Fiddleford's fourteenth-
century church. It is a few minutes' walk from the pub and
the primary school where she will be teaching, and within
shouting distance of the excellent Gatehouse Restaurant.
From the Alms Cottage front door, if she cranes her neck,
Fanny can see not only the restaurant but, right beside it,
the notorious, grand old iron gates of the Fiddleford Manor
Retreat, behind which so many disgraced public figures have
withdrawn to lick wounds and rebuild images.

It is April, bright and warm; the first morning in many
for the sun to shine and the year's first believable indication
that winter is moving on. Fanny and Brute scramble down
from the van. They stretch, dog and mistress, as engagingly
compact, vital and untidy as each other. Fanny breathes in

the spring-like air, glances across at the press people lolling beneath the famous gates, and waves. They gaze morosely back, having long ago made it a sort of Cool Club rule to be disdainful with the villagers.

'Bit rude, eh Brute?' she says vaguely. 'Go and bite.'

Brute, moronic but good-natured, sits on Fanny's feet in gay confusion, and dribbles.

Number 2 Old Alms Cottages is a minuscule affair. It's in the middle of a row of three two-hundred-year-old red stone terraced cottages, all of them empty. It has a single room and a bathroom upstairs, a single room with a kitchen downstairs and ceilings so low that the landlord has waited two years to find a tenant small enough to fit in. Fanny, at five foot three inches, fits the house as well as any modern human could hope to.

She stands in front of it now, jingling her new keys, pausing for a brief, thoughtful moment before launching on to this next new chapter of her many-chaptered life. She notices the faint, sour smell of old urine (old paparazzi hacks' urine, as it happens; with the pub being a few minutes' walk away, and the cottages empty, they often pee against her garden fence). She notices the paint-chipped, dirty-brown front door; the missing roof tiles; the sprawling ivy all but obscuring the single window upstairs – and feels a familiar rush of excitement.

New house. New job. New challenges. Another beginning. There is nothing quite like a new beginning, Fanny thinks – and she should know. This time, she tells herself (she mutters to Brute, still sitting on her feet), this time she is going to stick around to make it work. She is going to make roots. This small house and this fine spring day are to mark the beginning of Fanny Flynn's new life. Her real life.

She laughs out loud. *As if*. And immediately resents herself for it. 'Not bloody funny,' she says aloud, shunting Brute off her feet as if it were all his fault. 'Thirty-four years old next month. Thirty-four. Thirty-bloody-*four*. At this rate I'm going to wind up old and alone, and I'll be dead and rotting for a fortnight before anyone even notices the stink. Got to stop farting around.'

Truth is, Fanny is growing jaded. After eleven years of wandering from place to place, picking up jobs and boyfriends on passionate whims and then passionately dropping them again, she is in danger of running out of mojo, or worse still, of becoming a caricature of her ebullient, spontaneous younger self. She longs to find a job or a man – or an unquenchable passion for woodcarving (but preferably a man). She longs to find something which might give her a little meaning, or at the very least might persuade her to stay still.

Last November she was once again focusing her search for meaning on the very large Jobs section of the *Times Educational Supplement*, when her eye fell upon the advertisement for Fiddleford Church of England Primary School. It had, she thought, an engagingly desperate ring to it:

TO START AS SOON AS POSSIBLE.

Successful applicants should ideally have some previous experience as a Head or Deputy (although this is not essential) . . .

Perfect, she thought. Why not? A tiny village school, a challenge, a small and friendly community, a place where old-fashioned rural values might mean something, to someone – or something. Anything. Besides which Fanny had lived in many places before, but she had never lived in a village. And she had never been a head teacher. Perhaps, she explained to herself last November, perhaps those are the anchors which have been missing from my life . . .

Fiddleford Church of England Primary School opened its gates in 1854 with over a hundred pupils and has been shrinking steadily ever since. Now it has only thirty-eight pupils, and thanks to a damning report from OFSTED has been put into 'Special Measures'; promised a dollop of extra money by the LEA (Local Education Authority) and been given two years in which to improve itself, or else.

Mrs Thomas, the outgoing head, never had any intention of rising to such a challenge. Having called in sick with sneezes almost every day for the best part of three years, she immediately applied for early retirement on the grounds of stress-related ill health. By the time Fanny's application arrived she was killing time, waiting for a replacement so she could sidle away from the problem for ever.

But running a Special Measures school, in a small village deep in the middle of nowhere, is not an occupation very high on many people's Must-Do lists. By the time Fanny's application arrived, Mrs Thomas was growing impatient; there had only been one other applicant for the job. And that was the school's deputy head, the pathologically idle Robert White.

When Robert threw his hat into the ring, the remaining six governors called an urgent, secret meeting, during which they unanimously agreed to pretend the application had never been received, which was clearly impossible, since he had hand delivered it to them himself. They had hoped he might take enough umbrage to resign. He did not. Not quite. Lazy sod. He knew which side his bread was buttered, how hard it would be for them to get rid of him, and how hard it would be, as the long-standing deputy head of a newly 'failing' school, for him to get a job in the same salary band elsewhere.

Besides which, he'd taken a great shine to the school's very young new dinner lady/caretaker, Tracey Guppy, the thought of whose white-fleshed, wide-eyed innocence kept him awake for at least three delirious minutes every night.

The situation of head had remained vacant for yet another month. The school had staggered along. Governors began to wonder whether Robert White might have to be appointed after all. And then along came the letter from Fanny.

Fanny is, in fact, a very good teacher; intelligent and kind and instinctive – and reasonably industrious, if never yet quite truly dedicated. Children love her. And so do her numerous referees. She got the job.

When the summer term starts tomorrow morning, thirty-three-year-old Fanny Flynn will be the youngest and possibly the least experienced headmistress in the history of the south-west. There are plenty at the Lamsford Education Authority who sincerely hope she may also be its least successful. At which point, of course, and with minimum loss of face, they could save a lot of money and close the wretched school down for good.

2

The telephone is already ringing when Fanny pushes open
the Alms Cottage front door, so she is less demoralised than
she might have been by the pervasive stench which hits her,
of damp and human piss. The landlord said he would clean
the place up before she arrived, but the peeling seventies
wallpaper still lies in mouldy heaps on the carpet, and she
has to climb over two years' worth of junk mail and two
dead mice to get into the sitting room. He obviously hasn't
been near the place.

In any case Fanny's dealt with enough landlords over the
years to be surprised by none of them any more, and Mr
Ian Guppy's creepy, half-simple manner when he showed her
round in March led her to expect the worst. She has arrived
in Fiddleford equipped with dustbin bags, disinfectant etc.,
and even some large pots of white paint. She enjoys the
process of transforming a house into a home. It lends her
New Beginnings a little added emphasis, which – after so
many – is never unwelcome.

She clambers over the rubble and the mouse corpses and
dives for the telephone – a telephone, she can't help noticing,
which is so old it might have been fashionable again, except

that, like the ceiling, curtains, windows and walls, it's stained the patchy yellow-brown of ancient nicotine.

'Hello?' She holds the receiver a few centimetres from her ear, for obvious reasons, but is nonetheless half-deafened by the explosion of childish screams which comes blasting out. 'Hello?' Fanny shouts above them. 'Hello?'

An efficient feminine voice glides smoothly over the surrounding racket: 'Oh, lovely. You're there. I'm so pleased. I'm your neighbour, Jo Maxwell McDonald. Welcome to Fiddleford!'

Fanny recognises the name. General Maxwell McDonald, Jo Maxwell McDonald's ancient father-in-law, is on Fiddleford Primary School's board of governors for reasons neither he nor the school can quite remember. He participated most fulsomely during her interview, grilling her about the high turnover of jobs on her CV and then refusing, unlike all the others, to overlook her irrelevant replies. Fanny has developed a particular way of speaking during her job interviews, a sort of jargon-filled auto-lingo which kicks in as soon as the questions begin. She doesn't understand why it works, but it does. One way or another – partly, of course, because of the shortage of teachers everywhere, partly because Fanny tends to be attracted to unpopular jobs – she has never yet failed in an interview.

'I feel,' she said to the General, 'that multifaceted qualifications are essential for any modern head teacher in this day and age and I'm proud to have experience in a diverse cross section of educational establishments, enabling me to bring to Fiddleford a knowledge and understanding of children from a variety of backgrounds—'

'Hmm? Yes yes, I dare say. But didn't it occur to you you might learn something from occasionally staying in the same place?'

'I needed to balance objectives,' Fanny said solemnly. 'The

objectives of the students, first and foremost, and secondly the objectives of my own career development—'

'What? You're the restless type, are you?'

Fanny hesitated. She said, 'Erm, no.'

'You've not spent a year in the same place since you qualified!'

Fanny said, 'Yes. Well. As I was explaining—'

'Do you envisage spending longer than a year at Fiddleford?'

'Certainly I do. I envisage spending many years here, helping to establish and nurture a learning culture and environment which—'

'Mind you, that's probably just as well, of course,' he interrupted, ignoring her reply. 'Because the government *says* it's given us this time to improve. Ha. When we all know perfectly well –' he glanced around at his fellow board members, who were all suddenly staring very hard at their notes, 'what they're *actually* giving us is this time *not* to improve. Isn't that right? So they can feel quite justified in closing the ruddy place down. Thereby saving themselves a great deal of money. And frankly, Miss Flynn, with our track record I can't say I blame them . . . Had you thought of that possibility, Miss Flynn?'

Fanny blinked. Of course she had.

'Which gets you off pretty much scot-free, if I'm not mistaken. To continue your –' he glanced down at her CV once again, 'really – admirably adventurous life, as per before. With a short but impressive stint as a head teacher under your belt thrown in. Isn't that right, Miss Flynn?'

And all she could do was blink, and blink again. 'That's not true,' she said eventually, but she was blushing because of course, in a way, when he put it like that . . .

In the end Mrs Thomas (for fear of losing their one and only candidate) intervened to shut him up. Fanny, full of relief, and also guilt, threw the General a shamefaced sideways glance and caught him scowling at the outgoing headmistress with such intent ferocity that for most of the rest of the interview she'd had to struggle very hard not to laugh.

So Fanny remembers the General with a mixture of awe, annoyance and some affectionate respect. More to the point she knows all about the beautiful, businesslike daughter-in-law Jo Maxwell McDonald, and her ravishingly attractive husband Charlie, because she has read about them in magazines. Since opening their famous Retreat a few years ago Charlie and Jo have both become minor celebrities themselves.

Anyway, Fanny isn't used to speaking to people she's read about in newspapers. She's a little disconcerted. 'Hello, new neighbour,' she says goofily. 'How lovely. Thank you.'

'That is Fanny Flynn, isn't it?' Jo says briskly. 'Our new head teacher? Is that Fanny Flynn?'

'Yes. Sorry. Being silly. Yes, this is Fanny.'

'Only I thought it might all be terribly chaotic, since you've just arrived, and I wondered if you might like a bit of lunch . . . Plus I've got a small proposition to put to you. Hope you don't mind.'

'Ooh. Very intriguing!' Immediately Fanny pictures herself tipping up at the famous Manor, still in her worn-out combats and dirty trainers, her shaggy mop of curly hair unwashed for over a week. She imagines sitting down to eat at an enormous mahogany dining table; Fanny Flynn (and Brute of course), Jo and Charlie Maxwell McDonald – and whichever glamorous, wicked celebrities they have staying up there today.

But then she looks around her at the peeling wallpaper. She notices the skirting board at her feet is sprouting mushrooms. 'I'd love to, and I'd love to hear your proposition, whatever it may be, but really I can't, not today,' she says sadly. 'There's so much to do in here, and term starts tomorrow. I really ought to—'

'Plus actually, while you're on the line, I should remind you about the limbo evening on Friday night. You've heard about it, haven't you?'

'The limbo evening? No. I must admit—'

'That's what was worrying me, you see. I put a thing through your door but perhaps you haven't had time— It's in the village hall. Mrs Hooper – you'll meet her, she lives at the post office – she's brought in a man all the way from Exeter to teach us, and I'm terrified no one's going to turn up.'

'Oh, I'll come,' Fanny says cheerfully. 'Why not? What time does it start?'

'Six thirty. Very early. Everything starts terribly early in Fiddleford, God knows why.'

'Keeps us out of the pub, I suppose.'

'Hmm?'

'Nothing.'

'In any case, it should be a good opportunity for you to—' But her children's playful yells have by now reached a pitch which even their highly focused mother can no longer ignore. 'Oh God, hang on a moment—'

Fanny peers at her crop of mushrooms and listens idly while Jo, with stirring management skills, brokers a moment's silence from her two-and-a-half-year-old twins.

'Sorry, Fanny.' She comes back to the telephone. 'Where was I?'

'A good opportunity, I think.'

'Exactly. It's such a good opportunity for you to meet people. Tickets are only £3 and you have to bring your own drink, but don't worry about that because we'll be bringing plenty. And £1 goes towards repairing the disabled ramp in the churchyard. So it's all in a good cause. What are you up to right now? Shall I come and fetch you in the car? You won't want to run the gauntlet of that horrible wolf-pack at the gate, and lunch is more or less on the table. Why don't I come down and pick you up?'

'No, really, Jo. I can't—'

'Don't be ridiculous. It's no trouble at all. I'll be down in three minutes. And it's vegetarian, by the way. It's always vegetarian with the children. Obviously. So no need to worry about that!'

3

There are no wicked celebrities in Fiddleford Manor's worn and welcoming old kitchen that day; only the two rumbustious children and the elegantly jean-clad Jo, looking just as she does in the magazines, Fanny thinks. Possibly slightly better. She is long, lean and fit, clear eyed and clear skinned, and her sunkissed, clean brown hair is cut into a perfectly understated short, shaggy bob. She makes Fanny feel short, and as though she ought to have taken that bath this morning.

'No one else? Only us?' Fanny asks, peering hopefully round the corner of the door. But Jo explains (and she is infuriatingly discreet about who's staying) that Retreat guests usually pay extra to eat in a private dining room at Grey McShane's Gatehouse Restaurant at the bottom of the drive. 'Thank goodness!' she laughs. 'In the early days we never had any privacy at all!'

So while Fanny sits at the large oak table pushing salt-free kidney-bean salad from one side of her plate to the other and feeling dirty, there are only the twins to distract Jo from providing an uninterrupted run-down of who's who in the village.

'*So,*' asks Jo with a malicious glint in her eye, 'what do you make of your new landlord, Mr Guppy?'

Fanny's met Ian Guppy only once, back in March, when he showed her round the cottage. He is tiny – hardly taller than she is, with greased-back jet black hair and a gypsy-weathered face. She pictures him, leaning his filthy trousers against the dilapidated Alms Cottage kitchen sink and leering at her. She agreed to pay rent well over the odds solely so she wouldn't have to continue talking to him. 'Horrible,' she says bluntly. 'What a creep.'

Jo nods. 'And you should meet the wife. They bought those Old Alms Cottages off my father-in-law in the early seventies, and I don't think they've done a thing to them since. But one of these days,' she smiles, 'if I have anything to do with it, we're going to get them back.'

'Really? Why?'

'We need them, for the business. We need the office space.'

She and Jo are more or less the same age and yet Fanny – with her lack of twins, lack of thriving business, lack of representation in the tabloids, lack of outstandingly beautiful Queen Anne manor house, lack of direction, or of any serious acquisitive urges, lack of husband, lack of inches in the leg – feels a whole evolutionary species behind her. By the time the sugar-free herbal teas arrive Fanny's spirit is buckling. Jo still hasn't mentioned her proposition, and Fanny can't help wondering what she could possibly do for Jo Maxwell McDonald that Jo Maxwell McDonald couldn't do better for herself.

'. . . I don't know how she finds the time to organise it, what with the coffee ads, and all the boozing,' Jo burbles on, 'but the Fiddleford Dramatic Society is surprisingly good, thanks to her. They did *The Importance of Being Earnest* last summer. It was actually very funny. We had the soap star Julia Biggleton staying with us at the Retreat at the time.

Remember her? We had her playing Lady Bracknell down in the village hall! You should have seen the press! She's the one—'

'Do you know, Jo,' Fanny bursts out, suddenly desperate to keep her own end up, 'that tomorrow, when I start work, I'm going to be the youngest primary school head teacher in the whole of the south-west of England.'

'Hmm?'

And then Fanny blushes, and laughs. 'Crikey. Did I really say that?'

'Well, actually,' says Jo, not missing a beat, 'I'm glad you mention it, because it's just the sort of thing I wanted to talk to you about. Basically, Fanny— Have you got a minute?' She doesn't wait to be assured. She tells Fanny about her background in PR. 'Before I married Charlie,' she says, 'and became this dreadful sort of country bumpkin—'

'You!' interrupts Fanny with a burst of laughter. 'A country bumpkin?'

Jo shrugs. She knows she isn't really. 'I used to work in a big PR company in London. Used to represent nightclubs, restaurants, personalities. All very glamorous, I suppose. In retrospect . . . Anyway, it's pretty much how I – we – Charlie and I came to be doing this. I mean, it's one of the reasons why we thought of turning this place into a celebrity retreat.'

'I know,' Fanny smiles. 'I've read all about it. Like most people in Britain.'

'Right.' Jo nods. Smiles. 'But now the Retreat more or less runs itself and I want to broaden the business out a bit. Take on new clients.' She pauses for a small breath, leans a little closer. 'And what I want to do now, Fanny, is to use my public-relations skills, absolutely free of charge, to help you and your school!'

'Oh. That's very kind,' Fanny says vaguely. The idea doesn't excite her much.

'Not kind. Absolutely mutually beneficial. If I can show potential clients what I can do with a relatively high-profile, local issue like this one, well—'

'It's just that public relations isn't an especially high priority – for me, anyway. I think what we need—'

'Everything needs public relations, Fanny. Especially a school that's just been named-and-shamed! Unless you can persuade people that the school's turning itself around you're going to get every bright parent pulling their children out, and you'll be left with nothing but the dregs. I mean, you know. Not the *dregs*, but the—'

'I know what you mean.'

'Right. And you'll be sunk. Finished. Not only that, the General's convinced that what they really want is to close the place down. But it's the heart of the village, Fanny. And, speaking selfishly for a minute, I'd like the twins to go there one day. I certainly don't want it closing.'

'Of course you don't.'

'See? And I mean here *you* are, this young whizz-kid head teacher—'

Fanny laughs out loud. 'Hardly!'

'—Has anyone told the press? Of course they haven't. And yet it's the sort of thing local media goes mad for.'

'Oh!' Fanny says quickly. 'Oh, no. No, thanks.'

But Jo is already up and rifling through the dresser for a pen. 'Plus with you being pretty and so on. They're going to adore you.'

'No. No, I really don't—'

'Trust me, Fanny. I know what I'm talking about. That's if—' She stops suddenly and turns back to Fanny. 'I take it you are serious about saving our school?'

'What? Of course I am.'

'I mean, you do realise, don't you, how much people around here really care about that school surviving?'

'Of course I do.'

'Well, then!'

'It's just—'

'What?'

'It's just—' She offers an unconvincing laugh. 'You know, great if you want to put out a few nice stories about the school. That would be great. Just keep me out of it. I don't like personal— There are people I don't want—' Fanny stops again. But she really doesn't want to be drawn into details. 'Basically, I don't want my face in the paper.'

'Why? What are you hiding from?'

'No one. Nothing. I didn't say that.'

Jo laughs. 'I'm sorry. I don't understand.'

'Plus I've got a lot of unpaid parking tickets . . .' Fanny lapses into gloomy silence. She turns away from Jo's neat, determined face, to the open kitchen window. The birds are singing out there and a delicious, soft breeze is blowing through the giant cedar tree. She gazes out at the park and, beyond it, to the afternoon sun on the river and the distant tower of Fiddleford's church, and her old terrors seem briefly very distant, even a little ridiculous.

The desire to be outside, on the other hand, alone, striding through that fresh, bright grass, is altogether more immediate; in fact, it's suddenly quite overwhelming. She stands up. 'Anyway,' she says, 'I should be getting off. I've got a lot to do. Come on, Brute! . . . And thanks so much for a lovely lunch . . . It was really . . . absolutely . . .' But she can't quite bring herself to finish off with the customary 'delicious': 'Very nice to meet you and the twins.' Fanny is already reaching for the door.

'I'll make a couple of calls then,' Jo says, standing up. 'Get them writing something positive about our school for a change.'

'But please – try and keep me out of it.'

'I'll try, but I can't promise.' Jo giggles suddenly. 'You obviously hadn't been warned.'

'What about?'

'Most people refuse to eat lunch here any more.'

'They do? Why?'

'Because of the food, of course. Too healthy for them! By the way,' Jo shouts after her. 'Hope you haven't too many skeletons in the cupboard. Along with all the parking tickets! They'll be coming after you now you're going to be famous.'

'Not funny,' mutters Fanny. 'Not funny at all.'

But Jo is spooning soya into her twins' neatly opened mouths. She doesn't hear.

Fanny calls Louis, her oldest and closest friend, as soon as she gets in from the Manor. She leaves a message on his machine, sounding more cheerful than she feels, emphasising the quaintly rustic attractions of her new village, and inviting – or possibly imploring – him to come down for the weekend.

After that she feeds Brute and sets to work. She works for several hours without stopping, with the same ferocious energy with which she does everything: teaches, flirts, drinks, and even once fell in love. She pulls down the nicotine-stained net curtains, washes the windows, rips away what is left of the wallpaper, scrapes off the mushrooms and throws the junk mail out. She scrubs the skirting boards with disinfectant, and the 1950s oven, the 1950s kitchen sink, the 1950s basin and bath upstairs, so that they dazzle with shiny-white retro-chic. She pulls up the dank, sick-coloured carpets and discovers there are oak floorboards underneath.

By eight o'clock she has unloaded everything from the Morris Minor except what's on the roof: her solitary piece of furniture, a vile, thirty-year-old reproduction dressing table left to her (along with the car itself) by her late grand-mother and which she longs, one day, to be heartless enough to throw out. She is standing in her front garden beside the mountain of discarded carpet, gazing at the van and puzzling over how to get that final piece inside when she spots two magnificent-looking men strolling down the village street towards her. She recognises them both at once.

Charlie Maxwell McDonald – owner of the Fiddleford Manor Retreat, son to the truculent General, father to the rumbustious twins and husband to Perfect Jo, tall, dark and absurdly handsome – is, Fanny realises with a thrill of excitement, like his wife, every bit as good-looking as his photographs. He has his hands in the pockets of his old black jeans and the buttons of his pale cotton shirt half-undone . . . And he is muttering to a man even taller than he is, and even darker, with hooded eyes and wild hair and a great black coat which swings open behind him: a man whose press photographs do him no justice at all. Grey McShane, the notorious tramp-turned-poet-turned-pin-up-proprietor of Fiddleford's Gatehouse Restaurant, is possibly the best-looking man Fanny Flynn has ever laid eyes on. She feels, suddenly, as though she's walked on to the set of a soft-porn movie. Any second now, God bless them both, the men are going to start stripping their clothes off.

'Hi there,' Charlie says, drawing to a halt in front of her.

She stares at him. Tries to stop the soundtrack in her head and manages, somehow, not to smirk.

'You must be Fanny Flynn,' he says. 'I'm Charlie Maxwell McDonald. From the Retreat. And this is Grey . . .' He looks at her curiously. 'My wife thought you might need some help unloading things. Are you all right?'

Fanny laughs. And hates herself for it.

'What's funny?' asks Grey.

Fanny says, 'Nothing. It was just, you know, coming towards me there.' She grins at them. 'Had to pinch myself.

Thought I was dreaming!' Clearly they don't understand. 'I mean I thought I was in a magazine . . . Or something. I mean – not a magazine, but a – you're quite a striking couple . . . I mean, not couple. But together . . .'

The job barely takes a minute, and afterwards both turn down her offer of a drink. When they leave her alone in her newly scrubbed cottage she feels unreasonably let down. Lonely. Did she flirt too much? Probably. She usually does. She can't help imagining them now: Charlie and exquisite Jo, having a drink together in their exquisite house, putting their exquisitely rumbustious twins to bed; and then Grey, rampaging around the kitchen of his celebrated restaurant, lovingly preparing an exquisitely delicious dinner for his no doubt exquisite wife.

It is only half past eight. She hasn't eaten (there is nothing to eat) and Louis still hasn't rung, but she has had enough of today. She picks up a worn-out file with the exhausting words 'NEW JOBS: APPLICATIONS/ ACCEPTED ETC.' scrawled across the front, pours herself a dusty tumbler of red wine and takes them up with her to bed. She will have a bath in the morning.

4

Fanny Flynn met her husband while they were waiting to be served at the bar of a pub just outside Buxton and they fell in love at once. There and then. Six weeks later they had treated themselves to a spontaneous Wedding Day package in Reno, Nevada.

But the marriage turned sour within moments of their leaving the Wedding Chapel. It ended abruptly, three bitter months after it never should have begun.

They were fighting as normal when he suddenly broke the single civilising rule left between them. He lashed out. He kicked her in the stomach – and fled, tears in his eyes, jointly owned credit card in his hands. 'I'll come back for you,' he said wildly. 'I will. When it's safe for us. OK? And I'll always be with you, baby, in my heart. Because I love you. I always will.'

'You're a nutter,' she said in amazement, seeing it all – there and then – in a flash of horrible clarity. He wasn't poetic, he was insane. And she passed out.

It was Louis who found her – unconscious, blood from her damaged womb congealing on the kitchen floor, and the husband who loved her nowhere to be seen. Louis laid her down in the back of his van. She slid from side to side between dust sheets, tyre jacks, paint pots and coils of rope. (He was working as a freelance decorator at the time.) He crashed every light between her house and the hospital, but he probably saved her life.

That was in 1994, eleven years ago now, and he hasn't come back for her. She's moved many times. (Too many; since the marriage she has found it very difficult to stay still.) She moved from Buxton to London, four or five times in London, then from London to a refugee camp in northern Kenya, where she worked for a year, and from there to Lichfield, from Lichfield to Mexico City, where she taught businessmen to speak English; from Mexico City to Weston-Super-Mare, and now to Fiddleford. She tries to forget him. Yet, still, wherever she is, whenever it's dark and she's alone, the questions flit through her mind: Has he followed? Is he out there? Is he looking in?

She never mentions him to anyone, except to Louis, but she believes that he sometimes tries to communicate. And it frightens her. There was an anonymous valentine card in Lichfield: a picture of roses speckled with yellow-brown drops of dried blood, and tucked inside it a message linking American Imperialism with Cryogenics, with Fanny's 'Frozen Passion, unstarched by eternality'. She threw the card in the bin.

Then in London she thought she saw him leaning against a postbox outside her flat. She closed the windows, locked them, and called Louis, who rushed over on his new motor-bike. By the time Louis arrived the man was gone. He asked her if she had been certain. She wasn't, of course. But the following week Fanny moved yet again.

And finally, in Weston-Super-Mare, there was the puppy – sitting in a cardboard box and dumped inexplicably on her doorstep. She had picked it up, thought she smelt him

23

and gagged. But she was lonely. She kept the puppy – it was a cross between a golden Labrador and something mysterious. It was small and wiry, and it was very charming. She called him Brute. Now of course, except for Louis, Brute is probably her best friend in the world.

5

She wakes up having dreamt of him again, as she often does at the start of her New Beginnings. She dreams of him turning up at every new front door, with a stupid grin, as if she'd be pleased to see him, and a pathetic little offering – a box of cheap chocolates, a jigsaw puzzle – as if that would make up for it all. Usually, in her dreams, she doesn't let him into the house. But last night, for some reason, she did. He was coming through her door, stepping over her mushrooms, just as the alarm clock went off. So she wakes up in a nervous sweat. When she opens her eyes and looks around her new, small room, she remembers the day which lies ahead, and feels a lurch of a very different kind of terror. She springs out of bed.

For her first day at Fiddleford Primary Fanny puts on the clothes she always wears on the first few days of a new job; a newly washed knee-length denim skirt (her only skirt in the world) which, for the moment, fits like rubber, and a dark blue polo-neck jersey. The effect is unfussy, like everything about her; simple and attractive, quite sexy, and scruffy. Fanny always looks scruffy. She can't help it.

Feeling faintly sick with nerves she forces down half a

cup of black coffee (still no milk in the house), picks up her bag of heavy files, takes a deep breath and steps out from her little cottage, which smells of yesterday's disinfectant, and out into the sweet, fresh morning air of the village street.

The school is a small, russet stone Victorian building, pretty and symmetrical, with a broken bell tower in the middle, and just two large, arched windows at the front. Three gates open on to the front yard. The one on the right is marked BOYS, the one on the left, GIRLS. The middle one, non-specific, is the only one unlocked. Everyone uses it.

It's as pretty a little school, Fanny thinks as she draws up in front of it, as any little school could ever hope to be. She feels a swell of warm pride. It looks more like a school in a story book. Nothing too alarming could possibly happen inside such a place.

Children scurry around her, nudging each other and giggling. Fanny ignores them – for the moment. She looks at her feet. Doesn't want to speak to any parents just yet. Nor to anyone. She takes one more long, slow breath, mutters something to Brute about his wishing her luck, and pushes on, through the yard, up the path, into the central hall and right, to the door of the staff room. Pauses for a second. Opens it.

'Morning all!' she says, sounding unnaturally breezy.

The youngest head teacher in the south-west does not have a large staff to manage. There is Robert White, who wears a patchy beard and socks beneath open-toed sandals. He is the notoriously idle deputy head, still too idle to resign after being overlooked for promotion, but not, Fanny will soon discover, too idle to feel bitter and obstructive as a result of it. Robert teaches the younger class – when he turns up. There are the only two classes in the school.

There is also a part-time teacher's assistant, Mrs Tardy;

an elderly secretary, Mrs Haywood, who entertains the children occasionally (or so legend has it) by popping her glass eye in and out; and a dinner lady playground attendant who doubles up as caretaker.

The playground attendant/caretaker was a pupil here herself not so long ago, and she still has a brother and several cousins at the school. She is Tracey Guppy, the nineteen-year-old daughter of Fanny's landlord, Ian, the same girl who used to keep Robert White awake at night (his attention has shifted now to a girl in the Lamsbury Safeways). Tracey Guppy doesn't speak to Ian or to her mother, who threw her out of the house when she was fifteen. She's been living ever since with her Uncle Russell, wheelchair bound as a result of emphysema. They live together in a council-owned bungalow directly opposite the school.

'Morning all!' Fanny says breezily.

But only half the staff is yet present: only Linda Tardy, the part-time teacher's assistant, and Robert White the lazy-bones deputy head.

At the sight of the dog, Robert's shoulders jolt in surprise, making the Lemsip he has been blowing to cool spill on to his sock-covered toe. 'Ow!' he says irritably, and then, apparently too preoccupied with the accident to look or stand up, adds a grudging and slightly pert 'Good morning, Miss Flynn' in the direction of the carpet.

He places the mug of Lemsip on the floor, lifts the damaged sandal on to his knee and carefully undoes the buckle.

'No one else here yet?' Fanny asks brightly, looking from Robert White to Linda Tardy and back again. Linda, who is trying to swallow a mouthful of the same fish-paste sandwich she has vowed not to touch before lunch, holds a hand in front of her jaw and shakes her head.

'It's usually a bit slow on the first day,' mumbles Robert,

removing the sandal and unrolling the sock. 'And I'm afraid to say I'm only really popping in myself. I'm a bit under the weather.' He examines his toe, which looks bony and a little damp, but otherwise undamaged, and stands, at last, to arrange the sock on a nearby heater. 'I thought I should put a nose in, so to speak.' He smiles at her, keeping his pink lips closed. He is skinny, in his mid-forties, with eyes of the palest blue, and thin sandy-coloured hair cut into a well-kept bob. He is surprisingly tall when he stands up, Fanny notices; over six foot, or he would be if he pulled his shoulders back. 'I'll nip back to bed later,' he continues, 'but I wanted to say welcome . . . So –' with a burst of energy he flaps open one of the long thin arms and winks at her, 'welcome!' he says.

'Thank you.' It is unfortunate for Robert, especially since this is their first meeting (Robert having been off sick on the two previous occasions she visited the school and off sulking when the other governors were interviewing her for the job), but there's almost nothing Fanny finds more irritating than a man with a well-kept bob, open-toed sandals and a cold. 'Who's going to take your class then?'

Robert looks taken aback. 'Linda,' he says, as if it's obvious.

'You mean Mrs Tardy?'

'Linda always does it. They're ever so used to her. The kiddies like you, don't they, Linda?'

'They like it with me because we always do the fun stuff,' Linda Tardy chuckles, 'and then when Robert's back he has to do all the catching up for us, don't you, Robbie?'

'I do my best.'

'Though generally,' she adds, 'there's more to catch up on than he can manage. Isn't that right, Robert? With you being poorly so much . . . But they're lovely little children, and

28

that's what counts. Isn't that right, Robert? They're super kids.'

'But Mrs Tardy,' says Fanny, 'if you don't mind me being frank—'

'Oh, say what you like, dear. Don't worry about me!'

'But you're not a teacher.'

'Oh, I know that, dear. It says it loud and clear in my pay packet every month!' She rocks with laughter.

'Well . . .' Fanny hesitates. It's a bit early to be throwing her weight around but she feels she can't let it pass. She turns to Robert White. 'I think,' she says politely, 'with the children being so behind, and with Mrs Tardy tending, as she says, to stick with the fun stuff – it might be a good idea to get a supply teacher in, don't you?'

'It isn't ordinarily a deputy's duty,' he says, 'to administrate that sort of thing.'

'Isn't it? Wasn't it? Well, it is now!' Fanny forces a laugh. She's not used to this; ordering grown men about. It's awkward. 'Anyway, Robert, Mr White, to be frank – you don't exactly look like you're dying . . . Couldn't you stick around, now you've made it this far? As it's my first day. Would you mind?'

'I had no idea,' he says pertly, 'that our esteemed employers now insisted we should be dying before we're allowed time off sick.'

'Oh, come on.'

'And the last thing I want is to feel responsible for the kiddies catching my germs.'

'Children,' Fanny says, 'are pretty resilient.'

'In my experience, parents tend to be not unduly impressed by the sort of staff who insist on spreading their germs around. And if the parents complain—'

'Yes, but they won't,' she says.

There are blotches of pink at his cheek-bones. 'But they might,' he says.

'Well,' there are blotches at hers, too, 'then I'm willing to risk that.'

A long silence. It's a battle of wills. She may be young and small and new and female and disconcertingly attractive, but it begins fuzzily to occur to Robert that she might not be the pushover Mrs Thomas had been. They stare at each other, until finally, with a huffy, superior shrug, Robert nods.

'Thank you,' Fanny grins at him. 'You're very kind. Thank you very much.' Without another word he picks up his briefcase, bulging with exercise books he has failed to mark over the Easter holidays, and leaves the room.

With a great sigh of relief Fanny throws herself into the beaten-up, brown-covered armchair beside Mrs Tardy's. 'Sorry,' she says. 'That wasn't at all how I'd intended to begin.'

'The thing is, what I've learnt in my experience, Miss Flynn, we all have to begin somehow,' replies Linda Tardy nonsensically, but kindly, patting Fanny on the knee. 'But you mustn't mind Robert. He has his ways. And the main thing is, we've got some really super kids here at Fiddleford.' She nods to herself. Safe on safe ground. 'That's the main thing. Super kids. That's right, isn't it, dear? Now then,' slowly she heaves herself up from her seat, 'we've got a few minutes. How about I make you a nice cup of coffee?'

'I'd love some coffee,' Miss Flynn says. 'And please, Mrs Tardy, call me Fanny.'

Linda Tardy hesitates. 'It's a strange name though, isn't it, Miss Flynn?' She gives one of her bosomy chuckles. 'Not one you'd wish on a girl these days. Not really. You never thought of changing it, I suppose?'

6

The school hall is light and airy, with worn wooden floors, high ceilings and enormous windows set high in white-painted brick walls. Like the two classrooms on either side of it, it is clean and handsome but strangely bare; there are hardly any children's paintings anywhere, or charts, or wall displays. Robert's classroom has nothing at all except a laminated sign which reads:

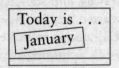

Today is . . .
January

Fanny sits, for the moment, swinging her feet over the edge of the school hall's tiny stage and feeling a mite peculiar. The children, all thirty-seven of them, all cross-legged on the linoleum before her, gaze up, placidly expectant, each one entrusting their fate to her as if it were the most natural thing in the world, as if she had a clue what she was really meant to be doing with it.

This is her first assembly and, although there will be complaints about it later, she has decided on the spur of that moment to tell the students of the shadow which hangs over their school's future. It seems only fair, she thinks, that they should know as much as she does. 'So you see,' she says emphatically, 'I don't think we've got all that much time. And unless we can *totally* and *completely* –' in her zeal her shoulders, her entire body, give an unconscious leap of enthusiasm, and the children chortle, they like her; children always do, '*transform* this place, work some kind of *miracle* and somehow improve every single thing about it, well then—'

The door is kicked open by a gangly boy in loose-fitting Nike nylon. He stands facing her, arms crossed and legs apart. He can't be more than eleven or he wouldn't still be at the school, but he's tall for his age.

'O'right, miss?' he says. His voice is breaking.

'Thank you. I'm OK,' she says brightly. 'Why don't you sit down?'

'Eh?'

'"*Eh?*" . . . I said why don't you—'

'Yeah, I know. But what if I don't want to?'

Fanny looks at him briefly and shrugs. She turns back to the other children, leaving him standing there, bewildered, brimming with thwarted urges. 'So the thing is,' she continues, 'unless we all decide to make a *massive effort*—'

'And my mum says it's disgusting as well, because I know what your name is, and it's disgusting. Your name's Fanny.'

Fanny smiles. 'And what's your name?' she asks. There is something vaguely familiar about him.

'Never mind what my name is. I tell you it ain't John Thomas! At least I ain't called penis!'

A wave of uncertain laughter.

'That's very fanny,' she nods. More laughter. 'You are a fanny boy. Well done.' She's made a similar joke at every school she's ever worked at. 'We were talking about how a lot of influential people think this school is utterly useless and that unless we can prove them wrong, it may one day have to be closed down,' Fanny continues. 'Aren't you interested in that? Wouldn't you like to see the school close down for ever?'

'Of course I would.'

'Well, if you sit down and shut up you might get a few hints on how to bring it about.'

Fanny doesn't show her astonishment when he sits. She's good at that. Instead she leans forward. 'Basically,' she says conspiratorially, and without missing a beat, 'for those of us who want it *not* to close, this is the plan . . .'

They wait.

'John Thomas, you should pay attention of course, because you'll be wanting to do the opposite . . .'

That first morning goes well, she thinks. In spite of the local radio reporter who pitched up at break demanding to speak to her, claiming Jo Maxwell McDonald had assured him it would be OK. (Fanny finally agreed. She dispatched him with a harmless little interview, and managed, or so she believed, to make herself sound relatively professional. Incredibly professional actually, since every time the reporter had referred to Fiddleford's 'head teacher', she'd had to pause for a millisecond to work out who the hell he was talking about.) In any case the interview went out live, so she didn't have to suffer the discomfort of listening to it.

Her children, all seventeen who made up her class (and what a luxury that was!) seem bright, and for the most part, gratifyingly energised by the prospect of joining forces to save the school. They have peppered their morning's lessons with suggestions on ways to keep the place open.

Having kicked off with some sensible maths problems, and gazed, while they counted quietly on fingers and thumbs, around her barren white classroom, Fanny had suddenly burst out, 'Oh, it's horrible in here!'

There was a moment of astonished silence. They stared at her, and at her dog, vacantly wagging its tail against the leg of her desk. And laughed.

'Isn't it, though? Don't you think? It's like an operating theatre. We'll all drop dead from *boredom* if we sit in here a moment longer. What shall we do to brighten the place up?'

There followed a passionate class discussion, after which she set them to making a frieze of Fiddleford, an enormous one, with each pupil painting a part of the village they liked best.

It had been lovely. A lovely morning. Now her first lunch-hour is drawing to an end and she's gazing out of the window of her tiny, upstairs office feeling unusually pleased with herself. She can see her pupils racing around in the sunny playing fields, and beyond the children the village of Fiddleford nestling around its church – and beyond the village, the river and the cedar tree rising majestically from the Manor Retreat park. It's beautiful; the way the English country is meant to look.

She finds herself daring to wonder if this new job might indeed turn out to be the new beginning she has been hoping for. A possibility, she realises with a start, which had never seriously occurred to her until now. But she likes this little school, the pretty village, the good-looking neighbours, her tiny ivy-covered cottage . . . It is a peculiarly happy moment, immediately interrupted by a feeble tap on her office door.

'Come in, come in!' she cries bravely, since she's already caught a whiff of Lemsip and knows perfectly well who to expect. 'Hello, Mr White – Robert!' she smiles. There are little red marks around the edges of his nostrils. He looks pale and stubborn and intolerably self-pitying. 'Feeling any better? You look *much* better!'

Robert feels robbed of many things as he turns the corner into her office: robbed of this room and that desk, robbed of her salary, robbed of her job, and above all, above everything else, robbed of his right to spend the morning in bed. So he says nothing. He wraps his two hands around the hot mug of Lemsip, hunches his shoulders and regretfully shakes his head.

'Sit yourself down!' says Fanny, jumping up and pulling out a second chair.

With the two of them and Brute in the room, it's a struggle to make enough space. Robert stands by, shivering and watching, while Fanny heaves a battered filing cabinet to one side. 'I'm glad you came, actually,' she pants, 'I wanted to talk about the walls. Why are they so bare? Why is there nothing on your classroom walls?'

He's not interested in walls. 'The fact is, Miss Flynn—'

'For heaven's sake, call me Fanny.'

The chair prepared, Robert carefully lowers himself on to it. 'The fact is, Fanny . . .'

Fanny has turned her own chair away from her desk so she can face him. It leaves them without any space at all. They both shuffle their bodies backwards, but the chairs, her desk, the filing cabinets are jammed together. There is absolutely no room for manoeuvre.

'Oops,' says Fanny, laughing, 'sorry. Bit of a squash! Perhaps we'd be better off standing?'

'Standing? Where?' asks Robert facetiously. He has her knees trapped between his long bony legs and it's nice. It's *nice*. Besides which he has a cold. He's not feeling very well. So he stays put. 'Fanny, as you know, the last thing I want is for you to get an impression that I'm letting you down,' he says, 'but I have to tell you I'm feeling pretty dreadful. I'm almost certain I've got a temperature. I really ought to be in bed.'

Without thinking, as if he were one of her pupils, Fanny leans over and puts a hand to his forehead. 'You don't feel like you have a temperature,' she says. 'Perhaps you're just hot. Why don't you take one of your jerseys off?'

She glances at his face, flashes him a brief, busy smile. And for one ghastly second their eyes lock. Fanny looks away. But it's too late.

There it is in the room between them: a tiny spark, the smallest flicker – it's not attraction (certainly not on Fanny's part), only a faint, disturbing recognition of their different genders. Fanny drops her hand at once. She stands up and tries, as elegantly as possible, and with minimal contact, to create some kind of gulf between them.

She has to clamber over his bony thighs.

'Bother,' she says irritably, nearly treading on Brute with her free foot and then having to grasp hold of Robert's shoulder to recover balance. 'It really is bloody cramped in here. I'm going to open the window.'

Robert watches her confusion with sly enjoyment and doesn't bother to help. 'I'm ever so sorry, Fanny,' he says. 'But you know what it's like with these colds . . .' He smiles at her, keeping the pink lips closed.

'I do,' snaps Fanny, free at last, grasping the window latch in relief. She opens the window, turns back to him with a forced smile of sympathy. 'Bloody awful. You poor thing. But couldn't you just hang on until school finishes? And then after school you can go straight to bed and you'll probably feel so much better in the morning . . .'

Outside, Tracey Guppy, the nineteen-year-old care-taker/dinner lady, rings her bell. Lunch-break is over.

Robert looks quietly at his hands.

'Please, Robert,' Fanny says, 'I know it's awkward, me storming in here, taking a job which you probably feel – probably rightly feel . . .'

Robert purses his mouth.

'But I need your help . . . to get this school back on its feet.'

Robert's chapped white hands clench tight around the Lemsip.

'Not that you haven't already done so much for the school, I'm sure. But we need to work *together* . . .'

A silence between them. Robert sits, thinking, his long thin legs neatly folded in the space where Fanny had once been. She stands by the window waiting for his decision, wondering if she should stop begging and begin to flatter, or stop flattering, if that's what she's doing, and start to bully. She has no idea. She's never been a boss before. Not to an adult. Not to a chippy, insecure male. And looking at Robert, she has her first blinding flash of just how complicated it's going to be.

The telephone rings. Fanny hesitates. She has no choice but to stretch across him to pick it up.

'There's a gentleman here says he's an old friend. Says he just heard you on the wireless,' Mrs Haywood the glass-eyed secretary growls into her ear. 'Of course, they'll all be coming out of the woodwork now.'

'Oh!' A flicker of fear.

'He wants to talk to you about it—'

'No! I mean, no. Sorry. I'm a bit busy at the moment, Mrs Haywood. Could you—' But Mrs Haywood has already put him through. 'Hello?'

She hears the laugh. She *recognises* the laugh. 'Hello, sweetheart,' he says. 'Remember me?'

She throws down the receiver as if it's burnt her. Stares at the telephone. All the colour has drained from her face.

'Hey,' says Robert, jolted briefly to concern. 'What's up? Are you OK?'

'I'm fine.' She's still staring.

'Who was that?' Robert asks.

'No one. Nothing. I'm fine.' She tries to collect herself. But then it starts ringing again and she leaps immediately away.

'*Hey,*' he says, almost kindly. He puts a hand on her shoulder. 'It's OK. It's *OK*. What's up?' He nods at the telephone. 'Do you want me to answer it?'

'No. Don't. I mean, yes, do. Answer it! *Answer it!*'

He leans across her for the receiver: 'He-llo?' he says. 'Thank you, Mrs Haywood. Fiddleford Primary? Can I help you?' And listens a minute. Fanny scrutinises his face. And then, 'Oh, yes.' Smile. 'That would have been myself . . . I requested a supply teacher for this afternoon . . .' Another pause. A show of heroic stoicism. He looks across at Fanny and shakes his head. 'Mmm, actually no,' he says at last. 'On second thoughts, not to worry. No. But thanks for getting back. I'm going to battle on today, after all.' He winks at Fanny. 'If I can . . . Yes . . . Looks like there's a young lady here in need of a little help! First-day jitters . . . Yes . . . Nothing serious!' He laughs. 'I'll give you a call tomorrow, yes? Depending on how I feel . . . Thanks ever so much, Sally. It is Sally, isn't it? Super. Bye-bye.'

He hangs up and slowly, meticulously, with a secret smile hovering over those lips, he uncoils his long bony body until he is on his feet again. He looks down at Fanny, who is too ashamed to ask him any details about the call. 'As it's your first day, Fanny, I'm going to make an exception, and sweat it out until home time. OK? But you should know this is not a precedent. Working in this kind of hyper-stressful environment, we teachers have a responsibility to look after ourselves.' He pauses in front of her as he passes to the door. 'And that includes you, young lady.' She can feel his hot Lemsip breath on her cheek. 'You and I won't be doing the kiddies any favours if we go forgetting that . . . So *relax*, OK?' He motions at the telephone. 'It's not going to bite!'

'Of course not,' she says. 'Thank you, Robert.'

'My pleasure,' he says, and winks.

7

While Robert relaxes at home, nursing his long thin body back to full strength, Fanny works harder than she ever has before. She teaches morning and afternoon and spends the evenings at home, alone at her kitchen table, wading dutifully through school paperwork. It occurs to her at the end of her third solid six-hour stint that she's made no noticeable dent in the stack of papers still waiting to be dealt with: she could spend the rest of her life filling in forms and then what? Some poor sod would only have to process them. She picks them up and stuffs them tidily into a damp cupboard beneath the kitchen sink. To be looked at another day. In the future.

And even then Fanny can't quite bring herself to stop worrying. Instead of calling friends, or sitting in the pub getting drunk with the locals, as she had previously imagined she would spend evenings in her new bucolic life, she puts brushes, paint pots and a long folding ladder into the back of the Morris Minor mini van, drives through the village to the school, and she stays up most of the night painting the central assembly room bright yellow.

*   *   *

Friday arrives – the day, as everyone in Fiddleford would tell you, of the great limbo cotillion. Fanny and her seventeen pupils, as a result of a deal cracked earlier in the week, spend the day dedicated to their village mural, which, by mid-afternoon, takes up an entire wall-and-a-half of her classroom. It's a multi-spangled, multi-styled, glorious, uneven affair, and it transforms the room, just as Fanny had hoped it would.

'It's beautiful,' Fanny announces, standing back to admire. 'But CARTOGRAPHERS might find the total DISREGARD for any kind of CONSISTENT SCALE, quite INFURIATING . . . if not altogether INTOLERABLE.' Her pupils write the words on the board and compete with each other to see who can use which one most effectively in conversation.

And so on. Fanny's a good teacher. The children aren't accustomed to being taught by someone with so much energy, so little regard for dreary adult protocols, and with a dog called Brute. They think she's wonderful.

By the time they leave her alone, at the end of Friday, she is truly exhausted. Exhausted and, with the building quiet at last, even a little flat. She's thought of nothing but the school since she walked into the building that first morning of term. And now it's the weekend. Now what?

Somewhere on her desk, under the piles of paperwork, lies Mrs Haywood's extended list of telephone callers, among them, calling for a second time, an ex-boyfriend from teacher training who was driving through the area and heard the radio interview; also Jo, who heard the radio interview; her mother, calling from her retirement flat in southern Spain, who hadn't, and a triumphant message from her previous landlord, announcing he had discovered a coffee stain in the bedroom and would therefore be withholding her £950 deposit. But still no message from bloody Louis.

So. Unless she can make a friend at the village hall tonight, or she gets lucky with another call-up to eat sodium-free pulses at the Manor, she faces spending the rest of the weekend alone. Which is OK. Of course . . .

Slowly, more slowly than she needs to, Fanny first closes her office, and then locks up the school. (Tracey Guppy the caretaker won't do it, having recently declared the building spooked her. She won't go near it when it's empty.) She heads out, turns down the lane towards the village and begins the short trudge home.

But the gloom soon leaves her. It would be very hard, after all, not to be soothed by such a commute. The air smells so sweet, and the sun is warm on her back. Before long she is plucking idly at the long grass by the side of the road, and her mind has buried itself in her work. She has plans – for the school, for her tiny cottage, for making new friends in the village. Hundreds of plans. She thinks about Robert White, who's a lecher, she decides, on top of everything else, on top of being an overall creep. She makes a mental note to find out the union rules on lechers and skivers, wonders how she might ever be able to get rid of him. Reminds herself to buy paint for her front door. Red, perhaps. Or dark pink. And to dig out her copy of *Tom's Midnight Garden* to read to the older children. She is far from unhappy.

8

Fanny's put on make-up for the Fiddleford limbo: sweeping black lines around her large grey eyes, and a lot of lip gloss. She's wearing a pair of very fitted low-slung jeans, a transparent grey silk shirt with the top four buttons undone and a fancy black bra on show underneath.

She's pulled her curly, paint-speckled hair into a pony-tail to camouflage the fact that she still can't be bothered to wash it, and on her feet she's wearing trainers – suede and still quite clean. All in all the look she has gone for is not, perhaps, ideal for a village headmistress on the evening she first properly meets her students' parents. But Fanny's not yet used to being a village headmistress, so she doesn't think of that.

She decides it would be a friendly gesture to take a bottle of vodka with her because in her experience a lot of people, herself included, prefer drinking spirits to wine. So, with a pack and a half of Marlboro Lights, and a bottle of vodka only short of a few shots, she heads out.

The village hall is a few minutes' walk away, beside the council-owned bungalow (where Tracey Guppy lives with her uncle), and just opposite the school. It's a dreary little building; a 1940s pebble-dashed hut, usually musty and empty, with a noticeboard outside advertising Wednesday Morning Bridge Club, Tuesday and Thursday Toddler Group, and not much else.

But that Friday evening it is throbbing. Fanny can hear the calypso beat, jaunty and foreign and completely incongruous, as soon as she steps out of her front door. In fact, though Fanny couldn't have known it, Fiddleford village hall hasn't seen so much action since the previous summer, when half the nation's hacks squeezed in to witness the famous soap star Julia Biggleton (staying at the Manor Retreat after being outed as a transsexual) attempt to resuscitate her career by playing Lady Bracknell in Fiddleford Dramatic Society's *The Importance of Being Earnest*.

This evening there is no Julia Biggleton expected. And yet by the time Fanny arrives, half an hour late, there must be sixty people standing awkwardly around that pebble-dashed hut, wishing they were somewhere else. It is an unlikely crowd for a limbo dance. At least half the people present are over seventy and by the look of them, too creaky even to stand for more than a few minutes without having to call for an ambulance. But a social occasion in a small village, even if it must include bending backwards under poles, is something the majority would be unwilling to miss. Needs must, as Jo would say. In the country. Needs must.

Fanny, of course, knows hardly anyone. She pauses at the door, vodka in hand, and casts a hopeful eye over the crowd. She sees old General Maxwell McDonald in blazer and tie, deep in conversation with the glass-eyed school secretary, Mrs Haywood. And his good-looking son Charlie at the far end of the room, smoking a cigarette with the limbo teacher from Exeter, who is wearing leggings. And there is Jo, of course, working another corner, in low-slung jeans and trainers, like Fanny, but with no make-up on, shiny clean hair, and an opaque, exquisitely cut white shirt with not a hint of any underwear showing.

She spots Ian Guppy, her wily landlord, cowering in a space near the door immediately behind her. Clasping a can of cider in one hand and the burning butt of a cigarette in the other, and wearing a patterned brown jersey which seems to be choking him, he's staring into the middle of the room desperate – or so it appears – to avoid eye contact with anyone.

Standing guard beside him and all around him is the reason why: a vast mountain of flesh which Fanny correctly assumes to be his wife. She is alarmingly large. Actually, she is obese. Next to her, Ian Guppy appears like a frightened pixie, half the man – an eighth the man – he was the only other time Fanny saw him, and with no trace of the horrible leer which had previously been stuck to his face.

On this occasion Mrs Guppy happens to be wearing a blue nylon leisure suit with a pair of new lilac slippers. But the main point about Mrs Guppy is her size. She is very large. And, in spite of her efforts with the talcum powder, which she has sprinkled liberally over her thick wiry hair and her great body, she smells strongly of frying and sweat.

She and Ian have eight children, so Mrs Haywood the glass-eyed secretary has informed Fanny. Three of them are currently in jail. One, now twenty-five, has been missing since he was fifteen. Two are in foster homes. Tracey Guppy the school caretaker, nineteen, is honest and drug free but not on speaking terms with either parent. Their youngest is Dane Guppy, eleven. He is the student who interrupted Fanny's first assembly. (She's taken to calling him John Thomas whenever he's difficult, and each time he bellows with laughter. It lights up his waxy, suspicious face.)

At first glance Mr and Mrs Guppy look almost comical, Fanny thinks, huddled together, like Fatipuff and Thinnifer, in the corner of the room. And yet there is something menacing about them too. Perhaps she imagines it – after all that Mrs Haywood said. But Fanny gets the impression that everybody in the hall is a little wary of them. They stand very much alone; the husband cringing under her giant wing, the wife with beady eyes flickering suspiciously through the crowd. Mrs Guppy exudes a quiet proprietorial violence which, since the publican's wife was found with blood gushing down her legs and both arms broken, has kept libidinous females and her libidinous husband well apart. Or so Mrs Haywood said. Ian Guppy may leer, but after the incident with the publican's wife he never strayed again. Apparently.

Fanny knows she ought to go up and say hello. But they look very uninviting. She scans the room for a more appealing alternative and unconsciously, out of nerves, twists the lid off her vodka bottle and takes a swig.

Tracey Guppy is glancing her way; hovering a good distance from her parents and managing to look pretty and optimistic in spite of the gene pool; in spite of a wretched perm and a chilly, tatty lime green mini-dress. Fanny starts walking towards her just as a young man – tall, with curly russet hair – attracts Tracey's attention. The two of them fall immediately into animated conversation and Fanny hesitates, slightly embarrassed. She fiddles again with the cap on her vodka bottle.

'Hey! Teacher!' Fanny turns. Behind her Mrs Guppy, with an imperious nod of that vast head, is beckoning her over.

Shit, Fanny thinks. Never should have hesitated.

'Hello,' Fanny says pleasantly, walking towards them. 'And hello to you, too, Mr Guppy. This is quite a party.'

Mr Guppy mumbles something unintelligible, keeps his eyes to the floor.

'Go and get Teacher a cup,' snaps his wife. 'You seen her! She's been drinking out the bottle.'

He begins to move away.

'Go on,' she nudges him forward. 'Don't stand there with your eyes gogglin' out like you never seen underwear before. Hurry up!' Before Fanny has a chance to speak, Mrs Guppy motions her décolletage. 'I didn't know you head teachers was paid so short.'

'What's that?' smiles Fanny.

'I should cover y'self up before the men go shoving their cash down there.'

Fanny glances at her shirt. 'Well!' she says in astonishment. 'Ha ha . . . goodness! And there was me thinking I was looking quite nice this evening!' Mrs Guppy doesn't smile. Fanny tries again. 'Mind you – if there *are* any people shoving money around tonight, Mrs Guppy, I'd much prefer they shoved it down my shirt than anywhere else! You are Mrs Guppy, aren't you? I'm Fanny Flynn.' She holds out her hand. 'I teach your son.' Mrs Guppy doesn't take the hand. It hangs in mid-air. 'He's . . .' Fanny can't quite think what to add. 'Well – he has a wonderful sense of humour, doesn't he?'

Mrs Guppy is not impressed. She stares coldly at Fanny. 'It's not Stinglefellows in 'ere, Miss Flynn.'

'Yes. Yes, I noticed.'

'Go home and put something decent on. You look worse than a prostitute.'

Fanny's not easily bullied; not any more. Not ever again. She flushes, first in shock, and then anger, but she does not go home and put something decent on. She fixes her eyes on Mrs Guppy and slowly, deliberately, she undoes three more buttons, until her shirt is hanging open all the way to the navel.

'And now, Mrs Guppy, what do I look like?' she says. 'What do I look like now?' She turns away, without waiting for a reply.

9

Mrs Hooper from the post office, oblivious to everything but her own pleasure that night, bustles up to the limbo dancer from Exeter to suggest that it is time he began. She switches off the music, taps the microphone with impressive precision, as if she's been tapping microphones all her life: 'Testing . . . Testing . . . One two three,' she says. And then, very suddenly, with a great uplift of volume: 'Hello, girls and boys, ladies and gents! Welcome all and welcome sundry! CAN YOU ALL HEAR ME?'

'They can hear you in bloody Exeter,' shouts back Grey McShane. Fanny tries to smile. She has crossed the room and sidled up to Jo Maxwell McDonald, who was just introducing her to Grey's beautiful – pregnant – wife, Messy. Her shirt still hangs absurdly open and she longs to do it up but she won't as long as she knows Mrs Guppy's eyes are on her, and they are. They still are. Burning into her back. She can feel them.

'I said CAN YOU HEAR ME!?!' Mrs Hooper bawls.

'Hey!' Messy McShane leans over to Fanny, 'Do you realise your shirt's undone?'

'I know.' Fanny tries again to smile but finds, to her horror, that her bottom lip is quivering.

'RIGHT THEN. I'M MARGE HOOPER, AS MOST OF YOU PROBABLY KNOW.' Mrs Hooper's voice is making the windows rattle. 'So welcome everyone and thanks ever so much for coming. We've got an action-packed evening ahead, and it's all in a good cause, so—'

'Switch off the microphone, would you?' calls out Grey. 'We'll have animals aborting all over the fuckin' county.'

There are grumbles of assent. Grey has been living in Fiddleford for several years – first at the Manor with the Maxwell McDonalds, then at the Gatehouse Restaurant – and though his relationship with the villagers certainly opened badly, with a violent brawl at the Fiddleford Arms, nowadays he is almost a popular figure. He's a good employer, and though his rudeness is legendary he's usually only saying what most people wish they dared to say. And he is often surprisingly kind.

On this occasion, however, Mrs Hooper chooses to ignore him. She's been waiting many years to have a turn at the microphone, and not even Grey McShane is going to make her switch it off. '. . . So I hope you've all got your dancing feet on! Yes, you too, Albert! No excuses! It's have-a-go Friday in Fiddleford this evening. Doesn't matter how old you are, you're never too old to learn! . . . So. Well! I suppose it's time for me to introduce you to our fabulous expert coach, Mr Timothy Nesbit, who's come all the way from Exeter . . .'

'Hey, Fanny!' giggles Jo suddenly. 'Look down! Your shirt's completely undone!'

'So Timothy, if you're ready, it's over to you— Oooh!' she pulls the microphone back from him just in time, 'and I'll be going round with raffle tickets in a minute. We've got some fabulous prizes . . . Mr McShane's donated a dinner for two at the Gatehouse Restaurant, and for those of you with nice, big freezers, the Maxwell McDonalds have donated half a bullock! . . . We've got a month's supply of young Colin and Chloe's bantam eggs; and Mrs McShane's offered a giant hamper of her award-winning veggies, so there are loads of super prizes . . . A bottle of wine, a great big box of chocs from Mr Cooke; a super Ladyshaver from Pru. Absolutely unused, isn't it, Pru? Unwanted Christmas present, I believe you said.'

Grey McShane, sitting at the back of the hall with his long legs stretched out in front of him and his arms crossed, starts snoring ostentatiously.

'. . . Tickets are 20p each, or five for £1. Which is the same price, of course . . .' Grey snores louder, and everyone begins to laugh. 'But it makes it a nice round number, doesn't it?' Mrs Hooper shouts over them. 'So – get your wallets out, ladies and gentlemen. Right then! Timothy? Are we ready? Let's take it away!'

People mill about waiting for Timothy to finish his limbering up. They are mumbling quietly to each other, eyeing him distrustfully, dreading the moment when he insists they join in. Jo turns once again to Fanny, this time with a hint of impatience. 'Fanny you do realise, don't you? Your shirt—'

'Of course I realise,' says Fanny.

'Well then, why—'

'You'll have to forgive us country bumpkins, Fanny,' Messy interrupts tactfully. 'We've been rotting away down here so long, haven't we, Jo? We're probably too damn dozy to realise it's the absolute height of chic.'

'No, we bloody well aren't,' snaps Jo. Who certainly isn't. 'Don't be ridiculous, Messy. It's not chic. Her buttons have come undone.'

'They *are* undone, Jo. They haven't necessarily *come* undone. Anyway,' Messy adds unconvincingly, 'it looks great.'

Fanny takes a deep drag on her cigarette and then exhales, puffing smoke out of the side of her mouth, before leaning closer to the two women. 'Tell me,' she whispers fretfully, 'only be subtle. Is Mrs Guppy looking at me?'

They glance over Fanny's shoulder to the corner where Mr and Mrs Guppy had been standing.

'Mrs—? Oh. Oh, dear,' says Messy with a nervous laugh. '. . . Oh, dear . . .'

'Christ! Don't say "Oh, dear"! "Oh, dear" *what*? What's going on?' She searches their faces, frantic for clues.

'Oh, crikey—' Jo's eyes widen in alarm. 'What have you done to her, Fanny? She's on her way over, and she doesn't look too . . . *Bloody hell*. Hey! Mrs— *HEY*!'

Fanny gasps as an icy blow hits her between the shoulders. She feels the shock working its way down her spine and she has no idea – she wonders if she's been stabbed. She spins round.

'Oh, excuse me,' says Mrs Guppy, yellow teeth glinting. 'I was only bringing Teacher a nice cup of cola . . . You shall have to go home an' change, now. Shan't you, my lovely?'

Fanny looks up at her. They all do; Messy, Jo, various people nearby have noticed Mrs Guppy move in, and she doesn't move often. A space has somehow cleared around them, and now a silence, which is quickly spreading across the room.

Fanny smiles. 'Not to worry, Mrs Guppy,' she says lightly. 'It's a warm evening. And we're all friends here.' She drops her cigarette into the pool of Coca-Cola at her feet, undoes the final two buttons of her soaking shirt, and peels it off. The limbo enthusiasts of Fiddleford pause in amazement at their new head teacher, who stands before them all in her uplift plunge-cut black lace magnificence, Marlboro Light packs bulging from her low-slung pockets, an open bottle of vodka in her hand. She's stuck there. She's dying out there. Time stands still . . .

The silence is broken at last by a wolf-whistle, long and low. Everyone turns towards it. Standing framed at the entrance is a tall, lean, suntanned man in his mid-thirties, with shoulder-length sun-streaked hair, his hands in jeans pockets, his mouth wearing a languid, admiring smile. He has a cigarette hanging from a corner of his lips. He is almost, but not quite, laughing.

'You're kinda naked,' he comments amiably, in his soft Louisiana drawl.

Fanny gives a short, strangulated laugh. 'LOUIS!' she chokes. 'Thank God! Thank God for you!' She runs through the space and throws herself into his arms. A series of flashes follow as the man from the *Western Weekly Gazette* springs from the melee to snatch pictures of the west of England's youngest head teacher introducing herself to the villagers. Louis glances up at the photographer, and then at the gawking crowd. He takes off his old suede jacket and drapes it over her shoulders. 'Come on,' he murmurs, 'let's get outta here.'

The Fiddleford Arms is deserted, except for the bar woman, because everyone's up at the village hall. Louis and Fanny – carrying the coke-drenched shirt and still in Louis's jacket – drink a lot, very quickly, and before very long Fanny finds she has forgotten about the dreaded Mrs Guppy and is instead telling Louis in neurotic detail about the telephone call which came through when she was in her office with Robert White.

'I actually dropped the telephone. It seems so stupid, but Louis, *I recognised his voice*,' she says, puffing away on her cigarette, slugging back the whisky mac. 'I knew it was him. I *knew* it was. He sounded so damn familiar . . . I hung up on him.'

'Has he called back?'

She hesitates. 'Not yet, no.'

'It probably wasn't him, Fan. It would be a pretty damn weird coincidence. But this kind of crap is going to go on and on – in your head at least – until you deal with it. I keep telling you. Talk to a lawyer. Talk to the police. *Talk* to someone.'

But she won't do that. She'll never agree to do that. She always says the same thing: she doesn't want to stir things up again.

'Until you find out where the sucker is, if he's still alive, for Christ's sake—'

'Of course he's still alive. Why shouldn't he be?'

'Whatever. Fine. But if you believe it was him on the phone—'

'But what if it wasn't?'

He stifles a sigh. He's said it all so often before; virtually every time they meet. 'Fanny, it probably wasn't. Either way. Talk to a lawyer. Talk to the goddam police.'

'No.'

'You could clear this whole thing up.' He snaps a finger. 'Gone. Like that.'

'No.'

'Well – I don't know what else to say, Fan. Anyhow, I guess this publicity idea isn't helping. I mean, if he *is* out there, which he *isn't*, then broadcasting your fabulous successes over the airwaves could probably be rated as "stirring things up". Don't you think?'

As he speaks they both remember the series of camera flashes which had followed her in her shirtless streak across the hall.

'Oh, Christ,' says Fanny, sinking her head into her hands. She lets out a low moan. 'Oh, Christ.'

Louis pulls her into a hug. He holds her tight, tighter than he needs to, and breathes in the sweet smell of her. And she breathes in the sweet smell of him.

They stay like that for a while, the two best mates, until one of them says something, makes some sort of brittle joke, and they both pretend to find it funny and slowly pull apart.

It's as they're awkwardly, reluctantly disentangling, that Grey McShane sweeps in. He stops at their table, towers above it. 'There you are,' he says, noticing her bloodshot eyes but showing no sign of being affected by them. 'You're not giving up on us already, are you?'

'What? No. No, of course not.'

'Well, you'd better get back there. They all think you've done a runner.'

She looks at him, confused.

'We've got the children talking about you like you're the bloody Messiah, Fanny.'

'Really?'

'We've got my stepdaughter, little Chloe, coming home every day, singing your praises. We don't want to lose you just because some fat cow doesn't like the look of you in your scanties.'

Louis snorts with laughter. Fanny turns to glare at him, finds it quite difficult to focus, and turns back to Grey.

'He's kind of right, though,' Louis says. 'You can't let the fat lady push you around.'

Fanny nods, takes another slug from her drink. 'Is she still in there? I don't think I can face it if she's still there.'

Grey shakes his head. 'They left pretty much straight after you.'

'Right then.' Slowly, and with obvious regret, she pulls herself up from her chair. 'Let's— I'd better get on with it then.' She pauses, sways backwards suddenly, steadies herself, and then with a scowl of concentration, 'Actually,' she adds, 'it turns out I'm quite – very – pissed.'

'Just don't try to say too much,' Grey says.

'And I think,' she tries to focus on Louis, 'I should probably do this on my own, Louis, don't you? If I just go back with Grey, it might maybe unruffle a few more feathers. I mean ruffle. Less. Fewer. Unruffle fewer feathers.' She frowns. 'It might go down better if I leave you behind.'

Louis is not especially disappointed. Fiddleford's great limbo cotillion did not strike him as much of a party. Besides which it's a nice evening. He thinks, instead, that he might roll himself a J and take a walk through the village. 'I'll meet you back here in an hour,' he says. 'OK? Good luck.' He grins at her. 'Don't get any more pissed. Less. Fewer less pissed. Don't drink any more if you can help it . . .'

PART TWO

PART TWO

10

Geraldine Adams looks rich. She is in her early forties and her hair, short and brown, with tasteful russet lowlights, is exceptionally well cut. She and her husband Clive used to be as important as Geraldine's haircut still implies but in actual fact, eighteen months ago, the Adams family joined that annoying group of former yuppies which newspapers call the 'downsizers'.

They've even been the subject of a newspaper feature themselves. (They have it framed in their downstairs lavatory.) There was a massive colour photograph of Clive and Geraldine and the son, Oliver, leaning smugly against a five-bar gate, with the village of Fiddleford nestling behind them. In the article Clive and Geraldine swear that they have never felt happier, and that their ten-year-old son Oliver is so happy with the new rural life that he's taken to voluntarily switching off the television.

'Ollie's got to the stage now where he can't stand processed food,' Geraldine told the journalist, called Richard. 'He simply won't eat it, Richard! Fortunately for us there's a marvellous commercial vegetable garden here in Fiddleford, so every morning before school, off Ollie and I trog to Messy

McShane's Organic Kitchen Garden. You know who Messy McShane is, of course, don't you? Absolutely! *Wife of*. Quite right! The notorious Grey. He's *charming*, actually. A sweetie. But for heaven's sake don't get me on to that. Where was I? Yes, Ollie and my little trips to the Garden – which allow him to play an active role in the choices about what he eats, and of course *choice* is what it's all about, isn't it, Richard? Messy talks Ollie through the vegetables that are in season, and then Ollie says, "Ooh, Mummy, I could murder a beetroot today," and so off she trogs, and picks it! Or whatever . . . You know what I mean. Picks it *up*. Picks it . . . *away* from the beetroot's . . . growing place. So to speak. Anyway, Messy's happy. I'm happy. Ollie's happy. And Ollie's eating beetroot! Who ever heard of a ten-year-old boy eating beetroot in this day and age! Ha! . . . No. No, I can honestly say to you, Richard, my only regret is that we didn't make the move sooner!'

Clive and Geraldine used to be partners in a firm of City solicitors. They used to live in Hampstead. Between them they used to earn not far off £1 million a year, if you included bonuses. They used to work twelve hours a day and pay their Australian nanny £600 a week. They used to do all that, and then rush off to the gym, and then have dinner with clients, where they would talk coyly and knowingly about the son they so rarely had time to see – and in truth they used to enjoy it that way. The life suited them perfectly. It probably suited Oliver, too. Because the £600-a-week nanny was usually too busy reading *Heat* magazine to forcefeed him any disgusting vegetables and, except when she could actually hear Geraldine at the front door, would absolutely never have been so cruel as to stop him watching television.

But Clive and Geraldine couldn't help worrying that they were somehow living life wrong. What with the return of terrorist threats in London, and a smaller-than-expected annual bonus from the City solicitors, the very distracting articles about downsizers in the newspapers, and then Geraldine, at forty-two, suddenly wondering if she ought to be wanting another baby, there came a time when Mr and Mrs Adams decided they had no choice but to take stock.

Geraldine's best friend, impoverished and non-productive 'children's author' Kitty Mozely, had already moved from London with her daughter, Scarlett, to a pretty cottage on the outskirts of Fiddleford. As part of their stocktaking process Clive and Geraldine went to stay for a weekend with her and, as they told her at the time, they were very impressed. Not only was Fiddleford a beautifully quaint little village, it was also at the heart of a 'fascinating' social whirl.

Kitty had pulled out all the stops that weekend, of course, because she wanted her friends to come and live nearby. She roped in people for dinner and for drinks, and managed to get them all invited out to lunch, so that by the end of the weekend, Clive and Geraldine had almost certainly experienced the peak of Fiddleford's sociability.

But it is true, too, that there is a generous sprinkling of 'fascinating' people in the neighbourhood. Apart from the McShanes and the Maxwell McDonalds, there is Daniel Frazer, the world-famous hat maker, who owns a cottage on the road to Lamsbury. He and his American boyfriend come down most weekends, and can often be spotted in the Fiddleford Arms, living it up with their fascinating friends. And then there's Annie Millbank, who was the love interest in lots of seventies movies and now stars in a series of coffee ads. She lives on her own, mostly drunk, in the Mill House about a mile beyond the Retreat. There are the people-friendly former government minister Maurice Morrison and his curiously hideous wife, who are renting the manor in the next-door village, and he can often be seen, sniffing around, glad-handing the locals; Solomon Creasey the art dealer comes down with his numerous beautiful children and a different beautiful girlfriend at least every other weekend. He owns a large house hidden behind a high wall, bang in the middle of Fiddleford, and on summer evenings, when the windows are open, the whole street can be filled with the smell of his cigars and aftershave, and the sound of him – laughing usually, or yelling very large figures into a telephone. Solomon Creasey, though not yet forty, is a man with an inscrutable past. Nobody really knows where he came from, but the main thing is that he once discovered a Rubens at auction and has since held the British record for achieving the greatest profit on any single painting ever sold. One way or another he is very rich. Kitty Mozely (the non-productive children's author) makes a courageous play for him every time they meet.

Anyway, after Clive and Geraldine's weekend visit to Fiddleford, non-productive Kitty, whose writing career has long since ground to a standstill, and who is often bored and lonely, became increasingly determined that they should follow her to the area. She would ring up Geraldine in her City office and regale her with stories of all the glamorous people who dropped in for drinks (nor was she above a little lavish embellishment), and she would swear that she and her daughter Scarlett had never been happier. She claimed that since moving to Fiddleford Scarlett didn't watch television any more. (Actually, enigmatic little Scarlett had never been that interested in television.) And she claimed that Scarlett's new favourite dish was baked fennel, which was an outright lie. 'I can honestly say to you, Geraldine, my only regret is that we didn't make the move sooner!'

Geraldine was not – is not – a woman who likes to be outdone. Certainly not in the social whirl. And not even over vegetables. So she and Clive finally blocked out an evening together to discuss their future. And by the end of dinner, in spite of all of Kitty Mozely's efforts, in spite of the wonderful – and fashionable – savings they would make by sending Ollie to the local village school, they had pretty much decided to stay put, which was a great relief to both of them. They slept better that night than they had in months.

Two days later Kitty rang to tell them that the Old Rectory in Fiddleford was up for sale.

They only had to see it once. It was perfect for them; built 250 years earlier, as if exclusively with the requirements of third-millennium Hampstead downsizers in mind. It was a small, symmetrical, irreproachably pretty Georgian manor, with six little sash windows on the first floor and two on either side of a wide, stone-pillared front porch. It was set back from the village street, with a drive that curled through a small copse of trees and down into a little valley. It was private, elegant, and not at all cheap. Clive and Geraldine fell in love with it. Their Hampstead house sold very quickly, and for the asking price of £1.85 million, making them an encouraging £790,000 profit, much of which they blew on their extravagant 'improvements'. They built the tennis court and the swimming pool, employed an interior decorator who specialised in a rustic-contemporary look, opened a small, exclusive practice in a converted town house in Lamsbury, and have been happily munching through Messy McShane's Fresh Organic Vegetables ever since.

Or quite happily.

Or actually (unofficially speaking) not very happily at all. Downsizing, they have discovered, is not quite as easy as it looks. And though the piece in the Saturday *Telegraph* was fun, it couldn't sustain them for ever, and there are times when Clive and Geraldine secretly feel quite breathless with horror at the smallness of their new lives. They might glance up from some exclusively priced little conveyancing job and hear the hideous, monotonous cawing of the ravens outside, or the pitter-patter-plop of the soft grey English rain. They might glance out from their rustic-contemporary, newly shuttered Georgian windows, and notice that it's already growing dark, and that the evening looms with only each other and the blip of Ollie's computer games for company.

Recently, Geraldine has been finding it increasingly difficult to sleep. She lies awake at night, next to Clive, and she can feel the quicksand of Downsizers' Oblivion closing in around them, sucking them in, and she wants to scream for help. And Clive, too, can lie quietly beside his wife, blinking in the absolute darkness, and he'll think about the important cases he and Geraldine might have been involved in if they had stayed in London, and he'll think of the humdrum papers on his desk, and of their practice, which is far from thriving and he'll think, *This is hell.* This is not what we worked so hard for.

But they always put on a brave face in public. Of course. Not even Kitty Mozely – not even each other – would have guessed how difficult they were really finding it.

11

So. It is tea-time at the Old Rectory on the Monday after the Friday-night limbo party and Kitty Mozely and Geraldine, who have both made a highly competitive point of stopping their non-existent work in time to pick Scarlett and Oliver up from Fiddleford Primary School, are stretched out on the lawn in front of the house discussing the *sujet du moment*, as they have chosen to refer to it: Fanny Flynn. Fanny is not a popular woman in Fiddleford at the moment.

Geraldine Adams and Kitty Mozely had both been present at the shirt-stripping incident, when she had swept out of the village hall with Louis's glamorous American arms around her, and they were still there afterwards, when she returned to the village hall with Grey. But neither has yet had a chance to speak to her, which is frustrating for them. It means they are unclear about exactly what happened to whom, and why, and are still, nearly seventy hours later, trying to piece the full drama together.

'I notice she didn't come out to the gate after school this afternoon. Did she? To have a chat with the parents – which she might have done. She ought to, really, every day. So the parents can get to know her. But really,' tuts

Geraldine, sitting up slightly to stir saccharin into her tea, 'after Friday . . .'

'After Friday it's the least she could do,' Kitty agrees.

'It's all very well. But she does have our kids in her care. I personally think she ought to have sent the children home with a letter of explanation. Don't you? I mean, so many parents were there at the limbo, witnessing . . . People like us can take these things in our stride of course but a lot of parents . . .' Geraldine is briefly distracted by the sight of a chip in the Chocolate Plum polish on her toenail.

'Absolutely,' murmurs Kitty, lying back, eyes closed, exhaling cigarette, soaking up the spring sun. 'That's absolutely right.'

They lapse into silence, listening idly to the birds twitter, the gentle breeze in the trees. 'Aaah . . .' sighs Geraldine. 'What a lovely day!'

From inside the Old Rectory they can hear Ollie and Scarlett talking animatedly, or – no, it's only Ollie, actually. Ollie's voice, yelling something angry, followed by a loud crash. The words 'stupid ugly bitch' ring out across the lovely lawn. But both women are relaxing, taking a well-deserved break from the stresses and strains of work, work, work and motherhood. They both pretend not to hear, and then, after a decentish pause, Kitty says (it could have been either of them; they tend to take it in turns), 'Isn't it marvellous how well the children get along?'

Scarlett Mozely is Kitty's only child, the fruit of a passionate month with a Moroccan cab driver, who has long since driven away. Scarlett was born with lopsided facial features and a twisted back which, though she doesn't need a wheelchair, means she will probably never be able to walk without crutches. She and Geraldine's son, Ollie, are both at Fiddleford Primary, and both in Fanny's class, although a year apart. They loathe each other.

'But I get the impression the *chap*,' says Geraldine, keen to stick to the *sujet du moment*, 'that incredibly handsome American who whisked her away at the end—'

'Louis,' Kitty prompts impatiently. 'He's called Louis, Geraldine.'

'Louis – he's not actually her boyfriend.'

'She must be mad. Why ever not?'

'They didn't embrace when they arrived, did they? They hugged in a sort of non-boyfriendy way, don't you think? . . . Plus, *Dawn* was behind the bar at the pub on Friday night,' Geraldine adds. (Dawn is Geraldine's daily.) 'She was watching them very closely. After all, she's got Derek at the school, hasn't she? Is he called Derek? I can't remember. Skinny boy. In Ollie's class. Ollie and Scarlett's class, excuse me.'

Kitty has no idea. Nor any interest. 'And the pub would have been empty, I suppose. With everyone being at the limbo. So she'd have got a good look . . .'

'*Dawn* says Miss Flynn was knocking back pints of Guinness. With whisky mac chasers. Guinness and whisky mac chasers!'

'Yes. And were they canoodling?'

'She said *not*. She said definitely just talking. But Miss Flynn was crying her heart out at one point. She must have been quite upset.'

'Christ,' bursts out Kitty suddenly. 'You don't suppose he's gay, do you? *What a waste!*'

Kitty adores young men.

As might be expected, given her frolicsome lifestyle, Kitty has aged a good deal less elegantly than her rich, self-disciplined friend, Geraldine. Kitty's long straight hair has been dyed so often it's devoid of any colour at all any more, and she's put on stones since the early days, when she and Geraldine were at Oxford together, and she, Kitty, was meant to be the sexy one; the doe-eyed Brigitte Bardot lookalike who was going to set the world on fire . . .

She still has the doe eyes, except nowadays they're watchful and puffy from alcohol. She's broke. Lonely. Lazy. She drinks like a fish. But she still has a certain blowsy allure. She dresses in white, always; wafts around in a cloud of musky scent and French tobacco, and when she flirts, which she does continually, she flirts with true and reckless intent. She's good company but a dangerous friend. Fortunately for Geraldine, her soft-speaking, cerebral husband Clive has never appealed to Kitty – and nor (though Kitty might not believe it) has she ever greatly appealed to him.

In any case, Kitty's action-packed sex life has always been a source of irritation for Geraldine. It's one area where Geraldine has always felt outdone. Especially since she's been married. She and Clive happen to have a strongish marriage (Kitty, on the other hand, has never maintained a relationship for longer than a few months). Clive and Geraldine work together, plan together, agree with each other on most things they consider to be important. They quite like each other. But they don't have much sex. 'Gay or not, my love,' Geraldine says, annoyingly brightly, 'young Louis is probably just a tad – too – young – for you, don't you think?'

Kitty chortles. 'I doubt that very much.'

'Either way, you'll probably never lay eyes on him again.'

'Ah-ha!' Kitty rolls over on to her belly, rests her chin in her hand. 'Top Secret gossip: Mrs Hooper says he was asking at the post office about places to rent! Apparently, Ms Flynn isn't allowed to know. But we are. He's a photographer, Mrs Hooper says. From Louisiana. Of course one can tell. He's got that innate masterfulness about him, hasn't he? From all that slave owning, I imagine. They all have it. In the Southern States . . . I can never resist a *Southern* boy, can you?' Kitty says 'Southern' with a silly Southern accent, and doesn't wait for Geraldine to reply. 'Anyway, Mrs Hooper says he works freelance for some of the London newspapers. She says he's looking for a place to live.'

'Oh. Well then, I'm wrong, aren't I?' says Geraldine. 'If he's moving down here – if he's keeping it secret from her – then he and Fanny Flynn must be lovers. Or if not then he certainly wants them to be. Which rather knocks you out of the frame, old girl. Sorry.'

'Not necessarily, it doesn't.'

They fall silent a moment, recover their good nature.

'I say, though,' Geraldine says brightly, 'you know Clive actually went up and talked to her, after she came back to the hall. And she's obviously rather a troubled young lady, because when Clive told her he was a solicitor she wouldn't stop talking about *stalkers*. Legal rights of. Imagine that!'

'So she's a stalker?'

'Either that, Kitty, or she's got a stalker. Which I think is the more likely scenario.'

'Oh! But who could possibly be stalking her? In Fiddleford!'

'Well, she wouldn't say, would she?'

Suddenly Kitty gasps. She even sits up. 'Geraldine! You don't think – *Grey McShane!*'

For one delirious moment they will themselves to believe it. Without success.

'One can't help thinking, though,' Geraldine moves blithely on, 'if a girl *does* wander through life ripping her shirt off at the slightest provocation, she is running the risk of attracting unwanted attention from – you know – these sort of ghastly, obsessive perverts. Don't you think so? I know it's not fashionable to say so. But that's just the way of the world.'

'Exactly . . . Absolutely.'

'Clive says she was being very obtuse. Absolutely wouldn't go into specifics. But one can't help wondering . . . I mean, it's certainly intriguing, isn't it?'

Just then Ollie comes rushing out of the house, screaming like a toddler. He, too, when he calms down enough to speak, remains stubbornly obtuse. Absolutely won't go into specifics. But it turns out his PlayStation is broken, and that Scarlett is to blame.

'Oh, baby,' coos Geraldine, 'never mind. I'm very proud you were generous enough to let Scarlett have a go with it.'

That isn't quite what he'd said.

'Yes, well done, Ollie,' says Kitty. 'Did Scarlett say sorry nicely?'

'No.'

Kitty clicks her tongue. She wishes Scarlett would remember that she's in Ollie's house, playing with Ollie's toys, and that really, given Scarlett's physical and material disadvantages, she should count herself lucky that such a nice-looking boy with so many nice-looking toys is willing to have anything to do with her. Besides which, weather allowing, Kitty very much plans to place herself and her daughter beside Ollie's lovely new swimming pool for most of the coming summer. It makes everything so much more awkward when the children refuse to get on. 'Where is she, anyway?' Kitty asks.

'Inside, probably. Smashing something else up—'

'Never mind, baby-boy,' interrupts Geraldine hurriedly. 'Never mind. If it's really broken we'll get you another one at the weekend. Fair?'

'But it's— What, the new one?'

'If you're good. As a reward for being so generous to Scarlett.' Geraldine leans across to give him a cuddle but he shakes her off and runs quickly back into the house. Geraldine hesitates. There are times when she is embarrassed by the contrast between Scarlett's and Ollie's fortunes, and this happens to be one of them. 'Perhaps,' she says, looking tentatively at Kitty, nervous that the suggestion might be thought patronising, 'perhaps I could get one for Scarlett, too? As an early birthday present . . .'

Kitty doesn't generally mind being at the receiving end of her rich girlfriend's largesse. Actually, over the years Geraldine has helped her out more often than Kitty cares to remember. But even Kitty has her limits. There are a few things she will not – she cannot – accept from Geraldine, and a PlayStation for Scarlett is apparently among them. So Kitty pretends not to hear. '*Children!*' she says irrelevantly. 'Anyway, how's work?'

'Oh. Work's OK. Work's great!'

She and Clive have slashed their prices since they first opened for business, but they still charge too much for country solicitors, and their whole Big City manner is too aggressive. It doesn't impress anyone around Lamsbury. So Geraldine's office is in fact more like a graveyard – very far from great – and with every month, as the negative word continues to spread, the situation seems to be worsening. Not only that, with the nest egg gone, and the big fat salaries too, Clive and Geraldine are beginning to fear that cash flow may soon become a problem. 'Work's fabulous, Kitty. Thanks. I mean, it's quiet, but we like it like that. And of course we're still relatively new. I was actually thinking I might slim down the hours I put in there. Just for the summer. Spend a bit of quality time with Ollie before it's too late, and we're packing him off to university!'

'They grow up so quickly,' Kitty says automatically.

'I was thinking I could take a couple of mornings and offer up my services at the school. They're clearly in need of it.'

'Mmm. Good idea. What fun.'

'I can do a bit of reading with the kids. Gosh, you know – all the stuff other mummies get to do, who don't have careers to worry about! . . . Because frankly, Kitty, what confidence I ever had in that establishment— I mean, never mind the three Rs. What about the others? What about Respect? What about Restraint? What about keeping your bloody clothes on?'

Kitty chortles.

'It's all very well having a young, attractive, spirited head teacher, and of course, in principle I'm 100 per cent behind her. One hundred per cent. But really . . . Personally, Kitty, I would have liked to have had some say in appointing her, wouldn't you?'

'Oh, yes.'

'It's because we aren't governors, Kit. Why aren't we governors? We should be governors.'

'Crikey, I don't know about that.'

'We should be. How does it work, do you think?'

'I've got a nasty feeling you'd have to go to church,' murmurs Kitty. 'And suck up to that bloody awful vicar.'

'*We*, Kit. Not me, *we*.' The idea is growing more appealing the more she thinks about it. Anything is more appealing than sitting in that silent office, watching her husband bend diligently over work he's too good for, listening to the ravens, waiting for the telephone to ring. 'I'll start by offering to do a bit of reading with the kids, I think. Don't you think? And then sort of work my way in. Because frankly, Kitty, after that display last Friday night I'd like to see for myself what's actually going on in that place.'

Kitty sits up suddenly. Mention of the Friday Night Display has once again reminded her of Louis, the masterful Southern boy, possibly not gay and possibly moving into the area; and she's felt a shiver of adrenalin run right through her. 'I say,' she says brightly, 'shall we open a bottle of wine?'

12

The photograph of Fanny and her fancy bra, arms outstretched and leaping into the arms of (an unseen) Louis, makes the whole of page 7 of the *Western Weekly Gazette* that Thursday. It is the same day that Robert White puts in his first appearance at the school since slinking off with a cold ten days earlier. And there is, most understandably, an air of repressed glee about him as he and his sandals and his thick polo-neck jersey shuffle into the staff room that morning. Behind the beard, his pink lips are upturned in wry, self-conscious amusement. He has the newspaper opened and folded under one arm.

Fanny, having ignored various *Gazette* telephone messages on her answer machine at home and here at the school, naively imagines that the newspaper has lost interest in the story, and has by now virtually forgotten it herself. So when Robert comes into the staff room she's sitting very peacefully with her feet on the coffee table, chuckling over a copy of *Private Eye*. It is only half past eight. School doesn't start for a quarter of an hour, and Fanny has once again been up for hours. (It's a new habit, and slightly disconcerting to her. She continues to work harder than ever before and yet recently she's been literally springing out of bed.) So she's already taken herself and Brute for a run, and put in a couple of hours' work on the increasingly damp stack of papers under the kitchen sink. Now she is relaxing. Beside her Linda Tardy the teacher's assistant is munching prematurely on her lunch-time sandwich, as usual, and staring blankly into space. Mrs Haywood the glass-eyed secretary is making herself coffee. Contentment reigns.

'Hell-o!' says Robert warmly. 'Morning all! Good morning, Fanny!'

They look up, mildly surprised. It's rare for Robert to come in at all. It's exceptionally rare for him to come in sounding excited.

'Morning, Robert,' they say. 'Welcome back. Good journey in?'

Robert lives in a village almost ten miles from Fiddleford, and he usually has a little observation to make about the traffic, or the inconsiderate behaviour of his fellow drivers. Today, most unusually, he says the journey was 'very good indeed'.

Mrs Haywood offers to make him coffee.

'Oh, that would be splendid!' he cries, rubbing his hands together. 'What a splendid idea, Mrs Haywood. Yes, please. Much obliged.'

'Glad to see you're feeling so much better,' Fanny says drily. Among all the other problems spinning around her head this week, the problem of Robert's absenteeism has not been forgotten. On the contrary, with every day he has failed to appear she has grown more resentful. She discussed it over the weekend with Louis, who was no help at all. On Friday night, after she reeled back to the limbo, she even found herself discussing it with old General Maxwell McDonald.

'Our real obstacle is Dr Curry,' General Maxwell

McDonald had shouted over the calypso music. 'Robert White's sister is Dr Curry's wife, of course. Excellent doctor, but weak-minded. That's the problem. He knows perfectly well his brother-in-law is a good-for-nothing layabout. I've spoken to him about it. But then Robert White turns up in the surgery, snivelling like a girl and asking for a "sick note".' The General shuddered at the words. 'Curry won't tell the man he's an idle bugger and pack him off back to work. I should, certainly. But then again,' he chortled, 'I'm not married to Dr Curry's wife . . .' At which the General had tapped his nose and added, incomprehensibly, 'Silent but deadly, see? Courageous work with Mrs Guppy, by the way. Thought you looked marvellous! Great success. Well done!'

Fanny smiles to herself, remembering the General's kind words, and Robert, hovering beside Mrs Haywood for his coffee, feels a squirt of glee. Fanny Flynn is looking very relaxed, he notes. She clearly hasn't seen the paper yet. Which means he can be the one to show it to her.

So. He looks thoughtfully at Fanny. With an effort, he suppresses the smirk he's been wearing all the way in to work – ever since the *Western Weekly Gazette* first plopped on to his doormat this morning – and pads, with his coffee, across the room to sit beside her. Meticulously, silently, he unfolds the newspaper and lays it out on the coffee table at her feet. Fanny ignores him, irritated by his proximity. She continues to stare at her magazine in the hope that he might move away, which he does not.

Silence. The gentle tinkle of Mrs Haywood stirring coffee. The passing of air through Robert's agitated nostrils. The squelching of tuna and watercress between Linda Tardy's teeth.

It is Linda Tardy who notices the article first.

'Oh, my gracious Lord!' she screams, making Mrs Haywood jump. 'Fanny! Mrs Haywood! Robert! Everyone!

Fanny, you're famous! We're all famous! LOOK AT THIS! This was— Oh, Robert, we were THERE! Fanny took her shirt off and— It's such a shame you didn't come; I know it's a journey for you but my goodness, look what you missed! What does it say?'

Robert watches Fanny's face as she glances up from *Private Eye* and slowly registers what is laid out before her.

'Oops,' she says. She lets out a sigh. 'Oh, dear.'

'I'm so sorry, Fanny, to be "the messenger",' Robert murmurs softly, 'only I thought you would probably want to see . . .'

'*What does it say?*' demands Linda Tardy impatiently, trying to nudge Robert out of the way.

'Bloody hell,' mutters Fanny. She takes the newspaper and stands up. 'Robert, I think you'd better take assembly this morning. It looks like I need to make a few calls.'

But as she speaks the telephone rings (as, in fact, it will continue to do incessantly now, for the rest of the morning; something about that picture has awoken the snake in every prude and pervert in the county). Robert doesn't notice the telephone at first, he's too busy watching Fanny. Unfortunately, the handset is on the window sill beside his elbow and no one else can get to it.

'Pick it up then!' says Mrs Haywood.

'Mmm? Oh!' He picks it up. 'Fiddleford Primary,' he snaps, his eyes fixed on Fanny, watching her as she digests the ribald picture caption at the bottom of the page. 'Pardon?' He frowns. 'No. This is Fiddleford Primary School. I think you've got the wrong number . . . Who? I can't hear you properly. You're sounding— Fanny Flynn? Oh,' he looks hesitant, 'I'm not sure. Who may I say is calling?'

In a rush of irritation – she's not sure if it's with the gloating Robert or with herself – she reaches across and snatches the receiver.

'Fanny Flynn here,' she says briskly.

She hears breathing. Panting.

Fanny Flynn used to do shifts on her university student helpline. Unlike Robert she knows at once what she is hearing. She ought to hang up, but she can't. Something's frozen.

Panting. And then her name.

Still, it doesn't sound like him. It *isn't* him. And yet somehow—

'Say something, Fanny.' And then nothing. Breathing. A long sigh. 'I've written you a poem, *Miss Flynn*. Want to hear it?'

'Fuck off,' she says at last, 'or I'll call the police.' She slams down the receiver, and without looking left or right, heads straight for the door.

The telephone starts ringing again at once.

'Don't answer it,' she says blandly. 'Nobody answer the telephone this morning, please. OK? Let this stupid thing blow over. And I'm sorry, everyone, about my terrible language.' She leaves the room in such a hurry that Brute is caught in the staff room behind her.

Alone at her desk, the first thing she does is to call Louis. Again. She hasn't heard a word from him since he headed back to London on Sunday and she's lost count of the number of messages she's left. She imagines he's already swallowed up in some new bloody 'love' marathon, since Louis is always falling in love, and it makes her wretched to think about it, even more wretched than she was before.

Louis's answering service picks up, as always, and this time Fanny hangs up without bothering to leave a message. The bell goes for the start of lessons but she doesn't react to it. She sits there, feeling sick. Was it him? She doesn't know. She can't even remember what he sounds like any more. *Was it him?* She doesn't know. But *it might have been.*

Half an hour later Robert follows her to her office. The school telephone has been ringing solidly, and though he isn't entirely clear what happened back in the staff room earlier, it had been disconcerting enough, annoyingly, to ruin his enjoyment of the scene. He taps on her door, waits, and when she doesn't answer, lets himself in anyway.

Fanny is sitting behind her desk, as before. She looks exhausted; pasty, tiny, vulnerable, unhappy. He feels, in spite of himself, a surge of pity for her. She doesn't look up, or invite him to sit down, so he rests his bottom against the radiator on the wall directly opposite her, and waits.

He clears his throat. 'Are you OK, Fanny?'

'I'm fine,' she says, glancing up at last, sending him a feeble smile. 'I'm fine. Sorry. Sorry not to er—'

'The kids are missing you. Lessons began quarter of an hour ago.'

'Yes, I know. I'm coming down in a minute. Could you—'

'Mrs Tardy's in with them.'

'Oh, good. Good. I'll be down in one minute.'

He sighs, a sigh full of teacherly, mature forbearing. 'Fanny, are you going to tell me what's going on?'

'Nothing's going on. You can see what's going on. That silly picture.' She stops, shrugs. 'You know how it is. Lonely people out there. They get the wrong idea.'

It takes him a moment to work out what she is implying. 'Ah, of course,' he says slowly, 'how very disagreeable.' A tiny flash of vexation that he hadn't worked it out before, and then he imagines it: the strange man, the photograph, Fanny listening. He feels faintly aroused. 'Well, I suppose you're always going to get these specimens, aren't you. They see these sort of images in the paper and they take them as an invitation . . .'

Fanny doesn't say anything. The room feels small with Robert in it, talking confidingly about things she'd so much prefer never to discuss with him. People wanking over her. She feels claustrophobic. She wishes he'd leave her alone.

'Perhaps we should call the police?' he says.

'No.'

'Well, Fanny, it's obviously upset you . . .'

'No. Robert—' She stops, forces herself to smile again. 'I'm fine. Forget it. So, anyway, you came to see me. What did you want? How can I help? Actually, I'm glad you came, because I've really been wanting to ask you about Scarlett.'

'Scarlett?' He looks confused.

'You know Scarlett. Little disabled Scarlett, with the thick specs.' Fanny speaks quickly, keen to move the conversation on. 'Scarlett Mozely. Only she won't show me any work and there are no notes. Mrs Haywood can't find any notes and I'm wondering—'

'Fanny, excuse me, but I return to work to discover photographs of our new head teacher in her bra and panties all over the press and you're talking to me about—'

'I wasn't in my "panties",' she snaps. 'Don't get carried away.'

'The telephone hasn't stopped ringing all morning. You're hiding away in your office here, refusing to pick it up, refusing to come to class. It's hardly the way— It's hardly a very good example.'

'I know.' She sighs. 'I know it isn't. And I'm sorry. Give me two minutes—'

'What were you doing in your bra and panties, anyway?' he persists. 'In front of everyone! What are the kids supposed to think? More to the point what is the *Local Authority* supposed to think? They're seeing images of our new headmistress in her bra and panties—'

77

'I wasn't in my pa—' She stops, glares up at him.

He smiles. 'And what about me?' he adds softly. 'Tell me, Fanny.' He moves across and sits down on the edge of her desk. 'Hmm? What am I supposed to think?'

She can't stand it. She can't stand him. What's he doing, sitting on her desk? She feels anger rising, and panic. She needs, she knows, to get on top of the situation. And yet— 'Please, think whatever you want.' She longs for him to go away. Instead he leans forward, over the table, and rests a light hand on her shoulder. 'No, really, Robert. Please,' she shrugs her shoulder, but the light hand stays in place. 'Thank you for trying to help. And I don't mean to be rude, but—'

'*Shhh,*' he says, and begins to massage ever so gently. 'You're so tense, Fanny,' he murmurs. 'You need to relax.'

'Please – seriously – piss off.' And from nowhere she notices that she's crying, and that he hasn't pissed off, far from it. And that the telephone is ringing again. He's slid further across the desk and now he has both hands on her shoulders, massaging, stroking and she's still bloody well crying.

'Shhh . . . Shhhh,' it's barely a whisper, '*relax. Relax, Fanny. Why so tense? Hmm? . . . Why so tense?*'

Out of desperation, to get him away – to bring a third party into the room – she picks up the telephone. '*Louis?*' she says. 'Is that you?'

Panting.

'Oh . . . Fuck off!' She bends her head to the desk, with the telephone still rammed to her ear.

Robert eases the receiver from her hand and gently returns it to its cradle, and as he does so his soft pink lips burrow beneath her hair, and he kisses her neck. 'Louis isn't here now,' he murmurs, 'I'm here . . . *I'm here.*'

And though she tells him to fuck off, more than once, it

sounds muffled, with her face on the desk. It's possible Robert doesn't hear.

And from nowhere, for the moment, can she seem to find the strength to push him off . . .

13

Louis grew up in Baton Rouge, the son of an Anglican vicar and a classics professor at Louisiana State University. His parents sent him to England for his degree, because it was something they had both always wanted to do themselves, and because he asked, and they could just about afford it. He and Fanny were both enrolled on the same course and have been friends since the first week of their first term together. Louis is happy in England (he tends to be happy wherever he finds himself), and except for the occasional holiday, he hasn't quite got around to going home since.

He spent a couple of years after university driving removal vans. Then he went to art school. He worked briefly as a children's illustrator. He trained as a TEFL teacher and for a year or two made a fortune giving private English lessons to Japanese bankers. He worked as a park attendant. He took a course in cabinet-making.

For the past year Louis has been working as a freelance news photographer which, with the occasional boost from painting and decorating jobs, more or less pays his way. He enjoys the work: it allows him to travel, and to chat to people (which he loves) and he's actually a pretty good photographer, too. But Louis isn't somebody who lays much weight on his 'career', nor has he ever been. In fact he's always found other people's career obsessions very comical.

And yet, to his own dismay, he finds himself more than a little undermined by Fanny's recent stride towards adulthood and respectability. He feels as though he's dragging behind. After all, he has two degrees, one in English, another from the Camberwell School of Art, and almost nothing to show for either of them: a rented flat in horrible Hackney, a part-time job, a motorbike with two helmets, an overdrawn bank account and a credit card that's just hit its limit.

When, the day after the limbo cotillion, Louis had ambled into the Fiddleford village post office to ask, on a whim, about local housing, Mrs Hooper had recognised him at once. Mrs Hooper (who was feeling a little lousy that Saturday morning) told Louis she was aware of only three places which were available in the area: one, a cottage on the road to Lamsbury, close to the famous hat maker's, large and newly refurbished, and likely to be expensive. The other two, she said with a smirk, Louis would probably already be familiar with. Numbers 1 and 3 Old Alms Cottages, she explained, on either side of Miss Fanny Flynn, had been empty for years and would certainly be going cheap. They, like number 2, belonged to Mr and Mrs Guppy.

'Ah . . .' Louis smiled with his usual deprecating charm. 'After last night I guess that might prove something of a problem.' To which Mrs Hooper had thrown back her aching head and cackled.

'Believe you me,' she said, 'nothing's a problem for Ian Guppy, except missing out on the chance to make money. You'll have no trouble with Ian! Just ring him up and tell him you want to take one of his cottages. No need to mention Miss Flynn; he'll realise soon enough . . . But hang on a moment, I've got his number somewhere.'

'By the way, ma'am,' Louis said, as she disappeared to rummage beneath the counter.

Super manners! thought Mrs Hooper. *Goes to show not ALL Americans are bad.*

'Would you mind very much— To be frank with you, I've only started thinking about this, so please, if you wouldn't mind, I'd be obliged if you don't say anything to Fanny.'

'I shan't breathe a word to anyone,' she swore, as she always did when people were delightful enough to entrust her with their secrets. 'Don't you worry!' And to Mrs Hooper's credit, it should be said that though she told Kitty Mozely, who told Geraldine Adams, and though she did mention it to Mr Guppy, and though she couldn't resist dropping a clue to Mrs Haywood the glass-eyed secretary when she came in to buy her weekly Lotto, and though she implied as much to Messy McShane, and though she vaguely touched on the subject to young Colin and Chloe when they came delivering the eggs, and though she sort of hinted at it to the General, Mrs Hooper did not breathe a word to Fanny. And nor, of course, since the gossip was directly related to her, did anyone else . . .

Which is a shame because it would have cheered her up.

'*Louis isn't here now,*' Robert White is murmuring, burrowing his soft pink lips into her hair, holding tight to that telephone receiver. 'Louis isn't here. *I'm here. Robert's here* . . .' And as he pushes her backwards towards the floor, she protests. She struggles, but her movements are restricted by her chair and desk; his wet mouth is covering her mouth, his wispy beard is soaking up her tears, and he has both arms around her.

Silence while Fanny tries to find some angle, beneath his bony limbs and wet, determined lips, to communicate more clearly her displeasure. She finds no angle. Can hardly breathe, in fact. Robert, more or less oblivious, moans in gentle pleasure. And both of Fanny's telephones strike up at once; the one on her desk, the land line, is Geraldine Adams, returning Fanny's returned call, and still trying to make that reading-with-the-kids appointment. The other one, her mobile, which has just been knocked to the floor and out of reach, is Louis.

Stepping out into the Canary Wharf sunshine, fresh from a surprisingly successful meeting with his picture editor, Louis holds his telephone to his ear and waits impatiently for Fanny to pick up. She has only just called him according to his own mobile, so she must be there . . .

This morning he telephoned Ian Guppy, who, after extracting an unfeasibly large deposit, agreed to leave keys to both Alms Cottages at the Fiddleford Arms, allowing Louis to choose between them in his own time. So he has a place to live. He has the promise of plenty of work from his editor. He envisages making this one call – just to be sure she's still speaking to him. And then sometime afterwards, sometime very soon now, tipping up outside the school with keys to the neighbouring Alms Cottage in one hand and all his worldly goods in the other, and surprising her. They would have the whole summer together.

Because he's been unable to get the picture out of his head all week. He can think of nothing but Fanny, standing all alone in that wretched village hall. Of the Coca-Cola glistening on her pale skin, of her absolute defiance as she stood there with all eyes upon her, absolutely isolated, foreign, misunderstood; absolutely, unbearably— It was the moment – or the image – which finally allowed him to acknowledge that he probably loved her. Probably had been in love with her for a very long time. They would have the whole summer together.

Maybe even the rest of their lives.

No answer. She's not answering. He hangs up. She must be in class, he decides. He pulls on his crash helmet, kicks his bike into action and accelerates away. Towards London, briefly, and then on, to the new beginning. Towards Fanny.

He doesn't believe he's ever felt so certain about anything in his life.

14

His lips are still pressed hard to hers. Somehow he's got her on to the floor. Her mobile has rung and rung off and now she can feel his hand at her shirt buttons. He lifts his wet mouth, to look down at her and smile.

'You're so gorgeous,' he murmurs. 'Has anyone ever told you?'

It's her first real chance to speak. 'You stupid fucking creep! GET – OFF me!'

Robert kneels up. He is still fully dressed; neat and clean in his thick woolly jersey, the ends of his open-toed sandals bending backwards against the carpet-tile floor. He is smiling at her, full of concern. 'Am I rushing you a bit?'

'What? What the fuck—'

And then a tippety-tap on the office door.

Another sunny day. Five minutes previously Geraldine Adams had hung up her telephone in irritation. She's been trying to speak to Fanny all week, without success, and Geraldine is the sort of woman who, when she decides to do something, likes to do it; likes to set the wheels in motion at once. After drumming her fingers on the Old Rectory breakfast bar once or twice, she picked up her house keys and marched over to the school in person. Geraldine didn't stop at Mrs Haywood's desk. She headed straight on up to Fanny's office. To tippety-tap on Fanny's door.

'He-llo?' she says pleasantly. 'Hello, Miss Flynn?'

Miss Flynn's and her deputy's eyes lock. An isolated flash of unity; a shared moment of unadulterated panic.

He leaps to his feet, pulls her up. She straightens her skirt. 'Miss Flynn?'

'Give me two seconds!' she calls.

She does up the buttons of her shirt. Quickly, with curious proficiency, he licks his fingers and neatens her hair. He rearranges her desktop, pulls out her chair and thrusts her down on to it, stands back to examine the effect.

He winks at her. Gives her the thumbs up. Fanny looks away.

'Come in!' she calls. 'Come on in! I'm so sorry to keep you waiting . . .'

Geraldine pokes her head through the doorway, a frown of utmost curiosity on her handsome face. 'Sorry to barge in,' she says unapologetically, her eyes darting this way and that. 'Do you have a minute, Miss Flynn? Only it seems we never manage to catch each other on the phone. So I've broken all the rules and just dropped in! Hope you don't mind.'

Fanny looks blank. What rules? Who is this woman?

Geraldine, who never forgets a face or a name or a pin number, or where she put her bloody keys, assumes quite incorrectly that Fanny remembers her from the school gate. It is, after all, Fanny's business to recognise the parents of her pupils. Besides which Geraldine owns the second-prettiest house in Fiddleford and she cuts, she thinks, a more sophisticated-than-average figure in the village. It doesn't occur to her to introduce herself.

'Do I mind?' says Fanny. 'Not at all! Come on in.'

Geraldine twinkles at Robert. 'He-llo, Robert!' she says flirtatiously. She has always made it a policy to flirt with Ollie's male teachers. She's not sure why, but she's convinced it helps the Adams Family Interest one way or another. 'And how are you, sir, on this sunny Thursday morning?'

'Just about bearing up.' He beams at her and then at Fanny. 'Just about bearing up under the new regime!'

'Yes. It must be quite a change.'

'Certainly is! Quite a change. But I think I can get used to it!'

Fanny feels sick. Why doesn't he leave? He's not showing any signs of it. On the contrary he's crossed his arms over his bony chest and settled his buttocks back on to the radiator opposite Fanny's desk.

Fanny looks from one to the other, waiting for Robert to leave, or for the unknown woman to explain her presence in her office. She takes a breath to take charge, to send Robert back to his classroom. But Robert likes Geraldine. She's an intelligent lady, he thinks. A sexy, intelligent lady. Plus she and Clive sent him a case of champagne for Christmas (which he sold to his sister for £120). So he's not going to leave if he can help it.

'Fanny, have you met Geraldine properly?' he asks chattily. 'Geraldine Adams is little Ollie Adams's mum. Ollie was in my class last year, and I must say, unlike most of the sprogs I have to deal with, I was actually very sorry to see him go, wasn't I, Geraldine? He's a remarkable lad, is Ollie. Very able.'

Geraldine smirks. 'Well,' she says, 'Ollie certainly likes to be challenged. He has a very active mind and, as you know, stimulating that little mind is something we specialise in at home.' She turns to include Fanny. 'We encourage him, Fanny, never to take anything at face value. We like him to be always asking "Why?"'

'You can tell,' nods Robert sagely.

'*Why* do we respect all religions equally? Why does a car need petrol? *Why* does the totality function in this manner as opposed to the other? *WHY?* It's the one word you'll hear bouncing around our house. And Ollie just adores it.' Fanny nods like a puppet; her eyes glaze over. More to the point, WHY is this awful woman in her office? (The Ollie Adams she teaches is lazy, catatonically incurious and thick as pigshit. But no matter.) And even more to the point, WHY hasn't the repulsive Robert White gone away yet?

By now Geraldine has edged herself fully into the room. She is pressed against the closed office door – the only space left for her – and to Fanny it feels unbearably crowded. But Geraldine and Robert seem quite oblivious, quite at home. Robert is advising Geraldine on how best to nurture young Ollie's enquiring mind, and they're both agreeing that a careful balance of verbal and visual stimuli is always important.

'And of course, as you know, Ollie simply won't *eat* anything with artificial additives. Which is marvellous, really . . .'

Robert asks Geraldine how her husband is doing. He's doing fine.

Geraldine asks Robert how his girlfriend Julie is doing. She works in the Environmental Health Department at Lamsbury District Council.

'Julie? Oh, Julie's doing fine,' he says. 'That is,' he adds, glancing significantly at Fanny, 'so far as I know.'

'Ah!' Geraldine smiles. 'It's like that, is it? I am sorry.'

'Don't be sorry! To be frank with you, Geraldine, it's a relief. Julie's a lovely lady, do you know what I mean? But she was one of these ladies who's after a ring on her finger, 2.5 kiddies in the back yard and all the kit, you know, the TVs, the DVDs, one of these Dyson thingummies. And I must say, I found myself,' he laughs, slightly hysterically, 'a *teeny* bit inhibited by that.'

'Of course. There has to be give and take,' says Geraldine vaguely. Robert White doesn't teach Ollie any more. She would have been satisfied with much less information.

And so would Fanny. 'Robert,' says Fanny firmly, at last, 'don't you think you ought to be getting back to your class? The children will be waiting for you.'

To both women's surprise, Robert completely ignores her. He turns again to Geraldine. 'So!' he says brightly, his arms still folded, his bottom still in place on the radiator. 'How can we help you, Mrs Adams?'

'Well—' Geraldine hesitates, slightly embarrassed.

'Robert,' says Fanny more insistently, but there is – and they all hear it – the faintest hint of a plea in her voice. (It's been a bad morning.) 'Robert, I really think—'

'Relax!' Robert smiles at Fanny, holds up a soft, white, long-fingered hand; Fanny looks at the hand, feels a wave of nausea. 'I've set them a little task which should keep them busy.' He turns his smile to Geraldine. 'The mummy of all numeracy problems, as a matter of fact. Ollie would enjoy this one: if you took all the players in the football premier division—'

'Oh, *super*,' bursts out Geraldine, clapping her hands with joy. 'I think it's so important to make mathematics relevant, don't you, Fanny? Relate it to things that actually *really* matter.'

Fanny smiles wanly. 'How can I help you, Geraldine? What do you want?'

'Ahh!' says Geraldine. 'Yes. Thank you. I know you must be so busy . . .'

Fanny glances distractedly at Robert, who is staring back at her, a small smile on his wet lips, and a light of jubilation behind the pale eyes. She scowls at him and he quickly looks away.

Gorgeous, he thinks. *Gorgeous little thing.*

Geraldine says it's more a case of what she, Geraldine, can do for Fanny, than what Fanny can do for her. 'I've found time in my schedule,' she says, 'and it sounds silly, perhaps, but you know I have so much in life: a husband, a wonderful, happy, healthy son . . .'

'Lovely,' coos Robert. 'So many people forget to appreciate the simple blessings, don't they?'

'They do, Robert. And I feel, now, that the time is right for me to *give a little back*. I want to actively support Our Little Village School, if you will allow me. And by extension, Fanny, if it doesn't seem too grandiose, the State Education System in general, which incidentally I firmly believe in.'

Geraldine is well aware (she clarifies) that there are several 'exceptionally fortunate' children in the school who may not require her help, but that there are others who concern her; one or two, the thought of whose difficult lives can keep her awake at night. 'It wouldn't be appropriate to mention any names, but I think we all know who the kids are, and I passionately believe they might benefit from some extra one-on-one care – something which, with all the best will in the world, you two marvellous teachers simply don't have the time or the resources to provide.' She grins, very assured. 'Am I right?'

'So right,' says Robert, stroking his soft hands together.

Fanny looks at her desk, manages to mutter something to the same effect.

'And I would love, Miss Flynn, if you will have me, to put two mornings of my week *entirely* at your disposal! How does that sound to you?'

Fanny says, 'Well, thank you. Sounds like a good idea. It's always welcome when parents lend a helping hand. Shall we say Monday and Friday mornings then, for extra reading? Does that suit you?'

'Erm – I – yes.' She is disappointed. After all, to give up two mornings every week for the State Education System in general is quite a thing; it's quite a sacrifice. Fanny, she thinks, might have shown a bit more appreciation of that fact. 'Yes, I imagine Mondays and Fridays— But, no. Let me think. I'll need to confirm that. Fridays can be difficult. The office tends to heat up before the weekends.'

'OK, just let me know,' says Fanny, pushing her chair back and standing up, unable to bear being in such a confined space with two such odious people for a single moment longer. 'Any days would suit me. I can work around you. Give me a call when you're certain and we'll get the police check in motion. But you know, it takes so long. Between you and me, you can start next week.' Fanny smiles as warmly as she can, and holds out her hand.

Geraldine stiffens with annoyance. After all, she isn't any old *bored mum*, looking for something to do with her bloody time. Doesn't Fanny realise that? Doesn't she realise that Geraldine Adams used to earn a great deal more money than Fanny Flynn ever has or ever will? Doesn't she realise—

'That,' says Robert, 'is a truly fabulous offer. And thank you, Geraldine. From the bottom of our hearts. Thank you, thank you, thank you! I know how busy you are, and I know what a tremendous sacrifice this must be for you.'

'Oh, no, really, not at all.'

'And when people like you can manage to take time out of their busy schedules to support their kiddies' schools—'

'No, honestly.' She glances significantly at Fanny.

'Thank you,' Robert says again.

'Stop! I'm just doing what I can. After all, we're all on the same side, right?'

'Oh, yes,' agrees Robert. 'Absolutely.'

She puts two thumbs in the air, cocks her head: 'WE'RE JUST DOIN' IT FOR THE KIDS!'

'That's right,' Robert nods. 'Kiddies first! Every time!'

Geraldine keeps the head cocked, offers the two of them a raised eyebrow, a winsome smile.

'Super,' says Robert. 'Well, Geraldine, if that's all, I know Fanny and I should be getting back to our young students.' He lifts himself up from the radiator and, with one soft hand on her shoulder, shepherds Geraldine towards the stairs. 'Thanks ever so much for dropping by. Lovely to see you! And send my regards to Clive, won't you?' Geraldine assures him that she will, though she won't. Of course. Clive wouldn't have had the faintest idea who she was talking about.

Robert White stands at the top of the stairs, smiling and waving until she is out of view. Afterwards he doesn't quite dare to return to Fanny's office. Some sense of personal preservation sends him instead to the toilet to wash his hands, where he finds that he can't stop grinning. Maybe he rushed her a little there, he thinks, but there's a chink, and he feels it; a chink of light in the tunnel of love; a teeny-tiny seedling from which something special and beautiful might yet grow.

Robert disposes neatly of his paper towel, checks his fingernails, and heads out to his classroom, where he orders the children to mark their own maths books and then switches a video on.

The video is called *Are We Being Served? An Overview of Service Industries in the West Midlands* and they have seen it many times before.

15

Robert White's previous hostility, his fluey colds, are all forgotten now. He turns up to work every day. He follows Fanny around the school like a puppy. She spoke to him only once, on the afternoon following the incident. She made it clear (she thought) that she never wanted anything similar to happen again. But he'd wandered off with the same serene smile stuck on his lips and it's been stuck there, now, for a week. No matter what she does. No matter how much she snaps and snarls and ignores him. She can't shift it.

The little interlude in Fanny's office has been re-shot in his mind, in softest focus and from all conceivable angles; it's been given a soundtrack, and a whole lot of dialogue that was never there. He's taken home the photograph from the *Gazette*, cut it out and stuck it on to sugar paper stolen from the school stationery cupboard. And this morning he brought pink roses into the staff room.

He made a tremendous drama of arranging them in a broken coffee mug.

'They're lovely,' gushed Linda Tardy; gushed Mrs Haywood. They called in Tracey Guppy from washing the floor next door to have a look.

'Bet you wish you had a young man giving you roses like that!' said Linda Tardy. 'I know I do!'

'They're revolting,' Tracey said.

Fanny, face buried in a newspaper, gave a muffled snort.

'Do you like them, Fanny?' said Robert, jiggling them ineptly about. The stems were too long for the mug, and they wouldn't balance.

'Hey, Tracey,' said Fanny (ignoring Robert), 'I spotted your naughty brother Dane in the post office yesterday. He didn't look very ill to me. Any chance he might come back to school one of these—' She looked round from behind her newspaper, but Tracey had left the room. 'Tracey?'

'Ouch!' Robert's mug of pink roses tumbled to the floor. He looked across at Fanny, pale eyes damp with yearning, a spot of red blood sprouting from his finger. 'I think I'm going to need a plaster.'

'Oh, belt up,' Fanny snapped.

'Have pity on him!' giggled glass-eyed Mrs Haywood, as Fanny slapped down her paper and stood up to leave the room. 'The man's soft on you, he can't help it. He can't concentrate on a thing!'

Through all this nonsense Fanny continues to work hard at her new job, and already the school is beginning to blossom. At least, there is a clear sense of energy to it now. The walls are covered in the children's artwork and poetry, and there are nature displays on the tables. She has made a small garden at the side of the school, where the junior class has planted flower and vegetable seeds. Last week her car hit one of the Maxwell McDonald pheasants, so she brought the bird in and dissected it for everyone, which was illegal on Health and Safety grounds, but popular with the children. Next week she wants to take them all out collecting wool. Together (the plan is) they will learn how to wash it, spin it, dye it, and weave it into scarves.

Fanny thinks of her school all day and most of the night. In the three weeks since term started she's had dinner a couple of times with Grey and Messy McShane. She's met Charlie, Jo, the twins and the General in the Fiddleford Arms for a weekend lunch. (They'd been unable to invite her to the Manor; one of their more troubled celebrity guests being so afraid of spies he'd demanded that even the post be left at the bottom of the drive.) Fanny's spent a couple of evenings on her own in the pub, chatting with Tracey and anyone else around (although she tries to avoid drinking with Kitty). And she gossips with Mrs Hooper for at least twenty minutes every morning, when she buys her milk and newspaper. But that, excepting the weekend Louis came, makes up the sum total of Fanny's Fiddleford social life to date. For someone so naturally gregarious, it's not much. And yet Fanny hasn't felt lonely for more than the odd few minutes in all that time. She's been so wrapped up in her work, and so exhausted by the end of each working day, often she can barely find the energy to talk to Brute, let alone to a human being.

Her evenings tend mostly to be dominated by the government forms: the progress reports, policy papers, target statements, assessment charts and time-allocation forecasts all growing steadily damper under her kitchen sink. It seems the more forms she fills in, the more they pile up, so that her desk at work and the kitchen cupboard are now stuffed and overflowing. And at night, even in her dreams, Fanny finds herself ticking boxes, evaluating performances, identifying ethnic origins, searching – endlessly – for that magical square which says 'other'.

Only two things worry her more than the paperwork: that Dane Guppy hasn't appeared at school since Fanny and his enormous mother had their disagreement at the limbo over a fortnight ago; and that Scarlett Mozely, Kitty's daughter, hasn't produced a piece of work or said a single word to Fanny, or to anyone else, since term began.

Scarlett sits at the back of the class with her crutches lying neatly beside her, as she sits everywhere in life, plain and silent and mostly ignored. She's been sitting at that same desk, with that same sullen face, ever since Kitty moved to Fiddleford, and until now no one has ever made more than a token effort to disturb her.

Mrs Haywood the glass-eyed secretary tells Fanny she has been unable to 'locate' any notes on Scarlett Mozely in either her office or Fanny's, which is no surprise since the notes on at least a third of all of Fiddleford's thirty-eight pupils have been missing for years. Robert White is equally unforthcoming when Fanny finally summons the strength to ask him for help.

They are in the staff room at the time, and not alone. (Fanny takes care that they are never alone.) He's chuckling self-consciously over something in the *Guardian*, and Fanny is in the far corner, as far away from him as possible, with her back to him, making coffee.

'Robert,' she barks. 'Tell me what you know about Scarlett Mozely.'

'Mmm,' he says happily, pretending to think about it but really only trying to make the conversation last, 'mmmm . . . No, I must say I don't know much about Scarlett, I'm afraid, Fanny. She arrived straight into Mrs Thomas's class.'

'Yes, I'm aware of that.'

'Mmm. So your best bet, Fanny, would probably be putting a call in to Mrs Thomas.'

'Mrs Thomas doesn't return my calls, as you know. And this is a small school. I presume you've had some dealings with her?'

'By the way, Fanny, I've been meaning to ask you, have you ever been on the Eurostar?'

'What?'

He tells her about a trip to Paris he took 'with a certain lady-friend. Call me an old devil, but what with *recent events* I've actually misplaced her name!' He asks Fanny to forgive him for quoting the old maxim, 'But Paris,' he says, 'really *is* the most romantic city in the world!'

Linda Tardy, eating McVitie's on the ink-stained sofa, shakes her head. 'I think you two would make a super couple,' she says, 'both being so brainy and international and everything. Wouldn't it be lovely, Mrs Haywood? Don't you think?'

'Linda,' Fanny says briskly, 'tell me. What do you know about Scarlett Mozely?'

'Well . . . To my experience,' Linda Tardy replies, after an incredibly long pause, during which she finishes her biscuit – and thinks, presumably, 'she's one of these *busy* ones who likes to buzz away at her own little projects. Doing her own thing. And who am I to say she shouldn't? Poor little mite.'

'But is she clever? Is she thick? Seriously, it seems ridiculous, but I've no idea if she can even read and write! You must have seen some of her work?'

Linda Tardy's lips disappear, leaving nothing showing but the outlying pink-smudged vertical creases, sprinkled with biscuit crumbs. 'Have *you* seen her work?' she asks sternly.

'No, but—'

'Well, then . . . And incidentally, Fanny, though I say it as probably shouldn't, but I personally don't appreciate descriptives such as "clever" or "thick" when it comes to our little kiddies. Not in this day and age.'

Fanny sighs. She glances out of the staff-room window, to where Scarlett sits alone on a wall, scribbling away in that red book of hers, and decides the time has come for her to contact Scarlett's mother. She takes her coffee and walks towards the door.

'Ooh, Fanny,' says Robert suddenly. 'I was wondering. Do you have a minute? Could I have a little word?'

A wave of ferocious irritation. She looks back at him. He's folded the *Guardian*'s 'G2' and placed it neatly back inside the main paper, and he's already half on his feet.

'What do you want?' she asks coldly.

'I mean, could I have a little word in the office?'

'NO.' She notices Linda Tardy looking at her curiously. 'I mean . . .' She corrects herself. 'Not really, no. Now isn't convenient. Can it wait?'

'Only I've been doing a little research.'

'Good good.' She looks at her watch.

'Into teachers' courses.'

'Oh, yes?'

'There's a one-day Saturday course in Swindon next month. Wait a mo'. I've got the leaflet here . . . It's for heads and deputies. I thought it might be fun if we did it together.'

'Ohhh,' drools Linda Tardy. 'Isn't that nice? Go on, Fanny dear. You deserve a bit of fun.'

He rifles around in the bulging briefcase at his feet, pulls out a glossy sheet and hands it to Fanny. There is a clammy mark where his fingers have been, Fanny notices, and she feels a wave of sympathy for him. She can see how hard he is trying. 'I thought it might be ever so helpful,' he says eagerly. 'A real, positive step forward for Fiddleford.'

She looks at the sheet. 'Robert, we've only got seven children in the football team!'

'Absolutely. But it says there that the course takes a "holistic" approach, thereby providing skills, not just refereeing skills but – other ones. Which may be useful in many scenarios. It's tailor-made for primary schools.'

She hands it back. 'I don't think so, Robert. No.' She flashes a smile. 'But thank you. Thanks for thinking of it.'

*   *   *

Scarlett's mother, Kitty Mozely, manages to sound impressively concerned about her daughter's refusal to participate in school life – for a good four minutes. She says that she, too, has noticed how Scarlett always carries a red notebook around with her, and how she only rarely speaks. 'But you know how it is,' Kitty says blithely, pausing to light one cigarette from the end of the other, and exhaling heavily into the receiver. 'Her father wasn't much of a talker either. Always sodding off without a word. Used to drive me bananas . . . So, but, yes. It is strange, isn't it? D'you suppose there's something wrong with her? I mean, aside from the obvious . . .' Kitty sighs, a fraction of her usual impatience just beginning to peep through. 'She worries me terribly, you know, Miss Flynn. She does. We've such a struggle as it is, with just the two of us. Because of course writers such as myself rarely earn a sausage. Others might, but me, no. You probably hear these Harry-Potter-type figures being bandied about—'

Fanny clears her throat. They seem to be veering off the point.

'But in this particular children's author's house, money's short, Miss Flynn.' (And so it is, in a way. It is for Kitty. She owns her pretty cottage and she lives off a small private income, about the size of Tracey Guppy's combined salary from the pub, where she works four nights a week, and the school, where she works as a cleaner/caretaker/dinner lady. But Kitty Mozely came from a very rich family once, plus she was spoilt for years by being so clever and pretty; her luck turned, she often says, from the moment she discovered she was pregnant with Scarlett.) 'Money's always a problem. We do struggle. And with all Scarlett's special requirements . . . Plus she eats like a— Really,' she adds bitterly, having just come back from Safeways, 'you'd be surprised how much that girl eats.'

'I'm just wondering if you have any idea,' persists Fanny, 'what she might be scribbling or drawing or whatever in that notebook of hers? I'm intrigued. And I think, maybe, I mean, if I'm going to help her I really do need to know—' Fanny is humiliated to have to admit it. 'To be frank with you, Mrs Mozely—'

'Ms. *Ms* Mozely, actually, Ms Flynn. But it doesn't matter.' She gives a wheezy, smoker's chuckle. 'Call me Kitty.'

'To be frank with you, Kitty, it sounds ridiculous, but I don't even know for sure if she can read or write!'

Kitty bursts out laughing. 'Read and write! *My* daughter? I have a degree from Oxford University, Miss Flynn. Of course she can bloody well read and write! Are you mad? What the bloody hell—'

'Good!' Fanny says quickly. 'Well, that's something at least.'

'She's been at your school for over a year!'

'I know,' Fanny says. 'I know. Only Mrs Thomas isn't – making herself available. She's not returning any calls. And I must admit we can't currently, erm, locate Scarlett's notes.'

Kitty isn't listening. 'I mean, of course she can bloody well read,' she says, but she sounds suddenly less certain. She tries to envisage her daughter either reading a book or writing a letter, and – absurdly – she finds she can't manage it. Her daughter is helpful in the kitchen. She's actually a very good cook. But other than that, what does her daughter do all the time? Besides squabble with Ollie Adams? Kitty laughs. She honestly can't think! The problem is, of course, Scarlett spends so much time in her bedroom.

'I'll tell you what I'll do,' promises Kitty hurriedly, keen now to get off the telephone before the true extent of her ignorance is revealed, 'I'll do a little detective work, shall I? See what the little monster's been getting up to! And I'll let you know what I find out.'

'Well, if you could . . .'

'Absolutely. I'll get on to it right away. I promise.'

A rash promise, made in haste, which, predictably, Kitty fails to keep.

Fanny waits. She tries again to get hold of Mrs Thomas, who has apparently taken her stress-related pay-off very seriously, and completely evaporated from the planet.

At the end of lessons a few days later Fanny's watching Scarlett, as usual, fastening her intriguing red notebook inside her battered satchel, and slowly limp towards the door. Scarlett is always the last out.

'Scarlett,' says Fanny, and she can see from the way Scarlett tenses that she's heard her, but she still walks on. 'Scarlett, don't ignore me. We need to talk. This is becoming ridiculous.'

Scarlett turns slowly, flushing with surprise. She limps towards Fanny's desk and stands there defiantly, waiting. Fanny pulls up a chair.

'Sit down.'

'I don't want to keep my mother waiting.'

It is the longest sentence Fanny has heard from her, but of course it's also not entirely true. By standing on her seat, which Fanny then does, she can see the school gate, and Kitty Mozely, as usual, is nowhere to be seen.

Fanny knows more about Scarlett's daily habits than Scarlett, accustomed to being ignored, could have possibly imagined. She knows that Scarlett often goes home with Ollie Adams. She's watched her, limping miserably behind as Ollie and the au pair march on in front, squabbling with each other. She knows that if Scarlett's not going home with Ollie, she usually has to hobble the mile home to Laurel Cottage alone.

'Your mother's not out there, Scarlett.'

'How do you know?'

'Because,' says Fanny, dropping back down into her seat again, 'I know what she looks like. I've seen her.'

'When? In the pub?'

'Since you mention it, yes. She's been pointed out to me. I've seen her a couple of times.'

'So you're in there yourself, are you, most nights? Just like Kitty. You must be lonely, then.'

Fanny gives a thin smile. 'I was beginning to wonder if you were a bit retarded, Scarlett.'

Scarlett sniggers.

'But you obviously aren't. So tell me. What's going on?'

Scarlett keeps sniggering.

'What's funny? Scarlett, I asked you to sit down.'

She sits. Finally Fanny says, 'Is your mother at home?'

'How should I know?'

'I'm going to call her and let her know you'll be staying late. So you can show me some work – OK?' She smiles; Scarlett doesn't. 'And afterwards I'll drop you off home in my car. All right, Scarlett? Do you understand?'

Scarlett doesn't answer.

'OK, Scarlett?' says Fanny again.

'Do I have a choice?'

Fanny hesitates. 'Er – you don't actually, no. So. Will you tell me your mother's telephone number, or are you going to make me go all the way upstairs to the office to look it up?'

Scarlett looks at Fanny as if she's an idiot. 'I'm going to make you go—'

'Of course. Stupid question.' Fanny opens a maths book to the page the rest of the class has been working from, and asks Scarlett to set to work. 'Do what you can,' Fanny says. 'And don't worry if you get stuck. It doesn't matter. It's what I'm here for. I'll be back in a minute, all right?'

Fanny pokes her head out into the hall. The staff-room

door has been left open. There is no one inside. She glances from left to right; no sign of Robert, then. She's spotted him a couple of times recently, skulking around after school, obviously waiting for her. Today it looks as though he's gone straight home. But she still runs across the hall, just in case, and takes care to close her office door, and even to lock it, before dialling the Mozely number.

She leaves a brief message on Kitty's answer machine and returns to the classroom, where she finds Scarlett leaning back in her chair, hands behind her head, pencil in the same place Fanny left it.

'Oh, come on, get on with it!' Fanny snaps. 'We'll be here all night. You're not going anywhere, Scarlett, until you've at least shown me—'

A tiny smile plays on Scarlett's lopsided lips. Her paper is filled with scrawls; it's an ugly, angry mess. But in those three minutes Scarlett has finished the same exercise her class has been struggling over all week. The arithmetic is there, scribbled randomly around the page. She obviously hasn't used a calculator. And every answer is correct.

'So,' Fanny says finally. 'So, Scarlett Mozely. That's what it's all about, is it?' Fanny laughs. 'So! Clever clogs. Well. Of course it is! I should have guessed as much. I mean, this is . . . this is . . . so . . . I mean, this is . . . phenomenal. Scarlett? I mean, seriously. What else can you do?'

And from the depths of Scarlett's chest there comes a disarming gurgle, long and deep; a laugh of triumph at having kept her secret for so long. Behind the moon glasses her eyes smart. She looks absurdly happy.

And so does Fanny. 'Honestly,' she giggles suddenly, 'I've never taught a Secret Genius before!' And without pausing for thought, Fanny has leant across the table, pulled Scarlett into a tight, untidy hug and given her a smacker on both cheeks.

'Oh, shit,' she says at once, releasing her hurriedly. '*Sorry*. I'm so sorry.' She tries to rub the kisses off. '*Sorry*. Not meant to do that. Very naughty. Child Abuse.' She giggles again. 'They could put me in jail for that.'

Scarlett says nothing. She is paralysed with confusion. When, after all, was she last kissed by anyone? Except for Clive and Geraldine's chillingly dutiful single pecks, always delivered to the pretty side, Scarlett can't even remember.

'Sorry, Scarlett,' says Fanny again, embarrassed to have so obviously embarrassed her. 'I am sorry.'

But Scarlett is too blown away to answer.

16

It's dusk by the time Fanny drops Scarlett back home. She and her mother live in a pretty-enough little cottage, with a moss-covered thatched roof and a buckling rose bush at the gate, but the path to the door is overtaken with brambles, and obstructed by an old fridge lying on its back. Inside, all the lights are off. The house looks empty and unwelcoming.

Fanny says, with her car engine still running, 'Will you be all right, Scarlett? You'd be very welcome to come and have tea with me, if you prefer. It looks as though your mother may have gone out.'

'I should think she has! I should think she ought to be allowed a life of her own while I'm at school and things. It's not easy, you know, having a child.'

'Well, no. But I think . . .'

Scarlett looks at her curiously. 'Don't you believe in a woman's right to have a life of her own?'

'What? Don't be idiotic, Scarlett. I didn't say that. Anyway, this isn't about women's rights. It's about you being not very old. You shouldn't be—'

'I can look after myself, thank you, Miss Flynn. I've been doing it for years.'

A drawn-out silence, while Scarlett struggles from the little car, and Fanny dares not offer to help for fear of offending her yet again. 'I shall see you on Monday then,' Fanny says at last.

It sounds unnaturally upbeat. They both notice it. Scarlett smiles awkwardly. 'Thanks for the lift,' she mumbles.

'It was a pleasure, Scarlett. And on Monday, bring me something to read, will you? I want to see how you write. Write me a story about . . .' She pauses to think of a subject.

'Actually, I'm writing a story at the moment,' Scarlett says, unconsciously tapping it, inside her satchel.

'Ah-ha!' Fanny laughs. 'The mysterious Red Book?'

She smiles. 'It's about Oliver Adams.'

'A story about Ollie? I was thinking of something more along the lines—'

'It's fiction,' interrupts Scarlett, her face glittering suddenly, full of mischief. She looks like her mother. She looks almost pretty. 'Don't worry, Miss Flynn. I'm writing it like a novel. At the moment it's called *The Most Boring, Feeble-Minded, Over-Indulged Little Pillock in the Universe.*'

'Pillock?' repeats Fanny, but she can't help laughing again. 'I mean, you can write what you want, of course. I'd love to see it. Only I don't think— I mean— Try not to make him too identifiable.'

Scarlett shrugs. 'If you like. But he's never going to read it.'

Fanny watches Scarlett as she hobbles through the dusk and over the brambles, fumbling with the keys before letting herself in. And pauses, engine still running, briefly at a loss. She feels less courageous than Scarlett about the prospect of returning to an empty house, with only the long, quiet weekend ahead. She turns the car around and heads back to the school where, as always, she has mountains of work to catch up on.

She had locked the place up when she left with Scarlett and it, too, as she draws up in front, looks far from welcoming. The encroaching darkness does something Gothic to its 150-year-old face; the enormous windows loom at her, the high stone walls, normally a warm and lichen-speckled russet, look cold and flat and grey. As she crosses the playground towards the shadowy front porch she's suddenly very conscious of the generations of childish figures that have passed through this place before; of the hopeful voices, the carefree laughter, the lives that have started here, and been, and gone; and she feels, for once, the full weight of her own responsibility. She may only be an outsider but she's also a link now, in a bigger chain, and it is up to her to keep this small place alive.

She shivers.

In the empty staff room she makes herself coffee, carries it up with her to her office and sets to work. She works for a couple of hours without noticing the time pass, wading doggedly through the interminable paperwork, marking books, filling in forms. She's about to take her mug downstairs to make a second cup of coffee when the creak of a distant pipe makes her jump. She pauses, noticing suddenly how dark it is outside, and how very quiet. There is a light shining in the bungalow opposite, where Tracey and her Uncle Russell with emphysema live. But Tracey's working in the pub tonight, and her uncle sits in his wheelchair with the television volume turned up high, so he can hear it over his own wheezing.

Another creak. Makes her heart thud. Makes Brute give a menacing growl. She reaches instinctively for her cigarettes.

Suddenly the telephone on her desk bursts shrilly through the silence. She stares at it. Who calls a primary school at this time? It rings four times and then it stops.

A wrong number. Of course.

She looks down at her desk, tries to remember what she was doing before, and it starts ringing a second time. Again, it rings only four or five times, and stops. Slowly, carefully, trying to breathe through the rising panic, she stands up to leave, and as she does so, knocks against a pile of papers at the edge of her desk. They scatter all over her chair and floor, taking the telephone and her car keys with them.

'Shit!'

She kneels down to pick them up and through the throbbing silence feels an unmistakable burst of cold night air, and then bang! The slam of a door. Silence.

A footstep.

She bites her lip.

Another footstep. It's coming closer, coming up the stairs . . .

One step . . . two step . . .

She should call the police.

. . . three step . . . four.

Fanny's-heard-a-maniac.

He's-just-behind-the-door!

The bloody telephone receiver's all tangled up with the back of her chair. She yanks at it—

Behind her, the office door bursts open. She hears a little thud and something square and purple skidding across the floor towards her. A box of Milk Tray chocolates.

'TE-DAH!' cries Robert. 'And all because . . . the lady loves!' He laughs merrily. 'D'you remember that ad, Fanny? The guy climbs into the lady's bedroom and—'

'No,' she snaps, clambering up. 'No, I bloody don't.' And then all at once the relief, the anger, the fear, the irritation overcome her. Robert's standing there with his shiny bob and his woolly jersey all rubbing up against his chin. He's twisting his fingers together uncertainly, shivering and grinning. Fanny bursts into tears.

'Hey, Fanny!' His face crumples. 'Don't cry! It was only a little joke. I saw the lights were on, I was just— I just happened to be passing. So I thought— Why didn't you answer the phone?' He puts an arm round her shoulders. 'Come on, Fanny. It's Friday night, what say you we go for a drink together, hmm?' He holds up his free hand in mock surrender, and beneath the blond facial hair, his pink lips stretch into another smile. 'And no hanky-panky, I promise!'

Fanny can't even bring herself to look at him. 'Robert,' she says, gazing down at the floor, 'I never want to have to say this again. The answer is no. It will always be no. OK? I'm sorry. I'm sorry if that's disappointing for you. So take your arm off my shoulder, please. Thank you. And— And have a good weekend. I really have a lot of work to do. I'll see you on Monday morning.'

He clicks his tongue. 'You work too hard, Fanny. You've got to learn to have fun.'

'Thanks, Robert. I know how to have fun.'

Robert takes a step away, puts his hands in his pockets, and gazes down at her. He chuckles, shakes his head admiringly. 'I'll bet . . . You're one feisty lady, aren't you, Fanny Flynn?'

'I'm your *boss*, Robert,' she snaps suddenly. 'Now fuck off. Oh, God—' He looks hurt. 'I'm sorry. I didn't mean to be rude.' She tries to smile. 'And thanks for the chocolates. OK? I've just got a lot of work on.'

'It's OK,' he murmurs, then he bends down and kisses her softly on the cheek. 'I can take the knocks. I can do that.' And because she sees that he's leaving, and she can see that he's pathetic and obviously lonely, she forces herself not to recoil, forces herself to stick with the smile. She waits until he has strolled out of the room before she wipes his wet lips away.

'Have a good weekend,' he calls out to her from the bottom of the stairs. 'You take care, now! And enjoy the chocs!' He sounds almost happy, she thinks.

17

She can't work after that. She can't concentrate. There is a single-screen cinema in the centre of Lamsbury, musty and almost always empty, but still just about open for business. The moment she's got rid of Robert, Fanny takes herself there, buys a ticket without bothering to ask what is showing, scans the cinema to be sure that he hasn't followed her, settles down to lose herself in another world and immediately falls asleep.

Afterwards, she's heading out through the foyer, feeling blurry eyed and incredibly hungry, when she bumps into Jo and her husband Charlie Maxwell McDonald, who is patiently re-explaining the film's plot to his father, the General. 'But they were *different characters*, Dad,' he is saying (again). 'There were *three* men, and they were all—'

The General catches sight of Fanny and immediately shouts out to her. 'Hello, hello,' he bellows. 'Thought that was you, nodding off in the front row! Kept your shirt on this evening, have you, Miss Flynn?'

Fanny smiles patiently, turns towards him. Since that evening the General has said the same thing every time they've met. 'I didn't see you all in there,' she says, and grins. 'Didn't see much of anything, actually. Was it any good?'

'Drivel,' the General answers, peering behind her. 'As per usual. Made no sense at all. Didn't miss a thing. Have you got your chap with you this evening, then? I can't see him. Is he here?'

'What chap?' she mutters. 'A chap? I don't have a chap. Thank you. No. I'm on my own.'

'On your own?' echoes the General indignantly. 'Attractive young lady like you!'

'She's been working so hard,' interrupts Jo, tactfully, 'she probably longs to spend an evening on her own for once. I know I do.'

'Mmm?' The General looks unconvinced. 'Well, well, I dare say. Nice to see you, Fanny.' He hesitates, on the point of marching onwards, but then in spite of what Jo says, he thinks she looks a little sad, a little lonely. 'I say, Fanny,' he adds, 'if you're not doing anything on Sunday, why don't you come to lunch?'

'Thanks—' She looks ready to accept.

'Oh, blast. Not this Sunday,' he corrects himself. Turns to Jo. 'We'll still have that paranoid bugger staying, won't we? D'you suppose he'll ever leave?'

'He says he wants to stay on at least another week,' Charlie says.

Jo and the General let out simultaneous groans.

'Well, next Sunday then,' the General says. 'Make it next Sunday.'

Fanny laughs. 'That would be lovely. Thank you.'

'And Grey McShane'll be cooking,' the General brightens a little. 'Meat. He always cooks on Sundays. Which means of course that we'll have the Ghastly Guestlies in loco. No way round it, I'm afraid. Wherever McShane cooks, the Guestlies tend to follow. But I'm sure you can cope. And God knows, they need diluting.'

'Right then. Well, I shall see you then.' Fanny hesitates,

tries hard not to ask but can't resist, 'So, er – who d'you suppose you'll have staying with you?'

'Mmm? Oh, no one much,' the General says airily. 'We've got a couple of bores from the television just arrived, who seem to think I keep a mental file on every aspect of their fatuous "careers". But they might have left by then. Fingers crossed. And a cold-fish adviser from Downing Street. Well, ex-adviser now. Ha, ha. Another raving ego maniac. As per usual. However. Mustn't complain . . . You'll have to sign a thing. Won't she, Jo? Sorry. It's ghastly, but we've come a cropper in the past. Things have turned up in the news.'

'You don't mean a "confidentiality agreement"?' Fanny giggles. 'General, I can't think of anything more glamorous!'

'Excellent. Jolly good.' He looks at her thoughtfully. 'Enjoying yourself down here, are you? Not too lonely?'

Fanny frowns. Enjoying herself? It's the question she and Louis always ask each other; it's their justification for always moving on. Enjoying her life in Fiddleford? She's been too involved in it to wonder. Suddenly it seems a ridiculous question. She's not even certain how to answer it. 'Funnily enough,' she says at last, 'and in spite of many things – yes. I suppose I am.' And the frown lifts, as if she realises the truth of what she's saying for the first time. She looks up at the General and laughs. 'Funnily enough, I love it here,' she says again.

'Good, good.' He nods. 'Well, maybe we should get Solomon Creasey over. Don't you think, Charlie? He'll have some Silent Beauty trailing along, of course. But not to worry. They come and they go. Have you met him, Fanny?'

'Not yet. I've heard a lot about him.'

'Noisy chap. Tremendous chums with McShane. In fact, I rather suspect they have some sort of a history together . . . Well. Excellent. We shall see you next Sunday!' He turns away without waiting for her reply. 'Charlie? Jo?' They are arm in arm, and nobody can fail to notice what an outrageously handsome couple they are, how happy they look together, and how incongruous in the foyer of the musty old Lamsbury Classic. 'Shall we get going?' he says briskly, and he charges out into the darkness, awkwardly tactful, leaving the lovebirds to amble slowly behind.

18

Among many other small improvements, Fanny has introduced a simple system at the school, involving letters and telephones etc., which makes it virtually impossible for the children to play truant without their parents finding out. Before she arrived some of the older children used to catch the bus into Lamsbury and roam around making a great nuisance of themselves, or, worse still, they used to roam around Fiddleford, stealing crisps and drinks from tables at the Fiddleford Arms, or standing outside the post office and imitating Mrs Hooper's laugh – which they could do sometimes, without any signs of boredom, for hours on end. Poor Mrs Hooper used to wake up in the night with their noises echoing inside her head.

But the truancy has stopped now, more or less. And Fanny, although still a long way from being forgiven for the shirt-stripping episode, has gained a handful of allies as a result.

The obese Mrs Guppy, of course, is not among them. Mrs Guppy, in spite of two letters and even a telephone call from Fanny (which ended before it ever began –

'Hello, Mrs Guppy. I'm sorry to disturb you at home. It's Fanny Flynn here. From the school . . .'

'And you can fuck off.' *Clunk*.)

– still keeps her son Dane at home.

And for Fanny the temptation to let him stay there is strong. Because she could just leave him to rot; make a nominal report to someone at the LEA who would of course make a nominal report to someone else, and nothing would be done. Dane Guppy is only one pupil. One stupid, troublesome, charmless, aggressive, thoroughly disruptive pupil, with a mother Fanny would be happy never to have to see again.

Fanny is brooding over this one lunch-hour. And feeling guilty, as she always does. She's on the verge – as she often is – of grabbing her keys and driving up to Mrs Guppy's house to confront her. And she's finding – as she often does – that being on the verge and actually doing, are two quite different things.

She gazes unhappily out of her open office window, away from the bungalows and the village hall, on to the view which she has already grown to love: the playing field, the winding lane, the church, the Manor's cedar tree. It's grey out there, she notices; it must be raining. Why are all the children in such a neat row? *Kneeling* in such a neat—

'*Oliver Adams!*' she yells through the open window. He jumps. The entire school jumps. 'Bring whatever that thing is you have in your hand and come and see me. Right now, please. And everybody else, stand up! Hurry up! You all look *completely pathetic!*'

They had been kneeling before Ollie, who was sitting cross-legged on a log with a boy-guard on either side of him, and a mobile with Internet connection on his lap. Fanny knows what it is because she's already caught him with it once before. He's been making the children grovel in front of him, in exchange for a glimpse of porn.

It is the sight of Ollie, in all his Boden finery, meandering his remorse-free path across the playground, which finally spurs her to action. Because she knows exactly how the scene will play out. Ollie will stand in front of her desk and mumble resentful excuses, and wait until she allows him to leave. She will probably confiscate the stupid machine until the end of term. And then Oliver Adams will go home and return with some other toy. And the children will form another line. And nothing will change.

Meanwhile the illiterate, eleven-year-old Dane Guppy will continue to fester at home while what future he might ever have had slowly decomposes in front of him.

It occurs to her she's like a police officer, fining a driver for not wearing his safety belt while there's a rape going on in the passenger seat beside him. She grabs her bag, her keys and her dog and heads for the door, passing Ollie on his way up her office stairs as she rushes down them. She skids to a halt.

'Hand it over!' she says.

'What?' says Ollie innocently. 'I haven't got it.'

Fanny points a finger between his eyes and prods him on the forehead. His head bounces slightly; recentres itself. He scowls at her. 'In case you didn't know,' he says, with lots of sarcasm, 'Poking and prodding pupils tends to be against the law.'

'And if I see that object again,' she says, ignoring him, 'I'm telling your mum. OK? And I'll tell everyone in the village you're a pervert.'

'You wouldn't!'

'Oh, I would.' She hurries on, taking the last three steps in a single leap, and colliding straight into Robert.

'Hey-hey-hey!' he says, grabbing the chance to touch her, holding her back with a vicelike bony hand on each shoulder. 'Steady! Where are you going in such a hurry?'

'I might be a bit late back,' Fanny says distractedly. 'Can you keep an eye on my class?'

'Will do,' he says. 'And you take it easy, young lady, hmm? OK? You'll be no use to any of us, lying in a hospital bed!'

19

Lazy days all roll into one around Mrs Guppy's dirty kitchen table. She sits at it, brooding, like an angry, asthmatic Buddha. She has an ashtray, a lighter and a pack and a half of Embassy Filter on one side of her, a cup of cool tea, thick with sugar, on the other. She has the Guppy sister-in-law sitting opposite her and a copy of the *Daily Star*, open at the horoscopes. She and the other Mrs Guppy live just outside the village, next door to each other, in large semi-detached houses which their husbands built in the late eighties and which are already falling apart. The Mrs Guppys are always together. They wait, while the time passes, mostly in silence, marking their presence with occasional wheezes and monosyllables, interspersed with isolated snippets of news. An example (from a couple of days ago):

INT. GUPPY KITCHEN. DAY.
MRS GUPPY, *on the telephone, is wedged beside the kitchen counter, dwarfing it, her back to* MRS GUPPY OTHER, *who sits at the table, smoking.*
MRS GUPPY
And you can fuck off.

MRS GUPPY *slaps down the receiver.*

MRS GUPPY
Miss Flynn, that were. From the school. (*Shuffles back to seat.*) Told her to fuck off.

MRS GUPPY OTHER (*Slurp.*) That's right.

Silence.

Dane Guppy, meanwhile, reclines in his tracksuit in the sitting room next door, with the curtains drawn, because Mrs Guppy believes the neighbours are all spying, and with the plasma-screen television's volume turned down, because Mrs Guppy hates the sound of recorded laughter. He has a pack of Top Trumps, which he shuffles, and a lighter, which he flicks, and he is bored. Every day for weeks now, it has been the same. Every day is the same.

Fanny has to go home to pick up her car and a newspaper article she cut out weeks ago, which she'd been meaning to send on to Mrs Guppy. It would only take ten minutes to walk there, but she knows enough about Mrs Guppy to be confident she'll be wanting to make a quick getaway.

As she starts the car and accelerates, back past the school and out of the village, she's remembering the story about Mrs Guppy and the landlord's bleeding wife. She's wondering which ditch, exactly, the landlord's wife was found in, and she has to swerve to avoid a motorbike coming very fast in the opposite direction. They're lucky; they don't hit each other, and since neither is hurt, and both parties feel vaguely to blame, they hurry shamefacedly onwards, waving apologies at one another without really looking back. It's only a few seconds later that Fanny realises – the silver bike, the black helmet, the old suede jacket, the lean, jeaned thighs . . . They all belonged to Louis.

Little fucker! she thinks. *Hasn't bothered to call me for almost a month, and thinks he's going to get a hero's welcome. Certainly bloody well not.* But she can't wipe the grin off her face.

It is Dane Guppy who comes to open the front door when Fanny at last summons the courage to bang on its lopsided knocker. Dane is desperate for any kind of distraction. He was up from in front of that silent telly like a shot. And when he first sees who it is, there's no doubt about it, an expression of pure, unguarded happiness flashes across his face.

'Oh,' he says, quickly recovering, pulling the door half-closed again so that only his sickly grey face pokes out, 'it's you, is it? What do you want?'

'What do you think I want, Dane? Go and fetch your mother.'

He laughs uncertainly. 'She don't like you very much.'

'I know that. She's already made that pretty clear. Why aren't you at school, Dane?'

He smiles. 'I'm sick,' he says.

'You don't look sick to me. Go and fetch your mother. I want to speak to her. Is she in?'

'No.'

'Dane?' comes a suspicious voice from behind him. Fanny's stomach lurches. 'Who's that?' calls Mrs Guppy, panting slightly as she makes her slow and heavy journey through the hall to the front door. 'Who're you talking to, Dane? Get back inside!'

'It's Miss Flynn,' he says, staying put, noticing the effect his mother's voice has on Fanny's face, and sending her a gloating smile. 'Come to take me back to school, Mum.'

'What's that?' Mrs Guppy wheezes up behind him, and

with a swing of one gigantic arm, cuffs him off balance and out of the way. 'You,' she says to Dane, 'do as you're told and get inside!'

He retreats, but as he does so he glances at Fanny one last time. The gloating grin has vanished and instead, behind the dull grey eyes, there is the smallest hint of an appeal; even a flicker of gratitude. Fanny sees it. She sees it, and it spurs her on.

'Hello, Mrs Guppy.' She bends to rest one hand on Brute's head, as if to reassure herself she's not alone. 'I'm sorry to bother you,' Fanny says. 'I hope it's not an inconvenient time . . .'

Mrs Guppy says nothing.

'May I come in?'

Mrs Guppy doesn't move. She keeps the door close to her but her size is such that there are still large gaps through which Fanny can glimpse parts of the hall. Except for a dirty beige carpet, it seems still to be unfinished. The windows are bare, the plaster walls unpainted, adorned only by cracks and the odd tuft of electrical wiring. From her place beneath the dilapidated porch Fanny smells frying, body odour and stale smoke. She's not desperate for her suggestion to be accepted.

Anyway, it's ignored. 'What do you want?' Mrs Guppy demands.

'I want – That is— Look, Mrs Guppy, I know we haven't exactly got off to a good start, and I'm sorry, because I know I have a terrible temper . . .'

(But it's too late for forgiveness; one lost child, four confiscated children, twenty-two stones of fat, one slimy, cheating, weak-willed husband – one long, cruel, lazy, hated life. Too Late.) Fanny's apology says nothing to her. She doesn't even hear it. 'What do you want?' she asks again.

Fanny sighs. 'I want Dane back at school, Mrs Guppy. I think he should be at school.'

Mrs Guppy smiles. 'Anything else?'

'Unless there's a reason he shouldn't be in school which I am unaware of?'

'Dane's not at school because I'm not sending him.'

'So he's not ill, then?'

'Dane's not at school because I'm not sending him,' she says again, and begins to shunt herself back into the house.

But Fanny's not finished yet. The adrenalin is pumping, and she moves instinctively. 'No, wait!' she says. She puts a foot in the closing door. 'It's actually illegal for you to keep your son away from school, you do know that, don't you?'

'Is that right?' Mrs Guppy mocks.

'And did you know that he's nearly twelve, and he still can't read and write? Did you know that, Mrs Guppy?'

'I'd be moving that foot if I was you.'

'And did you know that if you refuse to allow him to be educated, simply because you have a problem with the way *I* choose to dress, Mrs Guppy—' Fanny's voice begins to rise.

'I told you to move your foot.'

'I'm sorry. No. The dressing thing – that was silly.' Fanny taps impatiently at her own forehead. 'That's not what I meant. Please, don't keep talking about my foot. Please, just let me finish. Let me come in. I'm just saying that you're punishing him for something *I* did. And that's just so *unfair*.'

Mrs Guppy gazes coldly down, pulls back the door with her mighty arm and slams it against Fanny's foot. A gust of stale air. Fanny smells frying, smells body odour and stale cigarettes, and she winces in pain. But for some reason she does not move the foot. She doesn't even consider it.

'And if there's nothing wrong with his health,' she continues, 'if he's not ill – which, Mrs Guppy, I know he isn't – you do realise, don't you, that you can be sent to jail, you can be locked up—'

WHAM! The door hits against her foot once again. Another gust of stale air. And pain.

'Move it, Miss Flynn.'

'Mrs Guppy, I haven't finished!'

WHAM! Stale air. Pain. And coughing from inside the house, and something else; a bitter, distinctive smell. They both recognise it at once. Fanny stops, sniffs. Mrs Guppy, who's been watching her carefully – alert to possible reprisal – glances nervously back into the hall. Through the cracks of the badly fitted sitting-room door seeps a tail of black smoke.

'DANE?' thunders Mrs Guppy. 'Get out here! You stupid sod! DANE?' She stands there, not moving. 'DANE! What the bloody hell have you done now? Get out here this minute, or I'll—'

They hear choking from behind the door. He's rattling at the handle.

'Mrs Guppy!' Fanny can't get past her. 'For God's sake, get him out of there!'

'DANE. Get Out Here Now!' Quickly, again instinctively, Fanny somehow squeezes past her, reaching the sitting-room door just as it bursts open and Dane Guppy stumbles through. Mrs Guppy takes the four steps that had ever been required to rescue him, and whacks him around the head. 'You stupid bugger! You've done it again, haven't you?' she says. 'One of these days I'm going to lock you in there and leave you to burn. Go an' call Emergencies.'

Fanny peers into the sitting room. Beside the door the contents of a metal wastepaper basket are on fire. 'It's nothing,' she calls out. 'Half a bucket of water'll do it.'

'You still here?' asks Mrs Guppy. It sounds ominous.

'No. I'm just going,' says Fanny quickly, backing away. She fumbles in her back pocket, produces a folded piece of newspaper. 'But you should read this. I brought it for you.

124

It's an article about a mother who was sent to jail for refusing to make her children go to school.' Mrs Guppy does not move to take it. 'I think you should read it,' Fanny says again. 'That is – if you can.'

''Course I bloody can.'

'Ah,' Fanny smiles, 'lucky you.'

Mrs Guppy takes a step towards her, small eyes gleaming dangerously.

'OK! . . . OK . . . I'm leaving!' Still holding out the paper, Fanny edges round her towards the front door. 'I'll leave it here for you, then.' Awkwardly, because there is nowhere else to put it, Fanny lets the paper drop, and they watch it flutter slowly to the ground. It settles on the dirty beige carpet, where Fanny assumes it will stay for many months to come. 'The woman,' she adds as an afterthought, 'who kept her children at home, she was fined as well, you know. Several thousand pounds.'

And now it is definitely time to move on. With a final nervous smile, Fanny carefully withdraws. She manages to keep her voice steady as she calls for Brute, and her legs straight as she turns out of the short drive. She keeps walking until she hears the front door bang, and she knows she is out of sight, and then her knees buckle. She has to crawl the last few yards to her car.

She waits there, recovering, she doesn't know for how long, but until well after the fire engine from Lamsbury has scuttled past, discovered it was unneeded, and lumbered away again.

20

Less than half a mile down the road, in the school forecourt, Louis is parking up his bike. He stretches – it's been a long journey – and wonders how best to proceed. Suddenly he's not so sure. It's quiet, so the children must be in lessons. Should he walk straight into her classroom and surprise her there? Should he announce himself to someone, and then sit in some kind of staff room and wait for her? Neither option seems quite right, and Louis finds himself asking why, in all the days and weeks he's had to think about this very particular moment, it has never occurred to him to come up with a plan.

He takes off his helmet and saunters round to the back of the building, clanging the playing-field gate as he goes. The windows at the front of the school are seven or eight foot off the ground. He'd been hoping the windows on the other side might be lower but they aren't. He considers shimmying up the drainpipes. They look sturdy enough. And then maybe peering through each window until he finds her.

But he needs a smoke first. He's been five hours on the road without a break and now it comes to the moment, he discovers to his surprise that he's nervous. Louis is hardly ever nervous. He settles himself on the log which had previously served as Oliver Adams's throne, rests a foot on one knee and rolls a cigarette.

It's a grey, drizzly afternoon, but it doesn't matter, Louis thinks, as he pulls on that first drag. Nothing matters. He's going to climb the drainpipe. He's going to tap on the window. He smiles, allowing himself to imagine her expression, the struggle on her face between annoyance and amusement and pleasure. He imagines her, trying to keep it all together in front of the children, desperately trying not to laugh . . . And then maybe she's going to run out of the classroom— And she's going to— They're going to— But it doesn't matter anyway, because they have all summer. They have the rest of their lives. Nothing is going to dampen his spirits today.

'Excuse me. Can I help you?' He looks up with a start to see Robert, half-running across the playing field towards him. Robert's face is rigid with the effort of appearing calm. He is trying to smile.

'Hi there!' says Louis pleasantly. 'I was just smoking a cigarette here, hope you don't mind. It's a heck of a journey from London, isn't it? I'd forgotten how damn far it was. I'm Louis, by the way. Old friend of Fanny's. You must be . . .' Louis's eyes flicker over the shiny blond bob, the beard, the roll-neck jersey, and settle briefly on the open-toed sandals. He grins. 'You must be . . . Robin Grey, am I right? Fanny's told me a lot about you!'

Robert White isn't sure how to deal with this. He is torn between relief that Louis probably isn't, after all, a suicide bomber; jealousy that Louis probably is Fanny's lover; offence that Louis has confused his name; and delirium that Fanny has ever mentioned him at all. He struggles for a moment to come up with a response.

Silence. Louis waits, confused. 'You are Robin, aren't you? I'm not wrong. You teach the other class. The little ones.'

'Actually, I'm Robert,' says Robert, still trying to smile.

'Robert. I am sorry. Of course. Robert Grey.'

'Robert White.'

'Robert White!' Louis knocks the palm of his cigarette hand against his forehead, sprinkling ash on to his blond fringe in the process, and leaving it there. 'Stupid of me. Of course. Sorry. And I'm Louis, old friend of Fanny's,' he says again.

A mini stand-off. Louis waits for Robert to say, 'Ah! Louis! Not *the* Louis!?!' And when Robert doesn't, when Robert's lips purse and his head tilts in affected curiosity, as if the name means nothing to him, Louis feels a little thud of disappointment. 'Fanny and I,' Louis says, to cover the unkind silence, 'we go back a long way. We're very old friends.'

'Yes, you said.'

'I'm here to surprise her. She doesn't know I'm coming.'

Robert knows exactly who Louis is. Of course. He's heard all the gossip; heard in graphic detail from Linda Tardy about the moment Louis appeared in the village hall. He was burrowing his lips into Fanny's hair when she was calling his name into her mobile. '*Louis isn't here,*' Robert had said. '*I'm here. Robert's here . . .*'

More silence. Now they are both here, and Robert feels shrivelled and provincial beside him. And angry. Linda Tardy, Robert remembers, had described Louis as 'ever such a good-looking chap. Gorgeous, really. *American.*' But Robert, half-winded by his opponent's god-like grace and sensuality, notes bitterly that the woman did not even begin to do him justice.

Louis, with amiability dripping from every perfect limb, smiles expectantly. It occurs to him vaguely that Robert might be a little backward.

Finally Robert says, 'You shouldn't be smoking, you know. Not here. It's not permitted. Apart from anything, it's a bad example for the kids.'

'For the kids!' Louis laughs aloud. 'You think they haven't seen a man smoking before?' But he takes only one more drag before flicking the end on to the damp grass.

'Where did it land?' Robert scours the ground, pounces on it. 'It's a bad example for kids,' he repeats, churning up the mud, 'it's bad for your health, and it's a serious fire hazard. If I had my way it would be illegal.'

Louis doesn't seem to be listening. 'I was actually planning to climb up the drainpipe there, and tap on her classroom window,' he says with a laugh, 'but something tells me you wouldn't think that was such a cool idea.'

Robert, not amused, looks up from what's left of the butt end and shakes his head.

'So, er, perhaps you can just point me in her direction. Then I could—'

'No.'

'No?'

Robert casts around for a reason; can't believe his luck when he falls upon it. 'Fanny's not here! She's gone out!' he says triumphantly. 'She's not on the premises.'

'Oh. Where is she, then?'

'She rushed out at lunch-time because . . . Because . . .' Robert remembers that he doesn't know quite why she rushed out. 'She rushed out at lunch-time,' he repeats slowly, and finally he smiles. 'Well, you know Fanny, Louis. Rushing here. Rushing there. You know what she's like.'

Louis waits. 'She's gone?'

'That's what I'm saying.'

'So, where's she gone?'

Robert smiles mistily. 'Never stops, does she? I suppose we both know what she's like.'

'Yeah. I suppose so. So where's she gone?' he asks again.

'Pardon?'

'She's not ill?'

'Ill? Of course not. She's fine. I mean . . .' He glances at Louis slyly. 'I mean, it's not that she's ill. It's just – a *thing*.'

'What "*thing*"?'

'Look, if she hasn't already told you—'

'Of course she's told me.' But Louis's beginning to grow worried. 'What are you talking about?'

Robert has no idea. Not an idea in his head of what he's talking about, not an idea of anything except that he wants Louis to go away, quickly, before Fanny sees him here, looking so flamboyantly, disgustingly handsome. And yet . . . one way or another he can't help noticing that this nonsensical exchange is having an excellent effect on his opponent. Robert feels, from the depths of his despair, a small flicker of hope. Louis is a little jealous of him.

'I'm very sorry,' says Robert with a burst of new confidence. 'I shouldn't have said anything. But I thought you said you were friends.'

'We are. Bloody well friends. And you haven't said anything. Tell me. Is there something wrong with her?'

Robert looks squarely at Louis's left shoulder. 'There's nothing wrong with her,' he says. 'She's as healthy as any other thirty-something lady, I should imagine. But she's not coming back to school this afternoon, OK? And I should be getting back to my class. And for security reasons, which I'm sure you can appreciate, I'm going to have to request that you leave.'

'But where is she?'

Robert hesitates. 'Look. What I can tell you,' he says, as if he's doing Louis an enormous favour – and then stops. What can he tell Louis? Nothing. That he desperately needs time to think. That he desperately wants Louis to go away and preferably die and certainly never come back. Nothing else. 'I can tell you that Fanny will be at home at four. She will be back home by four,' he says at last. 'You know where she lives, I suppose?'

Louis nods, slightly irritably.

'Why don't you come round about fourish, then?'

'*Come* round?' repeats Louis.

Had he really said that? Oops. Stroke of luck! Robert sniggers. 'And I promise, I shan't breathe a word. OK? Top Secret. It'll be a surprise.'

Louis is certain of very little after his meeting with Robert – where Fanny is or why or, more to the point, what the relationship is with her weird, lanky, anti-smoking deputy. But he's still keen, if he can help it, to surprise her with his arrival, because he loves it when her face lights up. He decides to hide his bike in the car park behind the Fiddleford Arms, which he needs to drop in at anyway, to pick up his cottage keys.

What, exactly, Louis wonders, as he pulls off his crash helmet, had the lanky deputy guy Robert – or Robin (Louis's already forgotten which) – what in hell had he meant when he said 'come around' at four o'clock? Were they *living* together? Louis tries to dismiss it. Fanny may have hooked up with some geeks over the years. But Robin Green? Robert. Grey. Green? Fuck. Whatever he was called. Even at her most lonesome, at her most torridly, outrageously bloody lickerish . . . It wasn't impossible.

He tugs distractedly at the pub's side door, deep in troubled thought, and heads towards the bar.

Inside is warm and welcoming, imbued with a sort of low-key liveliness. A fire burns in a giant grate in the middle of the room, and everywhere smells of old wood and smoke and fresh draught beer. As he leans, waiting to be served, Louis very much intends to resist the temptation of ordering himself a pint. He needs to stick to his original plan. Or what's left of it. And on this occasion he's only come to the pub to pick up his new keys. He needs to buy some food at the post office, if it's open, check out the cottage, maybe open a few windows, unpack, make up a bed, and find a map because he's actually got a job tomorrow: he's meant to be miles away in somewhere called Crediton, photographing a mystics' herbal festival. By which time it will be—

'No, David. Darling. Don't be flip.' A husky female voice, brisk with irritation, rises above the general hubbub, interrupting Louis's train of thought. He turns idly towards it: the woman looks a little bohemian, in her mid-forties, dressed in diaphanous white, with long white-blonde hair and big panda eyes enhanced with heavy, smoky make-up. Her face is slightly puffy but Louis, who (being an artist) studies faces more closely than most, notices immediately how appealing she almost still is, and how stunning she must have been once. 'It's easy for you,' she's saying. 'You can *swish* off back to London in your marvellous car and forget all about it. But you're my *bloody agent!* So where does that leave me?'

The middle-aged man sitting at the table in front of her looks at his watch. He is embarrassed. He hadn't realised that Kitty Mozely, who's not produced a piece of work in nearly seven years, still considers herself one of his clients. Had he realised, of course, he wouldn't have dreamt of dropping in on her. But this morning, on the third and final day of what was turning out to be quite a lonely driving holiday in the West Country, he had remembered that she lived nearby, and he'd had a flash of her in her golden days, when they'd both been at Oxford and for a month or two – or maybe a fortnight, but anyway it was a bloody good fortnight – Kitty had allowed him to share her bed.

He'd headed for Fiddleford, stopped at the pub for directions and arrived at her cottage unannounced, brimming with warmth and goodwill. The look of rage she gave him when she came to the door, still in her dressing gown, had almost – very nearly – made him turn on his well-shod heel and run.

He hadn't. Actually, he'd taken pity on her. He'd taken her to lunch back at the Fiddleford Arms, and had been listening to her berate him for well over an hour by the time Louis sauntered in.

'Have you, darling boy,' Kitty is demanding, 'in your many *remunerative* years as a 'bloody agent', ever heard of such a thing as writers' block? *Have you?*'

'Oh, don't be silly, Kit,' he murmurs.

'You were supposed to *help me*. Not just abandon me to drown in my bloody creative juices. So help me! *Help me!* Give me a fucking *idea*!' She's drunk, of course. Poor old thing. Seeing him looking so dapper and so bloody prosperous at her front door – it had shaken her up a bit, brought back a lot of unwelcome reminders.

The agent fiddles with his lighted cigarette and prays to a God he doesn't believe in, for the bill to arrive. 'And how is Scarlett?' he lobs in half-heartedly. 'Is she thriving?'

'Scarlett's fine,' Kitty snaps. 'Her teacher doesn't seem to know if she can read or write. Which is a bloody joke. But otherwise she's fine. Angel, would you mind moving that cigarette? The smoke's going right up my nose.'

'Doesn't know?' He laughs. 'That's a bit feeble, isn't it? She always struck me as a very clever child.' He envisages her as he saw her last, a few years ago now; with the little lopsided face, the little twisted back, and the big blue

133

watchful eyes . . . kind of enthralling, in a funny way; that combination of knowingness and vulnerability, in someone so young. Very striking. Very Zeitgeisty, put like that . . . a tiny, twisted package of human life representing the *malaise* of a generation, and so on. Someone ought to paint her.

Suddenly he leans forward. 'I say, Kitty,' he begins. 'D'you have a photograph of her?'

'What? Don't be idiotic, David. We live together. Of course I don't.'

'But I take it she's . . .'

'What?'

'I take it she's . . .' He hunches his shoulders in embarrassment, at a loss as to how to put it.

'What?' Kitty asks coldly. A rush of savage protectiveness washes over her. It takes her by surprise. She can feel herself blushing. 'Spit it out, David.'

'Kitty dearest, believe it or not I think I've had a serious major brainwave!'

Louis fails to face down the temptation of that beer in the end (or very close to the beginning) and it's just as he is ordering a second one, that Kitty glances up from newly animated discussions with her agent and spots Louis at the bar.

'It's Louis!' she cries dramatically. 'He's come back to us!'

'Excuse me, ma'am?' Louis laughs, turning round to look at her. 'Are you talking to me?'

'I certainly am! You may not know me, but we know you! I mean we, not me and him,' she indicates the agent, not especially respectfully. 'I mean *we* – the People of Fiddleford! Come on! Come and join us.'

Louis has nothing else to do while he downs his second pint, and he's been half-eavesdropping on their conversation all this time. He's a little intrigued by her. He picks up his glass and walks over.

'Louis!' declares Kitty triumphantly. 'How do you do? Sit down!' She leans across and drags a chair from the neighbouring table, positioning it absurdly close to her own. 'Sit down!' she orders, patting it. 'I'm Kitty. Kitty Mozely. Author of excellent children's books, as this gentleman here,' she indicates the agent again, 'is duty bound to confirm; and mother to Scarlett.' She ponders that for a moment. 'And I do believe that you and I are about to be neighbours. Am I right? Aren't you moving into Alms Cottages? Next to our gorgeous stripping schoolmarm?'

'Next to Fanny,' Louis corrects her. 'She's not a stripping schoolmarm.'

'No, of course.' Kitty tips her head. 'Next to the ravishing Fanny Flynn. Louis, may I introduce you to my—' Suddenly she stops, half-closes her panda eyes and gurgles with delicious laughter. 'I was going to say "my-fucking-agent". Because that, frankly,' she turns to David, 'is all I've been calling you for years. But now it turns out you're not a fucking-agent after all. But a *marvellous*-agent, with a marvellous idea. And now it's completely thrown me, and I can't for the life of me remember your actual name!'

David smiles thinly. 'Don't be a bore, Kitty. You know perfectly well what my name is. In fact,' he smirks, 'I remember nights when you used to shriek it so loud the whole of bloody Oxford had to wear earmuffs . . . Don't you remember that?'

'So I did!' she says, as if she'd quite forgotten (which, to be fair, she may have done). She looks at him and chuckles, leans across the table and affectionately pinches his cheek. 'But I was only pretending. You know that. Now Louis,' she says, dropping the cheek and turning abruptly away, '*tell-me-tell-me. Tell me everything!* I want to know everything there is to know about you . . .'

135

The two men both catch her musky scent, her reckless-
ness, her magnetic wickedness and both – to their own slight
irritation – feel a surge of desire.

21

Robert's been pacing across the back of his classroom ever since Louis left. His students, as is often the way, are sitting quietly in front of *Are We Being Served? An Overview of Service Industries in the West Midlands*. Robert has said he's going to test them on it this time; he's told them the winner will get to go home five minutes early. Which is pointless, because nobody will be there to pick them up, and they won't have any friends to play with while they're waiting. But the children are making a good-natured show of taking the competition seriously – because he can be quite snappy when he wants to be, Mr White. So they're bored, but they're very used to that.

It leaves him free to pace, and to think about Louis. Arriving at Fanny's at four. Robert's stomach lurches, imagining their reunion; imagining their beautiful limbs, later tonight, coiling round each other in ecstasy. Robert is distracted by the sound of a car grinding abruptly to a halt outside. He frowns. Dangerous driver, especially so near a school. He hears the car door slam, and then the playground gate squeak open and closed. Nervously, he hurries to the front of the class and turns down the television.

'Shhh!' He holds up a finger.

Fanny spoke to him only yesterday about what she unreasonably called his 'dependence' on videos in lessons. She wouldn't be pleased to see him using them again so soon. But she hardly ever arrives in a car, and the individual walking up the path . . . has a limp. He turns the television's volume up again and returns to the back of the room.

Timing, he thinks. It's all about *timing* . . . Somehow he needs to prevent Fanny from going home until well after four. Until after Louis's been and gone. Or failing that, he needs to go home with her, and somehow be there to sabotage the moment when Louis turns up. But *how*—

A knock on the door. Fanny's head appears from around it. Robert jumps.

'Robert,' she says, very coldly. Her eyes are all puffy. 'Could I have a quick word?'

She's furious about the video – and justifiably, perhaps. But there are a lot of other reasons, that afternoon, which lead her to react as strongly as she does, and she doesn't manage the confrontation well. She is very rude to him. '. . . And I swear,' she says, well, she shouts, she *yells* at him, 'if you use that video machine again, believe me, I will fire you. Do you get that? *D'you understand that?*'

Robert shivers. She's so beautiful when she's angry. Right now, what he'd like to do to her . . . He'd like to—

'Wipe that fucking smirk off your face! I just asked you a question.'

Robert's smirk becomes a little more entrenched. He crosses his arms over his chest and looks down at her. A long, awkward pause follows, during which Fanny, in an unwelcome flash of self-awareness, pictures herself as she stands there, throbbing foot, angry face, craning neck. She flushes. Robert spots it. 'Hmm,' he says pertly. 'Are you quite finished?'

'I imagine,' she says, with a little wry grace, 'that I've made myself pretty clear.'

'Firstly, I appreciate how much you obviously care about your students' welfare and progress. You're overreacting; getting emotional about something which really doesn't merit it. But in my view that only illustrates your level of dedication to the job and *I approve*, OK? You have my respect for that.'

'I . . . What?'

'However,' he continues, and now he smiles (because in love or out of love Robert will always know his Rights), 'I don't believe, Fanny, that you can give a member of teaching staff a formal warning simply for using a very well established and respected teaching aid.'

'That's not the—'

'*If* this is a formal warning, Fanny, then I would appreciate it in writing, please, and I can proceed as per the union's advice. Is this a formal warning?'

She hesitates. Robert waits, crossing one sandalled foot over the other, tilting the head to one side, raising an eyebrow, smiling.

He nods. 'Secondly,' he says, 'and much more importantly. What's wrong with your foot?'

'What?'

'I notice you were limping. Are you hurt?'

'No.'

He frowns. 'You've got to take better care of yourself, Fanny. Charging around the place. Doing those emergency stops in that little car of yours. Did you have any lunch today? I bet you didn't. It's no wonder you get so overwrought.'

'I am not – remotely – overwrought,' she snaps. 'Switch the video off, Robert. And start doing some bloody teaching.' She limps away, furious, and he stands there, watching her. 'By the way,' she turns back, unable to resist it, 'did anyone

– I don't suppose anyone came calling for me while I was out?'

'Calling for you?' Robert looks masterfully blank.

'No? I just thought I saw a friend of mine . . . Oh, God, it doesn't matter.'

'Expecting someone special?'

She sighs. 'It's none of your business, Robert. I'll see you later.'

'Geraldine. Kitty here. I'm in the pub. You'll never guess who came to call on me this morning! David Prick-Like-a-Twiglet Watson. Remember him?'

Geraldine's in her office with nothing to do. She's spent the morning in school. It's her second morning doing her reading-with-the-kids, and she's already feeling a bit resentful about it. Because she doesn't feel, with her brain and qualifications, that her time at the school is being fully exploited. She could be doing so much more. And this morning, listening to a girl called Heather struggle drearily through another *Adventure with Biff* she found her eyelids very heavy. So heavy, in fact, that when Heather paused to clear her throat it made Geraldine jump. Heather didn't realise it, thankfully, but Geraldine had fallen asleep. So. Geraldine's husband is sitting opposite her, head bent over the leasehold details of someone's market stall, and Geraldine's feeling pretty listless, pretty disappointed, pretty gloomy. 'Hello, Kitty,' she says wearily. 'David who?'

'Oh, come on, Geraldine. Didn't you fuck him at Oxford?'

'No, Kitty—'

'I certainly did. Yuck! Prick-Like-a-Twiglet Watson. AKA my-fucking-agent . . . Drives a Jaguar now,' she adds as an afterthought. 'The little shit. Just waved him off in it. It's powder blue. So now of course I'm wondering if he's queer . . .'

140

'Oh, David Watson!' Geraldine smiles. She can't quite put a face to the name, and no, she did not fuck him, but she knows who Kitty is talking about. She and Kitty had both been at university with him, and suddenly she feels unreasonably hurt that he didn't come and call on her as well. He must have known she and Kitty lived in the same village. 'You should have brought him to see me. I would have loved to see him.'

'No you wouldn't. Anyway, the point is he's come up with a brainwave. As a result of which, my lovely friend, I am probably going to be even richer than you are! Imagine that!'

'Jolly good,' says Geraldine brightly. She hates it when Kitty starts talking about money. She strongly believes that their financial disparity issue should be left well alone. It's a can of worms. But Kitty's obviously drunk. 'So? Are you going to tell me what it is?' she asks.

'What?'

'The brainwave.'

'Hmm? Oh, no. It's a secret. Actually, I'm not sure you'll approve. Anyway, next piece of news. Guess which Deity of Masculine Perfection has been buying me drinks in the Fiddleford Arms this happy afternoon?'

'Can't,' says Geraldine, sighing. The conversation is beginning to annoy her. 'Kitty, I'm trying to work.'

'LOUIS, OF COURSE!' Kitty bawls. 'Come on, Geraldine. Wakey-wakey! And Christ, he's sexy, you know . . . I mean . . . *Christ*—' She hiccups. 'Ought to whisper, really,' she adds, doing nothing of the kind. 'He's only gone to the lav.'

Geraldine giggles. She can't help it. 'You're pissed.'

'Oh. And I did a teeny bit of trouble stirring, I'm afraid,' she adds proudly.

'Oh, God, Kitty. What have you said?'

'Well, it's only that General Maxwell McDonald was asking a couple of days ago whether Fanny Flynn was—'

'*You were at the Manor?*' It spews out before Geraldine can stop herself. She's never been invited to the Manor, not once in all the time she's been in Fiddleford. She's had Jo and Charlie and the General to dinner twice, now. Twice. Kitty hasn't. So what's Geraldine doing wrong that Kitty's obviously getting so right?

'Calm down,' chortles Kitty. 'I saw him in the post office. Mad as a tree, I think. But then, who isn't? And getting madder every day. He was asking if Fanny Flynn – who, let's face it, Geraldine, may be many things, but she's certainly not unattractive – he was asking if Fanny Flynn was having it off with that disgusting little teacher man, what's-his-name? Who taught Ollie last year. He had a bit of a thing for you . . .'

'Robert White? General Maxwell McDonald stood in the post office in front of Mrs Hooper, and asked if Fanny and Robert were *having it off?*'

Kitty creases up with laughter. 'Did I say that? God! If only. He may have said "stepping out" or something. But anyway, that was the gist. He bumped into Fanny at the Classic in Lamsbury last Friday night. Claiming she was on her own, he said. And then he spied that ghastly man skulking just around the corner.'

'Oh,' says Geraldine. 'That *is* interesting.'

'So obviously I assured the General he was absolutely right.'

Geraldine snorts.

'Only now of course I've told Louis. Well I didn't *tell* him, exactly. Didn't quite dare go that far. I sort of hinted at it . . . Funny?' She suddenly doesn't sound quite so sure.

'Kitty!' But then Geraldine's mind flicks back to the time she walked in on Robert and Fanny together up in Fanny's office. She remembers how weird and jumpy they had been. 'Mind you,' she says, 'the old General may actu-

142

ally be on to something. Because now I come to think about it . . .'

'What? *Geraldine?*'

'Well . . .'

Kitty almost gags on her curiosity. 'WHAT?' She hiccups, and it turns into a belch. '*WHAT?* Oh, Christ. Got to go. He's coming back.'

Geraldine giggles again. 'I think you should go home, have a strong cup of black coffee and a cold bath and maybe you can come round for dinner later. Are you up to anything this evening?'

'Well, that all depends . . .'

'Of course. I'll see you later, then.' Geraldine says goodbye, still with half a smile on her face. But the clunk of her telephone receiver returns her at once to her own humdrum surroundings. She looks across at her industrious husband, diligent as ever, and then down at her desk, at her own afternoon's work. She has written a list of people to call. They are people who have all contacted the practice once, with an initial enquiry, but who have never followed it up; people who she has already called a couple of times, to no avail. She sighs. Boredom.

Boredom.

Boredom.

Kitty's life is a mess, she thinks. And in many ways, disgraceful. But at least she's living it. At least Kitty gets highs and lows. She and Clive, meanwhile, are slowly withering to death. By Boredom.

'Clive . . .'

All the years of working so hard, all the years of gyming and juggling, and it has come to—

'Cli-ii-ive?'

Boredom. She needs more in her life. More meaning. More excitement. Either or both.

'Clive!' she says it more sharply.

'Hmm?' He looks up, startled.

'Are we happy here? In this office? Doing all this?'

'Doing all . . . what?'

'Are we?' she asks again.

'Well.' He lays down his pen. 'I'm happy, being here with you,' he says carefully. 'I'm happy that things aren't as frantic as they used to be in London. And I'm happy . . . that Ollie is happy.' He looks down at the work on his desk. He's taken aback by the question. Unprepared. They've been being stoical for so long, the two of them, he's finding it very hard to switch gear. 'Of course, the – money – thing. We're going to have to earn some more money at some point . . .'

'Oh, for Christ's sake,' she snaps. 'For once, let's forget about the money, can we? For a minute.'

'Well, I mean, Geraldine – apart from that, I'm happy if you're happy . . . Are you happy?'

Geraldine sighs. 'Am I happy?' she asks. 'Am I happy?' and she laughs. 'God, I don't know, Clive. What a ridiculous question!' She brushes it aside. 'But since moving to this –' she hesitates, *fucking backwater—*'

'Geraldine!' Clive chortles delightedly.

'The work hasn't exactly clawed at my attention . . . And since it's raining outside, and let's face it, neither of us has anything else to bloody well do . . .' She screws the lid on to her Mont Blanc fountain pen. She pushes back her chair and reaches across for her £1,349 Donna Karan overcoat. 'I think, just this once, we should cut loose! Shut up shop! Call Lenka and tell her she's going to have to give Ollie his supper tonight, and spend the rest of the day in a pub somewhere – not Fiddleford – getting plastered.' She smiles at him; a rare kind of smile for Geraldine, one brimming with promises. 'Are you coming?'

22

'Where are you going?' Robert stands at the foot of the stairs leading down from Fanny's office, more or less blocking her path. He rattles a sheath of papers under her nose, blocking her again. 'You don't normally leave this early, Fanny. It's not yet four o'clock. Look.' She tries to slide past him but he shoves his watch underneath her nose. 'See? Not even four. And I seriously need to talk to you.'

She stops. 'Really, Robert? What about?'

'Well – various things. Important school matters. Have you got a minute? I was just on my way up to see you.'

Fanny sighs. It was going to be the first day in ages she had managed to get home early. She's been up since six, as usual, and her toe is killing her. But if Robert wants to talk about 'important school matters' how can she refuse? It doesn't happen often. Plus, beneath the swirls of irritation which wash over her whenever Robert is close, she's still feeling shamefaced about having shouted at him earlier. 'Quickly then.'

'In the office?'

'I've just locked it. We'll have to talk here.'

'If you insist,' he says a little huffily, setting a shoulder against the wall, trying to make himself comfortable. 'Right then . . . Well, firstly . . .' He hands her a sheet of paper, advertising from what she can gather, a classroom white-board, very intricate, which can be linked to its own computer system, thereby— 'As you can see they're quite dear,' he explains, sending little spouts of warm breath over her shoulder, 'but a lot of the primary schools are getting fitted up with them, and I do think in the future they're going to be essential. After all, how are the kiddies supposed to learn if they can't—'

'What else have you got?' Fanny asks briskly. 'I'm not sure I can really see the point of this.'

'As I say, all the other schools are being fixed up with these gizmos and I really think—'

She sighs. 'Come on, Robert.'

'What?' he begins to sound peevish. 'I don't really see how I can be expected to effectively teach my class without access to a—'

She gurgles with laughter. 'You hadn't even heard of the damn thing before yesterday. But thanks. For pointing it out to me. Was there anything else you wanted to talk to me about?'

'Yes!' he says quickly, tucking the sheet away. 'I've discov-ered a fascinating course—'

She groans. 'Oh, please, Robert. I'm tired. Can't we talk about these things tomorrow?' She tries again to slide past him, but he doesn't budge, and the possibility of brushing against any single part of his body or clothing makes her shrink back to her narrow bottom step.

'It only lasts two days. And it's in Bristol,' he continues. 'I've got a cousin in Bristol, so I can stay with him. No overnight expenses!'

'I see. So what's the course?'

He pulls out another pamphlet. 'Dealing with Racism in

Predominantly White Schools: Preparing Kids for Life in a Multi-Cultural Society.'

'Don't dismiss this out of hand, Fanny,' he says, before she has a chance to respond. 'This is a sensitive and topical issue. And it's something we've been neglecting.'

'It may well be. But first things first. I mean,' she laughs again, in exasperation, 'you know as well as I do, Robert, OFSTED was hardly lacking in things to complain about us. Racism was probably one of the very few things that didn't even come up. And right now, so far as I'm aware, our school has the lowest literacy rate of any primary school in the county. Don't you think our time might be better spent—'

'*Tolerance*, Fanny, in this day and age, is the most important thing we can convey to our kids. Are you saying—'

'I'm saying find another excuse to go and stay with your cousin in Bristol. OK?'

He blushes. 'I don't appreciate that, Fanny,' he says, genuinely stung. 'As deputy head of this school I'm actually trying to help.'

She sighs. 'I'm sorry. You're quite right. That was rude. Again. I had no right to say that. Please, accept my apology.' Fanny smiles. 'I'm just quite tired today. But anyway—' She motions at the wedge of papers still in his hand. 'So what else have you got there? And before you go on, Robert, to save time, the answer, for the time being, is no to all teachers' courses. OK?'

'Oh!' He's shocked. 'But with the school in Special Measures, there's so much extra funding available, especially for courses.'

'Yes. Funnily enough I'm aware of that. But, as I explained at our last governors' meeting, which I don't believe you attended, and as I've set down in innumerable bloody policy statements – which I certainly don't blame you for not having read – I feel that what we need right now is continuity, not teachers sodding off on courses. We need *lessons*. So what else have you got?'

'Fine,' he says. Disappointed, obviously, and disapproving, of course. But nevertheless changing tack. He glances at his watch. Three minutes to four. He's got to keep her there for half an hour. An hour, to be safe. 'Do you mind?' he says. 'Only I've been on my feet all day,' and promptly sits down on the floor. He gives what he hopes is a cheeky grin. 'Good thing I do yoga, hey? You should see some of the other positions I can get into!'

Fanny's painkillers have worn off. She doesn't attempt to look amused.

'But seriously, Fanny, I do feel – I have come to feel, that in your drive to bring the kids up to a pre-designated educational "standard" which I think we both know is potentially as stressful to them as it is unrealistic—'

'No, it isn't,' she snaps.

He pulls a little face; he remains unconvinced.

'It's not either of those things, Robert. And it is certainly not unrealistic. OK? It is perfectly fucking realistic to expect children to learn to read. OK?'

He holds up a hand. 'I don't want to argue with you, Fanny. I'm only saying that we're in danger of neglecting an equally important aspect of the National Curriculum, one which, like it or not, Fanny, was put there by professional adults all of whom have the kids' best interests at heart.'

She waits.

'One word, Fanny. PSHE. Personal and Social Health Education.'

'Acronym, Robert,' she mutters.

Robert looks confused.

'One acronym. Five words. You're a teacher. You should probably check out the difference.'

'I was thinking we could host a series of little seminars,

Fanny. Maybe a talk on friendship, and one on litter, and then gradually work up to the knottier issues: under-aged drinking, domestic violence, STDs, paedophile rings, child abuse, of course, and "virtual" child abuse, where the kiddies are groomed by paedophiles over the Internet—' He stops for breath.

'Sounds interesting, Robert. Can we please talk about this in the morning?'

Robert steals a glance at his watch. Only four minutes have passed since they started talking. The attempt to delay her with school business isn't really working. In fact, he gets the distinct impression all he's succeeding in doing is irritating her. He's going to have to think of something else. 'Very well,' he says in a small, hurt voice, and slowly stands up. 'I was only trying to help.'

'I know. And thank you. Really. But let's discuss it in the morning.'

'D'you fancy a drink?'

'No, thank you, Robert.'

'No? Cup of tea?'

'No.'

'We could go to the pictures.'

'No. Thanks.'

He steps aside. 'Going home then?'

'Yup.'

'OK.' Very hangdog. Until— 'Oh! But I'm coming up that way in a minute. Got to stop off at the shop. Wait a mo'! I'll keep you company.'

She pretends not to hear.

'Or maybe I'll come and call!'

Sure enough, five minutes later, there he is, standing beneath the small porch on her doorstep holding another small box of Milk Tray. He peeps through the front window, glimpses Fanny moving around the kitchen at the back, putting the kettle on. No sign of Louis. So he waits. He enjoys the moment; relishes the sound of her footsteps on the oak floor, the sound of her murmured conversation with Brute, the sight of her as she moves closer, into the sitting room, and starts laying a fire in the tiny grate . . .

Louis can drink a lot of alcohol before it shows, so when, at ten past four, he finally picks up his cottage keys from behind the bar, waves goodbye to Kitty and various friendly others and meanders out of the Fiddleford Arms towards Fanny's place, he does it very respectably, leaving nothing but excellent impressions behind him. Nobody, except possibly Fanny, would recognise how drunk he really is.

But he is drunk. And feeling more than a little confused. The truth is, he's not really sure what he's doing here in Fiddleford any more. Not after what Kitty has said. Or hinted. Or half-hinted and then taken back and then hinted again.

Problem is, though, he's just paid £1,600 in deposit and advance rent to Ian Guppy, which has cleaned him out. Unless he sells his cameras, he won't have enough money for another deposit for at least a couple of months. So he's kind of stuck here. Not only that, he's got more work lined up than he's ever had. In anticipation of his new life with Fanny, and wanting to impress her, he had managed to line up local assignments from several different London newspapers and for several weeks ahead. If he lets them down they may never hire him again . . .

He looks at his watch. This was meant to have been a happy day – possibly even the happiest of his life. Now he envisages a summer of rural, sex-starved solitude, while Fanny and the repulsive teacher – *Robert*/Robin – fuck each other merrily on the other side of the wall. He groans. It's actually too disgusting to contemplate. Why, he wonders, as the cottages – his and hers (and the empty one) – come into view, why hadn't he spoken to her before he made this move? Why had he been so damn presumptuous?

The jasmine is in full flower now – it's crept all along their shared garden fence. It looks welcoming against the warm red stone, even in this grey light. It pulls the cottages together, makes them look like one. And she's lit a fire. There's smoke coming out of her chimney.

What's he going to do, anyway, when he gets there? When he bangs on her front door? What's he going to say?

Er.

Oh. Hi, Robin. Robert. Whatever the fuck your name is. It's you. Wasn't expecting you. Robin. Robert. Excuse me. Could you give Fanny and me a minute alone?

But Louis stumbles on, because in spite of everything Kitty said, he still hasn't given up hope. Not entirely. At least— Louis stops.

Robert White saw Louis before Louis saw him. He spotted Louis meandering down the road towards him and leapt into action. To Plan B. He's knocked loudly, confidently, on Fanny's door and she's come to answer it. Louis can see her standing there, her outline – not her face. She's maybe ten or fifteen metres away, no more. He hears Robert:

'SURPRISE!'

And then an exclamation from Fanny, some sort of exclamation – or possibly laughter.

'AND ALL BECAUSE THE LADY LOVES . . .' says Robert. *Yells* Robert. So Louis can hear. Surprising level of decibels, Louis thinks vaguely, from a man with such a delicate frame. Robert bellows with laughter. Even more incongruous. He passes her something – the chocolates, obviously – and then bends down and forward, out of view.

Silence.

Louis can't see what's happening. But he can picture them,

and it's disgusting. He feels like a pervert, listening in . . . Still more silence . . . He feels a cold sweat of jealousy breaking out on the back of his neck, a sour pain around his eyes and jaw, and, unseen, turns quickly and quietly back the way he came –

– a millisecond too late to see Robert reeling backwards, clasping his cheek in pain. He had leant forward to hand her the chocolates and his lips had puckered. When she took the chocolates he lunged. He pushed his luck just that little bit too far and Fanny's temper kicked in. She had slapped him very hard across the face.

'Oh, God, Robert. I shouldn't have done that. I'm sorry. I'm so sorry. I thought you were – I just – I don't want you calling. OK? I'm not interested! I never was. Please! How can I get the message across to you?'

He stands there, eyes smarting, rubbing away the sting. 'Well,' he says coldly, 'you have now. Message received. Loud and clear.'

'Robert, I'm so sorry. Do you want some ice or something?'

'I actually disapprove of violence,' he says. 'I strongly disapprove of violence.' And she notices that his voice has changed. It is dull and cold and distant. Without another word he turns away. Angry. Angrier than he can remember being. His love for her extinguished. Like that.

PART THREE

23

After that, Fanny decides she needs company. She calls Messy and Grey but there's a cabinet minister just arrived at the Retreat, and a corresponding frenzy of journalists in the bar and restaurant. It means Charlie and Jo will also be busy tonight. She briefly considers calling Geraldine Adams. But the thought of Geraldine, earnest and energetic, lecturing her as she had this morning about 'youngsters requiring nurture-to-go', quickly brings her to her senses. Crossing her fingers that Robert White isn't already there, nursing his stinging cheek, she takes herself to the pub.

Which is where she finds not Robert, but Louis. Sitting with his back to her at a little wooden table beside the fire; his head in his hand, a cigarette between his fingers. He is bent forwards, whispering into the ear of Kitty Mozely. Also drunk. For a moment Fanny thinks she's hallucinating.

'Louis?' she says.

Kitty is facing her. So Kitty sees her first. She glances up through her white-blonde fringe, and the drunken half-smile which has been sliding this way and that as she listens to Louis's mutterings, slides right off her face and hits the floor. She looks murderous.

'Louis?' says Fanny. 'Louis! Is that you?'

Slowly, without altering the angle of his body, with his head still resting on the one hand and his elbow still on the table, he half-turns towards Fanny. 'Louis! What the hell are you doing here?' She throws her arms around him just as she did in the village hall but, with a chilly shrug, he shakes her off again. 'Hey!' Fanny laughs uncertainly. She steps back. 'What's going on? Louis? What are you doing here? Why didn't you call?'

'Obviously I should have done,' he says.

Kitty gurgles.

'You're pissed,' Fanny states. 'God, Louis. Where the bloody hell have you been all this time? You haven't called me for a month. I was beginning to wonder if I'd done something . . .' And then she beams at him. 'Fuck it! I'm just so happy to see you! I've got so much to tell you.' Again she moves to put her arms around him; again he moves away.

'Aren't you going to say hello to Kitty?' he asks.

Fanny glances at her. 'Hi, Kitty. How are you?'

'Never been better,' growls Kitty, eyeing her malevolently, trying quite hard to aim a cigarette into her mouth.

'Scarlett's – doing very well. In everything. As usual.'

Kitty doesn't bother to respond, and Fanny can't be bothered to pursue it. 'Louis,' she says, turning back to him, 'what's going on? Have I done something? Why are you being so weird?'

'I was just telling him,' interjects Kitty, 'about this *marvellous* idea from old Twiglet Prick. What's-his-name.' She burps. 'Which is going to make us barrels and barrels of money, isn't it, dear? . . . Anyway, he's going to do my illustrations. He's frightfully talented.'

'So much confidence in me,' Louis smiles at her. 'And I haven't even shown her my work, yet. Isn't that nice?'

'It's idiotic,' Fanny snaps. 'Anyway, I thought you gave up illustrating ages ago.'

'Yes, I'm sure you did.'

'What's that supposed to mean? Louis—' Fanny turns to Kitty. 'Excuse me, Kitty. I don't want to be rude, but you couldn't possibly give us a minute? . . . Louis?'

'By all means,' Kitty says, but she doesn't move and neither does Louis. Fanny waits, bewildered. A silence follows, broken simultaneously by Kitty, slurring, '*WherezRobert?*' and then burping, and Louis, in a voice full of self-mockery and general bitterness, announcing, 'By the way, Fanny. I've moved into the cottage next door.'

'Next door to what?'

'To you.'

'*To me?*'

'Yes. Next door to you.'

'Well—' She laughs. 'But that's fantastic, Louis! Why? I mean, no, never mind why. It's the best news I've heard in my entire life!'

Louis feels the ground shifting again. Perhaps Kitty's wrong—

'Hey! *Wherezzz Robert?*' Kitty asks again, and disintegrates into snort-filled laughter.

'How the hell should I know?' snaps Fanny. 'More to the point, where's Scarlett?'

Kitty stops laughing. 'At Ollie Adams's house,' she lies. 'If it's any business of yours. Which it isn't . . . Anyway, excuse me. I need a pee.'

Which, when Kitty finally staggers up from her seat, leaves Louis and Fanny alone. The flicker of a glance they give to each other as soon as her back is turned is filled with so much confusion, so much misunderstanding, neither has any idea what to say to begin.

Finally, Fanny says, 'You two seem to be getting on well.'

'Oh. She's good fun. She's a laugh.'

'She's a bitch, Louis.'

'Well, I suppose beggars can't be choosers. Out here in the sticks. Isn't that right, Fan?'

She has no idea what he's talking about. 'So, anyway.' She shrugs. Tries another tack. 'When did you arrive?'

'What, in the village? Or in the pub?'

'I don't know. Both. Louis, what's the matter with you?'

'I arrived in the village at zero hundred hours plus fourteen. I arrived in the pub at zero two hundred plus twelve.'

'That's not funny. You're not making any sense.'

'Minus a small detour at the rutting-donkey show. *Eeeyyy-orrr!*' He stands up suddenly, impressively steady. 'Anyway. Got to go,' he says, without looking at her. 'Got to make up a bed and stuff. Open a few windows. Plus I've got to be in Crediton tomorrow. Don't suppose you know where that is?' He doesn't look at her but as he passes his arm reaches out, almost of its own accord, and gives her a quick, tight squeeze. Can't resist it. He's missed her. 'See you later, Fan.'

'No – hey – Louis, wait! I'll give you a hand.'

He hesitates, the arm still resting on her shoulders.

'*Hey-ho!*' bawls Kitty, bursting through the lavatory door, wiping her wet hands on her skirt. (She's never peed so fast in her life.) 'Where are you two off to? You're not leaving, are you?'

He drops his arm. 'I'm leaving, yes,' he says. 'Got loads to do. Nice meeting you, Kitty.'

'Wait. I'll come with you,' Fanny says.

'Thanks. But I can manage on my own. I'll see you around, Fan.'

'Wait for me!' shouts Kitty. The threat of his disappearing, plus the pee-break, have combined to sober her up a bit. 'Wait there, Louis. We haven't finished discussing our little plan. It's the chance of a lifetime! Darling boy, don't you *want* to illustrate the most talked-about children's book of the century?'

He strides out of the bar without looking back. Kitty, eyes wild with lust, brushes past Fanny without really seeing her.

'Oops,' she mutters vaguely, knocking Fanny into the table. 'Out the light, dear.'

The door bangs and Fanny stands alone, blinking in the aftermath. She hears someone behind her clearing his throat. 'Afternoon, Fanny.' It's the General, escaped from all the hectic activity at the Retreat. He's been sitting at the bar quietly observing everything. 'Came here for a bit of peace and quiet, I did. How about you?'

'God. I'm not sure any more,' says Fanny. 'I came for a bit of company, I think.'

He pats the stool beside him. 'Come on,' he says, 'over here.' He turns to Tracey Guppy, behind the bar, slicing lemons. 'Kitty Mozely going at full wattage this afternoon, eh, Tracey?'

Tracey rolls her eyes. 'Kitty's a pain.'

'She is,' he says. 'Indeed she is.' He looks at Fanny thoughtfully, moved, as he often is when he sees her, by the air of faint loneliness which always seems to surround her. 'I was thinking,' the General says, 'Fanny and Solomon might make an awfully good duo, Tracey. What do you think?' He turns back to Fanny. 'We must reschedule that luncheon.' Fanny's lunch at the Manor has been cancelled twice now – as lunches at the Manor, she is discovering, so often have to be, due to the very neurotic nature of so many of their high-paying guests. It's a mark of some optimism on the General's part that he continues to issue invitations at all, since at least 80 per cent of them have to be withdrawn later.

'Fanny and Solomon?' Tracey says dubiously. Considers it a moment. Looks critically at Fanny. 'Don't know about that,' she says. Tracey's too kind to tell Fanny she's not glamorous enough. Solomon Creasey's girlfriends always look like supermodels.

'Have you met Solomon yet?' asks the General. 'You must have done.'

'Not yet,' Fanny says. She sits down beside him.

'What? Haven't met him yet?' The General stares at her, finding it hard to imagine there's anyone in Fiddleford who hasn't yet met Solomon Creasey. 'How extraordinary! He's in the pub most weekends, isn't he, Tracey?'

Tracey shrugs. 'I don't work weekends, General.'

'Well. He's never in when I'm in,' Fanny says.

'What's that?' The General's not listening. 'Well, well. Plenty more opportunities. In the mean time, what can I get you two girls to drink?'

Louis moves into the cottage that night and continues, in spite of Fanny's efforts, to treat her with distant hostility. And although Fanny is truly bewildered and hurt by it, she is distracted, within a couple of days, by the arrival of the dreaded letter, announcing the arrival at the school of Her Majesty's Inspectors within the next couple of weeks. Fanny's been expecting to hear from them ever since her job began, since the inspectors come once every term to a school in Special Measures. Nevertheless the now very real prospect of their descent sends her into a spin of hasty amendments, and yet more intensive form filling.

The children are ordered to hide their descriptions of the pheasant dissection. They have to put their tadpoles back in the river, clear away their untidy nature tables, set aside their weaving looms and focus exclusively on the official Curriculum.

'But we can make it interesting,' Fanny pleads with her little students. 'And if we concentrate hard enough we can get through it all very quickly, and go back to the other stuff as soon as the inspectors have gone.'

Robert White, meanwhile, refuses to come to work at all. He won't even take her calls any more. After her fourth message on his machine goes unanswered, she grows worried; worried enough to call Robert's brother-in-law, Dr Curry. But Dr Curry refuses to give any information out. He's curt. Especially when she suggests that Mrs Curry (Robert's sister) should go round to Robert's house and check if he's all right. Dr Curry, font of so many unwarranted sick notes, has a feeling she may be mocking him.

'I'm sure he's perfectly fine, Miss Flynn,' he says briskly. 'Probably just another of his colds. Now if you'll excuse me . . .'

After a long week struggling to bring Robert's class, as well as her own, up to scratch for the inspectors, and with only the help of a series of dozy supply teachers and the feeble Linda Tardy, Fanny leaves Robert a final message, threatening to bring in the LEA if he doesn't call back at once. He calls back at once.

'I'll return to work as soon as I feel sufficiently able,' he says in the monotone he'd used at her front door, after the slap. 'I don't want to bring the union into this but I can and I will if you continue to harass me like this. And I would be grateful, Miss Flynn—'

'Miss Flynn?' repeats Fanny, with a burst of laughter. 'Sorry, Mr White, but last time I saw you you were trying to stick your tongue in my throat!'

'That isn't the case, Miss Flynn. And I find that suggestion exceptionally offensive. If you repeat that allegation, I can and will—'

'Oh, fuck off,' she says. 'Fact is, Robert, if you stay away another week I shall call in the authority and you can call in the union if you want.' She slams the telephone down.

Robert, who had been lifting weights in his garage when the initial call came through, replaces his own receiver with a little smirk, pads through the kitchen and into his bedroom, and pulls out his new diary:

10.45 a.m.
Acute migraine. Stress induced. Miss Flynn contacts me once again, making accusations of a sexual nature, also questioning veracity of my condition. Miss Flynn terminates call by telling me to f*** off.

He's put away the diary with the poems he wrote to her, and diagrams, and little fantasies. Once he'd cross-checked the dates of her other managerial misdemeanours, he locked the old diary into the little safe beneath his bed. Though he knows it can't stand as evidence, he has an instinct that the diary may come in handy when the time comes for lodging his complaints.

24

Geraldine Adams enjoyed riotous sex last night (unlike her friend Kitty, who was offered none to enjoy). Actually, astonishingly, Geraldine's enjoyed riotous sex for several nights in a row, and it's beginning to show in one or two minor details: there's a jaunty light in her nicely made-up eyes, a subtle loosening of the muscles around the side of her mouth. Or maybe she's just smiling more. And she and Clive are being embarrassing together: patting each other's bottoms at breakfast, giggling at the most tenuous *double entendres*. It all makes Ollie feel a bit sick.

But it won't last. Obviously. Because in spite of one very merry, drunken night, when they recaptured a glimmer of the fun they had together before money and success and offspring made life so very serious, and in spite of the astonishing number of passion-filled nights which have followed – nothing has changed. Their elegant offices in Lamsbury remain as dull and quiet as the grave, and their beautiful Georgian rectory still feels like a pointless toy they haven't yet learnt how to play with.

But at least, amid all that tumultuous shagging, they have finally found the time and the nerve to admit that not everything in their almost perfect lives is quite as perfect as they were pretending. They miss their important jobs, their frantic, adrenalin-filled lifestyles, all the money that used to pour into their bank accounts, and they have agreed that somehow or other, if they are ever to be happy in Fiddleford, they must find a way to recapture those things again.

Step One: Of course. To get the practice working.

'I don't think we *interact* enough,' declared Geraldine during one of their inter-coital breathers. 'People don't believe we're for real. They think we're stuck up. We need to get more involved with the community.'

She called on the drunken, former sex siren Annie Millbank (who lives a mile out of the village at the Mill House, and stars in a series of coffee ads) and has now signed them both up with the Fiddleford Dramatic Society, whose summer production rehearsals for *The Duchess of Malfi* are due to get under way shortly.

Geraldine has ordered a copy of the play to be sent to her by Amazon, and is, though she tries to sound weary when she discusses it with Clive, secretly quite excited about the whole thing. Cerebral Clive, on the other hand, is dreading it. But he understands clearly (very clearly; it's how his mind works) that spending a couple of evenings humiliating himself in fancy dress in front of the simple people of Fiddleford is merely a means to an end. He and Geraldine, if they are to expand their practice, if they are to put themselves in a position where they can pick and choose from the county of Lamsford's most important, interesting and remunerative cases, need to be liked and trusted. Need to be known about. Need to know what's going on.

'I ran into Jo Maxwell McDonald this morning. She's wanting to take on new clients. She says the Retreat more or less runs itself now.'

'Clever girl,' says Clive. He rather fancies Jo.

'Well, clever both of them, to be fair,' says Geraldine who, like every woman in the county, fancies Jo's husband, Charlie. 'I think Charlie does a hell of a lot behind the scenes. He just doesn't feel the need to show off about it. Anyway, I'm wondering if we shouldn't employ her. Not just for the practice, but for us. As the practice. Sort of thing. What do you think?'

Clive considers it. He always considers before he speaks. It can mean he sometimes misses the chance altogether.

'Because, Clive,' she continues, 'I don't think we really communicate to people how much we *care* about this village. This county. And about the issues that worry them. And we do. I mean, we care about the school. We care about the lack of public transport for our kids. About maintaining rural post offices and mobile libraries . . . the tax on petrol . . . *all* those sorts of things. I care about them passionately. Don't you?'

'Very much so,' says clear-thinking Clive. 'Very much so.'

'Well, I think we should try and get that across. And I think Jo Maxwell McDonald's the person to help us. So I'll give her a call, yes? . . . They've still got that ghastly Transport Minister up there, apparently. *Still* refusing to resign . . .'

To make her twice-weekly sessions at Fiddleford Primary more endurable, Geraldine has taken to spending less of each pupil's allotted ten minutes actually listening to them reading, and more time making them listen to her chat.

She was sitting fighting sleep again the other day, while a young plodder called Simon struggled over the word 'rug', when her own intense boredom forced her to interrupt him.

'It's *rug*, dear. Mmm. *RUG*. Do you know, Simon, before I was a mummy I was something else. I was something called a *law-yer*. And I still am a *law-yer*. When I've got my law-yer's hat on! Do you know what a law-yer is, Simon?'

Simon shrugged. 'Dunno.'

'A *law-yer* is somebody you call when you need help with the law. A *law-yer* is somebody who sticks up for people's *Rights*. Do you know what Rights are, Simon?'

Simon shrugged. 'Dunno.'

'What do you know about *children's* Rights, Simon? Do you think children have *Rights?* Can you think of a children's *Right*, Simon?'

Simon shrugged. 'Prob'ly it's about signs and so on. For your bicycling.'

The answer shocks Geraldine. ('As a lawyer and a mum,' she explained to Clive a little later.)

So now, in whispered ten-minute sessions in the corner of Fanny's classroom, Fiddleford's pupils are learning all about their legal rights: about how to protect themselves from police harassment, how to access their personal health and education records, what constitutes a physical assault and at what age they're allowed to decide on their own body piercings. And it keeps Geraldine awake.

25

'Hey! Fanny! Wait there!' Fanny, hurrying home that Friday night, tired, fed up and looking forward to spending a weekend in London seeing old friends, glances up to see Tracey Guppy rushing out from the bungalow she shares with her Uncle Russell. Fanny curses softly to herself, fixes on a well-mannered smile and crosses over to the wire fence which separates Tracey's garden from the lane.

'Hey, Tracey.'

'I've got *you-know-who* inside.'

'Louis?' (Two weeks now, and Louis still isn't speaking to her.)

'Louis? Don't be daft!' Tracey giggles. 'Not Louis. I mean Dane. I've got my brother Dane inside. Mum's sent him over because of the skiving fine. So he's shacking up with me and Uncle Russell. Only he's been with us a couple of days and he still won't go to school.' A gust of wind. Tracey, bursting out of a denim mini-skirt and spaghetti-strap electric-pink vest with FOXY LADY across the front, hugs herself with arms covered in goose bumps. She looks as anxious as a mother. 'You don't see it, Fanny. I know you don't. But underneath all the struttin' he gets ever so shy.'

Fanny manages not to glance at her watch. She has just over an hour to catch her train and the station is thirty-five miles away. 'Shall I come in and say hi quickly? Might it help?'

Fanny follows Tracey through a small, clean kitchen, into the front room, stuffy and stale with the smell of smoke. It has a sliding glass door looking out on to the grass, from which Fanny can see the school, the playground and most of the playing field behind. There is a large television at the far end of the room, and against the wall, an enormous turquoise sofa still covered in cellophane. In front of it, in a giant, modern wheelchair, sits Uncle Russell Guppy. He has a brimming ashtray resting on one knee and the mouth-piece of his respirator on the other. He and his apparatus are the only untidy things in the room.

The television is blasting out, loud enough for Uncle Russell to hear it over his own breathing, so he and Dane don't hear Fanny and Tracey come in. Dane isn't watching the television, Fanny sees as she draws closer. He's lying with his bored, grey face turned in towards the back of the sofa, melting bits of the cellophane with his lighter.

'Hello, John Thomas,' says Fanny. 'Watch out, there. You'll set fire to it in a minute.' At the sound of her voice Uncle Russell doesn't bother to turn around, but Dane Guppy jumps. Literally: his entire body jerks with fear and guilt. In less than a second he's on his feet.

Fanny giggles. 'Sorry. Did I startle you?'

'No. What're you doing in my house? I didn't say you could come here.'

Uncle Russell, who's watching *Changing Rooms*, says, 'It's not his house. It's my house.'

'Ah-ha! See?!' Dane Guppy cries victoriously, waving a finger at his uncle. 'It's not your house, Uncle Russell. It's the council's.'

Uncle Russell ignores him. As he has done ever since Dane moved in. As he has done, in fact, ever since the day he was born. Uncle Russell only rarely speaks to Tracey, either, though they've lived together for four years, and she cooks for him and cleans for him and sometimes, more recently especially, has to help him to the toilet in the middle of the night.

Uncle Russell hates both his brothers, and by association, all his brothers' offspring. In fact hatred for his only two brothers has been the ruling emotion of his adult life, ever since 1963 when their father died and they cheated him out of his inheritance. Uncle Russell has spent the intervening years (until his illness prevented it and he was forced to stay at home) sitting on the same corner stool in the Fiddleford Arms silently mulling over that injustice, while his brothers have become husbands, fathers and rich men. It would be hard to comprehend the depths of Uncle Russell's bitterness.

'It's not your house, Uncle Russell. It's the council's,' Dane is saying again. 'See? Plus my dad gives you cash, doesn't he? He gives you loads of cash, as I know. So it's not *your* house, Uncle Russell. It's more like my dad's house, and that's why we're staying here!' Uncle Russell, his eyes fixed steadily on the television, holds the respirator mouthpiece up to his face and inhales. He does not intend to respond.

'Anyway,' Fanny says brightly, 'I was just passing, so I thought I'd come and say hi. And maybe see if I could lure you back to school Monday morning. We're missing you.'

'No, you ain't,' snarls Dane.

Fanny tilts her head, takes a peep at her watch. It'll take five minutes to get back to the house, more if she meets someone on the way; five minutes to pack; it takes forty minutes to get to the station – if *she* remembers the way, which she almost certainly won't . . . And if she misses the train she'll be stuck in Fiddleford until tomorrow, at which point it'll hardly be worth making the journey.

She smiles at Dane. 'We do. Yes, we do miss you. I miss you a lot.'

'No, you don't.'

'OK. I don't.'

'You don't?'

'Yes, I do.'

He looks confused. 'You do or you don't?' he asks, voice rising, eyes brimming suddenly. 'I'm not coming back if nobody's even ruddy well noticed I ain't there!'

She sighs. Sinks on to the end of the plastic-covered sofa. 'Can I—' She turns to Tracey. 'I don't suppose I could get a cup of tea?'

26

Ten-year-old Oliver Adams, small, pretty, with golden-blond hair, pink, plump lips, and a sprinkling of delightful freckles, is instinctively ambitious, just like his parents, and he owns all the gear which most impresses his peer group. He's almost a year younger than Dane Guppy, one-time school supremo, and several inches smaller, but he slipped into the vacancy Dane left behind with the minimum of effort, as if he'd been born to the position.

When Dane stumbles into assembly the following Monday morning, filling the quiet hall with the squeak of his trainers, and the rhythmic chafing of his nylon-covered thighs – not quite his usual cocksure self, ill at ease, out of practice, with greasy hair laid flat and neat against his head, and eyes averted – Oliver Adams feels only a vague flutter of annoyance. In the month since Dane absented himself, Ollie has grown complacent.

His mother, on the other hand, is beside herself with excitement. Providing quality vocalising time to a bona-fide problem child is what she's been wanting to do all along – it's what she's here for, what moved her to offer her mornings to the school in the first place – and until now she's been frustrated by the stubborn levelheadedness of all the pupils.

That morning, when she's meant to be helping the seven-year-olds (who have their SAT exams looming), Geraldine Adams draws Fanny aside.

'The little ones are all focusing very nicely,' she whispers. 'And I'm wondering if I wouldn't be more helpful elsewhere. Perhaps having a little chat with Dane. Help him to settle back in. Could I have a little moment with him, Fanny, do you think?'

Fanny glances across at Dane. He's doing nothing very special. Staring at the window, picking his nose.

'I feel I could help,' Geraldine says. 'I know he can be combative, but he seems like such a sweet kid—'

'Sweet?' Fanny raises an eyebrow.

'Well – yes. You may be surprised by that,' says Geraldine. 'But I do feel, *having a boy of my own* in that age group, and being *a mother*—'

'Oh, yes,' says Fanny.

'Oh, but Fanny. Please, don't take that the wrong way.'

'Of course not.'

'I'd love to try to *reach* him, Fanny. Could I try that? Would you allow me to try?'

'Of course! The more time we spend with him the better. He can barely read, poor little sod. So please! Take him away.'

Geraldine inhales at the word 'sod', but manages not to comment. 'Is he dyslexic, Fanny?'

'No.'

'He's not?' Geraldine sounds shocked. 'How can you be so certain?'

'He's not dyslexic. He's very lazy and he's pretty thick and he hasn't been taught properly—'

'Fanny!' Geraldine laughs nervously. 'Really, I don't think—'

Fanny shrugs. 'So, you know, "reach him", by all means. Whatever it takes.'

Geraldine calls him over at once. But her unbridled enthusiasm – to succeed where all others have failed – leads her to break the cardinal child-reaching rule: she ignores the bell for break.

''Scuse me, Mrs Adams,' he says, ''scuse me . . .' She's leaning over the desk, her manicured hand only centimetres from his arm, her well-cut hair so close to his grey nose he can smell the shampoo. The reading book lies unopened between them, and he's grinning self-consciously, showing all the gaps between his blackened teeth. He's embarrassed. He's not used to people sitting so close to him, but more than that, he's desperate. *The bell just went.*

'Yes, Dane,' she interrupts her own flow, 'what is it?'

He gives a nervous giggle.

'Why are you laughing, Dane?' Geraldine gives him a flash of her porcelain-covered gnashers. A big, friendly smile to encourage him. She has perfect teeth. 'Go on, Dane. You can tell me! Whatever it is you've got to say, I'm a mum! I'll have heard worse and that's a promise!'

'It's because I don't think you heard the bell, Mrs—'

'Geraldine. Call me Geraldine.'

'Geraldine.' Snigger. A globule of spit flies from the back of his throat, across the desk, over the unopened reading book and lands on the back of her hand.

She glances at her hand and determinedly, because the last thing she wants is for this young lad to feel that she finds him disgusting, does not pull it back. She doesn't do anything. She leaves the spit exactly where it landed, glistening bravely above the age-defying moisturiser. '*Dane,*' she says softly, 'we were talking about— Can you remember what we were talking about?'

He shrugs. 'Dunno.'

'We were talking about intimacy, Dane.'

'But the bell's gone, Mrs Adams.'

'Geraldine. We were talking about feeling *safe* with *intimacy*. And I asked you if you felt safe, getting to know me, and you said— What did you say, Dane? Can you remember what you said?'

He shrugs again, more irritably this time. 'The bell's gone for break, Mrs Adams. *Geraldine.*'

'I'm in the middle of saying something, Dane,' she says, gently cajoling. 'We're in the middle of a discussion. Chat. And I want to know, do you feel safe talking to an adult, talking to *me*, because you should, you know; or do you feel . . .'

Outside he can hear the children whose company he's been starved of all these weeks. He can hear them running and shouting and fighting and laughing and he longs to be out there. He looks across at Geraldine, still jabbering away, weird blue eyes staring, and he racks his brain for something to say – anything – some password which will allow him to get out there in the sun.

'*. . . difficult time,*' she's saying, '*and I know family . . . confrontations . . . wanting love . . . concern for you . . . your future . . . confused . . . understanding and trust can feel isolating bewildering . . . so important . . . Tough decisions for adults as well . . . Lonely and vulnerable and lost. Even I feel unloved sometimes . . .*'

He stretches over the table. 'But you know what, Mrs Adams?' he bursts out. She jumps, but not fast enough to prevent him from clasping her bony cheeks, one in each dirty hand, ruffling the hairdo, spraying her face with spit: 'You don't need to worry about that no more, because I love you!'

'W-what's that, dear?'

'*I* LOVE YOU!' he bawls. 'So can I go now?'

She is confused, very confused; frightened, actually. He's

174

a big boy, behaving erratically. Worse than that, *he might be laughing at her*. Distantly, she hears the bell ringing again; break must be nearly over. Or nearly beginning. She's not sure. 'Of course, darling. Poppet. *Dane*,' she says. 'Of course . . . And I love you, too.'

He releases her, leaps up and scrams for the door, and Mrs Adams, trying to recover her composure, runs a hand over her expensive hair. 'Well,' she says out loud, willing herself to believe it. 'That went very nicely, I think.'

27

'And the fact is,' says Geraldine, 'I don't suppose that poor boy's uttered those three words together in his life before. "I LOVE YOU!" Not to anyone. So it was terribly, terribly touching . . . and it makes it all the more difficult to understand what happened afterwards . . .'

What happened, in a nutshell, was that later that day Dane, feeling overshadowed by Oliver Adams, nipped home to Uncle Russell's place and brought back a penknife and a dead blackbird, which he then handed to Ollie, daring him to saw off the bird's head. Ollie sawed, threw the decapitated head at Dane, and accidentally hit him with it on the edge of the mouth, which made nearby children scream in disgust. Fanny, glancing out of her office window, saw the knife blade glinting in Ollie's hand, and ran downstairs to get it off him.

'It's not mine, it's his,' Ollie said.

'It's not mine,' said Dane, wiping the blackbird's innards from his chin.

Fanny confiscated the knife. 'And you, Ollie,' she said, 'don't you ever bring a knife into this school again.' After lessons that day Dane and Ollie went for each other. It took

Lenka, Geraldine's au pair, Mrs Cooke from the pub, Mrs Norman, in her tight leather trousers, and Linda Tardy the teacher's assistant to pull them apart, and Mrs Norman (Matthew's mum) lost a gold hoop earring in the kerfuffle.

So that's what happened (in a nutshell). Two days later, as Kitty is discovering to her cost, Geraldine is still a long way from closure. 'I just can't help feeling a teeny bit let down. Why didn't Fanny speak to me first? I could have told her, Ollie doesn't even *possess* a penknife any more. Not since they took it off him at the airport, coming back from St Barts.'

She and Kitty are grabbing a quick lunch at the Old Rectory, and have been for several hours now. They've nibbled their way through rocket salad and sear-grilled tuna, and Kitty's nibbled her way through an entire camembert, and she's well into the second bottle of wine. It's a weekday. Clive is at the office, and Lenka the au pair has just set out to pick up the two children from school.

'I feel for little Dane. I do. And I want to *help* him,' Geraldine declares, not for the first time.

'I say,' interrupts Kitty, 'have you got anything sweet in the house? I could really do with a taste of chocolate. Don't you think?' She hates it when Geraldine talks about her school work. She puts on a soppy, conceited voice, Kitty thinks, and drones on, as if simply because she's doing something worthy, she has free rein to be as boring about it as she likes.

'The thing about Dane Guppy,' continues Geraldine, 'which Fanny simply doesn't pick up with all her mania about "reading", with the literacy *boot camp* she's got running up there, is that he's actually a very sensitive little person.'

'Which of us isn't, sweetheart? Have you got any chocolate?' Kitty glances, once again, at her mobile telephone. She doesn't normally carry it around with her (chiefly because she's never learnt how to work it) but today she has it, and she's made a great fuss of putting it in the middle of the table. She's asked Geraldine six times whether the Rectory kitchen has a signal.

'By the way, you know I'm with *Vodaphone*, Geraldine, don't you?' she adds, forgetting about the chocolate for an instant. 'Is that the same as Orange, do you think?'

'Of course it isn't.'

'Well, so how do you know if Vodaphone gets a signal out here?'

'I don't,' Geraldine snaps. 'Just look on your telephone. There are meant to be bars on the display thing.'

'I know, but how can you be sure—'

'Kitty, I'm in the middle of saying something. Something quite important, as it happens. Because frankly, Kitty, I'm beginning to have very serious doubts about that head teacher of ours. I think she's irresponsible, inconsistent, arrogant. She's unsettling Ollie and Dane. And I'm seriously considering lodging some kind of complaint . . . So I would have thought you might be interested.'

Last night, after supper, Kitty came into her daughter's bedroom to wish her goodnight. Scarlett couldn't see her mother properly because she'd already folded her pebble glasses on to the bedside table, but she could smell her – a familiar musky scent, French tobacco, alcohol – and she could hear her – brittle, awkward, *bored* – obviously longing to get away. But nevertheless, Kitty sat on Scarlett's bed. She said, 'Things are going to get better for us now, Scarlett.' She was slurring her words. But it didn't matter. She'd never said 'us' like that before, as though they were actually on the same side.

'You and me, darling girl,' Kitty said, and she patted

Scarlett's knee through the blanket. 'In spite of everything
. . . we're a fabulous team.'

She leant over and pecked Scarlett on the top of her head.
It was so quick, so light, Scarlett barely felt it, but her eyes
welled with tears, and as her mother stood up again and
then paused at the bookshelf beside the door, and then slowly,
excruciatingly slowly, opened the door and shuffled back
out on to the landing, Scarlett lay in her bed, afraid to move,
and the tears rolled down her cheeks, the snot rolled down
her nostrils and on to her upper lip; and she could do nothing
about either because she didn't want her mother to know
she was crying.

This morning, as she does every morning, Scarlett took
coffee in to her mother before leaving for school. Kitty, as
is often the way, only managed to mumble something sleepy,
didn't quite open her eyes, so they haven't spoken yet. But
today, of course, is the Big Day. *Their big day*. Scarlett hasn't
been able to think of anything else.

Right now she's in the hall at school, hiding from Lenka
the au pair, who is waiting with Ollie to take her back to
the Old Rectory. She knows her mother is having lunch with
Geraldine and that she's expected to join them. But there's
only one thing Scarlett hates more than going to Ollie's house
on her own, and that's going to Ollie's house with her mother.

She's spent her life watching out for Kitty's mood swings,
and she reckons she knows most of the triggers. Being At
Home with Geraldine is definitely one of the worst. Kitty
exhausts herself with her jovial not-being-jealous show, and
it's guaranteed to put her in a foul mood for several hours
afterwards. Scarlett can't remember the last time Kitty didn't
find something to yell at her about on the way home.

The minutes pass by, stubbornly slowly. It's a quarter of
an hour after lessons ended and everyone else has gone home,
but she can still hear Ollie and Lenka out there squabbling.

'Oh. Hello, there, Scarlett.' Scarlett jumps at the sound of Fanny's voice. 'What are you doing still here? I thought you'd all gone home.'

'I was just – resting my back,' Scarlett says. 'My back was hurting.'

'Oh. Well, shouldn't you be sitting down?'

'I'm OK.' She examines Fanny, standing there with a ramshackle pile of posters in her arms, and a staple gun. She looks shattered. 'Are you all right, Miss Flynn?'

'Me? I'm fine, Scarlett. Thanks for asking.' Fanny grins, quite touched. 'Spent the weekend in London. I think I'm still recovering.' As it happens, Fanny's weekend, when she and Brute finally made it up on the Saturday, hadn't had quite the effect she'd been hoping for. Instead of revelling in the big-city crowd and bustle she'd persuaded herself she was missing, she found herself longing to get away from it all. She missed the sound of the sheep in the field behind her house, and the smell of the jasmine outside her window. She missed the church bells and her early-morning walks with Brute along the river. She missed stepping out of her front door and seeing people she knew, and knowing that if she went into the pub somebody there would probably offer to buy her a drink. In fact, for the first time in her adult life, Fanny was reminded of what it felt like to be homesick. Fanny was homesick.

'Did you drink too much alcohol in London?' asks Scarlett.

'I'm afraid I did. By the way,' Fanny says, changing tack, 'I haven't seen your big red book out recently. Whatever happened to that story you were writing?'

Scarlett blushes. 'My novel?'

'That's right. I'd still love to read it.'

'But you can't!'

'Oh . . . Ok.'

'I mean, you *can't*. You mustn't even tell anyone you know about it.'

'I mustn't? . . . I mean, I won't, of course. But—'

'But seriously.' Scarlett looks terrified.

'OK. Well, never mind. Don't worry, Scarlett. I'm sorry I mentioned it.'

'Mentioned what? What red book? Miss Flynn, *I don't even know what you're talking about.*'

'It seems ridiculous, Kit, and you'll probably laugh at me, but I don't think Fanny really understands kids,' Geraldine says, closing her lovely larder door and tossing some dark organic chocolate on to the table. 'She certainly doesn't understand Ollie.'

'How can you tell,' says Kitty, squinting once more at her telephone, 'if this useless object's battery is flat?'

'What kids need these days is Nurture-to-Go. As I said to Fanny. Because every kid is special. Ollie, Dane, Scarlett. And by that I don't mean—'

'Geraldine, angel, I hate to be a bore but do you think if you just dialled my mobile number on your telephone . . . Only, then I could be absolutely sure it was working.'

'I'm sorry, Scarlett,' Fanny says again. 'I swear I'll never mention the book again. Ever. Which I can't. Obviously. Because I understand now that it doesn't exist – and never has.'

Scarlett glances at her through the thick glasses. 'Now you're laughing at me.'

'By the way, I've got the car today. Got so much to carry back. If you don't mind waiting I can give you a lift home.'

Scarlett doesn't answer. Her mother has sworn her to secrecy but now that Fanny's asked, now that it's more or less out in the open, she can't – she *can't* – keep it to herself any longer. 'I actually finished that story,' she bursts out. 'My novel. I mean, in the red book. I finished it and I showed it to Kitty.' (Kitty insists on the 'Kitty'. She says 'Mum', 'Mummy' etc. sound bourgeois and sentimental.)

'Really? That's nice. How nice. And did she enjoy it?'

Scarlett smiles slyly. 'I know what you're thinking, you know.'

'You do?'

'You think Kitty's a bad mother.'

'Oh!' Fanny laughs in surprise. 'Well, I wasn't. No, I wasn't thinking that.'

'I don't think you like her very much.'

'Don't be ridiculous. I mean, of course – I mean, yes, I do.'

Scarlett rolls her eyes. 'No, you don't. It doesn't matter. Loads of people don't.' She shrugs. 'She's hard to get to like, in a way. But once you're used to her you realise . . .' She falls silent, remembering her mother coming in to her room last night. She remembers the warm smell as she swooped down, and brushed her lips against Scarlett's hair. 'She's a bit of a *wild flower*, that's all.'

Fanny laughs. 'A wild flower?'

'I know,' Scarlett nods. 'You were going to say we're all wild flowers, really.'

'Was I?'

'Of course we are. Especially you.'

Fanny's not sure whether to be flattered or offended. 'I am?'

'But she's had a horrendous time, you know,' continues Scarlett smoothly. 'Having to look after me . . .'

Fanny frowns, shakes her head. 'I don't believe that, Scarlett. I can't think of a nicer child to look after than you. I think your mother's incredibly lucky.'

'No. I mean because of my back and everything. I'm very hard work.'

'You're not hard work. You're lovely,' she says quietly. 'And if, as you say, we are all wild flowers, Scarlett, then I reckon you're one of those rare wild orchids people risk their lives to steal from dangerous jungles.'

Scarlett giggles.

'And, seriously, if your mother doesn't appreciate that—'

'That's not what I meant. My mother appreciates me . . . She appreciates me a lot . . .' But suddenly Scarlett looks as though she's going to cry.

'Well, good,' Fanny says briskly. 'I'm glad to hear it. Right then, Wild Flower, where shall we put these wretched posters?'

They settle on a space outside Robert White's classroom and Fanny climbs on to a chair to staple them to the wall.

'Because you can actually read it, if you want. Would you like to?'

'Read what?' Fanny says vaguely, distracted for the moment by negative thoughts of Kitty.

'Kitty sent it off to her agent in London, who says he's going to sell it for lots of money to an actual publisher. He says he's very confident he can sell it. That's what he said.'

Fanny swivels round on the chair, dropping the poster.

'It's going to be all my words. And on the cover it's going to be by me and my mother: *by Scarlett and Kitty Mozely*. It's going to be like that.' *By Scarlett and Kitty Mozely*. The five words fill the room, Scarlett's pleasure in putting them together making them come out unnecessarily loud.

'By Scarlett *and* Kitty? But Kitty didn't—'

'It's better like that. Apparently, we'll get lots of "sympathy votes".' Scarlett rolls her eyes. 'With us being mother and daughter, and me — Looking like this. He says we'll get our pictures in all the newspapers.'

'I'm not sure I understand. Am I being stupid, Scarlett?'
Fanny jumps down from the chair and sets herself on the
edge of a nearby table. 'I mean, it's fantastic. Obviously. But
I don't see why a novel which you've written— That's right,
isn't it? *You* wrote it.'

'I told you I wrote it. You saw me writing it. In my red
book.'

'No, I know you wrote it. I'm just saying I don't understand why your mother's putting her name on it as well.'

Scarlett sighs. 'I just explained.'

'Yes, but—'

'Anyway, it doesn't matter,' Scarlett snaps. 'For God's
sake, who cares?'

Fanny takes a second to absorb this. 'Of course. I'm sorry.'
She laughs. 'Well, congratulations!'

Scarlett nods. 'You can read it if you want,' she says again.

'I'd love to.'

Immediately, Scarlett undoes her satchel and pulls out the
red book. 'Only don't show it to anyone. If they see it like
that, they'll know it was all written by me. And that would
be awful.'

Fanny bites her tongue. She opens the book, flicks through
it. Every page is dense with Scarlett's tiny, neat handwriting.
'Are there going to be pictures?' she asks and then remembers Kitty in the pub, shouting about Louis doing her illustrations. She snaps the book shut and stands up. 'Anyway,'
she says quickly. '*Well done*. Will you let me know what
happens? When do you hear?'

'The agent'll call Kitty,' Scarlett says, with a sweet hint
of grandeur, 'and then, I suppose, Kitty's going to call me.
She might even telephone me here at the school. She might.
If it's good news. Or there might already be news at home.'
Scarlett indicates the book. 'You can take it with you if you
like. Just for tonight. It's all been typed out by someone in

London anyway.' She giggles. 'It's amazing, isn't it, Miss Flynn? I keep thinking I'm dreaming.'

Just then the door bursts open and Ollie barges in. 'Oi, ugly!' he yells. 'Oh. Hello, Miss Flynn. Didn't see you there.' He turns back to Scarlett. 'What the hell are you *doing*, you idiot? Lenka and me have been waiting for you for about three hours!'

'Really?' says Scarlett, trying to look surprised. 'Why?'

'You're supposed to be coming back with us. Don't pretend you didn't know because you did.' He steals a sideways glance at Fanny. 'Anyway, I want to get home so I can do my homework.'

Fanny chuckles. 'You haven't got any homework, Ollie. Scarlett was just helping me with some posters.'

'And then I'm getting a lift home with Miss Flynn.'

'Yeah, right. Come out and tell that to Lenka. She's refusing to leave without you. *So hurry up.* Your mother's there. Oh! Hey! *That's unusual!* What a surprise! *Scarlett's mother's sitting around in my house for a change.*'

'No need to be rude, Ollie,' Fanny says.

'I wasn't. I was just commenting on the fact that it was a surprise. Because Kitty's never at our house, is she, Scarlett?' He flicks on a smile; it's very cold. Scarlett blushes. She's frightened of him. 'Come on,' he says to her, 'hurry up. Stop wasting my time.'

Kitty's opened a third bottle of wine, and finished the organic chocolate, and her telephone still hasn't rung. Geraldine has moved on from complaining about Fanny's maltreatment of Ollie and is now bullying Kitty about putting herself forward to be a school governor.

'Only trouble, I don't think Fanny Flynn likes me very much,' says Kitty, smirking slightly, and pouring herself another glass of wine.

'Yes, but it's not up to Fanny, is it?' replies Geraldine. 'We can do it through the vicar. Actually, I've already mentioned your name to him.'

'Oh, really?' Kitty pulls a face. 'And how did he take to that?'

'As a matter of fact,' Geraldine says smugly, 'he's expecting us both at church this Sunday morning!'

Kitty scowls. 'Annoying of you. I might be doing all sorts of other things on Sunday morning.'

'Yes, well, I dare say. Talking of which – what news on Louis? You've gone rather quiet on that. Not having any luck?'

'*Louis!*' Kitty says irritably. 'I had him round to take some photographs of Scarlett and me. At the crack of dawn as well, because the little sod refused to come round any later, even though I was paying him.'

'You did what?' Geraldine hoots with laughter.

'Shut up.'

'And you actually *paid* him?'

'Well, I *will*. Almost certainly. If he ever sends me an invoice. Anyway, it's not the point. He took the photographs. It all went very well and he's sent me some prints and I've sent him a marvellous fan letter and so on. Which he'll adore. Because creative people like Louis love that sort of thing. We *crave* encouragement.'

'And?' Geraldine demands impatiently.

'Well – exactly. *And?* Not a peep. Obviously he's dashing around the county, taking pictures of geriatric lottery winners or whatever. But one way or another he's playing bloody hard to get.'

'Maybe, Kit, *maybe* he actually doesn't want to be got. Has that occurred to you?'

'Don't be annoying, Geraldine.'

'No, but seriously. Perhaps he and Fanny—'

'No, no, no. They're *definitely* not. She was in the pub with Messy McShane last night – who's looking grotesquely pregnant, by the way. Disgusting. When's she due? And Fanny Flynn was looking about as bloody miserable as a thirty-whatever-she-is spinster can look . . . *Urghh*.' Kitty shudders. 'I really don't like that woman. Something about her. She's so bloody *smug* . . .'

'Which is why,' Geraldine says, 'if we're going to be governors, which we *are*, we need to go via the vicar. Right? As I say, I dropped a note through his door, and Clive and I have invited them for a drink after Sunday's service, he and his wife – though I'm not entirely certain he has one. Does he have a wife? I don't suppose you know?'

'He did, until about a year ago. Don't you remember? She died.'

Geraldine clicks her tongue. 'How embarrassing . . . But you will come, won't you?'

Kitty glances restlessly around the room. She hates to be pinned down, least of all to a date with a bloody vicar, a *grieving* bloody vicar. 'Anyway, where the hell are the children?' she asks irritably. 'Shouldn't they be back by now?'

Just then, just as she's giving up on it ever ringing, her mobile bursts into life. Kitty jumps and all the layers of white clothing jump with her; she's not reacted so fast in fifteen years. She lunges for her telephone and her white organza shirtsleeve catches on a wineglass. She knocks the empty camembert plate to the slate stone floor and sends the telephone skidding across the table after it. Both land at Geraldine's feet. The plate smashes into several pieces, but the telephone rings on. Geraldine stoops to pick it up.

'Out the way!' orders Kitty. She snatches the telephone from her. And stares at it, panic-stricken. 'Fuck! Geraldine, *fuck!* Help me! How do you answer this fucking thing?'

Geraldine takes it from her, pushes the appropriate button

with her shiny, painted fingernail, and coolly hands the telephone back.

'*Yes?*' says Kitty. 'Is that you?'

A long pause.

'Is it you?' Kitty spits it out again.

A chuckle from old Twiglet Prick. Gleeful and sadistic.
'Depends which "you" you're referring to, really, doesn't
it?'

'Don't be fucking clever,' snaps Kitty. 'I'm having palpitations. David, sweetheart—' She tries hard to pull herself
together. Breathes in deeply. Exhales. Makes herself smile.
'Lovely to hear from you. How are you? So tell me. I'm
having . . . heart . . . palpitations. What's the news?'

'The news, my dear, is *very good.*'

'It is? So—' She pauses, offers a light but hysterical laugh.
'David, you're killing me. What's "good" when it's at home?
What is it exactly?'

'It's actually better than good . . . It's actually *better* than
better than good. Are you ready, angel? Are you sitting
down? . . . They think you and Scarlett are going to be, not
the next J. K. Rowling, unfortunately, but the next Roald
Dahl. Which, of course, as you may remember, is how I
pitched you. Anyway, they fell for it.'

'Yes? . . . Yes?'

'Is Scarlett with you?'

'*What?* No! For Christ's sake, David. What have they
offered?'

David says, 'Don't you think that she ought at least to
be with you when I break the news? Shall I wait? When's
she getting back?'

'I don't know. *Now.* I mean later. It doesn't matter. I'll
tell her when she gets in.'

'She's a very talented girl, you know, Kitty,' he says,
suddenly serious. 'I mean it. A real talent. Little did I know,

when I suggested you write something together, what a little gem—'

'I know, I know,' Kitty says impatiently. 'I know that. Of course, she's got youth on her side. Obviously. I mean, if *I'd* started younger— If I'd been *encouraged* the way Scarlett has— David, stop messing about. Tell me, before I have a heart attack and actually die and you'll have death on your hands. What's the offer?'

'£250,000.'

Kitty screams. She throws the telephone in the air and this time when it lands on the slate stone floor it smashes into several pieces. Kitty doesn't even notice. 'Geraldine!' she yells, and she takes Geraldine in her arms and starts dancing around the table. 'I'm rich! I'm rich! I'm-rich-I'm-rich-I'm-rich! Ha, ha! Fuck everyone! *Fuck them all!* Because I'm RICH! Does old Mrs Hooper-Dooper sell champagne at the village shop? I'm RICH. Of course she doesn't, the silly old bag. Let's go to Lamsbury and buy champagne. Fuck it, let's buy a case! Geraldine, I've done it! I love you. *I love you!* I love everyone. I love the world!'

Geraldine's holding the dustpan and brush and several pieces of the smashed camembert plate in her hands, and she has a nasty feeling that the telephone which Kitty threw into the air has left a mark on her expensive floor. But she manages to put all that aside; to put aside, for a moment, the current of resentment that Kitty's fortunes should be rising just as hers and Clive's appear to be settling in for a freefall. She has never seen her old friend look so happy.

'No need for Lamsbury,' she says cheerfully, trying tactfully to disentangle herself. 'We've got tons of champagne in the cellar. Anyway, the children are due back in a minute.' She grins at Kitty. '*Well?*' she says. 'This suspense is all a bit much, Kit. Are you going to tell me? What the hell is going on?'

Kitty takes a deep breath. Her head is still spinning. 'I can't,' she says. 'Not until we've opened the champagne.' And then, before Geraldine has moved a muscle, she blurts everything out. The way she understands it.

'Scarlett and I have been plotting away, you see. Working *terrifically* hard – which is why you've seen so little of us recently.'

(Had she? Geraldine hasn't noticed it.)

'Actually, we've been working harder than I've ever worked in my life!'

'How marvellous.'

'And I've been longing to tell you, Geraldine, but Twiglet insisted we keep it absolutely *top secret*, because – well, I don't know. People just love to see other people fail. Anyway, so we had this wonderful idea of doing a book together. I thought, Geraldine, between you and me, I thought doing something like this would work wonders for Scarlett's confidence – and so on. Anyway. Cut a long story short. Old Twiglet Prick's come up absolute bloody trumps. He's sold our little book for – well,' Hell. Why stop at £250,000? 'Four – I mean, *five hundred thousand pounds!*'

'Good God!'

'£500,000!' she says again.

'Yes, I heard . . . I didn't realise you'd even finished one. You are a dark horse!'

'£500,000.'

'Kitty!' She's rich, but even so – not as rich as Geraldine. So Geraldine can take her friend in her arms and give her a giant, heartfelt hug. 'I'm so happy for you. You deserve it. *You deserve it!* Come on, let's get that champagne.'

'Actually, would you mind. I really need to call Louis. Why don't you go and get the champagne and I'll put in a quick call. Oh. And can I use your phone?'

28

Like many other women over the years, Kitty Mozely has learnt Louis's telephone number by heart. And for once he picks up.

'Louis, darling!' (*Gotcha!*)

He's photographing a prize-winning, EU-subsidised organic tofu supplier on the other side of Lamsbury, and when he recognises Kitty's voice, his heart sinks. But he doesn't show it. Louis is always polite.

'Hey, Kitty,' he says pleasantly. 'How's it going? I was just going to call you.'

'I'm so well! I'm *so well!* And I'm just so flattered you found the time to do those marvellous pics of Scarlett and me when you did. And I must pay you. Have you sent your bill?'

Louis hasn't. Of course. He's hopeless at that sort of thing.

'No, but do listen. It's not what I called about and I don't want to take up any more of your precious time. Do you remember our little project? Which I was so excited about? Do you?'

'Oh, God – yes,' Louis says guiltily. 'I meant to send you some of my illustrations . . . I'm sorry. I'll do that tonight.'

'Never mind the illustrations now. I mean, they're very important, obviously,' she adds quickly. 'And we'll have a little meeting with Twiglet about them. Very soon, I promise . . . No, the point is, sweetheart, I've just heard from the old Twiglet himself, and we've actually *sold* the bloody thing for – well—' She laughs. 'You're not going to believe this, but for – well—' Hell. '£650,000 . . .'

It's a funny thing, how a piece of news like that can alter one person's perception of another. Louis can't help it. He is impressed. And nor does he mind admitting to it. He is profoundly impressed.

Kitty listens to him stuttering amazement for some time before she finally interrupts. She says, 'And I'm such an admirer of your talent. Your *photographic* talent, Louis. Of course, I can only guess about the rest . . .' She gives a fruity, suggestive laugh and Louis (though the subsidised tofu maker is by now beginning to look quite impatient) finds himself laughing along with her. 'I think the photographs you took of us last week are so splendid, I really want you to do more. What I'm going to do, Louis— Have you got a pen? I'm going to give you old Twiglet Prick's telephone number, OK? Only do remember he's actually called David.' Another fruity laugh. 'So talk to him. Because this is going to be a terrific news story – obviously. You know, mother love, self-sacrifice, hope-conquering-all, *my* career resuscitated and so on – and, of course, dear little Scarlett. So I want you to talk to him and make sure that you're doing the photographs. OK? Tell him I simply refuse to be photographed by anyone else.'

'Sounds great,' he says. 'I'll call my editors and—'

She's not listening. 'Your scoop, my love!' she yells. 'You can thank me later. Oh, and I don't want any weirdo begging letters arriving at the cottage, so we'll do it at the school. Hokey-cokey? No pics at the house. Not any more. Shall

192

we say eleven o'clock tomorrow? And then we can go and celebrate afterwards. Ah – here comes Geraldine with some champagne. At last. I shall see you there! Got to go. *Very* thirsty.'

She hangs up, watches greedily as Geraldine loosens the wire on the champagne bottle and eases out the cork. 'Oh, you are a spoilsport!' she cries. 'You might have let it pop.'

'By the way, Kit, you know who you ought to get in on this. Clive and I have just taken her on, and I must say she's frightfully impressive. Jo Maxwell McDonald! If anyone can get you media coverage, she can.'

'Oh.' Kitty hasn't thought of that. *Extra* media coverage, what fun. But then she frowns. 'I suppose she'll charge a fortune.'

'I thought she was fairly reasonable. When you compare her to London prices. Anyway, Kitty, you're rich now. What does it matter?'

'Good point.' They clink glasses. 'To me!' Kitty says, and takes a swig of champagne. 'Ha, ha! Yes, very good point. What's her number then?'

But Geraldine likes to let people know personally when she's doing them a favour. It's what she and Clive call '*Basic Good Business Practice*'. She holds out a hand. 'Pass me the phone. I'll call her now.'

So Kitty's sitting on the edge of the kitchen table, her feet on a chair, lapping up Geraldine's side of the conversation, which is peppered with passionate avowals of her own delight. 'Well, I'm so pleased for her, Jo. I'm so happy for her. She's my oldest, dearest friend. I'm so proud . . . Yes, she's been scribbling away for so long. I've always known she has talent and— What? Scarlett too, that's right. Yes, isn't it sweet? A real fairy tale come true . . . Because it hasn't been easy. Kitty's such a trouper. If anyone deserves it, she does . . .'

At last the kitchen door opens. In come first Lenka, and then Ollie, and finally Scarlett, bringing up the rear. Ollie and Lenka are squabbling about something. It doesn't matter what, but it's preventing Kitty from hearing Geraldine's conversation.

'*Shhhh!*' she says.

'Hello, Kitty!' It's Scarlett, moving faster than usual, talking louder. She's smiling. She's shiny with hope. Her mother looks pissed – but there's nothing new in that. She also looks happy, and though Scarlett had promised herself she wouldn't ask until they were at home together alone she can't – of course she can't resist. 'Any news?'

'Shhh! Please, darling. I can't hear what she's saying.'

'Why? Who's she talking to?'

'Never you mind, darling. Shhh.'

'*Any news?*' she whispers.

Kitty turns on her, rigid with drink-fuelled irritation. 'For crying out loud, darling, *what about?*'

29

Several times recently the sound of Louis coming and going on his motorbike has woken Fanny in the middle of the night. She's lain there, with the blood thumping in her ears, imagining him and Kitty together on the other side of the wall, until eventually all she can hear is the sound of her own listening and she has to get out of bed.

She and Louis are still avoiding each other; hurrying proudly in and out of their neighbouring cottages without glancing to left or to right, always busy, always nursing their wounds. It doesn't help that they both also happen to be working unusually hard. Louis, because newspapers keep on commissioning him and he's not yet confident enough to turn any of them down, and Fanny to satisfy the phenomenal bureaucratic expectations of the school inspectors, due to descend on her within days.

She finds it hard to work at home on the evenings she can hear Louis moving around next door. This evening she doesn't even attempt it. She fetches wine and cigarettes, and immediately settles down to read Scarlett's novel.

A Revolting Boy. By Scarlett Mozely.
Mr and Mrs Oliver used to be very important London
lawyers, but when their revolting son, Adam, was nine
years old they worried that being quite so important all
the time meant they never had time to have fun. So they
moved to live in the country. They bought a large house
in the middle of a quiet village called Pigsbury . . .

Fanny chuckles nervously.

And with the money they had left over they built the
world's first vegetarian dog food factory. This would
have been very good, and much more fun than being a
lawyer, except that vegetarian dog food smells
TERRIBLE when it's cooking, and Mr and Mrs Oliver
had built the factory right there in the middle of their
garden! The people of Pigsbury were furious.

Fanny doesn't look up again. She doesn't notice when the
cottage next door falls silent and Louis's footsteps shamble
up their shared garden path and into the village street. She
doesn't notice her log fire burning down to its embers, or
how dim the room has grown – until the story is finished,
and nine-year-old Adam Oliver has been accidentally tinned
and served up to the hunting hounds. When the telephone
rings Fanny's head is still buzzing with Scarlett's story. She
answers it with a smile on her lips.

'Hello there!' she says. 'Hello? . . . Hello?' No one speaks.
She glances instinctively towards the window: her curtains
are still open. 'Hello? Who is it?'

Silence. Nothing. He hangs up.

She replaces the receiver. Number withheld. Of course.
Quickly she crosses the room and closes her curtains. She
made the curtains herself, from gold embroidered wedding

saris brought back from India years ago; it's only now, in Fiddleford, that she's finally bothered to put them to use. And it's only now, this instant, that she notices quite how badly. They don't fit the window. There are large gaps on both sides. She feels very exposed.

When the telephone starts up again Fanny doesn't hang around. Doesn't hesitate. She grabs her keys and makes a run for next door.

'Louis? It's me.' Fanny knocks again. 'Louis? I know you're in there . . . Please, come to the door.' She can hear the telephone in her own house still ringing; ringing on and on. 'Louis?' She takes a step back. *He's up there*, she thinks, *hiding under the duvet with Kitty*. 'LOUIS! For Christ's sake . . . I thought we were friends!'

'You won't be for much longer, not if you carry on like that, angel.' It's Grey McShane. Plastered. Eyes and teeth gleaming through the semi-darkness. A bottle of spirits in one hand, a burning cigarette in the other. Fanny screams, and he laughs, his deep rich laugh, staggers forward and puts an arm round her. 'Och, calm down, girl,' he says. 'Only me! Nothing scary about me, now is there? I'm only goin' for walkies!'

'Like a bloody vampire going for walkies,' says Fanny, and tries to smile, because she likes Grey. Pissed or not, he always makes her laugh.

'What's up?' he asks.

'Nothing. Just—' Inside, her telephone falls silent. 'Nothing.' But something catches in her throat, her face crumples and she starts to cry.

'Hey!' says Grey. 'Hey! What are you cryin' for?'

'I'm not crying.'

'Yes, you are!' Carefully, Grey balances the spirit bottle at his feet and wraps his other arm around her shoulders.

197

'Never mind Louis,' he says, squeezing her into a clumsy hug. 'You got loads of friends in Fiddleford. We all like you. Well, most of us. Apart from the odd prick. But who gives a bugger about them, eh?' She shoves him away, laughing in spite of herself. 'Jesus, Grey, you stink!'

'And that,' he says proudly, 'is because I'm pissed. I've been drinking since I woke up this morning. And I tell you, Fanny, it feels bloody good!'

Fanny clicks her tongue. 'Where's Messy, anyway?'

'Messy,' he says, 'is in the Lamsbury hospital. Fast asleep. And sleepin' right beside her is—'

'Oh, my God! Grey! Congratulations!'

'Aye. Eight pounds and seven ounces . . . and he's got hair an' everything. God, Fanny. You should see him. Fuckin' beautiful. Called Jason . . . Jason McShane. What do you think about that?'

Fanny puts her arms around him, in spite of the stink. She reaches up and kisses him on the cheek.

'An' I'll tell you something else for free,' Grey says. 'Solomon Creasey fancies the fuckin' pants off you!'

'He – what?' Fanny giggles. 'That's lovely. Lovely to hear. I'd be flattered, I expect. Except we've never even met.'

'Aye, no,' Grey brushes it aside. 'But he *would* fancy you. If he had. Met you. That's what I keep telling him . . . I've got one o' those espresso machines at my place,' he adds. 'You can come back wi' me. If you want. I'm sure I could cheer you up.'

'Thanks, Grey. But I think I'll pass on that.'

He shrugs. 'Please yourself.' He staggers slightly as he bends to retrieve the bottle at his feet. 'If you change your mind . . .'

'Are you sure you're going to be all right?'

'Better than all right, Fanny!' he shouts impatiently,

weaving away. 'And Messy'll be home tomorrow. I'll be sober as a fuckin' judge.'

'Send her my love, won't you?' Fanny calls.

'And no crying now,' he calls behind him. 'Two lovely pieces of news there. Nothin' to cry about. Not when you're here in Fiddleford, see? We'll always look after you. Don't you worry about that . . .' But he's talking as much to himself, or to the cool summer air, as he is to Fanny, and Fanny doesn't catch the end of it.

As Grey sways on past the Manor Retreat gates, a solitary paparazzo steps up with his flashgun. Grey's enormous frame, his giant black coat, and all his inebriated footwork are briefly illuminated, but he doesn't even bother to look up. 'Och, fuck off, you little sod,' he yells carelessly. 'Can't you see I'm celebratin'?'

She watches him disappearing, glances one last time at the window which is Louis's bedroom and then, with a sigh, takes the torch which she keeps hidden under a stone beside the dustbins, and heads on out to the pub.

It sounds like a busy night at the Fiddleford Arms as she approaches. She can hear laughter from halfway up the street. And as always she can hear Kitty's voice rising above everyone else's, mostly yelling at people to shut up.

'May I speak— Oh, do shut up, Clive. May I speak? This is meant to be MY evening. Shut up. Everyone shut up. All I'm saying is— Of course, she's good at her job. Of course. I'm just saying that in-house bonking – call it what you will – no, it's not funny. Rogering one's employees is not – is not – MAY I SPEAK? Oh, come on! Is not all that professional. And all I'm saying about Fanny—'

That's when Fanny pushes open the door – too early by half a second. Kitty Mozely misses a beat. Geraldine, Clive, Louis – they all do. Beneath his golden West Country tan, Louis blanches. In spite of so much noise it turns out that the pub is almost empty; only the four of them and a couple of white-haired tourists – and a youngish man with curly russet hair leaning over the bar, talking to Tracey.

'What's that you're saying about me, Kitty?' Fanny asks pleasantly. 'I must say, from the looks on all your faces, I would hazard a guess it wasn't especially nice.'

It's Kitty, of course, who is the first to recover. Her open mouth reforms itself into a brazen, baby-toothed grin and she cries, 'Fanny! Ha, ha! Come and join us. You're quite right. We were just this minute talking about you, weren't we, Geraldine? In fact, we were only just saying how bloody good you were at your – sort of – teaching job. Anyway. Never mind all that. What are you drinking?'

Fanny wavers. But she's arrived alone. She can't think of any way to get out of it.

'Come on!' snaps Kitty, already growing impatient. 'What are you standing there for? Like a stuffed goose.' She chortles, nudges Geraldine who ignores her. Geraldine, at least, has the grace to look embarrassed.

'I'm afraid you're catching us in the middle of rather a heavy evening,' says Clive. 'We're celebrating Kitty's success. Have you heard? Can I tell her, Kit?'

'Of course you can!'

'Of course I can! She heard this afternoon that she's actually sold one of her children's books to a publisher for—' He glances nervously at Tracey. But Tracey's distracted, chatting animatedly to the boy at the bar. 'They're paying her £500,000!'

'£650,000,' Louis corrects her.

'More or less,' Kitty nods.

The four of them watch Fanny as she absorbs this piece of news. 'Oh,' she says, frowning. 'OH!' she says again. 'You don't mean— You mean *Scarlett's* book! £650,000! But that's fantastic! She must be so happy! Where is she?'

'We're both very pleased,' says Kitty.

'Your daughter,' Fanny beams at her, hostility fleetingly forgotten, 'is a very, very talented little writer.'

'Yes. So we finally discover,' Kitty drawls sourly. 'Last week, if I remember rightly, her teachers weren't even certain if she could manage to write her own name.'

'Well, congratulations, Kitty.' Fanny smiles. 'On having such a brilliant daughter. Well done.'

'Yes, aren't we awfully clever? Louis darling,' Kitty continues, more or less carelessly, 'do get your friend a chair. Or perhaps— Should we get two?' She offers a sly smile. 'Do you have anyone special coming along, Fanny?'

'Anyone special?' Fanny looks blank. 'Like who?'

Louis stands up. 'Anyhow,' he mumbles, 'I should be getting along.' He looks miserable. 'Got an early start tomorrow.'

'Oh, no, you haven't!' cries Kitty. 'I'm seeing you at eleven o'clock, remember?' She leans across the table, runs a light finger over his hand as he reaches to pick up his tobacco. 'Oh, don't go, Louis, darling. Don't be a bore. The evening is still so young!'

He smiles at her. Fanny notices that he doesn't move the hand. 'I only came in for a pack of Rizlas,' he says. 'Well done, Kit.' He bends down to kiss her cheek, but she moves quickly, catches him on the lips, and smirks. Louis is too good-natured to manifest anything except slight, well-mannered pleasure. He smiles at her, raises an eyebrow, throws a wave at Clive and Geraldine. 'And thanks for the drink. I'll see you tomorrow morning.'

As he turns to leave he looks evenly at Fanny, and Fanny looks evenly back at him: neither knows, any more, exactly what's gone so wrong between them. Neither knows how to begin to make it right again. 'Goodnight then, Fanny,' he says coldly, and brushes quickly past her.

She doesn't even reply.

Another silence. For the three remaining – and especially for Kitty – Louis's departure has taken the edge out of the evening. They all feel suddenly rather flat, and Fanny's wounded presence at the door certainly doesn't help matters.

'Well!' says Geraldine, standing up. 'I don't know about anyone else, but I'm exhausted. I think I'll toddle up the road to bed. Clive, do you want to stay here and finish your drink?'

'No, no,' he says hurriedly, knocking it back. 'I'll come with you.'

Kitty also clambers to her feet and they begin to move as one towards the door. 'Kit, sweetheart, are you up to driving?' asks Geraldine. 'Why don't you stay with us tonight? Since Scarlett's already there . . . I mean, I presume Lenka put her to bed. I didn't actually speak to her about it, did you?'

'Of course she did,' Kitty says. 'Don't worry about Scarlett.'

Clive holds open the door for Kitty and his wife and they jostle through it. 'The bed's already made up,' continues Geraldine, 'if you don't mind sleeping in your own sheets. You were definitely the last person to sleep there . . .'

'Goodnight, Fanny,' says Clive. 'I'm sorry if we're a bit boisterous. Goodnight, Tracey.' He nods at the lean, russet-haired figure: 'See you, Mack.'

Mack, dressed in baggy, worn jeans and mud-caked desert boots, has been leaning his long arms and broad, bony shoulders over the bar, muttering with Tracey ever since Fanny arrived. All Fanny has seen of him is the back of his untidy russet head. Now he turns towards Clive and she is struck – as everyone is the first time – by the size and light of his bright green almond eyes. He sends Clive a saucy wink. 'Tell Kitty well done on the book deal,' he says.

'What's that?' says Clive, embarrassed. 'Gosh. Did you hear?'

'Tell her I'll be round in the morning, collecting what she owes me for the bookshelves.' He has a strange accent; a rough mixture of West Country, Geordie and posh. Geraldine has employed him a couple of times to do bits of carpentry work around the Rectory, and he's done the work better than any of their smart London people, and for half the price. Even so Clive wishes Geraldine would stop employing him. Clive finds Mack uncomfortable, because although Mack always seems reasonably impoverished himself, Mack's father happens to be one of the richest men in the county, and much, much richer than the Adamses. Consequently, Clive can never quite decide whether to treat him, as he puts it to himself, as one of *them*, or as one of *us*.

'Hmmm,' says Clive, trying to look concerned. 'Owes you money, does she?'

'Macklan!' Tracey giggles. 'It's not Clive you should be talking to about Kitty Mozely's carpentry bills.'

'No, I know that, Trace. But there's no sense to be got out of Kitty tonight, is there?'

Fanny looks around her. Apart from the two white-haired tourists, still whispering in the far corner, only Mack and Tracey remain. She feels like an intruder, doesn't want to polish off an already rotten evening by being made to feel like a gooseberry. She takes a subtle step back towards the door.

'Where are you off to?' Tracey asks sharply. 'I should think you need a drink after that! What can I get you, Fanny? This is Mack, by the way. Macklan Creasey. Solomon's son.' She smiles. 'You know Solomon, don't you, Fanny?'

Fanny shakes her head. 'No. Amazingly, we still haven't met.' The General's promised lunch at the Manor has yet to materialise, of course, but as the weeks go by she learns more about the fabled Solomon. She knows he donated something in the region of £350,000 (actual figures vary) to put a new roof on the church a few years ago. She knows he has three young daughters of primary school age, and a stream of magnificent-looking Euro-splendid girlfriends who follow him about everywhere. And she had understood he was in his late thirties. Still quite young. Macklan looks much too old to be his son.

'I'm twenty,' Macklan says, reading her thoughts. 'My dad was just seventeen when I turned up.'

'Oh! Sorry, was I—'

He smiles. 'Save you the trouble of asking. Different family set-up. Well, "family's" probably putting it a bit strong.' He laughs. 'I don't suppose him and Mum would even recognise each other now. Anyway, nice to meet you, Fanny. At long last. Everyone I meet seems to think you're the bee's knees.'

'Really?' says Fanny, astonished. 'Who?'

'Well, my dad, obviously.'

'Oh.' She sounds deflated. 'Him again. I told you, I've never even met him!'

Mack shrugs, doesn't seem to think much of it. 'But Grey McShane keeps telling Dad what a catch you are.' He laughs. 'And frankly, anyone's better than the usual tarts he drags round with him . . . But Dad listens to Grey. We all do. Grey's no fool, is he, Trace?'

'You obviously haven't seen him this evening,' Fanny says, laughing.

'Certainly have. But he was celebrating! Poor chap's got to celebrate once in a while . . . Want to know who else says lovely things about you?'

'Of course I do. But only if they've actually met me. Or it's hard to see how it counts.'

'Well, there's Tracey. True, isn't it, Trace?'

'Shut up, Mack.'

'And Dane.'

'Dane?'

'And Robert White,' Mack says, warming to his theme.

'Oh, no,' Fanny laughs. 'You're a bit out of date there, Macklan. Robert hates me. Won't even come to work any more, he hates me so much.'

'Anyway, fuck Robert,' Tracey says. She doesn't often swear. Fanny and Macklan stare at her.

'I'd rather eat my own eyeballs,' Fanny says at last. 'To be frank,' but Tracey doesn't smile.

'Right then,' declares Mack, standing up from his stool. 'I'm going for a piss. Why don't you get Fanny a drink, Trace, since she's come all this way, and you're supposed to be the drink-getter. You can tell her about the other fellow who's been mooning after her these past weeks.'

Fanny asks for a pint of Guinness and a whisky mac and settles herself on a stool at the bar. 'So?' she says. 'Who, exactly, in this village of strangely attractive but unavailable men—'

But when Tracey plops Fanny's whisky mac on the counter, she's not looking amused. 'And before you go saying anything stupid,' she mutters, 'he's not my boyfriend.'

'Who?'

'Him.' She nods at the door. 'Macklan, of course.'

'Oh.'

'He's not my boyfriend.'

'No. Fine. That's a shame. He's lovely. I'm sorry, did I—?'

'He's not my feller, all right? I've got enough problems.'

Fanny takes a moment trying to make sense of that. 'OK,' she says slowly. 'Well, are you going to tell me then? Which

205

guy's been mooning after me? It is a guy, isn't it, Tracey? Tell me it's a guy!'

Tracey manages a sulky smile. 'You're supposed to be the brainy one. Can't you guess?'

'No! Of course I can't.'

'Oh, come on. Have a guess!'

'I can't. I've absolutely no idea . . . It's not What's-his-name. The hat maker?'

'Daniel? Don't be stupid, he's gay!'

'It's not the General, is it?'

'NO! Don't be disgusting, Fanny.'

'Then who?'

Tracey shakes her head. 'He flops in and out of here like a ruddy love-struck Romeo. All he talks about is you. And Fanny, if you don't know who it is by now, you don't deserve to know.'

'Oh, come on! That's not fair.'

She laughs. 'No. I'm not telling you.' She glances up as Macklan Creasey lopes back into the room. 'And neither will he. You'll have to work it out for yourself.'

30

Jo Maxwell McDonald, now in charge of Kitty and Scarlett's book publicity as well as Fiddleford Primary School's, has escaped briefly from the neurotic demands of her cabinet minister guest and organised, with Fanny's approval, a press call in the school playground for eleven o'clock. She has ignored Kitty's sex-driven demands regarding Louis's exclusive rights to the event and he will, after all, be only one of several invited photographers. She calls Kitty at half past eight that morning to warn her.

'You are *mean*, Jo,' Kitty moans. 'It's too awful for poor Louis not to have his little exclusive.' Kitty has woken in the Old Rectory's front guest room, and is still in bed, propped up against Geraldine's crispest linen-covered pillows. Clive (to keep Kitty out of the way) has already brought coffee, newspaper and the telephone up to her bedroom. He's pulled back the double-interlined cream silk curtains and opened the pretty sash windows so she is bathed in soft, early-morning sunlight. 'Poor Louis. I did promise him.' On the other hand the prospect of a whole gaggle of young men aiming their cameras at her is hardly torture. 'Well, as long as you tell Louis that I tried. Would you do that, Jo? Would you be kind? Tell him I've fought *tooth and nail*. But I suppose we must bow to your superior knowledge. I imagine you understand how these things work . . .'

There is a knock on the door. Scarlett, already dressed and breakfasted, comes in as she does every morning before leaving for school, carrying a plate of toast and Marmite, and a second cup of coffee for her mother.

'. . . But will you make it clear to him, Jo dear,' says Kitty, 'how important it is to me that he's there? In fact, could you ask him to call me, just to confirm? That would be terribly kind.'

Scarlett clears a space on the bedside table and very carefully lays down the plate – without incident. Which is good, considering how nervous she is. This is the first time she and Kitty have been alone since hearing old Twiglet's news and Scarlett's coffee-and-toast delivery, even on ordinary mornings, usually involves at least one spillage.

She smiles at her mother but Kitty is still engrossed in her conversation. She's discussing what she should wear for the photo call: 'You know I'm wondering, actually, Jo, if it isn't worth contacting that little shop in Lamsbury – do you know it? The only place that sells decent clothes in the entire bloody county. I'm sure you do know it. What's it called? Couldn't we get them to donate something in exchange for a little free publicity?'

Scarlett waits patiently, but Kitty shows no sign of getting off the telephone and after a few minutes Scarlett gives up. She leans over the bed and drops a noiseless kiss on her mother's cheek. Suddenly, and still without actually looking at her, Kitty snatches hold of Scarlett's arm.

'Jo, angel,' she says, 'can I call you back? I've got my daughter here. And everything's happened so fast, we haven't even had time to congratulate each other. Could you give me half a minute?'

After she's hung up Scarlett and Kitty look at each other for a short, quiet moment. They can hear Lenka the au pair standing at the bottom of the stairs shouting that it's time to go to school, and then Ollie, yelling at her to hurry. Normally, Scarlett would have jumped. Kitty would have snapped at her for keeping them waiting. This time they both ignore it.

Kitty's eyes slide away from Scarlett's, to the floor. 'Well done, old girl,' she says at last – more quietly than Scarlett has ever heard her say anything. 'Clever girl.' And then more quietly still, so quietly Scarlett isn't even sure she heard it, '*Thank you, Scarlett.*' Scarlett can think of nothing to say to that, but she can see her mother's eyes are brimming and quickly looks away. 'SO ANYWAY,' adds Kitty, pulling herself together. 'Didn't we do well!' She beams at her daughter. 'We're going to be fine now, darling. Everything's going to be *fun* again.'

Scarlett pitches forward to give her mother a second awkward kiss and her foot catches on the bedside table, sending the toast and coffee to the floor. She watches in horror as the dark brown liquid spreads slowly over Clive and Geraldine's 190-year-old silk Chinese rug. But for once her mother laughs.

'Go on,' Kitty says. 'I'll clear it up later. No one'll notice. And if they do we can buy them a new one! Ha! Can't we? So run along. They're waiting. You'll be late for school.'

Fanny tells the children they can come out to the playground and watch when the press arrives to interview Scarlett and her mother. '*BOR-ING*,' moans Ollie Adams. 'What's so interesting about watching somebody having their photo taken?'

'It's not just "somebody", Ollie. It's Scarlett. And there won't only be photographers there. There'll be people from radio stations, possibly. Maybe even someone from the telly, and they'll all be here, in our playing field, not at the Manor, and they'll be firing all sorts of interesting questions at Scarlett. Can anyone think what sort of questions they might be asking her?'

A long pause.

'They might ask her if Jesus exists,' ventures a boy called Carl, whose mother ran away with the woman from the mobile bank last summer.

'They might well ask her that. What else might they ask?'

'They might ask her what it feels like to be so brilliant,' suggests little Chloe Monroe.

Fanny grins. 'Well?' She turns back to Scarlett. 'Feel like telling us?'

But Scarlett is tongue-tied, as usual. She smiles and shrugs, finally opens her mouth to speak—

'Anyway, everyone knows it's her mum who wrote it. They're only pretending it was Pebble Eyes to make people buy the book.'

'That's horrible, Oliver Adams!' pipes up Chloe bravely. 'You're only saying it because you're jealous.'

'Of course he is,' Fanny agrees. 'Oliver Adams, you're being loathsome. Either apologise to Scarlett or get out of the room.'

He chooses to leave the room. He stands up, burning with self-righteous anger, and begins the long, humiliating walk from the back of the yellow assembly hall to the door beside Fanny's chair.

'*Jea-lous . . . jea-lous*,' mutters Dane Guppy merrily, as Ollie trundles by.

'Stop it!' snaps Fanny.

'*Jea-lous!*'

'Dane, that's enough,' says Fanny irritably. 'Ollie, get a move on. Go on. Get out of the room.'

Ollie pauses in front of Dane, points his small white finger into Dane's large, greasy face. '*You've had it*, Penis Guppy. I'm gonna get you.'

Dane goes, '*Ooooh. Scary*,' and every child in the room starts to giggle.

31

Jo Maxwell McDonald arrives at the school half an hour early, as arranged. She's brought armfuls of white clothes from the shop in Lamsbury for Kitty to try on, and a full-length mirror. Kitty said she was feeling too hungover to go back to the cottage so she borrowed from Geraldine's glorious collection of make-up and is using the school staff room as a changing room. Jo's assistant, meanwhile, has gone to arrange some chairs in the playing field.

'You do realise, don't you, that these clothes are not free-bies,' says Jo, trying one more time to pull up the zip of a long white velvet evening dress which Kitty is insisting on trying on, in spite of its being at least two sizes too small and with a neckline which plunges halfway to her navel. 'All these clothes are only on loan.'

Kitty gives one of her fruity chuckles. 'We'll see about that,' she says.

'No. We won't, Kitty. You have to give them back.'

'Yeah, yeah, yeah.'

'No, Kitty.' After her last few years running the Manor Retreat, Jo is entitled to think she's an expert when it comes to managing spoilt and difficult customers, but there is something unruly about Kitty which makes her harder to control than any of them. Because, unlike the streams of cabinet ministers and television presenters who come tripping through the Manor Retreat doors, Kitty doesn't care. She doesn't care about anything, except fun. It makes her difficult to work with.

'As I just explained,' Jo tries again, 'I've got to give these clothes *back* at the end of the day, OK? It's not a joke. And by the way, this dress doesn't fit. I think you should choose something else.'

'Of course it fits!' cries Kitty. 'Are you mad?' She tilts her head, examines her reflection. 'You've got to admit it looks bloody marvellous from the front.'

Jo doesn't say anything.

'Seriously. Look at my boobs. For someone of my age, they're bloody amazing!'

'They're certainly big,' Jo says sulkily.

Kitty laughs. 'If you could just stand next to me, where the zip is. That's right. Then nobody's going to see if it isn't done up, are they? See? And look, if I keep my arm here. It'll be fine!'

'It won't be fine,' says Jo through gritted teeth. 'You look ridiculous. By the way, where's Scarlett?'

'Scarlett? In lessons, I should think. You couldn't just move the mirror up a bit – that's better . . . What I really need to set this all off is some sort of hairpiece . . . sparkly . . . I don't suppose you brought anything like that? In your bag of goodies? . . . Or maybe just a very long feather.'

'We need to talk about how you're going to answer the questions, Kitty. We've got quite a few people turning up today and I don't know if you've ever been to anything like this before, but they'll all be throwing out questions. It can be quite disconcerting. So we need to be sure you and Scarlett know what your answers are before we begin. It's very important you're both reading from the same prayer sheet, so to speak.'

'Prayer sheet?' repeats Kitty, slightly alarmed. She hasn't been listening.

'We need to prepare what you and Scarlett are going to say,' Jo repeats patiently.

'Oh, don't worry about Scarlett,' Kitty says. 'She's awfully shy, poor little mite. She'll probably leave all the talking to me. More importantly, Jo. Did you speak to Louis?'

'I did. Louis's coming. He's going to be a bit late.' Jo glances at her watch. 'I'm going to ferret out your daughter now. I feel terrible. I haven't even congratulated her yet.'

But Kitty won't allow her to go, and the more insistent Jo is the more demanding Kitty becomes, so that when, already fifteen minutes late and still in her ludicrous bulging white evening dress, Kitty is finally escorted by Jo to one of the two chairs which have been set up in the sunny playground, Jo has broken the rule of a lifetime. Because the press is already waiting (all except Louis), and so is Scarlett. She is sitting in her chair in front of the cameras, with her crutches beside her and with Fanny and Jo's assistant standing protectively behind her. And she and Jo haven't even met.

'Oh, *I say*, she's bloody well starting without me!' cries Kitty to the pressmen, settling her merry velvet arse on to the chair beside Scarlett's. 'Next thing we know, she'll be saying she wrote the damn thing, won't you, darling?' There is an edgy silence. They had been expecting somebody mousy and careworn, someone so overwhelmed by gratitude at the turn her life had taken she would need to be coaxed to speak. And here was Kitty, dressed all in velvet and with bulging breasts on show, not showing a hint of remorse for having kept everyone waiting. '*But don't you believe it*,' she continues blithely. 'She didn't write a damn word!'

Kitty leans across her daughter's chair, so that only Scarlett can see her face, and gives her a giant wink. Scarlett bursts out laughing.

'OK,' begins Jo, 'I think most of you probably know me already. But for those of you who don't, hi. My name is Jo Maxwell McDonald, of McDonald PR, and also, of course, the Fiddleford Manor Retreat. Thank you very much for coming. I think my assistant has already handed you a little press release, so I'm going to kick off straight away . . . It is my great pleasure to introduce to you the incredible mother–daughter double act, Kitty Mozely and her brilliant daughter Scarlett, who is, of course—'

'By the way, boys,' interrupts Kitty (though of the ten or so people before her, at least half are women). 'As you may notice, the zip on this marvellous dress I'm wearing doesn't actually *do up*. Not on me, anyway! So please, please, please, be kind. Don't photograph the rolls of flesh that may possibly be bulging out of it. Jo, you promised you were going to stand beside me – here. That's right. So they wouldn't be able to see . . .'

It happens to be one of the mornings when Geraldine is providing her surreptitious civil rights classes to the juniors, and since Fanny has given the children time off to witness Scarlett's moment of glory, it would have been churlish of Geraldine not to come out and watch it too. But of course it's one thing, getting drunk with an old friend the night before – it's actually quite another having to stand on a netball court with sundry staff members (Linda Tardy the teacher's assistant, Mrs Haywood the glass-eyed secretary, and some unknown supply teacher) and a gaggle of yokel children, to applaud her through each individual moment of her glory.

She might have felt a bit better if it weren't also for the fact that her son is in disgrace as a result of something he did in assembly this morning, and is the only member of the school forbidden to watch the show. Fanny refuses to tell her what he's done wrong. Which Geraldine thinks is outrageous, after all she's done for the school.

'So, *Scarlett*,' a female journalist ventures, about twenty minutes in, 'would you tell us in your own words, what's the story actually about?'

'Do you want to tell her, darling? Or shall I?' But then Kitty makes the grave mistake of pausing for breath, and Scarlett's small voice can be heard, clear as a bell. 'No, it's all right, Kitty,' she says. 'I'll explain.'

Kitty double-takes. A look of irritation flits across her face. But she smiles, not unpleasantly. 'Oh!' she says. 'Jolly good. Well, go on then, darling. Tell-tell. What it's really about, of course,' she adds, turning back to the journalists, 'as always with my work, for those of you who haven't read it, is the indomitability of the human spirit. And, need I add, the truly unpackageable magic of childhood!'

Fanny's been listening to Kitty bombast her way through this whole process. She's watched the journalists, like putty in Kitty's hands – and even she can't quite deny that Kitty is funny. But beside her, she sees Scarlett, bursting with pride and yet never, not even once, getting a chance to speak. 'Scarlett?' she blurts out. 'Is that how you would have described it?'

Scarlett chuckles. 'Not really, no.'

'Oh!' says Kitty, not in the least put out. 'Scarlett, you are awful! But she's quite right, of course, I'm talking absolute nonsense. As always.'

'So? What is it about then, Scarlett?' persists Fanny. She has to raise her voice to be heard over everyone's laughter.

Scarlett doesn't mind sharing credit for having written the book. She doesn't mind sitting here and smiling while her mother enjoys herself, showing off – in fact, she loves it. She's never seen her mother on such good form. But there is one thing she wants to make clear to everyone, and it's this:

'The book,' she says, 'is about a real boy, who I know very well. He's spoilt and stupid and nasty. He bullies the children. He bullies me. And yet his parents think he never does anything wrong . . . I wanted to write – *we* – *we* wanted to write a story where he gets his just deserts.'

Kitty cackles wickedly. She steals a glance at Geraldine; she is standing next to Linda Tardy, wearing a tired, distracted grin. Obviously not listening. Lucky.

'Who's the boy? Does he go to school with you here in Fiddleford?'

'Well,' she says solemnly, 'I don't think I should probably tell you that. But I'm hoping his mother will read it to him every single night as a bedtime story, since he's probably too thick to read it himself. And that one night, in a terrible, blinding flash, he'll suddenly realise the story's all about him.'

Kitty cackles again. Naughty Scarlett, teasing everyone like this! She'd never realised her daughter was such a good sport.

'So it's revenge against the playground bully, is it?'

'Yes, it is.'

'No, but it's only pretend, though, isn't it, darling?' says Kitty suddenly, remembering Clive and Geraldine's swimming pool, and the fact that they are lawyers. 'Those people don't really *exist*. The horrid boy and his ghastly parents and so on. It's just pretend.'

Scarlett gives her mother a strange, cold look. 'No, Kitty. It's not pretend. I really hate him.'

'No, but sweetheart, he doesn't actually thump you or anything horrid like that. Of course not.'

'That's not the point.'

'OK,' interrupts Jo, sensing danger. 'I think that's probably enough questions.'

'So *who's the bully?*' demand the journalists. 'What's his name, Scarlett? Can you tell us that?'

'Of course I can,' she says, stung by her mother's uncharacteristic attempt at diplomacy. 'His name is—' at which point Kitty and Fanny and Jo, too – who doesn't know the name but most certainly knows that nobody else should either – all start shouting at once.

'*What? Who?*' The journalists turn in frustration from Scarlett to one another. '*Did you catch that? What did she say?*'

'His name is—' Scarlett tries again. But it's too late. Everyone's making too much noise. Jo has moved in front of Scarlett and is yelling about coffee being available in the village hall. Kitty is yelling about authors believing their characters are real. Journalists are shouting that they can't hear. Photographers are shouting that they can't see. And Fanny is clapping her hands, yelling over everyone that it's time for the children to go back inside.

She feels her mobile telephone vibrating in her jeans pocket.

'Yes? Hi! Who is it?'

'Louis,' he says coldly.

'Who?' She walks away from the noise. 'I can't hear!'

'It's Louis. I'm standing in front of the school and I think you might like to get out here.'

'What? Why?'

'I should hurry if I were you.' He hangs up.

Fanny turns to look back at the school. There is a tail of smoke rising from the far side of the building. 'Keep them here until I say,' she mutters to Jo. 'I'll be back in a minute.'

The bonfire, on the tarmac just in front of the girls' cloakroom, is raging a metre high by the time she turns the corner. She sees him laying something on top of the flames: another dead bird, by the look of it, with a couple of fireworks strapped on to its back.

'Dane Guppy!'

He jumps, obviously guilty, but still can't drag himself away. His fireworks could go off at any moment.

'*They're going to explode!*' shouts Fanny.

'I hope so.' Dane bends closer over the fire to get a better look.

'*Get back, you idiot!*'

He doesn't move.

'*Get down!*' Fanny, not much larger than he is, throws herself on top of him and knocks him to the ground just as the first firework fires off into the morning sky . . .

. . . and the last frame Louis takes is of Fanny, scrambling up from on top of her pupil, a furious finger pointed at the camera while the bird and remaining firework explode above the bonfire's flames. As he lowers his camera Louis is weeping with laughter.

'Give me that fucking camera. It's not funny, Louis.'

'Oh, sure, it's funny.'

'Why didn't you stop him?'

'I did, didn't I? I called you.'

She looks down at Dane, still flat on the ground. 'Dane, you idiot. Go and wait for me outside my office. I'll be there in a minute. And you,' she spits at Louis, 'give me that film!'

'What?' He laughs. 'No. Of course not.'

'Give it to me!'

Louis smiles, indicates the playing field on the other side of the school. 'By the way,' he asks lightly, 'about how many journalists you got over there right now?'

She gazes at him. 'Oh . . . fuck.'

He gazes back. Gives another burst of laughter.

'Louis . . . please. *Please* . . . There's a fire extinguisher in the hall.'

Somehow they manage to put the thing out and sweep away most of the embers just as the first few reporters begin

219

to file out through the front door, so that the only telltale signs of Dane's experiment are a lingering smell and the black smears on Fanny and Louis's clothing.

And then Fanny and Louis are left alone. They are standing side by side where the fire had been, Louis with his hands in back pockets, Fanny absorbed by her shoe stitching, both uncertain whether their shared adventure constituted any kind of a truce.

'Thank you, Louis. Thank you very much.'

'Where's Mr White when you need him, huh?'

'What's that?' she asks hopefully.

'Robin Grey. Whatever he's called. The skinny teacher.' He shrugs. 'Doesn't matter.' He looks at her, at last. Most of Fanny's hair has tumbled out of its clip and she's got a smear of soot across her nose and cheek. She looks slightly mad, he thinks, and wild, and – it demands all his willpower not to take the cheek in his hand; not to bend down and kiss her. 'I'm late, Fan,' he mutters. 'I should get on. Scarlett and Kitty are waiting. They'll be pissed.'

At the mention of Kitty's name the spell is broken. 'Well, well.' Fanny smiles sourly. She can't help it. 'Heaven forbid you should keep Kitty waiting.'

'That's right,' he says. 'I'm supposed to be working.'

'"Work" is it now, Louis?' Stupid and spiteful. She knows it, and yet still can't seem to stop. 'Business must be very bad.'

'Don't be a jerk,' he says coldly and begins to walk away.

'Oh, come on, Louis,' she calls after him. 'Louis, I was joking. I didn't mean—' But the moment is gone. He doesn't turn back. He ignores her.

He wanders off, leaving Fanny standing there alone. Briefly she considers Ollie and Dane, both of them waiting for her upstairs – no doubt beating the life out of each other. She ought to break them up. She ought to do that.

She ought to do a lot of things, and yet she stands there, waiting – hoping that for some reason Louis might turn round and come back. So they can try having the whole, stupid conversation again.

32

Macklan Creasey spent the first seven years of his life in Durham shuttling between a handful of foster homes and the tiny, dirty flat of his ageing mother. During that time he never once set eyes on his father. He was barely aware that he existed – until one strange afternoon, at the end of a month-long visit to the foster home, it had been not his depressive forty-seven-year-old mother, but a twenty-four-year-old Solomon who turned up to take him away.

By that stage Solomon the art dealer had already spent a short spell in prison, for fraud, and had learnt from his various mistakes, definitely not to make identical ones again (although he would return to prison for tax evasion several years later). He was also already well on his way to making his first million. He spent some of it on Macklan's mother whom he'd deserted seven years previously. He was guilt ridden; a rare state for Solomon (and not wholly justified since, at the time of Macklan's birth, Solomon, at seventeen, was twenty-three years younger than Macklan's mother, his former art teacher). He found her treatment for the depression, paid for it, even pre-booked the thrice-weekly mini-cabs that were due to take her to her appointments with the shrink. He bought her a brand new house in a brand new close in a refined corner of Durham. And he took Macklan.

Solomon promised his former art teacher that as soon as she felt well enough Macklan would be returned to her. But the months passed and she never asked for him. A year passed, and Macklan's mother stopped telephoning. She stopped replying to Macklan's letters. Finally, Solomon and Macklan travelled north together to find her. And there she was, still living at the lovely new house Solomon had bought for her. She looked well – and neither pleased nor particularly displeased to see them. She had a job at Boots, she said, and a new boyfriend. She probably would have taken Macklan back if Solomon had insisted on it, but then, when it came to the crunch Solomon found, most inconveniently, that he couldn't quite bring himself to be separated from him. He loved his goofy son, and his goofy son appeared to love him. So he bundled Macklan back into the car and drove them both south again.

Macklan didn't shine at school. He was academically slow, physically uncoordinated, tone deaf, not even any good at art – and dyslexic. But people loved him. He was good-looking in a fey, haphazard sort of way, and incredibly good-natured. His mixture of vulnerability, self-possession and humour made him hard to resist, especially for women.

He left school at sixteen without a great deal to show for it and took a year-long course in cabinet-making, since when, because he is a perfectionist and he constantly undercharges, Macklan has always had more work than he can keep up with. He moves around, sometimes staying with friends or a girlfriend, often staying with his father in London. But he's spent the last couple of months on his own at Hawthorne Place, Solomon's weekend house in Fiddleford. He's rented part of the disused stables up at the Manor Retreat, which he uses as a workshop. It is the first workshop he has ever had.

Solomon worries that Macklan, alone in the country all week, might sink, as his mother did, into depression. Solomon is always trying to persuade Macklan to return with him to London.

But Macklan is far from depressed. He is in love with Tracey Guppy. Macklan and Tracey have been in love with each other since the evening they met, seven weeks ago, on the night that the people of Fiddleford were meant to be learning how to limbo dance.

On the Sunday that Kitty and Scarlett Mozely's faces are splattered over a handful of newspapers' inside pages, Macklan Creasey ambles gracefully into Solomon's study, hands in pockets. He waves vaguely at his father, who is on the telephone, as ever; feet up on the desk, mid-negotiation with an Austrian packaging tycoon, and speaking in effortless, fluent German.

They have the same long-limbed, athletic physique, Macklan and his father; the angular cheek-bones, set jaws, long, straight, bony noses (although Solomon's looks as if it might once have been broken), and yet nobody who didn't already know it would ever guess they were related. It would be hard to find two men with such opposing styles. Macklan's large green eyes are full of light and humour; Solomon's are black, hooded and watchful. Macklan, with his pale skin, careless clothes and shaggy russet hair, looks like a Romantic poet. He is beautiful. Solomon is not. He is a long way from beautiful. He is smooth and swarthy, impeccably dressed and deliciously scented. He looks and smells like a Hollywood villain.

'*Etwas ist passiert,*' Solomon lifts his long legs from the desk, nods at his son, '*ich rufe sie zurück,*' and hangs up without waiting for a response.

'Sorry,' says Macklan. 'I could have waited. There wasn't any hurry.'

'Not at all. He's always very repetitive. So what can I do for you, Macklan? Want a lift back to London?' he asks hopefully. 'Or you can take one of the cars if you want. Drive yourself.'

Macklan frowns. 'Actually, I came to tell you I'm getting my own place. I've decided to move to Fiddleford properly.'

A moment's frosty silence while Solomon absorbs this, then, '*Macklan, you fool, you'll be fucking miserable!*'

'Of course I won't.'

'You haven't got any friends down here.'

'Yes, I have.'

'But all your family's in London. We're all in London!'

'We can see each other at weekends.'

'But what the bloody hell are you going to do with yourself down here all alone?'

'There's plenty of work around. Charlie Maxwell McDonald's got loads of work at the Manor.'

But his father isn't listening. He won't listen. Though he himself ran away at fourteen and has never once contacted his parents since, he believes Macklan, at twenty, is still too young to leave home. Will always be too young. 'There's fuck all to do in the country. You do realise that, don't you?'

'And I'm renting one of the Old Alms Cottages off Ian Guppy,' he says. 'The last one. I'm lucky. There was only one left.'

'*Lucky?* Have you gone mad? Macklan, the roof of those cottages hardly reaches your ankles!'

'Well, then I'll just have to bend. There's no point going on, Dad. I'm moving in tomorrow . . . Cheer up.' Macklan smiles. 'You can come and have supper with me next weekend if you like.'

'But *why?*'

'You might be feeling hungry.'

'Don't,' Solomon shudders, 'for Christ's sake, Macklan – don't be facetious.'

'Sorry.' Macklan smirks.

'I simply don't understand what attraction this village could possibly have for a young man like— Oh. Unless you've met a bird?' Solomon chortles suddenly. 'Is it a bird, Mack?'

'Mind your own damn business,' snaps Macklan. 'I just like it down here.'

'If it's a bird there's not much I can do about it . . . Does she— Is she—' Solomon throws his son a sideways glance – and decides against it. Sighs. 'Never mind.' Instead he turns to the bookshelf behind his desk, taps in a code on some invisible keyboard. The spines of ten adjoining books ping abruptly open. 'Will you at least take this?' he says, pulling out a wad of banknotes. There is, beneath the bluster, a hint of pleading in Solomon's voice. Mack shakes his head. As usual. 'But you'll need something to set the place up. You've got to have some cash, Mack. I mean, for example, do you have a kettle?'

'I can get one.'

A look of triumph from Solomon. 'And do you have any idea how much a kettle costs these days?'

'I've got a pretty good idea,' Macklan laughs at him. 'What about you? How much do you think a kettle costs?'

'What? Well . . . Christ.' He thinks about it. 'I haven't got a fucking clue. It's got nothing to do with it. Macklan – please – I'm ordering you, just this once, take the cash.'

'No.'

Macklan's a fool. He never takes the cash.

226

33

Solomon spends the entire, long journey back to London worrying about Macklan's decision. He drops off his Silent Beauty at her elegant address somewhere in Chelsea and heads for an early bed. Solomon does all his best thinking in bed.

At three in the morning he telephones the ex-Mrs Creasey, currently living it up in Miami with an Iranian plastic surgeon, to tell her that he and the children will be moving to the country. Mrs Creasey has never been to Fiddleford. He bought it after they split. But even the thought of the English countryside, from her air-conditioned sea-view splendour, makes her shiver with fear and loathing. She wishes him and the children heartfelt luck, which Solomon accepts with a gust of laughter so loud it wakes the children. They come down one by one – Clara, seven, Dora, six, and Flora, five – in search of breakfast.

'Good news,' he says, pulling toasted crumpets from out of the grill. 'Ouch. Bugger. As from next week, we're all going to live in Fiddleford and you'll all be going to school in the village. Which of you wants Marmite?'

* * *

'You'll die o' boredom, Solomon, you ass,' says his old friend Grey McShane when Solomon telephones to tell him the news. 'What the bloody hell are you going to do with yourself down here?'

'Work, of course. And I thought I might buy a bit of land,' Solomon adds vaguely. 'Buy a little tractor . . . The children would love it . . . Or perhaps I might become an MP.'

Grey belly laughs. 'With your record?'

'No. All right. Fair enough. What else do people do in the country? I don't want to just flop there like a rich bastard.'

'Like you do at the moment.'

'Exactly.' Solomon rests his large feet on top of the seventeenth-century dining table which serves as his desk at the London gallery, and lights himself a cigarette. 'Any ideas? Maybe I could sponsor a croquet competition. Or darts. Nothing too strenuous, so we can get the geriatrics in on it too. Since Fiddleford seems to be half-populated by the over-nineties. Do you think they'd enjoy a croquet and darts knees-up? Might do. I certainly would. To celebrate our arrival.'

'Sounds good,' Grey says distractedly, prodding at a tray of dover sole being held out for his inspection.

'Macklan could build a podium, for giving out the prizes. And I'll get trophies made. Anything else? You must do us a banquet. With a pig on a spit. Can the restaurant stretch to that? I'm sure it can.'

'Of course it can.'

'Excellent. This is beginning to take shape. Perhaps I should organise hot-air-balloon rides. Flora and Dora are obsessed—'

'Right then,' chuckles Grey. 'Well, I've forty covers for lunch today, so I'll leave you to mull that over, shall I, Solomon?'

They arrange for Solomon to come round, discuss suckling pigs and pay homage to the new baby that Friday, and hang up only for Grey to call back sixty seconds later. He suggests that Solomon might like, as part of his non-flopping policy, to volunteer at the village school as a governor.

A stunned silence. 'You're joking, right?' Solomon says. He sounds like a true Londoner, for once. Always does when he's surprised.

'No, I'm not fucking joking,' snaps Grey. 'Don't be a bloody snob. We'll talk about it when you get down here on Friday.' And with that Grey slams down the telephone.

34

Fanny gets the HM Inspectors' report back a week later, on the Friday they are due to break for half-term, and slightly earlier than expected. Mrs Haywood the glass-eyed secretary hands it to her with a knowing smile, and lingers a moment, fiddling ineptly with the untidy papers on Fanny's desk while Fanny, with cold, sweaty hands, fumbles to open the envelope.

'Well? . . .' says Mrs Haywood at last. 'What does it say? . . . I expect they're delighted, are they?'

'I'm not sure,' says Fanny, too nervous to know where to start. 'I doubt it.'

'Look at the summary, dear,' orders Mrs Haywood. 'And don't look so worried! You've worked ever so hard for us. You've done ever so well. If they can't see it then they're blind as bats, and I'm sure we'll all have a few things to say about that . . .'

Slowly, Fanny's face breaks into a grin.

'There. You see?' says Mrs Haywood, surreptitiously dropping a random bunch of papers from Fanny's desk into the bin, as she always does when she's in here, if she thinks Fanny's not looking. As she's been doing for years, in fact, for every boss she's ever worked for. (It never seems to matter.) 'I told you, dear!' She leans across the desk, gives Fanny a hurried pat on the shoulder. 'Well. That's all I needed to know. I'll leave you to read it on your own. Many congratulations, Fanny. You deserve it.'

'Thank you, Mrs Haywood,' Fanny says in amazement. 'Thank you. I had no idea you— I had no idea you thought I was any good. You never said.'

'Didn't I, dear? Well, of course I do.'

'Thank you very much.' Fanny beams.

Mrs Haywood closes the door behind her.

Fanny has to read the report's conclusion once, twice and again before she begins to take it in. In spite of the shortage of governors, she reads in numb amazement, and the shortage of paperwork, and the protracted absence of one member of staff, *rarely, if ever,* it says, *have Her Majesty's Inspectors noted such improvement in a school over such a short period of time. Miss Fanny Flynn is to be highly commended.*

. . . Highly commended . . .

Fanny shouldn't have been so surprised. Most of the children's parents, like Mrs Haywood, would have told her the same. With or without the forbidden dissected pheasants, nature tables etc., Fanny's hard work and imagination have indeed worked miracles over the school. It's evident not just in the brightly coloured walls, the murals, the clay models, the weaving looms, the poetry and science displays, the small vegetable garden outside the cloakrooms (just now sprouting carrots). Above all of that, all the variety and imagination on show, Fanny's success is evident in her students' faces. Nobody, unless by some fluke Robert White happens to be working, nobody at Fiddleford Primary School ever looks bored any more.

A copy of the report is sent to the vicar (chair of the board of governors) and to its seven other members.

Fanny sits at her desk, grinning to herself . . . *Rarely, if ever* (she reads it again) *have Her Majesty's Inspectors noted such improvement in such a short period of time . . . Rarely, if ever . . . Rarely if ever . . . such improvement . . . in such a short period of time . . . Miss Flynn's achievements must be highly commended . . .*

There is a tap on her office door: the light, efficient tap she has come to know so well, accompanied as it always is by the infuriatingly upbeat 'Only me!'

Only Geraldine. Wanting to talk about Ollie. Again.

The feud between Ollie and Dane has spiralled, over the last week, to the point where they now have to be sat at opposite corners of the classroom. Earlier this morning Dane had taken the unprecedented step of contributing a non-aggressive comment to a class discussion. The fact that it was garbled and irrelevant didn't matter; the will had been there.

'Eh?' interrupted Ollie, scratching his golden curls and looking facetiously around the classroom. 'Is Penis Guppy talking German again?'

Once again Fanny sent Ollie out of the room.

'Do you mind, Fanny? I know you're busy . . .' says Geraldine, pushing open the door and firmly closing it behind her. Fanny has rearranged the furniture in her small office. She's thrown out the broken filing cabinets and replaced them with a chair. Geraldine doesn't wait to be asked. She is already sitting in it.

But Fanny's had a glowing report from the inspectors. She's off to Spain tomorrow morning to spend half-term with her mother. She pats the wad of paper in front of her, grinning. 'Got the inspectors' report back, Geraldine.'

'Oh! What does it say? Is it nice?' Geraldine leans across the desk towards it. '*May I see?*'

'I'm amazed it's come back so quickly,' Fanny says. 'They said it would take at least a week.'

232

'*Is it nice? May I see?*'

'It's incredibly nice, actually,' Fanny says.

A flicker of surprise on Geraldine's face. 'I knew it! See? You shouldn't have worried so much! I'm so happy for you. *May I see it?*'

'I was thinking of zooming out to Safeways, actually. Thought I'd get us some champagne to celebrate.'

'*May I see it?*'

''Course you can.' Fanny slides it across the desk. 'Not supposed to, mind. Supposed to be confidential. For governors' eyes only . . .'

The bloody vicar had cancelled last Sunday's drink at the Old Rectory, and though he has promised to come this Sunday instead, Geraldine is beginning to suspect that he's a flake. There is only one thing in life Geraldine fears more than a flake, and that is to be left outside of a loop. Any loop. Even a loop of people officially allowed to read the HM Inspectors' Report of Fiddleford Church of England Primary School. She wants to be on that governing body. Now.

She clears her throat. 'It's not what I came to see you about, but it's something I've been meaning to discuss with you for some time. As you probably know, *lovely* Reverend Hodge is doing his level-lovely-best to get Kitty and I rush-elected on to the body. Via his little church council.'

'Oh.' Fanny didn't know. Geraldine has taken care not to mention it to her. Obviously. But the fact that the lovely Rev. hasn't mentioned it either only confirms Geraldine's suspicions that he's a flake.

'*Dear* Reverend. He's a sweetheart and I adore him,' Geraldine continues. 'But of course, you know how it is with these *old soldiers*. Their idea of a "rush" isn't quite . . .' Geraldine rolls her eyes, smiling, 'the same as one's. Meanwhile, Robert White tells me that you're desperately short of governors—'

'When did you speak to Robert?'

'A couple of weeks ago now. Poor little chap. I gather he's terribly sick?'

'Depends how you define "sick",' mutters Fanny.

'Hmm?' Geraldine's beady eyes try to look confused, but she's heard. She's taken it in. 'So, no. We – Robert and I – were talking about it a few weeks ago, and he happened to remark that we were heinously short. Of governors . . . I must admit I had rather hoped, Fanny, you would have invited me to join the board.'

'Oh!' is all Fanny can think of. Again. Her mind races for an excuse. 'Oh! . . . How silly . . . why didn't I think of it?'

'And as I say,' continues Geraldine, 'Kitty, too. She's keen to join, too. And with her all over the papers she might be quite a useful person to have on board, don't you agree? We'll need to organise a little election. But I can do that.'

'Oh, absolutely. Let me, erm— Only I'm not quite sure . . . how many we need. Or if we need . . . But it's such a lovely thought. Can I think about it?'

Geraldine smiles brightly. 'What's to think about, Fanny? Since I'm here . . .'

'Yes,' Fanny laughs. 'But Geraldine, you're *always* here.'

Geraldine looks faintly bewildered. Faintly hurt. 'OK,' she says in a smaller voice. 'OK. Well. Have a think about it.'

'Thank you, though,' Fanny says limply, 'I don't mean to . . . Was there anything else?'

'Hmm? . . . Oh. Yes,' Geraldine rallies at once. 'I'm afraid there is. Fanny, I found Ollie *in tears* outside your office this morning.'

'He was in tears, was he?' Fanny sounds sceptical. 'Are you sure?'

Geraldine won't confirm or deny. She tilts her head. 'Fanny, Ollie has never been in trouble at school before. Not

234

in London. Not here. Never . . . And I don't know what to tell him, Fanny. He's convinced you're picking on him.'

'Ollie—'

'And I personally believe,' Geraldine closes her eyes for emphasis, to block any interruption, 'that when a child is engaging in challenging behaviour with only *one* authority figure, and with no one else, then that authority figure *must* examine her own behaviour to see if it's actually her behaviour, *and not the child's*, which is at the root of the problem. Because Ollie,' Geraldine's eyes pop open again, 'is perfectly well behaved with Clive and me. And he was always good with Robert.'

35

Fanny bumps into Grey McShane at the Safeways checkout as she's paying for the champagne, but is still so consumed by the threat of Geraldine Adams on her governing body that she forgets even to explain to him, her fellow governor, the reason for buying it. *'We've got to stop her!'* she cries, without telling him who to stop, or from what, or anything about her recent triumph. Without even remembering to say hello. 'She'll take over the school!'

'Who's that?'

'Geraldine Adams! She's demanding to be a governor. Can you believe it? And Kitty Mozely, too! God knows . . . I couldn't think of a single reason to say no . . . and she just sort of *sat* there, looking hurt. But it can't happen! It can't. I'd end up killing them both.'

Grey laughs his deep, rich laugh. 'You'll have a job stopping either of them, Fanny. The vicar's got the General down for a meeting Monday evening to elect them in. It's as good as done. So,' Grey gives her an evil grin, 'much more interesting than that – what did you make of him, Fanny? Handsome, eh? He's bloody rich, too.'

'Who?'

'Who? Solomon Creasey, of course. What did you think of him?'

'Solomon? Grey, this is serious.'

Grey clicks his tongue. 'Come on, Fanny. He must have made some impression.'

Solomon Creasey had spoken twice to Mrs Haywood the glass-eyed school secretary, during which Mrs Haywood, thinking he was a delightful gentleman and much better than his reputation, had blithely assured him there was 'more than enough space' for his three children to join the school after half-term. But Mrs Haywood hadn't seen fit to pass any of this on to Fanny. And what with the darts and croquet to organise, and all the other house-moving diversions, Solomon Creasey had failed to pursue the point himself, or tried to talk to Fanny in person. In truth, having been so reassured by Mrs Haywood, he too had forgotten. And this accidental gossip with Grey McShane, in Safeways on the last day before half-term, is the first time Fanny has heard that the population of her small school is about to be increased – by almost 10 per cent.

'But he can't do that!' Fanny says angrily. 'Doesn't he realise? There are *systems* and *procedures* and things. I'm not just a dropping-off place for his children. I mean, doesn't he realise this school is a publicly funded— It's a government— I mean, fuck, Grey. Doesn't he realise there are probably about six million forms to fill in?'

Grey just giggles. 'I take it you don't know about the petition, then?'

'Hmm?'

Last weekend Dora, Flora and Clara Creasey, riding small ponies and dressed as ancient Romans, delivered darts and croquet day invitations around the village. (Fanny must have been out. She found her own invitation on her doormat.) At the same time they presented a petition: 'SIGN HERE IF YOU

WANT SOLOMON CREASEY AS SCHOOL GOVERNOR'.
The girls had collected almost seventy signatures – more signatures than there were parents in the school . . .

'Which makes him one of us, eh?' Grey McShane smirks. 'Solomon's very keen to play an active role in his children's schooling,' he deadpans. 'He takes that sort of thing very seriously. He told me so himself.'

'What? He's a governor? But why didn't he tell me? For God's sake, this isn't how it's supposed to work!'

'Och, Fanny. Who cares? You just said you needed governors, and he's better than Geraldine. Don't be so bloody prissy.'

'I'm not being prissy,' says Fanny. 'I'm just saying, I can't believe I'm having to find this out in Safeways. Who the fuck does Solomon Creasey think he is?'

It turns out nobody wants to drink champagne with Fanny that afternoon. Linda Tardy the teacher's assistant announces she never drinks; Tracey Guppy takes one look at the bottle and runs out of the staff room; Robert is off sick; Geraldine Adams has left the building; and Mrs Martin the supply teacher has to rush off to pick up her own children from school. They leave Fanny and her champagne all alone, still smiling to hide the fact that she minds, and then her mobile rings.

It's her mother. 'Is that you, Fanny, sweetheart?' she says, sounding a bit feeble.

'Hello, Mum!' Fanny cries, feeling full of warmth, feeling suddenly less lonely. 'This time tomorrow! . . . I can't wait!'

'*Oh, Fanny love*—' Her mother bursts into tears. She and Derek (a retired tax collector, also her mother's new boyfriend) have been vomiting all night. 'There's a bug going round. We've all got it in the Pueblo, and I'm sorry, Fanny,

238

because I've been so looking forward to seeing you. And Derek's been so excited. But I think you'll be better off staying at home.'

Fanny swallows her disappointment, listens patiently, even when information begins to emerge regarding the tax collector's high turd count. She assures her mother that she isn't too disappointed, that she'll come out in the summer holidays, that she has plenty of things to do instead . . .

. . . except Louis's not speaking to her, and her three closest girlfriends (all teachers) have gone off to Helsinki for half-term. They had asked her if she wanted to come.

She hangs up the mobile, glances across the empty staff room at the unopened bottle of champagne, decides that if she's going to drink it alone, which of course she is, then she'll drink it alone at home, at least.

Fanny approaches her little cottage in a fog of loneliness. It's the proudest day of her professional life. And she can find not a single soul to celebrate it with. Not even Brute, whom Fanny, thinking she was going to Spain, has already consigned to the local kennels.

As she pushes open the front door her foot slides on a large brown envelope. 'Fuck it,' she mutters irritably, wrapping her arms protectively around the champagne, and in doing so, knocking her head against her newly repainted red hall wall. Fanny's cottage is fully adorned now with all the trinkets – the Indian sari curtains, African woodcarvings, Mexican lanterns, Chinese wall hangings, Turkish kilim floor cushions – all the junk she has picked up on her travels and which she has lugged, but never unpacked until now, from one unloved place to another.

Without bothering to close the front door behind her she bends over to pick up the envelope. On the front her name has been enclosed by a large heart shape, marked out with Xs. She opens it up and laughs as the contents fall out: prints of the photographs of Dane's bonfire, which Louis took the last time he and Fanny spoke. In the first picture Fanny is flying through the air towards Dane Guppy, mouth open, screaming; the next shows her landing beside the bonfire, on top of him; the third has her finger pointing at the camera, her face distorted with rage, while Dane Guppy struggles for breath underneath her.

Darling Fan,
Sorry I've been such a jerk.
I'm a bit lost without you. Can we be friends again?

L.
P.S. I guess you may not enjoy these photos as much as I do . . .

She hears him behind her, clearing his throat. It's a sound she would recognise anywhere, half-contrite, half-confident – it's the noise he uses to attract her attention whenever he tips up to surprise her. As he loves to do.

He loves it because each time it has the same effect. Her face breaks into a smile, she spins around – just as she's doing now . . .

. . . and Fanny sees him looking back at her with that same sexy, easy smile. She feels her heart leap and more than that, the familiar lurch of desire. She doesn't return the smile.

'Hey, Louis,' she says, sounding bemused. She walks the few steps towards him.

'I missed you, Fan,' he murmurs. 'I'm so sorry.'

'You should be . . .'

'I mean, what I meant to say is—'

'What did I do wrong?'

'Nothing. I've been a jerk.' Hands both deep in his back

pockets, shoulders hunched, he falters, suddenly uncertain, insecure. She's never seen him look so ill at ease. A gurgle of laughter escapes her. 'What's up, Louis? Are you OK?'

'*Fine.*' Suddenly, in one swift movement, he pulls his hands from the pockets and pitches towards her, grasping her head in both hands –

'Hey!'

– *and kissing her.*

It takes a minute to adjust, after so many years of not, but then Fanny lets the photographs flutter to the ground and within moments they are both lying on top of them, a tangled mess of limbs and long-repressed yearnings. They are tugging at each other's clothes, oblivious even to the front door, still half-ajar behind them.

After so long waiting for each other (and imagining it) neither lasts too long. A glimmer of time, and then they have both collapsed into a heap, the one on top of the other, both scarcely undressed, and the front door still banging softly in the breeze behind them.

'Well!' laughs Fanny, lying back on the wooden floor beside him, her body still glowing. 'Hi, Louis. Nice to see you, too. How's life with you?'

Louis doesn't reply. He traces a thumb over her cheek, down her neck. 'I love you,' he says simply.

Fanny sits up. 'Oh, Jesus, Louis. *The door!*'

Louis turns to it incidentally, without interest; maybe he saw a figure flitting by, maybe he didn't. It doesn't matter. 'You're beautiful,' he says to Fanny. 'I love you. I've loved you for years.'

She smiles. 'What? Me as well? As well as all those others? Are you sure? What about . . .' She looks at him gazing levelly back at her, with such certainty. And of course she loves him too. And she has for years. But she can't say it. Yet.

His hand slides under her T-shirt, strokes the small of her back 'What about . . . ?'

She realises she doesn't want to mention names. Not right now. She doesn't want to mention all the women he's declared he was in love with over the years. 'It doesn't matter. For God's sake, Louis. Close the door!' But then she can't stop herself. She half-sits up. 'I mean – I suppose I mean what about Kitty?'

'Kitty?' he laughs, kicks the door closed with his foot and pulls Fanny back down to the floor again. 'You're joking, aren't you?'

Later, when they're upstairs – Fanny in the bath, Louis sitting on the edge of it, sharing the champagne and one of Louis's oversized spliffs – Fanny mentions her aborted trip to Spain which was meant to have started tomorrow.

'But Mum and the new boyfriend are both sick,' she says.

Louis isn't really listening.

'She gave me half an hour's worth of details about the state of his'n'her bloody bowel movements, which I could have done without.'

Louis pulls on the spliff, watches the Badedas bubbles sliding slowly between her breasts. 'I bet,' he says vaguely.

'And then she cancelled me!'

He holds the cigarette to Fanny's lips. She inhales, flinches slightly as the hot smoke hits the back of her throat.

'So,' she says, exhaling, 'what was I saying?'

'Bowel movements?' Louis says politely.

'That's right . . . Waste of a ticket, really.'

'Ticket to where?'

She rolls her eyes. 'Spain, of course. Weren't you listening?'

'I most certainly was,' he says.

'What?'

He laughs, slightly uncertain. 'What?'

'You . . .' she frowns, trying to remember. Louis's spliffs are always too strong. 'Most certainly was what?' She giggles suddenly. 'Scarlett Mozely reckons we're all wild flowers.'

'Mmm?'

'So what does that make her mother?'

'Mmm?'

'Deadly nightshade! Geddit?' She slaps her thigh, spraying water around the bathroom.

'What are you talking about?'

'If we're all flowers . . . see?' she giggles pointlessly.

'Flowers?' Louis repeats.

'Wild flowers. I'm a dog rose. You're a – dandelion, let's say. OK? Or a pimpernel. Tracey Guppy's probably a buttercup.'

'What's a pimpernel?'

'Geraldine Adams is obviously a thistle. And Kitty Mozely's deadly nightshade . . .'

'You're talking crap, Fanny,' he says amiably, leaning forward to kiss her. But she's still laughing. She can't stop, and then neither can Louis.

In the morning Fanny wakes to see him, head propped up on one arm and gazing down at her. He smiles. He says, 'Were you saying something last night about going to Spain today? Or did I dream it? Or was everything that happened between us last night a dream?'

'I bloody hope it wasn't,' she says, pulling him towards her. 'Oh. And by the way,' she pulls back, takes his head in her hands, 'Louis, you never actually answered. About you and Kitty Mozely – or Deadly Nightshade, as I shall now be calling her.'

He smiles. 'What about us?'

'Are you and she having a – thing?'

'Come on, Fan. Don't be disgusting,' he says mildly,

243

moving on top of her, his words muffled as his lips work down her body. 'Oh.' He looks up. 'And I finally worked out she was jerking me around about you and that skinny-ass teacher from school, right? I was right, wasn't I? To decide that?'

'Robert White?' Fanny laughs in disbelief. 'Kitty Mozely told you Robert and I were— And you believed her? Louis! You met him! He's repulsive!'

Louis considers her for a second. 'Yeah,' he says. 'Stupid of me.'

'It certainly was.'

'I guess I should have asked you earlier.'

And then, later still, while they're lying in each other's arms, Louis suddenly frowns. 'What was that you were saying before, about Spain? It's pretty damn goofy, you know, us starting conversations over and over . . .'

'I said,' she says, 'several times, in fact, but I don't think you were listening—'

'Sure I was! I hang on every word you utter, Fanny Flynn. You know that.'

'I was saying that I was meant to be flying to Malaga this afternoon.' She looks at the clock beside her bed. 'In five hours and forty minutes, to be exact. But Mum's ill. So . . .' She shrugs. 'It means we can spend the week together. Which is nice. Which is much nicer. Isn't it?'

'You've got a ticket to Malaga?'

'Yes. Well, I did have.'

'And you've got a week's holiday?'

'A week and a day. Not due back until next Monday.'

'*So what are we waiting for?*' He leaps out of bed. I've got . . .' he pauses, 'three jobs lined up so far this week, and I can cancel them all on the way to the airport.'

'Louis, I said *I've* got a ticket. You haven't. Anyway—'

'I'll buy a ticket when we get there. Come on, Fan! Hurry up. Get it together. Stop lazing around! Let's get going!'

They had both forgotten to recharge their mobiles overnight, so they plugged them in while they packed, and carefully arranged them, so they wouldn't forget them, side by side at the foot of the stairs, right in front of the front door. Half an hour later they both stepped right over them. They climbed on to Louis's bike and sped away.

36

Sunday morning. The church bells of St Nicholas ring out across the village of Fiddleford, calling its small congregation to matins.

Clive and Geraldine Adams, all togged up in their Anglican finest, sit in the car outside Kitty's cottage, their engine still running. The vicar is once again expected for pre-lunch drinks, and Geraldine is adamant that she, Clive and Kitty should arrive at the service on time. As a mark of respect, if not for her own faith, which is non-existent, then for everybody else's. She honks her horn impatiently, waiting for Kitty to emerge.

Solomon Creasey, in grey silk dressing gown open at the top to reveal a dark, hairy chest, and with the usual faint and delicious suggestion of expensive cigars, and Czech & Speake's lavender and sandalwood aftershave around him, sits in his breakfast room drinking thick, black coffee. The Silent Beauty is upstairs, expertly emphasising her lovely features with some light, subtle make-up. His three youngest children are outside, squabbling merrily on the trampoline, and Solomon, for once, has a little time on his own. He is thinking about his children's new headmistress, Miss Fanny

Flynn. After speaking to Grey in Safeways Fanny had left a brisk, not especially friendly, message on his Fiddleford answer machine, agreeing to welcome his children to the school Monday week, and to tackle related formalities later. Since when Solomon has repeatedly tried to speak to her, without success. It's his first weekend as a full-time Fiddleford resident, and he realises he hasn't made a great beginning.

General Maxwell McDonald, meanwhile, hair spruced, blazer pressed, is walking briskly across the Manor park, in perfect time for morning matins.

Charlie and Jo, having had their good-morning shag rudely interrupted, are lying in bed pretending to sleep while their young twins clamber over their heads.

Messy McShane, exhausted, is sending a disgruntled Grey downstairs to fetch a freshly sterilised baby's dummy from the kitchen.

Macklan Creasey, lying in bed beside Tracey Guppy, at number 3 Old Alms Cottages, is running a worshipful hand over her sleeping body – and pausing, briefly, at her belly. She's getting a little tubby, he thinks. Not that he cares, of course. (So long as she doesn't end up like her mother, whispers a tiny voice.) But she is. Getting a little tubby.

In a tiny pueblo up in the hills behind Fuengirola, southern Spain, Louis and Fanny have woken simultaneously. They have opened their eyes, smiled, reached across for each other . . .

And outside the girls' cloakroom at Fiddleford Primary School, a hand strikes a match, puts it to the petrol that has been spilt all over the windows and door and stands back, mesmerised. He watches the flames licking greedily at the dark red paint; licking higher, higher, higher . . .

The church bells fall silent. For half an hour nothing further disturbs the pretty peace which is Fiddleford. The sun shines. The birds sing. The vicar delivers a sermon about renewal. Clive and Geraldine sit quietly side by side, worrying about money. Mrs Hooper sits quietly behind them, worrying about death. The General peers through his glasses and wonders whether the vicar has shaved properly that morning.

Kitty Mozely thinks about lunch, and then about Louis, and then about the contact sheet he put through her door yesterday morning. The images on it were mostly of her and Scarlett after the press conference. Her belly rumbles. She smothers a yawn. But the other images . . . What the hell was Fanny doing, rolling around in front of a bonfire with a bloody schoolboy? She chortles, a little too loudly. The old bag from Glebe Cottage turns around to scowl.

'I say, Geraldine,' Kitty whispers noisily.

'Shhh.' Geraldine frowns.

'Remind me. I've got something bloody funny to show you afterwards.'

Later, inside the church, the small congregation hears the fire engines racing by, sirens briefly drowning out their reckless singing. They glance at one another – '*Morning has broken, like the first morning*' – but keep belting it out – '*Blackbird has spoken, like the first bird*' – and surreptitiously try to calculate where, exactly, the sirens might be stopping.

> *Sweet the rain's new fall, sunlit from heaven*
> *Like the first dewfall on the first grass;*
> *Praise for the sweetness of the wet garden—*

Dane Guppy bursts into the church, soot all over his face, greasy hair on end, eyes glazed with excitement.

'Vicar!' he shouts. 'I can't find Miss Flynn nowhere. But it's all burning up out there. You got to come!'

PART FOUR

37

Morning matins are brought to an abrupt end and the twenty-strong congregation move as one, following the smell and then the billowing smoke, out through the churchyard, through the village, to the scene of the fire.

They find three fire engines and two police cars parked up in front of the school and smoke engulfing the whole west half of the building – the girls' cloakroom, the stationery cupboard, Robert White's classroom, the assembly hall, and above it, Fanny's and Mrs Haywood's offices. In the middle of the chaos, Dane Guppy, giddy with excitement, jumps between firemen offering help and suggesting causes.

It was Dane who called the emergency services half an hour after that match was struck, and he is proudly announcing it now to the gaggle of horrified churchgoers.

'I saw the flames,' he says. 'Well, no. I smelt them first. Then I looked out the window—' He turns and points to Uncle Russell's bungalow: 'There. That window there. See it? I looked out the window, and I think to myself, *crumbs*.' Dane pauses to wave at one of the firemen. 'I know him. I know the other fellow, too, the one behind him. See?'

Nobody replies. Dane Guppy's exuberance is embarrassing.

With the exception of the vicar, on his mobile telephone trying to get hold of Fanny, and the General, who nods at Dane, eyeing him thoughtfully, the gaggle from church stare at the flames as if they haven't noticed he was there.

Dane doesn't seem to mind. 'They came round to Mum and Dad's not so long ago. That's how I knows 'em. I knows a couple of the others, as well. So I'm thinkin', *Oh, my crumblin' Mondays!*' he continues. 'Because the school's on fire. And I call the emergency services. I pick up the telephone and I call 999. That's what I done . . .'

'Good thing too,' says the General. 'Dane, isn't it? Aren't you Ian Guppy's boy?'

'That's right!' Dane says a little skittishly. He was killing time throwing conkers at passing cars not long ago when he made the mistake of aiming one at the General's Land Rover. The General slammed on his brakes, wound down his window, and bawled at him so loud it actually gusted Dane's greasy hair off his forehead. They haven't spoken since. 'All I done was call 999, Mr Maxwell McDonald. That's all I done. I was with Uncle Russell. I looks out the window. And then it's 999.'

The General shakes his head sadly. 'Lovely old building,' he says. 'Don't you think, Dane?'

Dane glances at him foggily, with maybe a fraction less respect. '*Lovely*, General Maxwell McDonald?' He laughs. 'I don't know about that.' He feels a tap on his shoulder.

'Mr Dane Guppy?' It is a policeman.

'That's right. What do you want? All I done was call 999. That's all. You can ask General Maxwell McDonald.'

'Do you mind if we have a little word?'

38

Geraldine spots Kitty, her white clothes flowing behind her, sloping off down the lane towards the pub.

'Are you off to fetch Scarlett?' Geraldine shouts over the roar of the flames. 'I thought you said Scarlett was making her own way?'

Kitty turns back. 'Her own way to where?' she asks guiltily. She had been hoping the fire might be a good excuse to skive out of the vicar's drinks.

But Geraldine says they have *ovolini* awaiting them at the Old Rectory, and quail's eggs, and baby artichoke hearts wrapped in prosciutto. And champagne on ice. 'Plus the vicar's bending over backwards to get us on to that governing body. I do think the least we can do is spare the time to have a drink with him to celebrate. I also think, actually, Kitty, that with the school in obvious crisis, and with bloody Fanny Flynn completely vanished, it's our duty as almost-governors to put our heads together and come up with some sort of a rescue package. Don't you? So it's drinks at the Rectory, as per before. We'll just be running a little late.'

Kitty gets snappy when she's hungry. She likes the idea

of the *ovolini*, but her empty belly is demanding urgent satisfaction.

'Well, how long are you going to be?' she asks plaintively.
Flakes of debris from the fire rain down on her. 'Can't I go
on ahead?'

Geraldine looks across at the vicar, bent into a mobile
telephone, still trying to track down Fanny. There is a
policeman standing by waiting to speak to him, and also a
fireman. She itches to get back to them, back into the thick
of the action. 'Let's give it half an hour, shall we?' she says
distractedly. 'I'll see you there. Oh, I say, General—' She
catches him just as he's taking a sad last look and turning
away. There is nothing he can do. 'I'm pleased I caught you.
I wanted to thank you, on behalf of Kitty and myself.'

He looks blank.

'I understand that as a member of Fiddleford PCC you'll
be very kindly voting us on to the school's governing body
tomorrow evening! And I'm so terribly grateful.'

'Mmm? Oh, yes. Yes, of course. Well, well. Welcome
aboard,' he says, not with overwhelming enthusiasm. 'We'll
need as much help as we can get after this.'

'Absolutely. Quite. In fact, I was wondering—'

He indicates the burning building. 'Hard to see how much
damage has been done beneath all the smoke. But it's a
bloody awful mess, whichever way you look at it.' His son
Charlie, and his late, much loved daughter, Georgina, had
both briefly attended the school, many years ago. Until his
wife had died, and they had both been packed off to boarding
school. 'Ah well,' he sighs, to himself rather than to
Geraldine, and turns slowly away.

'I was actually wondering, General, if you'd like to pop
in to the Old Rectory for a pre-lunch drink. We've got the
vicar coming. And Kitty. And Robert White . . . It was meant
to be a sort of celebration. Can't think why we didn't invite

you before! Now, of course – well, I think we could all probably just do with a drink.'

'Very kind,' says the General, who dislikes Kitty and Geraldine, loathes Robert, and has endured more drinks with the vicar over the years than he would ever care to remember. 'What a shame. Would have loved to. But I ought to be getting back.' His eye is caught by Dane Guppy, in heated discussions with the police. 'They're putting him through it rather,' he mutters. 'Poor chap. Seems a nice boy.'

'Yes, that's Dane,' says Geraldine vaguely. 'You're certain I can't persuade you?'

'Thank you so much, Mrs Adams.'

Geraldine isn't quite ready to give up. 'But I thought we might have an impromptu sort of emergency meeting,' she says. 'I mean, heaven knows. Under the circumstances—'

'No, no, no,' booms the General, suddenly very impatient. 'Good morning, Mrs Adams. Good morning, Miss Mozely,' and marches resolutely away.

He's deep in thought, lost in the past, marching back through the village, when he spies a lanky, bearded figure up ahead. Robert White has parked up in front of the Alms Cottages and is peering into Fanny Flynn's front garden.

And because the last person the General wants to see on his sunny, ruined morning is Fiddleford Primary's repulsive, malingering deputy headmaster he does something uncharacteristic. He spies the telephone box beside the post office and quickly, shamefully, hides himself behind it.

Robert hesitates at Fanny's gate. Inside, he can hear her mobile telephone ringing unanswered. The windows are closed. The cottage is clearly empty. He glances up and down the street, spies no one, not even the General's polished toes peeping from behind the telephone box, and lets himself in to the front garden. Furtively, he peers through her window.

'*What the bloody hell—*' thinks the General.

New silver lanterns, Robert thinks. *To go with the ruby-red walls. A bit like a brothel*, he thinks, with a shiver.

He glances anxiously at the other two cottages. No sign of life coming from either. So Robert proceeds a little further. He has always wondered about her back garden. Is it large? Is it small? Does she hang out her clothes to dry?

'*What the devil—*' thinks the General.

The garden is communal; the same garden for all three cottages. Large, untended, chaotic, more like a paddock than anything else, with a few rose bushes sprouting out of the grass and a perfect peach tree at the far end. Robert notices none of this. He sees there are several windows overlooking it, but all with their curtains drawn – and that on the washing line, between the red duvet cover, the red pillow cases and the pinky-grey tea-towels, is a tiny pair of gauze-and-lace silky-look scarlet knickers. He breathes deeply, rooted to the spot. And he can't resist taking them. He snatches. He snuffles them away.

Robert thinks he hears a sound from the third cottage (Macklan Creasey's cottage) and he darts immediately back towards the front of the house. He hurries out on to the village street and collides with the General, who feels duty bound to bring himself out of hiding when confronted by such suspicious behaviour. He's on his way into Fanny's garden to haul Robert out.

'Oh!' they both say at once, with equal displeasure. They step back. Scowl at each other.

'She's not there,' the General says. 'What are you up to, Mr White?'

'Yes, so I discover. I was just popping a letter through her door . . . I've been invited for a little drink,' Robert can't quite keep the pride from his voice, 'at the Old Rectory. Geraldine kindly invited me . . . But how are you, James? On this beautiful morning?'

The General screws up his eyes, considers him. 'Well, you're looking awfully shifty. Why aren't you up at the school?'

'Shifty?' repeats Robert indignantly, slipping his hand into his trouser pocket and closing it tightly over his silky red booty. 'I thought I might find Miss Flynn in the garden. As I say. I was only trying to post a letter.'

'Right. Well. Good, good.'

Robert sniffs. 'Smells like there's a fire somewhere.' Ordinarily, from his house ten miles away, Robert would have had to drive past the burning school in order to get into the village.

'That's right,' says the General, without offering any further details, disinclined to extend their conversation a syllable longer than necessary. The man would find out soon enough, if he didn't know already. 'I'd have thought you came past it on your way in.'

'*No*. I mean, no. Past what?'

'The fire. Well. Good morning to you, Mr White. See you again. No doubt.'

Robert watches the old man striding off and thinks he's probably got away with it – whatever *it* may be. For some reason Robert doesn't think he's done anything wrong. In fact, he vaguely resents the General for making him feel as though he has.

He climbs back into the white Fiat Panda, drives it the fifty-odd metres to the Old Rectory drive and, with a wave of skittish nausea, swings in between the Adamses' newly restored eighteenth-century stone gateposts.

'Hello?' he calls tentatively, having stood in the porch for over a minute, rung the bell a couple of times, and failed to attract anyone into the hall to greet him. The door is wide open. Robert takes a little step in. 'Anyone home?'

257

'In here!' It's the muffled sound of a woman, slightly irritated, shouting through a mouthful of food. Not Geraldine, he thinks. Certainly not. She would have come to the door.

'Anyone home?' he says again.

'I'M IN HERE!' Kitty Mozely yells.

Robert finds her in what the Adamses call the 'parlour'. She is the only one there: Scarlett is already in the television room reading a book, Ollie, he presumes, is still in his room, Lenka is still in bed, and all the others are still down at the fire.

The parlour is small, perfect, immaculately proportioned; light, airy and peaceful, with sash windows that stretch from ceiling to floor. The room smells of orchids and freesias and furniture wax and there is not a painting or an ornament – or even a book – whose position hasn't been thought about, which doesn't blend with an overall theme. There are creamy brown worsted silk curtains against the windows, and smooth, oatmeal-coloured walls. There are a pair of eighteenth-century rosewood side tables flanking a creamy white sofa imported from a company in New England which has also made sofas, Mrs Adams likes laughingly to explain, for the last three American First Ladies.

Kitty's presence slightly ruins the effect. She looks particularly slatternly in an armchair beside the real gas fire, which she has lit in spite of the sun streaming in through the open windows. She's got her nose buried in the *style* section of the *Sunday Times*, and all the other sections are spread haphazardly at her feet. Though she hasn't quite dared to open her hosts' champagne in their absence, she's helped herself to some vodka and tonic, and she's obviously been munching hard on the *ovolini*. There are only a couple more left.

'Hi,' she says, without smiling or standing up. 'Nobody's here yet. They're all still down at the fire. Want a drink?'

258

'Oh, well!' says Robert, rubbing his hands together. 'If you're offering! Why not?'

'Drinks are over there,' says Kitty, indicating a heavily stacked table between the long windows. 'But I don't think we ought to open the champagne. There's tonic water in the little fridge . . . there. That's right. Underneath. The thing that looks like a cupboard.' Kitty returns to her newspaper. She hadn't realised Wetty White was invited. She probably wouldn't have come if she had. *Ovolini* or no. As Geraldine bloody well knew.

'Super!' he says. Pads over to the drinks table. Hesitates. He's suddenly not quite sure how to begin. A silence falls: awkward for Robert, self-conscious of the fizzing noises while he pours his Diet Pepsi, but unnoticed by Kitty, reading a fascinating piece about a wrinkle-eradicating laser gun. 'So! What's all this about a fire?' he asks at last. He asks three times, before he gets an answer.

Kitty tells him.

'Goodness!' His eyes are smarting, just thinking about all that smoke. His eyes are red and dry, he knows it. 'But that's *awful!*' he says, edging his bottom towards the unnecessarily warm hearth. 'It's just *awful!*'

'Isn't it?' she says. 'You should be up there, really. Since it's your school, and nobody seems to be able to find Fanny Flynn. You could send the others back down.'

'Mmm,' he says, without moving. 'Though really it seems more sensible to wait for them here, I think, Kitty. As Geraldine's expecting me. Otherwise we'll probably end up crossing paths for the rest of the day and never actually catching up with each other!'

Kitty doesn't respond, and though Robert makes a few attempts at conversation, she doesn't speak again until Clive, Geraldine and the vicar arrive about ten minutes later.

Robert doesn't drink often, and never normally during

the day but Geraldine insists that he has some champagne. He was too nervous to eat breakfast. And he's far too nervous now to tuck into what Kitty's left of the quail's eggs. *Ovolini* all gone. One single glass goes to his head. Before long he is nodding along happily while Geraldine engages him with a meticulous analysis of The Weaknesses of Fanny Flynn.

'I mean, of course, *let's be fair*,' says Geraldine, 'she's a marvellous, dedicated teacher – when she's around.'

'Well, that's right,' says Robert. Head swimming slightly.

'And how could she ever have guessed that the place was going to go up in flames? She couldn't. But I do think that if a person finds themselves in a position of unique authority, as of course Fanny does, it's just plain *irresponsible* to waltz off, God knows where, without leaving some sort of contact telephone number.'

'Her car's there,' says Robert.

'That's what's so frustrating.'

'But Louis's bike isn't . . .'

'I mean, where is she?' continues Geraldine, not quite picking up. 'That's all we want to know. We're not asking who she's with, for heaven's sake. Or if she's in bed with somebody—'

'No!' He's worried he's blushing, so he looks down, takes a nervous gulp from the glass just refilled. '*Certainly not*,' he reiterates. But he still can't resist. 'Although since you happen to have brought that subject up, Geraldine, I think she does get – how can I put this? I think she does get very easily distracted by certain matters. By the male . . . gender, if you like. I actually think she's a very, very, very *sexual* person. And Louis—'

'Ye-es,' agrees Geraldine, trying quickly to accommodate this new weakness into her analysis of Fanny Flynn. A very, very, very *sexual* person. She hadn't particularly thought of that. 'Mmm, well, I suppose you'd know . . .' she says, suddenly remembering and smiling at him slyly. 'Since a certain little bird told me that you and she were seeing a teeny bit of each other. Am I wrong?'

'*Fanny and Me?!?!?*' So highly pitched only a bat could have entirely made it out. '*Fanny and Me?!? Ha! Geraldine! Fanny and Me?!?!?*'

'No?'

'Certainly not! Gosh, no. No. Certainly not!'

'Oh. Well, anyway. Sorry, no offence, I hope?'

'What? NO! Of course not. Don't be absurd, Geraldine. *Really*. No, no, no.'

Geraldine shrugs. Hard though it may be for Robert to understand, she's not actually that interested. 'However, I agree with you, she's certainly hot-blooded. Of course, you weren't there when she stripped off half her clothes in front of the entire village.'

'Mercifully!' Another nervous swig from the champagne. 'But perhaps she'll simmer down a bit now. Now she and Louis have finally got it together.'

'Have they? Are you sure, Robert? I got the impression they'd fallen out. How do you know?'

Mistake. How does he know? Another bubbly swig. *He can see their feet now, all tangled together. Louis with his trousers round his thighs, all the moaning and groaning, and the front door banging against the ruby red, open and closed, open and closed . . .* How the hell does he know?

Geraldine laughs merrily. 'Seriously, unless you've been spying on her from your sickbed, Robert, I don't honestly see—'

Empty glass. 'Well, I don't know. No. Of course not. No. I don't know. But between you and me, and judging by her track record, I think that young lady will open her legs for just about anyone.'

Geraldine pauses. Glances at him uneasily. It's an odd

261

thing to say. It's an unattractive way of saying it. In fact, everything about it feels entirely – to use one of Geraldine's favourite words – *inappropriate*. Robert smiles at her; soft lips, mouth closed. It's meant to be reassuring. 'Not,' he adds quietly, 'that Miss Flynn's sex life has anything to do with me.'

'No,' says Geraldine coolly. 'No, it doesn't.'

Robert senses his blunders. Acutely. But, dizzied by so much creamy-brown prosperity, by the smell of those freesias and orchids, by all the champagne bubbles knocking around his brain, he doesn't yet feel inclined to backtrack. He breathes deeply and continues. 'You may think that was an odd thing to say, Geraldine.'

'Well.' A very tight smile. 'Just a tad, Robert. I didn't have you down as a misogynist.'

'Me? Ha! A misogynist? Geraldine, I'm offended! I *worship* ladies. Absolutely worship them.'

'What, all of them?' she asks drily.

'The fact is, I do have a little experience of Fanny's . . . well, what can I call it?'

Geraldine raises one of those nicely plucked eyebrows. She waits.

'The fact is, Geraldine, I've had a few problems with Fanny of my own.'

'Really, Robert?' She smiles. Robert thinks it's patronising. 'Fanny's a terribly attractive woman,' she says. 'I don't imagine you'd find many men complaining.'

That annoys him. 'You can laugh, Geraldine. People usually do. But suffering from sexual harassment in the workplace isn't really a joke. In this day and age. And it isn't the sole prerogative of women, either. As I'm surprised I should need to remind you.'

'Oh!' A few buzz-words to jolt her. Magic words. 'Apologies, Robert,' she says hurriedly. 'I am sorry. I certainly

262

didn't mean to be insensitive . . . Gosh. Well, you should have said. So what exactly . . . ?'

Robert shakes his head. 'I don't really think it would be appropriate to go into details. Suffice it to say—'

He's rescued from saying anything at all, by Clive suddenly shouting across the 'parlour' to his wife. 'Geraldine – sorry to interrupt – what's the name of that terribly nice man, Ollie's godfather? Ex-boyfriend of yours . . .'

'Where is Ollie, by the way?' Geraldine asks vaguely. 'Don't tell me he's still in bed?'

'He does Portakabins,' continues Clive. 'Reverend Hodge and I were just thinking – they're going to need to come up with some temporary classrooms ASA, if the school's to reopen by the end of half-term. And your friend, What's-his-name, might be able to help us out. Don't you think?' Clive turns back to the vicar. 'I'm saying he "does" Portakabins. I think he's actually the largest portable-cabin manufacturer in Europe – isn't he, Geraldine? And as luck would have it—' Clive laughs. 'If only either of us could remember his blessed name.'

'He's called Tony Milson,' says Geraldine succinctly. 'What a smart idea, Clive. Why didn't I think of it?' She looks at her watch. 'I could call him now, before lunch. Get the ball rolling. But I should know first exactly what we need up there. Wouldn't want to waste his time.' She sighs. 'Robert,' she says decisively. 'You haven't seen it yet, have you?'

'Not yet,' he grimaces. 'I'm worried I'll find it terribly upsetting.'

Geraldine, still feeling wrong-footed re male gender sexual harassment and her own insensitivity to it, gives his shoulder a comforting pat. 'It is upsetting,' she says. 'I'm afraid you will be very upset. But with Fanny gone AWOL—'

'She hasn't gone AWOL,' Kitty looks up suddenly. She's

been so bored by the company, and apparently so engrossed in the *Money* section of the *Mail on Sunday* she's barely contributed a word all morning. 'She and Louis have buggered off to Spain for half-term. Oops.' She glances unrepentantly at the reverend. 'Sorry, vicar.'

'Believe you me,' chortles the dreary reverend, 'I've heard it all before.'

'Honestly, Kitty. You might have *said*,' snaps Clive. 'Saved us all a lot of bother.'

'Thought you knew,' Kitty shrugs. 'Didn't you see Macklan Creasey in the village?'

'And that, effectively,' interrupts Geraldine, very businesslike now, 'leaves you, Robert,' she gives him a dazzling smile, 'in charge! You are now the acting head teacher. Am I not right, Reverend Hodge?'

'Indeed, you most certainly are.'

'Robert! Mr Deputy-Headmaster, sir!' she twinkles at him, swaddling him in warm approval. 'Congratulations – and thank goodness that one member of our little school's staff can see his way to being available at such a crisis!'

'Well, of course,' says Robert uncertainly, 'somebody has to—'

'Exactly. Everyone, a little toast for the acting head,' orders Geraldine. 'To our marvellous acting head. And then, Robert,' she takes a hurried gulp, 'you and I are going to pop up to the school so you can have a quick look at the damage.' She's already slipping into her creamy-brown linen cardigan. 'And Clive, I think you should go and see what Ollie's up to. Get him out of bed.'

'He's in the bath. Or he was twenty minutes ago.'

She turns her attention back to Robert. 'It'll be upsetting for you, I know, but we'll need your expert opinion, Robert, on the portable-cabin issue. How many. For which functions. And so on. And of course you're going to need to speak to the police, who'll no doubt still be there.' Robert is still clutching his glass, his lean bottom in front of the fire. He looks torn: proud and flattered by her attention, and yet struggling with an inclination to disobey. He is, after all, off sick at the moment. And it is a Sunday. And this is, strictly speaking, Fanny's job, not his. 'Did you come with a jacket, Robert? Clive, dearest,' she turns to her husband. 'I think Robert left his coat in the hall. Could you be sweet . . .' She turns to the vicar. 'Reverend, I hope you won't think I'm rude.'

'No, no, absolutely not.'

'Kitty, I'm sure, will get you another drink. If you prod her hard enough! And I shall be back in a tick. I'm just going to run Robert up to the school. In fact, I shall probably leave him there because, Robert, there'll be various bods wanting to talk to you: Health and Safety and so on. I'm only wondering whether we should get on to the Maxwell McDonalds. Kitty, what do you think? You seem to get on with them frightfully well.'

'Do I?' says Kitty. 'Which ones?'

'Oh, I don't know. All of them,' says Geraldine, as if she didn't care. 'They'll have to loan us the area beyond the playing field, I imagine. Tony's people are going to have objections to putting their cabins too close to a burnt building. For obvious reasons.' She smiles at Robert once again, who hasn't yet moved. Her voice has a little ice in it now. 'Are you ready, Robert?'

Robert jumps. Places his empty glass on the mantelpiece, stretches an obedient arm into the jacket Clive is holding out to him. 'You're a *star*,' says Geraldine. 'I honestly don't know what we'd all do without you!' She leads the way out of the room. 'Honestly, Fanny had better watch out or she'll find herself holidayed out of a job, don't you think, Robert?'

Robert laughs. 'I don't think the union would take too kindly to that!'

'Well! Or she'll find we've all staged a little coup and the governing body's voted the deputy head to take over. What do you think about that?'

His excitable laughter can still be heard as they close the front door behind them.

39

Fanny and Louis spend a lazy, blissful week dodging the Andalusian sun, mostly in bed or on shady wisteria-clad terraces. They drink Rioja, eat paella (the only two things they understand on the menu), talk, squabble, laugh – and make love. And return to Fiddleford on a rainy Saturday evening, as happy as either can ever remember being.

Tracey Guppy tells them the news. She bangs on Fanny's door just as the two of them are settling down in front of Fanny's hearth for a good-natured argument about who should do what, and when, about their collective lack of groceries.

'All right, you two?' Tracey says, smiling on the doorstep.

She looks a bit chubby, it occurs to Fanny. Poor girl. Obviously inherited her mother's genes. Fanny smiles at her kindly. 'You look very well,' she says stupidly. She needn't have said anything. 'How's it all going? Come on in.'

Tracey shakes her head. 'Macklan's cooking sausages. D'you want to come over?'

'Oh. Well, yes. Please. Fantastic. We would, wouldn't we, Louis? You've just saved us a trip to Lamsbury.'

Tracey searches Fanny's carefree face, feels a flash of sympathy. 'You still don't know, then?'

'How did it start?' asks Fanny, as the four of them tramp through the rain towards the school. 'It was an accident, wasn't it?'

Nobody answers. They walk in silence for another minute, until the building comes into view. They stop. Louis gives a low whistle. The front playground is a wreck of abandoned building materials. The school – what's left of it – is black with soot; Robert's classroom and the cloakroom beside it are draped in a giant green tarpaulin. Thanks to Geraldine's turbo efficiency, repairs have already begun. But the place looks terrible.

Fanny feels a lump in her throat. '*Oh, my school!*' she whimpers.

'It's not as bad as it looks,' Tracey says softly. 'You can still use your classroom, and the assembly room. And the boys' cloakroom. And your and Mrs Haywood's offices. They're all OK . . . It's only this end, see? Robert's classroom, mostly. Girls' toilets. And the stationery cupboard. It's one reason it burnt so well, apparently. Because of all the stationery . . .'

Fanny looks at her. She can tell from the nervous way Tracey's talking but she still has to ask, 'How did it happen, Tracey?'

Tracey looks away. Macklan puts a protective arm around her. He says, 'Nobody knows. But there are some unfair rumours. A lot of people are jumping to conclusions.'

'About Dane?' demands Fanny. 'For God's sake, you two. Spit it out! I'm going to find out anyway.'

'He didn't do it,' Tracey says stubbornly.

'Has he been charged?'

'No, he hasn't been charged. No one's been charged,

268

Fanny,' snaps Tracey. 'And no one's going to be. It was an accident.'

Fanny wanders ahead to look more closely at the damage. She walks slowly across the front, weaving through the scaffolding, between the sacks of cement mix, the planks, bricks and wheelbarrows . . .

Rarely, if ever, have Her Majesty's Inspectors noted such improvement in such a short period of time. Rarely if ever . . . She continues around the side of the building towards the playing field. There is a mountain of sand and a cement mixer where last week the children's vegetable garden had been. And onwards, beyond the playing field, churned to mud by the wheels of the tipper truck, there is a Portakabin, vast and oddly luxurious, with pink curtains hanging at the windows and a pair of elaborate brass lanterns on either side of the door.

Tracey comes up behind her, breaks the sombre silence. 'We've Geraldine Adams to thank for that,' she says quietly. 'Geraldine's been amazing. She's organised everything.'

'I bet she has,' mutters Fanny.

'She organised a Village Scrub-a-Thon, she called it, didn't she, Macklan? And Mrs Maxwell McDonald brought down all her newspaper people.' Tracey laughs. 'They were all elbowing each other out the way, posing for the cameras with their scrubbing brushes . . . Maurice Morrison the politician chappie. He was there. And Kitty Mozely, and Clive and Geraldine and Ollie. And Scarlett, and the General and everyone from the Manor . . . and Grey and Messy . . . and Mrs Hooper was here. Even your dad was here, wasn't he, Macklan? With the three girls.'

'And Robert White,' adds Macklan, 'giving little interviews and so on.' He smiles slyly. 'Should have been there, Fanny.'

'I should, shouldn't I?' she mutters. She feels sick. Standing there, looking at the wreckage of her lovely school, hearing everything that's been done to save it in her absence, she feels sick, and very threatened. She glances across at Louis, smiles at him guiltily, as if he could read her thoughts.

He smiles back at her ruefully. 'I guess you're kind of wishing you'd never gone away.'

'Oh, no. Not exactly,' she says.

They return to Macklan's cottage, where Macklan lights a fire and the four of them sit around it, eating sausages, cold and burnt, and washing them down with a bottle of Louis's whisky.

'So,' says Macklan finally, pushing his plate away, stretching his legs out in front of him. 'One minute you're storming out of pubs not speaking to each other. Next minute you've buggered off to Spain on the back of his motorbike! Is there anything else you might want to tell us?'

Fanny laughs. 'No,' she says, looking back at them both. 'And what about you two?'

Tracey stands up. Abruptly. 'I'm going to head home, Macklan.'

'What? Just like that? Don't go, Trace! Stay here with me. It's much nicer.'

She shakes her head. 'They'll be wondering where I've got to. Dane will. And Uncle Russell.'

'I guess we should waddle off home ourselves,' mutters Louis, hauling himself up. 'But thanks, Macklan. For some of the most outrageously delicious sausages I've ever eaten. Thank you.' Macklan barely hears him. He smiles distractedly as Louis claps him on the back. 'Wait!' he shouts at Tracey, already heading for the door. 'Wait, Tracey. I'll go with you. Wait for me.'

As Fanny draws closed her upstairs curtains she glimpses them walking tightly arm in arm up the rain-drenched street, Tracey's hideous white, belted macintosh shining in the moonlight, her permed head resting on Macklan's shoulder. They look so young, Fanny thinks, and yet welded together; a natural couple. As if they were born never to be apart.

She wonders if she and Louis appear like that, or if . . . She's distracted by his hands on her waist, his lips on the back of her neck. She turns around to face him – and stops worrying, at least for a while.

40

The next couple of days are fraught for Fanny as she tries to settle her children – including the new Creasey trio – into what is left of the school, and to grapple back the control of it from the new power duo: Geraldine Adams and her suddenly not-so-work-shy deputy, Robert White. Geraldine's been strutting around the school like a newly appointed Minister for Education, barging in and out of classrooms, clutching various forms, her thin face stiff with business as she arranges all the various donations from her own very influential friends.

There has also been an anonymous donation of £50,000 which is to be spent, when the rebuilding is done, on extra library books and artwork for the walls.

'And I think it would be nice, Fanny,' Geraldine says, 'if you dropped a line to the marvellous Maurice Morrison. Have you met him?'

'No,' Fanny says sulkily. 'Not yet.' While she was away in Spain Mr Morrison, the former New Labour minister, and now Lamsbury's prospective MP, had been billeted by the LEA to be Fiddleford's eleventh – and final – school governor, and the high-handed manner of his appointment is just one more reason for Fanny to feel her position threatened.

'Only we're fairly certain,' (We? Who the bloody hell is 'we' in all this? Fanny is much too proud to ask) 'he's our secret donor. He's very rich, as you probably know. I've already sent him an enormous bunch of flowers, by way of implied thanks. And I'm hoping to get him over to dinner shortly. You must come, Fanny! You must come! Wouldn't it be nice?'

'Lovely. Thank you,' says Fanny dutifully.

'Nothing to thank me for, Fanny dear. At times like this we've all got to pull together.' Of course, if Geraldine does manage to lure the mighty Morrison to din-dins, Fanny Flynn would be the last person on her list of glamorous guests. Charlie and Jo Maxwell McDonald would be invited, perhaps. And Solomon Creasey, of whom she and Clive instinctively disapprove, but who is, after all, handsome, extremely rich, and possibly in need of a new, Lamsbury-based solicitor. Geraldine snaps her mind back to the matter in hand. 'In any case, Fanny, Maurice has been inordinately generous, not only with his purse but with his time. So maybe a little letter of thanks wouldn't go amiss . . .'

'Yes. I'll do that, Geraldine. Thank you. Was there anything else?'

The same few days have been noticeably less busy for Louis, whose mobile, since he picked it up from Fanny's hall, has remained disconcertingly silent. He still has a couple of jobs lined up, but – as he is now learning to his cost – news-paper editors forget nothing more quickly than a freelancer who doesn't answer his telephone. After a handful of wasted evenings in the Fiddleford Arms, talking to passing traffic and waiting (always waiting) for Fanny to tear herself away from her work, Louis decides he has to go back up to

London, briefly, to jog their memories and try to drum up some more commissions.

He and Fanny spend a final evening in the pub together before he leaves. But she is distracted. And though he tries to understand how terrible she must have felt, coming back to such carnage after a week in the sun, her subsequent inability to stop thinking about anything else is beginning to get on his nerves.

He relights his cigarette, pulls a strand of tobacco from his mouth, takes a slurp of his Taunton cider, and still she burbles on. 'I should have reported Dane to social services after that first bonfire. That's what I should have done. And I should have called the police . . .'

'What's done is done,' says Louis, soothingly.

'I should have insisted he saw a psychiatrist. I should have talked to his parents . . .'

Louis sighs. 'For all you know, he didn't even do it.'

Fanny laughs. 'Yes, right.'

'Frankly, Fan. It could have been any number of people. Let's face it. It's not like you're the most popular girl in the village.'

'Shut up,' she says. 'OK. So who do *you* think set fire to my school, then?'

'"*My school*",' mimics Louis.

Fanny ignores it. 'Maybe you think Kitty Mozely did it? Overcome by jealousy when she saw us riding off into the distance on your motorbike?'

'Wouldn't rule it out,' he shrugs. 'Or Robert White . . . Now there's a man with issues.'

'That's ridiculous . . .'

'It's possible,' he says idly. 'Does anyone know where he was when it started? People go mad in the country, Fan. Haven't you noticed? They get things out of proportion.'

'Robert wouldn't have it in him,' she says, frowning.

Louis shrugs. 'Or Mrs Fatty Guppy might have done it,' he continues. 'Come on, you've got to admit, she *hates* you . . . Or Geraldine Adams. You said she was pretty pissed with you.' He chortles, beginning to enjoy himself. 'Or maybe it was someone from LEA trying to find an alternative way of shutting the place down.'

Fanny gives a grudging laugh.

'Or maybe it was the vicar,' he continues. 'Maybe he's fallen in love with you. Maybe he knows he can't have you . . . And would rather see you burn than have you give yourself to another . . .'

'Very possible. Except then he would have set fire to the place when I was in there, don't you think? Anyway, this isn't funny, Louis. It's not . . . Because I'm beginning . . .' Carefully, she puts aside the seductive prospect of Robert's guilt; it would have been too good to be true. Besides which, though Robert has many weaknesses, so far as she knows being an arsonist is not among them. 'I'm beginning to think Dane Guppy's a real danger, not just to himself, but to everyone. I mean, to all of us. And I don't think he should be allowed in school until this thing is cleared up.'

'He hasn't even been charged yet, Fanny.'

'He was *there*. He called the fucking fire brigade. Yesterday some of the children found a petrol can in the field behind the school. Louis, *it had Russell Guppy's name on it!* He lives with his Uncle Russell, and – seriously, Louis, *he's done it before! I* mean, come on!'

'Mmm,' he says blandly. 'Put like that it doesn't sound so good, does it? You should throw him out before he tries it again. D'you want another drink? Or shall we go home where I can ravish you? What shall we do? Your choice.'

But Fanny doesn't seem to be listening. She shakes her head. 'It could *only* have been Dane . . .'

'Actually, no. Second thoughts. My choice.' He stretches

across the table and takes the half-filled beer glass from Fanny's hand, and knocks it back in one.

'Hey!'

'You're being boring, Fan. Come on. Let's go back to yours.'

41

Last week Solomon Creasey recognised the unsigned other half to a well-known portrait by Sargent. He reunited it with the owner of the original half and came away with a profit of just under $1 million. The following day his Beauty, whom he'd been seeing regularly since early spring, broke a three-month stretch of almost total catatonia, put on a shimmering Diane Von Furstenberg wrap dress and a black silk g-string with diamanté studs going all the way up the back crack, which must have been agony, slipped into his office on Duke Street, closed the door behind her, untied the dress with a single, expert flourish, and proposed to him.

He smiled, because he could see that she'd made an effort, but the exhibition made him feel depressed and oddly lonely. He couldn't help wondering if she would have gone to so much effort, if he'd been the same man, only without the money. It's not a question which usually troubles him – or not until recently, anyway.

That night he chucked her – very politely. She seemed to take it well, at first. Afterwards he took her out to dinner at the Caprice, drenched her in gratitude, apologies and gentle compliments and finally he drove her in his big, vulgar

Bentley, back to her lovely Chelsea flat. He waited patiently for her to climb out of the car.

He waited and waited. But she stayed where she was. After a while he noticed she was trembling, and asked her if she was all right. That was when hell broke out. The floodgates opened, and out gushed a torrent of hatred – not just against Solomon but against all the men she had ever known; every gift-bearing, bill-footing escort she's ever deigned to share her great beauty with.

On her lovely, skinny hands, she began to list her many admirers – and a truly impressive collection of names it was too, in a way; a veritable *Who's Who* of Europe's Most Eligible.

'I'm sorry, angel,' he interrupted, with the engine still purring, stifling a little yawn. Cursing himself, actually. Feeling more lonely and detached than ever. 'I don't deserve you. I never did. If I'd had any idea—'

'*Fuck off*,' she yelled in her sexy, mysterious Ruski-Euro-Texan accent. (Solomon had never properly noticed it before.) 'All di money you make and you give me *sorry!* Fuck you and fuck your sorry!' But she still didn't get out of the Bentley.

Eventually, with a resigned, apologetic sigh, he climbed out of it himself. He left her there in the passenger seat, screaming at him above the purring engine. He left the key in the ignition. 'Vait!' she howled. 'Vhere are you going? I haven't finished—' And then, in blank astonishment, 'But, Solomon, vat about your motor car?'

Solomon, already heading off towards the taxis on the King's Road, turned briefly and winked at her. 'You keep it, angel,' he said. 'As a token of my – ah – a token of my . . .' But he couldn't think of what. *Desperation to get away?* That would have been rude. And Solomon didn't feel she deserved rudeness. So he watched her beautiful jaw dropping and waved a final goodbye.

A moment's stunned silence while she wondered if he was joking, shattered almost immediately by a final 'Fuck you!' It echoed shrilly down the white-stuccoed Chelsea street. And then, very quickly, before it had died, before he could change his mind, she clambered into the empty driving seat and accelerated away.

The following day he remembered to ask his assistant to transfer the car's ownership into her name. As a bonus, really, for all the lovely things she'd done for him. It would bring an amicable conclusion, or so he hoped, to what had always, until the very end, been a very amicable arrangement. A businesslike arrangement.

All of which isn't strictly relevant. Except that Solomon, in spite of having been through such an action-packed and glamorous week in London, has now returned to Fiddleford to find his mind still dominated by just one thing, and he's bewildered as to why it's bothering him so much. His children have already been welcomed into Fiddleford Primary (thanks to Fanny's magnanimity. She could well have refused to take them), and from what Solomon can gather, they are very happy there. Yet he still hasn't managed to make contact with Fanny Flynn, let alone apologise, and he feels extremely uncomfortable about it.

He sent flowers to her cottage during half-term, while she and Louis were away in Spain. Macklan, painting his front door at the time, intercepted the flower deliverer and had the flowers returned to Solomon, but forgot to include any kind of explanation with them.

Solomon called Fanny at the school on the Monday morning, the first morning his three children began, but in all the chaos of the fire, the message he left went astray. She never received it. That was over a week ago now. He has called several times since, but his children tell him that the school is still in chaos as a result of the fire.

Sitting at his desk in Fiddleford, gazing uncharacteristically listlessly over the freshly mowed lawn, Solomon mulls tenaciously over the offence he must have caused. He is unaccustomed to women who return his flowers but not his calls. Which is partly why, in spite of dramas with the diamanté underpants, the Bentley, and the Sargent sales, he finds he can think of nothing but Miss Fanny Flynn, and of the increasingly extravagant ways he might try to make his amends.

42

Louis calls from a noisy pub somewhere in Paddington just as Fanny is heading out to the Lamsbury Safeways to buy him a welcome-home dinner.

'Not going to be able to make it home tonight, Fan,' he shouts. 'Sorry. But it'll give you a bit of time to get some work done without me getting in the way.'

'But you're never in the way,' says Fanny politely.

'What? Can't hear. Anyway, I'm missing you, Fan.' He is, too. 'Can't wait to get back.'

'So why don't you?'

He says he can't hear, and Fanny doesn't push it. He sounds happy. And he's right, of course. She'll be able to get a lot more done. He says he'll be back on Friday.

On the Thursday evening she arrives home after a long and hard day at work, to find a package leaning against her door. It is large and flat, beautifully wrapped in brown paper and thick green cotton ribbon. She stares at it. A present from Louis, perhaps? Missing her, after all?

She dumps her bag and takes the parcel into the kitchen. Stares at it. Sniffs it. It smells delicious. Cigars and sandalwood. She's never received such an elegant-looking parcel.

Nor, she soon discovers, has she ever received such a gift. Inside is a painting. Fanny knows almost nothing about art, but it's an oil, about 75 centimetres x 50 centimetres, framed in worn gilt. A dark-eyed woman wearing a long grey crumpled dress and dishevelled cap stands in front of a village school surrounded by a gaggle of children. At first glance, the rosy children, the merry schoolmistress, look a picture of rustic mid-Victorian perfection and yet— Fanny stares at them. Not all the children are laughing. There are three children, hungry looking and awkward, hovering apart from the group, gazing on resentfully. And the woman is smiling, certainly. But there is something disturbing about her, too: the intent brown eyes, the bony white hands, the tiny lines around her mouth – in spite of her laughter, in spite of all the jovial activity surrounding her, she looks restless, harried, worn out. She looks miserable.

Fanny rummages through the brown paper in search of a note, turns the painting over and finds, wedged between canvas and frame, a thick creamy envelope with his card inside.

With many thanks for taking on my trio, and many apologies for my appalling manners,

Solomon Creasey

The painting doesn't match with the ruby-red brothel theme of Fanny's eccentric sitting room but Fanny's not like Geraldine Adams. She shunts aside the gold-and-purple Chinese embroidery currently above her mantelpiece, tugs out the silver candle holder from Mexico – which never attached properly to the wall anyway – and immediately hangs her new picture in pride of place.

She stands back to wonder at it, and at the mythical benefactor, Solomon Creasey, about whom she has already heard so much. She writes him a letter.

> . . . *I have never possessed anything so beautiful. Thank you. Your apology was completely unnecessary, since I must admit I couldn't even remember what you were apologising for when I first read your note, and anyway it's hardly your fault Mrs Haywood didn't pass on the message. However . . . unnecessary apology entirely accepted! Thank you.*
>
> *Your lovely daughters are a pleasure to have in our school, and seem to be very happy. I'm glad they've joined us. Here's hoping we meet one day.*
>
> *With best wishes and the best of luck in your new Fiddleford life—*

She spends a long time worrying about how to sign off: Fanny Flynn? Unfriendly. Or just Fanny? Or Fanny (Flynn)? Or . . . She signs it Fanny, and beside it, in the same flourish, automatically scribbles a couple of Xes.

> *Fanny XX.*

Shit.

She copies it all out again, without the XXes this time, and slips it through his letter-box on her way to work the following morning.

43

Louis's week-long mission to meet with newspaper editors and pick up work has been hampered slightly by his pleasure at being back in London and meeting up with his friends. His search for commissions was interspersed with a lot of parties, exhibitions, and pub crawls and he has returned from London with just one photographic assignment, which will pay him very slightly less than the figure he put on to his credit card last night when he paid for himself and two old girlfriends to eat curry.

In spite of this he is full of the joys of summer as he bounds into Fanny's cottage that Friday evening. He notices the painting at once. He and Fanny are in the sitting room, mid-reunion embrace when he stops suddenly—

'Bloody hell, Fan! Have you been robbing galleries? Where the hell did you get that?'

'Solomon Creasey gave it me. To say sorry for sending his children to my school without asking. Stupid, really.' She giggles. 'Because I'd completely forgotten . . . It's beautiful, isn't it?'

'I guess he wants to fuck you.'

'Don't be annoying, Louis. We haven't even met.'

He steps around her, closer to the mantelpiece, to get a better look. 'Seriously, Fan,' he says. 'That's not some piece of crap he picked up in a junk shop. Personal taste aside, that's a fine piece of work.'

'I can see that,' she lies. 'Anyway, who cares? It's here now. And it's mine. And it's the most beautiful painting I've ever owned. Actually, it's the only painting I've ever owned. And I love it.'

'It's OK.' Louis pulls a face. 'Kind of sentimental.' He pats the pockets of his suede jacket, pulls out a pouch of tobacco. 'Victorian paintings of rosy-looking kids always make me feel a little nauseous.'

'It's not sentimental,' Fanny says coldly. 'Not if you look at it properly. So don't be a smart arse.'

'Can't help it, Fan,' he says mildly, rolling a cigarette with one hand, peering closer at the painting. 'I hate to sound like those guys on the *Antiques Roadshow*, but do you have any idea how much this thing is worth?'

'It doesn't matter, does it? Seeing as it's not for sale.'

'You sure about that?' He flicks her a glance. 'You might change your opinion when you find out what you could get . . . Know what?' he adds, peering closer still. 'The guy's signed it! We should look him up on the Net.'

Fanny is beginning to feel uncomfortable. The question of the painting's value has, in fact, been niggling at her all day, and she's been trying to ignore it. Because if the painting really is valuable she'll feel duty bound to give it back. 'Oh, don't, Louis,' she says quickly. 'Please. Don't look it up. I don't want to know.'

'Besides which,' Louis adds slyly – urbane, good-natured, easygoing, cultivated he may be, and a fine lover and a very old friend, all those things, he may be, but he doesn't appreciate unattached millionaires plying his girlfriend with works of art while he's away – 'you might decide that accepting it isn't so cool. I mean, it's probably not illegal. But it sure isn't— My guess is, a painting as fine as that's going to be worth at least £20–£25,000. And I don't know, Fan,' he says, looking away from it at last, lighting his cigarette, '*corruption and bribery inside the English education system*, or whatever, it's hardly my area, but . . .'

'What are you talking about?'

He picks a loose strand of tobacco off his tongue, smiles at her. 'But I think you should give it back.'

'Don't be ridiculous! Honestly . . . Don't be ridiculous.'

He shrugs. 'I'm only saying what I think.'

They don't talk about the painting again that night. They open a bottle of wine, and then another. It's a horrible rainy evening. They smoke a spliff together and stagger up to bed. But long after she and Louis have rolled away from one another, and while Louis lies snoring peacefully beside her, Fanny stays awake.

She lies there, thinking about her painting, listening to Louis's snores and the heavy patter of the rain against her window until the day begins to break.

At five o'clock she dresses quietly in winter jersey and jeans, since it's early and cold and still raining, and tiptoes downstairs. In the sitting room she stands before her mantelpiece, takes one last, long look at her painting and carefully takes it down from the wall. She wraps it in a dustbin bag.

Fanny had been planning to write a letter to him, explaining why she couldn't accept such a valuable present, and had spent much of the night composing it in her head. But now that it comes to the moment of setting pen to paper none of the words she prepared seem to make any sense. She can't think of anything to say. She feels a fool. Angry with herself for accepting the thing. Angry with Solomon for having given it to her. Angry with having to give the painting back.

She gives up on the letter. She throws it away, half-finished, picks up the dustbin bag and heads out. Solomon's house is very close. Sometimes, if the breeze is right, and Solomon is outside, she can catch wafts of his delicious lavender and sandalwood aftershave from her front garden. Not today, however. It's pouring with rain and it's still only five o'clock in the morning. She doesn't want to see him, anyway. She just wants to leave the painting on his doorstep, as he left it on hers, and then, if possible, never have to think about it again.

Half an hour later she is sitting at her kitchen table marking exercise books while Louis still sleeps upstairs, when she hears a loud clattering noise outside her door. Fanny tiptoes to the window to discover the cause of it. She peers nervously out from behind the ill-fitting sari curtains and discovers a man, tall, lean, with a face not unlike an eagle: nose, bony and straight, with a dent, as if it's been broken once; eyes heavy; jaw dark with early-morning stubble. He has tripped on one of her metal dustbin lids.

He's out there in the pelting rain dressed only in his pyjama bottoms and a grey silk dressing gown. And he has the painting. He raps impatiently on the front door – an economic, graceful movement, pent with energy. And the cottage rattles. Fanny hesitates.

He bends down and flicks open the letter-box. 'FANNY!' he yells. 'MISS FLYNN?'

Miss Flynn? She smiles. She tiptoes back to her seat at the kitchen table and waits silently for him to go away again.

But Solomon has no intention of leaving. She hears him laughing through the open letter-box. It's a nice laugh – heartfelt and infectious. 'I know you're up because you've just been to my house and left a bloody good painting outside in the pouring rain. And I know you're there, because I've just seen the bloody curtains moving . . . And not only that,' he adds, after a pause, 'not only that, the curtains don't fit! Fanny, I can *see* you. For heaven's sake, come to the door.'

She's not sure what to do. She feels cornered.

'Come to the door.' An edge to the voice now. She can smell sandalwood and lavender. Solomon Creasey is apparently unaccustomed to waiting.

Kind of sexy, Fanny thinks. Except it's half past five in the morning. Why should she come to the door just because a delicious-smelling, unattached multimillionaire James-Bond-Villain lookalike in a grey silk dressing gown is demanding it?

As she pulls back the latch he straightens up, surveys her, and reminds himself never to listen to Grey McShane's thoughts on women ever again.

Very small, he thinks. *Very scruffy. Is that last night's make-up she has smudged all over her face?* He is confused, briefly. He doesn't know any other women who would open the door looking like this. The women he knows spend hours locked away in their bathrooms. And when they finally emerge, they look sensational. They look— *But does that*, he wonders wildly, as Fanny looks up at him, apparently waiting for him to speak, *does the fact that she comes to the door looking like a draggletail make her better or worse than the other women? BETTER OR WORSE??*

Well, worse, *obviously. Stupid bloody question.*

Solomon gives himself a mental shake. The incident with the Bentley has clearly unsettled him more than he realised.

He still hasn't spoken but otherwise his examination of Fanny – and ensuing disappointment – have been meticulously hidden. Solomon hides everything from his face. Instinctively.

Finally, Fanny speaks, with more hostility than she meant. (His silence is making her awkward. The aura of ruthlessness about him, and confidence and faint depravity, combine to quite an intimidating effect. There is, she thinks, without doubt, something horribly, deliciously carnal about him as he stands there. Not helped by his still being in his dressing gown.) 'What do you want, anyway?' she snaps. 'It's half past five in the morning. I'm trying to work.'

'What do you think I want?' he says. 'I want to know why you've left this excellent painting outside in the rain, where it would have been destroyed if I hadn't happened to be up.'

'I wrapped it in a dustbin bag.'

'And rested the dustbin bag in a fucking puddle.'

'There wasn't a puddle there when I left it,' she says. Though there might have been. She had been keen to get away.

'Apart from which, yesterday you sent me a thank-you letter saying how much you liked it. Actually,' he adds, 'one of the loveliest thank-you letters I've ever received.'

'I didn't.'

'Yes, you did. I have it here.' He reaches into his dressing-gown pocket, produces a sheet of paper. 'What changed? What happened between yesterday and this morning?'

'Nothing. I mean, I should never have written that letter. I'm sorry. But at the time I had no idea how much . . . And I'm sorry, but I really don't think it's appropriate . . .'

He rolls his eyes, groans.

'And the fact is, when I found out,' she continues, 'I mean, I certainly don't mean to be ungrateful, but I was a little annoyed. In a way. Because I'm not some sort of – I don't know – one of your *mafioso* business associate . . .'

'*Mafioso?*' He laughs. 'You've been listening to village rumours.'

'I'm actually your children's teacher,' she continues, feeling silly.

'I'm aware of that.'

'And I'm certainly not the sort of person who . . .' She stops, uncertain how to finish.

'What?'

She shrugs. 'I dunno. Gets given lovely paintings.'

He smiles. Lets the comment hang there for a moment. 'Well, you should be,' he says, his voice rich as velvet.

She looks away. 'I mean, I just can't be seen to be taking bribes . . .'

He bursts out laughing. 'Fanny, I hate to be rude, and I'm not in the least averse to providing bribes when necessary – but what reason on earth would I possibly have to bribe you?'

'I don't know . . . How do I know?' She's beginning to feel very stupid. 'I'm just *saying* I don't want to be a part of it. I mean, the school isn't for sale. And nor am I.'

The sound of Solomon's heartfelt laughter wakes Macklan and Tracey in the house next door, wakes Mrs Hooper at the post office, wakes the vicar in his bungalow vicarage behind the church. Upstairs, even Louis stirs.

'You can laugh as much as you like,' snaps Fanny. 'I'm sure in *your world* people accept bloody great presents like that without thinking twice about them.'

'They certainly do,' says Solomon.

'Well, bloody well bully for them.'

He looks at her. His children had been quite right, of course; the woman in the painting looks just like her. 'Only I don't know any other anxious, brown-haired, untidy-looking village schoolteachers to give this to, and since you happen to be teaching three of my children . . .' He pauses to wipe the rain from his eyes, looks up at the sky and then down at the offending painting. 'Look, I don't suppose we could discuss this inside? This painting's going to be destroyed.'

She looks at him. Never mind the painting, he's drenched. With a sigh she stands back. 'Come in, then. I'll make you some coffee. But be quiet, though. Louis's upstairs, sleeping.'

'Ah yes. Louis,' he says. 'The photographer.'

'That's right.'

A silence. She can feel him watching her as she turns away to switch the kettle on. 'Sit down,' she says.

Solomon doesn't walk, he prowls: three long steps from front door to sitting area. He stretches himself out on her small sofa, his large frame and that aura of power which surrounds it, making her sitting room feel suddenly uncomfortably small. 'I don't suppose you could drop a bit of whisky in that coffee, could you? It's bloody cold outside.'

'I could forget the coffee and give you straight whisky if you prefer.'

'No, no, no.' A flicker of a smile. 'That would be disgusting.'

She hands him his cup and stands beside him, feeling awkward in her own house. There's nowhere left to sit except the floor cushions – and somehow she doesn't like the idea of sitting at his feet. 'Anyway, look, enjoy the coffee,' she says, watching him gulp it down, 'and it's nice to meet you at last. But to be honest with you, Solomon, as far as your painting's concerned I'm not sure that there's really a hell of a lot to discuss. I can't accept it and that's that. Thank you very, very much. And everything. *Really*. I mean it was beautiful—'

'It still *is* beautiful, Fanny. Or rather, it was.' He half-props himself up, pulls back the sodden dustbin bag with a surprising delicacy. 'Before you left it to rot in a fucking puddle. Let's have a look . . .'

A silence between them as he holds out the painting and watches her gazing wistfully at it. It is still beautiful – more beautiful, she thinks, than it had been even half an hour ago. A tiny, regretful sigh escapes her and he laughs.

'The children said you and she were alike,' he says thoughtfully. 'Look . . .' He leans forward and casually traces a finger over the tiny frown line between her eyebrows. 'It's uncanny . . . I dare say she would have left the bloody painting in a puddle too.'

Fanny, not expecting to be touched, rears backwards. She bumps her head on one of her wretched Mexican lanterns and sends it crashing to the floor.

'Oops,' says Solomon, taking another slug of coffee and settling back on to the sofa again. 'Anyway, it's all yours. I shall probably sell it if you don't take it. But to be frank with you, Fanny, it's more of a bother putting it up for sale than leaving it here with you. So for Christ's sake, take it. As Grey McShane would say,' he adds, watching her through dark, half-closed eyes, '"*Don't be so fuckin' prissy.*"'

She laughs out loud. 'That was pretty good.'

'It was, wasn't it?' He takes another gulp of the coffee, winces slightly. 'I couldn't have a touch more whisky in this? I loathe the taste of neat coffee first thing in the morning.'

'You know what,' Fanny says, 'I'm feeling hungover enough. I might even join you.'

'Hair of the dog that bit you,' drawls a familiar voice, and Louis strolls into the room, bed ruffled, sleepy, having pulled on boxer shorts and a T-shirt. 'Always works. Hey, there,' he adds pleasantly to Solomon, reaching automatically for his cigarette pouch, on the counter behind them. 'Bit early for visitors, isn't it?'

'You'd have thought so,' agrees Solomon. 'But your girl-friend has already been out calling this morning. Leaving this painting in a large puddle on my doorstep.'

'There wasn't a puddle when I left it there,' Fanny says again.

'Hard to believe,' drawls Solomon, who often doesn't sleep, 'since it's been raining hard all night.'

'Louis,' Fanny says pointedly, 'Solomon and I are drinking whisky for some reason. Do you want some?'

Louis shrugs. Looks at Solomon. 'Sure. Why not?'

'Do you two know each other?' asks Fanny. 'Louis, this is—'

'Yeah, I know. Hi, Solomon.'

'Oh!'

'We've met a couple of times in the pub,' Louis explains.

'With La Mozely,' adds Solomon. 'Since your Adonis-like boyfriend arrived, Fanny, I've been let off very lightly. It's wonderful . . . I no longer have to put on a fucking flak jacket every time I feel like going to the pub.'

'Oh, come on,' Louis smiles. 'She's not so bad. She can be very funny.'

Solomon nods. 'True.'

'So,' Louis says pleasantly, 'excited by this whisky idea . . .'

With a glass of whisky in her hand – and a third person in the room – Fanny feels more comfortable about the floor cushions. She and Louis take one each, on either side of the painting, and the three of them lie back, turn their eyes to the ceiling. They sip on their whisky-coffees, listen to the rain – and chat happily, lazily, for an hour or maybe two. It's an oddly intimate occasion. They get a little drunk as the rain thunders down outside, and tell each other things they might not have done if the sun had been shining, or if they'd been properly dressed, or if they hadn't been drunk and it wasn't so early in the morning.

'In all my thirty-seven years,' Solomon says after a small, thoughtful pause, and apropos of nothing much. 'I've never been in love . . . Strange, don't you think?'

'Really?' asks Fanny. 'What about Macklan's mother?'

'Macklan's mother was my art teacher at school. *Macklan's mother* bloody nearly put me off women for life.'

'Oh . . . OK,' says Fanny. 'Well, what about your ex-wife? Weren't you ever in love with her?'

'Christina . . .' He smiles. He thinks about it for a while. 'No. Never. And what about you two?' he asks abruptly, turning his laser-like gaze on Fanny. 'Are you in love?'

'Oh—' Fanny hears herself laughing. 'Louis falls in love about once every couple of months, don't you, Louis? He can't help himself.'

'True,' Louis agrees, tilting himself forward to reach the whisky bottle. 'But this time it's different.'

Fanny rolls her eyes, chuckles.

'And what about you, Fanny?' Solomon asks. He hasn't taken his eyes off her. 'I gather you were married before.'

'You do?' Fanny asks. Less warm suddenly. 'How did you gather that, I wonder?'

'Well—' He notices Louis isn't looking at him. Louis has his eyes fixed on his cigarette end. 'Grey,' Solomon says smoothly. 'Grey McShane told me, I think.'

'He did, did he?' Fanny mutters. 'Well, I wish he wouldn't.'

'"*Och,*"' says Solomon, his Scottish accent slightly rougher this time, after the whisky, '"*don't be so fuckin' prissy!*" We've all been married before. What's the big deal?'

Fanny frowns. 'Strange, though. I don't remember telling him.'

'"Cause you were popped, I imagine,' says Louis lightly. 'It's happened before, Fan.'

'Seriously. I thought no one in Fiddleford knew anything about it.'

Solomon snorts. 'Everyone knows everything about everyone's business in this village. And if they don't, they invent it. Hadn't you worked that out? In fact, I probably know more about you than you know yourself. And vice versa.'

Fanny looks ready to argue.

'One word,' he says, holding up a hand. '*Mafioso.*'

She smiles. 'Oh, yes. But—'

'I rest my case. So. Go on. Were you in love with him? Was he in love with you? He must have been. Louis, I'm not being tactless?' he asks, though he knows the answer. The first time he and Louis met, Louis was goodnaturedly regaling half the Fiddleford Arms with the story of Fanny's ex-husband.

'Of course not,' Louis says. 'Lived through most of it first hand, didn't I, Fan? That is,' he adds, 'as long as Fanny doesn't mind talking about him. You don't, do you, Fan?'

Fanny shakes her head. It feels odd to be talking about him to a stranger: odd, and oddly comforting. 'Well,' she begins slowly. 'He was a teacher. Like me. A few years older . . . Taught PE and Latin.' She pauses, remembering him; remembering the moment they met, and then immediately fast-forwarding, as she always does, to the flight to Vegas, when she'd had her first moment of doubt. Their first argument. For nothing. For no reason. Because she'd been looking at an air steward. She should have realised then. 'He was a teacher, like me,' she says again. 'And yes. For a short time I was in love with him. But we used to fight. God, but we used to fight.'

'What about?'

'Oh – anything. Everything. He was very jealous. Insanely jealous. Obsessive. He used to call me up twenty-thirty times a day just to – *impose* himself, really. It became— Anyway.' She laughs. 'The whole thing only lasted a couple of months. Got a bit nasty in the end, didn't it, Louis?'

'Certainly did,' agrees Louis, propping himself up on one

elbow to roll himself another cigarette, this one with grass in it.

'Yes,' murmurs Solomon. 'Grey – said you wound up in hospital.'

'He did? Well, how the hell—? What did he say? I'm certain I wouldn't have . . . I'm *certain*.'

'Fan, you always underestimate,' Louis stretches across to run an affectionate hand down her arm, 'how much you like to blab when you've drunk a bit. Besides,' he grins at her, 'I always think I come out of it very well.'

She turns to Solomon. 'But what did Grey say, exactly?'

'I don't know.' Solomon looks more impatient than embarrassed. 'That Louis found you in a terrible state – and that you haven't seen him since. Honestly can't remember the details. Probably because there weren't any. Is it true?'

'He damn nearly killed her,' says Louis. 'Didn't he, Fan?'

'But did Grey say *I* told him?'

Solomon shrugs. 'I don't think I asked. Does he have a name, this geezer? What happened to him?'

'*Nick* something,' Louis says helpfully. 'And the funny thing is I can *never* remember . . .' He frowns in concentration. 'Nick . . .' He waves a hand in front of his head, snaps his fingers. 'Surname . . . gone! Hopeless, isn't it? Not even an initial.'

'It's the spliff, Louis,' Fanny says blandly. 'Your memory's fucked, in case you hadn't noticed.'

'Surely *you* can remember, Fanny,' persists Solomon. A lean smile. 'If I'm to send one of my "mafioso" people out to hunt him down I shall need a name.'

'His name,' says Fanny, 'was Nicholas Faraday. Nick Faraday.' She shudders. 'And you can keep your "people" out of it, Solomon. Thanks.' She glances at him, and her own subdued smile dies on her lips. His long arms and legs are still crossed, just as they were, his head and shoulders are still propped against the sofa, just as they had been. But the languid, sexy, early-morning affability has vanished, replaced by something else, an air of watchful attention. She laughs unsteadily. 'God knows if you're actually joking. But I'd prefer to forget all about him . . . Thank you.'

'Nick Faraday, you say?' Fanny catches a hint of an accent in his voice. South London. It surprises her.

'Nick *Faraday*!' cries Louis. 'That's the one. God! How could I forget? Poor old Fan,' he turns to Solomon. 'She thinks he's started telephoning her.'

'Nick Faraday's been telephoning you?' repeats Solomon. He has propped himself up, the better to look at her. 'When, exactly?'

She shrugs. 'Last week. And then again a couple of nights ago. He didn't say anything. But it was him.'

'And you tried 1471?'

'Of course I did. Number withheld. Always is.'

Solomon collapses back on to the sofa and slowly, as if he's trying to fight it but can't, his face breaks into a broad grin.

'I wasn't trying to be funny,' she says coldly.

Louis stands up. 'I'm starving. Is there any bread in the house?'

'But Fanny, darling,' says Solomon, 'you're a very attractive woman.' He pauses. Squints at her. 'I mean, in a way. And you're knocking around the world, dropping anchor wherever the whim takes you. Flashing your tits in village halls and so on. Being photographed in newspapers in your underwear. You're bound to get a few crank admirers. For heaven's sake, I shouldn't have to tell you that. It comes with the territory.' He stops again and then adds, after a brief gurgle of laughter, 'Nicholas Faraday! What on earth makes you think it was him?'

'Because he's done it before!' she snaps, feeling stupid,

vulnerable, intensely regretful of ever having confided in him. 'And it's not funny. You have no idea, Solomon. You have no fucking idea . . .'

'Take it easy, Fan,' mutters Louis, from the far end of the room, his nose inside a half-empty box of Shreddies.

'I'm sorry.' Solomon holds up a hand. 'It's not funny. Of course it's not funny. Only if somebody calls,' once again his face breaks into an unwilling grin, 'and doesn't say anything and withholds his number, then how on earth can you know—'

'These are a bit stale,' Louis says. 'I think I have Corn Pops next door. I'll be back in a sec.'

'I *know*,' shouts Fanny, 'because he's done it before! I mean, he's done things. Other things. He's sent me things. Stupid cards . . . horrible cards. He left me Brute – my dog, Brute – three years ago. I came back to my flat one day and found Brute on the doorstep.' To her horror, she finds her chin trembling. 'And Brute even smelt of him. That's why I called him Brute. Poor little thing.' It's that – the naming of Brute – which finally tips her over the edge. She drops her head and begins, very quietly, to cry.

Solomon sits up, leans forward. 'Fanny, angel,' he says tenderly, wrapping an arm around her. 'You may well have smelt Nicholas Faraday on your poor dog on the day you found him. You may well have done. All I'm saying—' he stops. Starts again. 'All I'm saying, sweetheart, is that Faraday can't have had anything to do with it, because three years ago he was already dead.'

44

Solomon is very sweet after that; says almost nothing, in fact, just sits there, waiting to be questioned, watching her curiously, trying to match her with the pathetic, angry junkie he'd known in jail. Nick Faraday, one-time Latin teacher, had used to lie there, limp, on his thin grey bunk and talk about a girl he'd met in Buxton, a teacher called Fanny; and though nobody said so exactly, it was obvious he was dying. One afternoon he slipped into a coma. Somebody called for help and they carted Faraday off to hospital for the last time. A few months later they came and took away his things. It was how Solomon and the rest of them learnt he was dead.

She wants to know how he died – of course – but Solomon doesn't know how to tell her.

'But did he have any friends in jail?' she keeps asking. 'Were you his friend when he was ill?'

Solomon shrugs. 'It's not really how it— I wasn't *not* his friend. But I mean—'

'So he was all alone?'

'Well,' he hesitates. 'I mean, of course he was, Fanny. He was bloody well dying.'

'But why did he die? *How* did he die? What was wrong with him?'

Again, Solomon shrugs. 'They didn't tell me.' But it was obvious. Everybody knew. 'Fanny, how long ago did you, er— How many years ago is it since – you were married?'

Which is when Louis comes back from next door, with his bowl of Corn Pops. He sees Fanny, face shocked colourless. 'Fan?' he says.

'Nick's dead,' she says dully. 'Died in jail, seven years ago. Which means Brute . . . All the times . . . and the telephone calls . . .' She falls silent. Louis plonks the Corn Pops on to the nearest surface and rushes to take her in his arms.

'Sorry, Fanny,' mumbles Solomon. 'I'm so sorry. Stupid of me to— I might have broken it to you more gently, I suppose. But it's such a peculiar coincidence. And I couldn't quite believe— I don't understand why somebody didn't tell you.'

Louis shoots him a look over Fanny's shoulder, indicating that Solomon ought to leave. 'And maybe you should take the painting, yeah?' He glances at Fanny. 'Right, Fan?' She doesn't reply. Louis gives an amiable, apologetic smile. 'Sorry, Solomon. I know it was well meant, but—'

'Of course.' Solomon, remorseful, keen to do the right thing – and yet unwilling to leave Fanny still in this numb state – lingers awkwardly for a moment. 'I really am sorry, Fanny. Anything I can do. Any questions you may want to ask – any time at all. Whenever you're ready . . .'

'Yes, of course,' says Fanny, offering him a mechanical smile. 'Thanks, Solomon. Thanks for everything.'

He pats her on the back, beneath Louis's protective arm, and she feels its warmth, catches the smell of sandalwood and lavender. 'See you soon, Fanny.' He picks up the painting without even bothering to wrap it, and prowls unhappily back out into the rain.

* * *

Fanny doesn't cry for long. In fact, soon after Solomon leaves, she appears to rally completely. Perhaps she is a little vaguer than usual but beyond that she behaves as if nothing has changed. Louis misinterprets it. He congratulates her on taking the news so well, when she hasn't actually taken it in at all, and spends the rest of the day calling her 'Widow Flynn' in what is meant to be an amusing medieval accent. Each time it makes her wince, and yet she can never quite summon the energy to object to it.

Later the following day she announces she wants to question Solomon more about the circumstances of the death. She is on the point of leaving when Louis, lying on her sofa reading a Patrick O'Brian, persuades her to think again. Fanny couldn't hear, or wouldn't hear, what Solomon had been trying to tell her, but Louis, having heard from Fanny all that Solomon told her, clearly understands what killed Nicholas Faraday. Fanny will work it out in her own time, of course, but in the mean time, rightly or wrongly, Louis instinctively wants to protect her. He suggests, with feigned carelessness, without even looking up from his book, that she should spend time getting used to what she's already learnt before going after the details. 'You've got to ease yourself into this,' he says.

It irritates her. When he looks so bloody easy himself, lying there reading novels. Almost as if he'd forgotten.

And yet, Louis has helped her through all the years of husband-related damage – and what now turns out to have been husband-related paranoia. It's not unreasonable that he should voice an opinion now, or even that she should listen to it. So, out of gratitude, if nothing else – and confusion – she sits mutely back down again, picks up a book of her own.

But the words on the page only float in front of her eyes. She slumps there for a minute or two and then a sigh escapes her, a great juddering, choking, sigh, and finally she melts into tears.

'You should be happy, Fan,' Louis says, laying down the book, holding her tight, stroking her hair. 'At least it's all over now. You'll never have to be terrified of him again . . .'

They wind up with their clothes all over the sitting-room floor, which helps her for a shortish while. Stops the tears. But which later only makes her feel worse.

After that, Fanny's reflections, and her grief for Nicholas Faraday – or her grief for what might have been – become a very private thing. She doesn't mention his name again.

45

It's exactly a fortnight after the Fiddleford fire before the police come calling at Uncle Russell Guppy's bungalow again. They find him in his wheelchair, surrounded by breathing kit and cigarettes, staring morosely out of his front-room window. The telly, he complains between gasps of air, has been broken for almost three weeks. He's keen to know if they can fix it.

But they've come to talk about Dane. They want to take him to Lamsbury police station for questioning.

'Well . . . he's in his . . . bedroom, I expect,' says Uncle Russell, bored and sour.

'Yes, sir. An officer is with him now . . . As you know, Mr Guppy, Dane insists he was with you when he first spotted the fire. Last time we were here you were unwilling to confirm that. But you didn't deny it, either. Do you have anything to say about it now?'

Uncle Russell sends him a surly, sideways look. 'Nothing to do with me,' he says, just as he said before. 'I've got enough . . . trouble. Keep me out of this.'

'So you're unwilling to substantiate Dane Guppy's alibi. Am I correct?'

'No bloody . . . comment.'

'Is there someone,' asks the plod with a patient sigh, 'who might be able to accompany him to the station?'

'Not . . . me,' says Uncle Russell. 'I ain't going . . . nowhere. Can you do anything with that . . . telly, then? . . . Or can't you?'

'Not really, sir. No. His mum and dad—'

'*Them!*'

'Suggested there was a sister. Tracey, I think.' He glances at his notebook.

'Dunno where Tracey is . . . Probably at . . . Macklan Creasey's place. Little . . . tart.' Slowly he turns his head from the window, looks at the policeman for the first time, his grey face a map of pain, isolation, anger. 'Tell my . . . brother,' he says, 'the ruddy TV's broke, will you? . . . Tell Tracey to tell him. Can't . . . do nothing without . . . the telly.'

'I'll do that, Mr Guppy,' the policeman says kindly, flicking his notebook closed. 'Many thanks for your time, Mr Guppy. I'll certainly pass that message on.'

Kitty Mozely is driving back from the supermarket in Lamsbury just as the police car, with Dane in the back, is parking up outside the Old Alms Cottages. She slams on the brakes – utterly brazen, in the middle of the street – keeps the engine running, and waits to see what happens next.

A few minutes later Tracey emerges from Macklan's front door, and from the jumbled look of her, she's come straight from bed. She is followed by an equally tousled-looking Macklan.

Tracey snarls something at the policeman (something, annoyingly, that Kitty can't quite hear). Then she notices Kitty staring at her, and something snaps. 'What are you staring at, Kitty Mozely?' she yells. 'Haven't you got a daughter to look after? Fuck off and mind your own business.'

Kitty, slightly put out, offers Tracey a defiant smirk and stays put.

'*I asked you what you're staring at, Kitty Mozely.*' Tracey ducks under the policeman's arm and starts charging the car.

With a throaty chuckle, Kitty flicks her a finger and quickly accelerates away.

Back at Laurel Cottage she dumps her groceries on the kitchen table and shouts out to Scarlett to come and unload. She's distracted. Dane's face in the back of the police car has reminded her of the contact sheet Louis put through her door, with the peculiar photographs of Fanny and the young boy, rolling about in a heap in front of a bonfire. She'd forgotten all about them. Where the hell did she put them?

She rummages around in the mess on her kitchen dresser, among the neglected bills on her desk, in the cupboard under her bathroom sink – and eventually finds them, folded and scrumpled, in the pocket of a skirt at the bottom of a pile of dirty laundry.

'Scarlett!' she yells. 'How many times do I have to ask you? *Check* the bloody pockets before putting things in the laundry pile!' (Scarlett doesn't respond, and nor does Kitty expect her to. The quiet harmony at Laurel Cottage is routinely punctured by Kitty's bad-tempered exclamations, bellowed from different corners of the house. Kitty, if she thought about it at all, would have been quite disconcerted were her daughter to respond to any of them.) 'I'm going round to Geraldine's,' she shouts, thumping down the stairs. 'I bought us a chicken for lunch. Do you want to put it in the oven? I'll be back in about an hour.'

Scarlett is in the kitchen, watching *Breakfast with Frost*, tutting quietly at the Member for Kensington and Chelsea's approach to monetary union, and already sorting out the shopping. Her television screen flickers as the front door slams.

The Adams family is still perched at the breakfast bar when Kitty breezes in. They're not even dressed. Clive and Geraldine are bent over their newspapers, munching toast and organic marmalade and frowning with concentration, perfectly engrossed in the vital task of remaining *au courant* with the big bad world beyond their own small patch of oblivion. Ollie sits between them, a pile of toasted waffles in front of him, untouched and swimming in organic maple syrup. Apart from the adults' methodical crunching, and the occasional broadsheet rustle-and-fold, the only sound emanating from the Old Rectory breakfast table is the *blip-blip-crrr* of Ollie's computer game.

'Morning all!' Kitty bawls. 'Only me!' She halts at the kitchen door. 'Good God! Not even dressed! I'd have thought you'd be out campaigning for a Fiddleford bus route or something by now. What's the matter with you? Are you ill?'

With a guilty start, Geraldine jumps up and begins to clear the plates.

'Kitty!' she says shrilly. 'How lovely to see you! No, no, no. Not ill! Certainly not. It's just that now the school governor issue's been settled it's the first Sunday we've had a chance to sit round *as a family* for weeks. Isn't it, Clive?' She glances at him nervously. '*For once* we felt we didn't have to go to church.'

'For once?' scoffs Kitty. 'You only went twice altogether.'

'Four times, actually, Kitty,' Geraldine reminds her. 'You may remember, we went without you on the first week. And we went again, last week. Out of courtesy.'

Kitty turns to Clive, sensing his lack of pleasure at her arrival, vaguely noting that he hasn't yet bothered to look up. 'How's life, Clive?' she barks at him. 'Business *thriving*?'

Clive doesn't smile at Kitty. He's been feeling increasingly irritated, recently, by her presumption of free and apparently absolute access to his house at any time of the day or night, and he's complained about it to Geraldine.

'Kitty,' he says, nodding at her sullenly, then returning to his newspaper.

'*Clive*,' mimics Kitty.

Clive ignores her.

The problem, as even Geraldine agrees, has grown significantly worse since Kitty signed her megabuck book contract, because now when she turns up unannounced, she's taken to bringing the drink with her – and it's almost always champagne, as if each and every one of her interminable arrivals demanded celebrating. Neither he nor Geraldine particularly likes champagne but Geraldine insists on accepting each new bottle with dutiful whoops of gratitude and excitement. After which, of course, they're more or less obliged to drink the thing together, which makes it doubly hard to get rid of her.

'Oh, I say!' exclaims Kitty, eyeing up a three-quarter-full cafetière. 'Is there any of that coffee left?'

'It's a bit cold,' Geraldine says.

'Not to worry. I'll heat up some milk . . . If that's all right?' No words of reassurance from Clive or Geraldine, who are engaged in a silent warfare, exchanging shrugs of non-responsibility behind her. But Kitty is unabashed. She's already pulling at a small green Le Creuset saucepan which hangs, beside its matching brethren, from a meat hook above the green Aga.

'You'll never guess the excitement,' Kitty continues cheerfully.

'Ollie!' snaps Geraldine. Because she has to take it out on someone. 'Switch off that wretched machine and say good morning to Kitty.'

'Morning,' he says drearily, over the blips.

'By the way,' says Geraldine, trying to sound a bit more friendly, 'when're you going to give us a glimpse of the Great Novel, eh, Kitty? Clive and I were just saying – you're being awfully secretive about it. And I know you've got the proofs back, because Scarlett told Ollie. Didn't she, Ollie, sweetheart? Scarlett told Ollie she couldn't wait for Ollie to read it. Which was rather sweet, I thought.'

'Did she?' says Kitty nervously. 'Well, I shouldn't pay any attention to what Scarlett says.'

'Oh, Kit,' Geraldine says, looking disapproving. 'That's not fair, now is it?'

'Anyway, never mind Scarlett. Forget about the book.' Kitty waves it aside impatiently.

'I shall have to call the publisher myself, if you don't hand it over,' Geraldine says skittishly. 'Seriously, Kitty. I can't wait!'

'I wouldn't waste your time doing that because they won't give it to you,' Kitty snaps. 'Anyway, *much* more interestingly, guess who I saw being taken away in the back of a police car this morning! The boy! I've forgotten his name. You know, the horrible Guppy boy! Who barged into church the other week – who called the fire brigade. What's his name again? Tracey Guppy's brother—'

'Dane?' says Geraldine sharply (skittishness gone). 'They've arrested him? Gosh! I thought they never would . . .' Geraldine can never quite hear Dane Guppy's name without a tiny, secret, gush of shame; a rush of bubbling hostility. She has never again asked to have a 'reading session' with him, not since he took her head like that, and shouted that he loved her. 'Well. And about bloody time, frankly,' she mutters.

Crrr-blip-blip. Crrrrr beeeep.

'They had the police car parked outside Macklan

Creasey's, and they both came tumbling out of the house. Tracey was screaming like a fishwife. It was quite funny . . .' Kitty pictures her, and pauses. 'Poor little thing. She was weeping . . .' Anyway,' she adds quickly, pulling her merry old self together. 'Imagine – what a stroke of luck. There was I, up with the lark, on my way back from Safeways, *just* as they were carting the little sod off to jail.'

GAME OVER – GAME OVER – GAME OVER.

'Ollie, I told you to switch off that machine.'

'And it's the best place for him, the stupid little sod,' Kitty adds approvingly. 'Too many out-of-control children in this bloody country. They get away with murder.'

'Since, Kitty, you have difficulty even remembering the boy's name, and you weren't, so far as I know, actually present when the match was struck,' snaps Clive, though he'd been intending to ignore her, 'it's somewhat contrary of you to be so bloody confident that he's guilty.'

Kitty looks at him, mouths a silent '*oooh*'. 'Who's rattled your cage this morning?' she asks mildly. 'I say, I don't suppose you've got any more of those waffles, Geraldine? And anyway,' she turns back to Clive, 'I do know he's guilty, Clive, actually. If you want to know. Because I've got photographic evidence . . . I've been meaning to show it to you for ages, Geraldine. I've actually got photographic evidence that the boy is a pyromaniac. If you can believe it! It was only when I saw him this morning in the back of that police car that I finally put the two faces together.'

'What does pyromaniac mean?' asks Ollie, in a burst of unprecedented curiosity.

Nobody answers. Kitty produces Louis's folded, crumpled contact sheet and with a flick of the wrist, sends it spinning across the breakfast bar.

'Oh,' says Geraldine, catching it before it spins on to the floor, bending over to have a look. 'Oh, they're rather nice . . . *Lovely* one of Scarlett, there. You'd hardly notice—'

'Yes, yes, never mind that. Look at the top row . . . See? The exploding bonfire?'

'OH!'

'Isn't that Dane Guppy there, being sat on by Miss Flynn?'

'Well . . . *goodness*!' exclaims Geraldine, picking it up and holding it to the window. 'How *extraordinary*! Clive, do look.'

'Can I see?' says Ollie.

'Good God!' Geraldine cries. 'It's outside the school! It's in the playground. It's actually— Kitty! It's outside the girls' cloakroom, where the fire began.'

'Is it?' says Kitty happily. She hadn't noticed that.

'When do you suppose this happened?'

'Well, if you look at the numbers, it was obviously on the same reel of film as the press conference, which means—'

'I know when that happened,' says Ollie. 'Can I see? It was when you were doing your press thing, and Miss Flynn sent him up to her office. Where I was. Remember? He told me all about it. He put a dead bird on the fire with rockets attached, and—'

'Pretty damning, aren't they?' interrupts Kitty smugly. 'What do you suppose the police would make of *them*? There's bound to be a legal term. Clive, you'll know. Proven Predisposition or something? Being an Obvious Pyromaniac. Who cares, anyway? He's as guilty as sin.'

Finally, Clive can control his curiosity no longer. He lays down his paper and leans to look over his wife's shoulder. He frowns, moves closer, puts on his spectacles and studies the series of photographs long and hard.

'Is this the boy,' he asks, 'who was playing truant most of the term, Geraldine, whom you felt you made some connection with during one of your reading seminars?'

'Mmm. Yessss,' says Geraldine, still examining the

pictures. 'Yes, I'm afraid it is. He was at school very much against his will, I think. Poor little thing.'

The comment hangs. Kitty ferrets in the bread bin in search of waffles and Ollie stands behind his parents, straining to be allowed a glance, until Clive breaks the silence with a cold, clear, 'But what we're looking at here doesn't constitute evidence, Geraldine. I don't need to tell you that.'

She laughs. 'No,' she says quickly. 'Of course not. But I mean, seriously, Clive. You can't honestly think . . .'

Clive turns his cold clear eyes on to Kitty. 'How long ago was it you saw the boy being driven off?'

'Well, just a second ago!' she exclaims. 'Literally! Dumped the shopping, grabbed the pictures and came straight over. Because really I thought,' she adds, delighted by the weighty turn her snippet of gossip has taken, 'well, I was sure that *you*, Clive, with your *brilliant* legal mind, would want to be versed . . .'

'Clive,' says his wife, reading his brilliant legal mind, 'dear Clive, it's our *family* morning . . . and you and I are *not*— Clive, I hardly need to point out, we are company lawyers. We're not equipped— And I will *not*— Clive?' But he's already on his way upstairs, taking the steps two at a time, fumbling with the belt on his Ralph Lauren towelling robe. 'We didn't move to Fiddleford,' she shouts after him, 'so we could bloody well ambulance chase on our *family* morning!'

He pauses on the top landing. 'And we didn't move to Fiddleford to sit on our fannies all day, and piss all our savings down the drain.'

'Don't be disgusting.'

'We need the work, Geraldine.'

Geraldine glances across at Kitty, munching on her bloody waffles, gleefully taking it all in. 'Please, don't be melodramatic, Clive,' she says, making herself smile.

'It's a good job. High profile. It'll get us some attention.'

'It's a ghastly job, Clive. It's a foregone conclusion. *He's* as guilty as hell. And *we* are company lawyers. We know nothing about criminal law.'

'I do. You conveniently forget, Geraldine . . .'

(She doesn't. She was vaguely hoping Clive had. He only switched to company law after they were married.) 'And it's bloody well *Sunday morning*.'

'I'm going to call Jo Maxwell McDonald. Make her do some work for all the money we've been paying her . . . Come on, Geraldine. *Hurry up!* What are you waiting for? Go and get dressed!'

'What's going on?' says Ollie.

He's talking sense, of course. Clive always talks Geraldine's kind of sense. But he should never have talked so much of it in front of Kitty. Geraldine is furious. 'Yikes,' she says, with a little laugh, 'do you think the country air has finally got to him?'

'On the contrary,' smirks Kitty. 'I've never seen him so masterful. As a matter of fact,' she wipes a trickle of maple syrup from her chin, 'for the first time in fifteen years or whatever it is, I begin to get an inkling of what you actually see in him.'

'Oh, piss off.'

Geraldine stalks out of the room.

46

The Lamsbury police have never come up against such an *überforce* as the Adams Duo. Within minutes of arriving at the station, Clive and Geraldine, working together despite Geraldine's lack of qualifications, have persuaded Tracey they should be allowed to take on the case (free of charge, for the moment). They have dispensed with the lawyer already provided, and are sitting on either side of Dane in the interview room. They learn that Dane's fingerprints have been identified on the petrol can with Dane's uncle's name on it, which was found in the field behind the school, and they listen to him being formally charged. The case is conclusive, and yet, to Clive's hidden dismay, the police (nervous of the *überforce* and wanting to please) suggest that Dane should return home without waiting for police bail. The whole process takes less than twenty minutes.

'*Well*,' says Geraldine, tossing her bag among the breakfast things still spread out on the kitchen table, 'I hope you thought that was a worthwhile way to spend a family morning, Clive. One pyromaniac, guilty as charged, and free to roam. One pair of *company* solicitors. Over-qualified. Or under-qualified, depending on how you measure. Not charging at all. One hell of a lot of evidence. One foregone conclusion. One hell of a waste of time.'

'It'll go to court,' mutters Clive. 'And we'll get him off. One excellent way of drawing attention to ourselves. Don't be so bloody childish, Geraldine. You know perfectly well we can't live on nothing a year. We need to work. Just like everyone else does.'

'And one very lonely little boy,' she continues, ignoring Clive, running her hands through the golden locks of her beautiful son, and bending to kiss his cheek. He is sitting at the breakfast bar, as he had been an hour before, playing with his Nintendo, with marmalade, butter and the remains of his and Kitty's waffles still spread out around him. He doesn't look up. 'One *wery wery lonely boy*,' blubbers Geraldine, pushing her lips forward and out, 'who's had to spend all his morning *alone* because his mummy and daddy wanted to do some silly work. On a Sunday. I'm *so sorry*, baby.'

Ollie doesn't reply.

Neither does Clive, standing with his back to her, doing something fiddly with a mobile telephone. Nobody's listening to her.

'And by the way, Clive, *thank you so much* for letting Kitty know the practice was in trouble. I must say, that was brilliant.'

'Hmm?'

'*Absolutely brilliant*. You realise she'll be telling bloody everyone.'

'I thought she was your best friend.'

'And by the way, I'm still a long way from being persuaded,' she adds, taking some of Messy McShane's organic courgettes from her walk-in larder-fridge, 'that this morning's desperate little ambulance chase didn't actually impair the good name of our bloody practice, Clive . . .

314

Clive?' In a flash of rare temper Geraldine slams the organic courgettes on the kitchen-island slate counter. 'For God's sake! You could at least have the bloody decency to *answer me*.'

'What?' With a jolt, Clive puts the mobile into his pocket. 'Sorry, Geraldine. What did you say?'

'I said—'

But cerebral Clive is the sort of man who can take things in even when he isn't listening. 'I don't know whether it helped directly,' he interrupts. 'We shall see. Look on it as an exercise of neighbourly goodwill, if you like.' He gives a thin smile and his eye strays towards the *Sunday Telegraph*, spread out on the kitchen table. 'It's often the most futile-seeming exercises which pay off in the long run. Don't you find?'

At last Ollie comes up from his computer. 'So,' he asks, with a big smile, 'what happened then? Is Dane Guppy going to prison?'

'Instead of reading that paper, Clive, you might be kind and start peeling the potatoes. Lunch is late enough as it is.'

47

At the Fiddleford Arms, meanwhile, Fanny Flynn and Louis are spending an equally ill-tempered afternoon. The day had begun badly, with Fanny waking to the sound of Tracey outside on the street, yelling at Kitty and the police. Fanny had clambered out of bed in time to see Dane, Tracey and Macklan being carted away in the police car.

'Louis!' she said. 'Louis, wake up. They've taken Dane. They've taken him off to the police station. D'you think I should go down there and help him out?'

Louis barely grunted.

'Louis? Louis!'

'Mmm? . . . Why? What's the day?'

'It's Sunday. It doesn't matter what day it is. Poor Dane. He's one of my pupils, Louis. He's a part of the school. I can't just—'

'Ahh,' Louis murmured, very wry. 'Sunday. The day of rest . . . Come back to bed, Fan.'

She felt guilty then. Louis has to put up with her school rants from the moment they wake until the moment they fall asleep together, and she knows it isn't fair on him. She forced back the impulse to ignore him – to drive straight to the police station – and instead climbed back into bed. They've not spent a morning in bed since they came back from Spain; Fanny's barely spared the time for a drink with him.

Louis made a noise of warm, dozy satisfaction as she rested her head in the crook of his arm and she was shocked by how that little noise could irritate her. She stared at the ceiling for a while, worrying, waiting. And within minutes Louis was asleep again. Snoring gently.

She crept downstairs to the telephone, but by the time she got through to the station, Dane Guppy had already been charged and released.

Now she and Louis are in the pub. They've eaten the lunch – disgusting, as it always is at the Fiddleford Arms, but better than having to make their own, or so they thought beforehand. They're feeling overfed and a little sick, and Fanny's so preoccupied with worries about Dane that she's hardly managed to speak. Tracey and Macklan wouldn't come to the door after they got back from Lamsbury; not when Fanny knocked, nor when she sent Louis to try. So she still knows nothing. No more than she did first thing this morning. She daren't call Dane's mother nor, quite, his emphysemic Uncle Russell. It's frustrating for her, and her ignorance is beginning to make her unpleasant.

'I suppose you could call Kitty Mozely,' she says sourly, breaking a long silence, during which Louis perused the soccer reports in the *Observer*, and belched a couple of times, very softly.

'Hmm?' he says, without looking up.

'Well, she was *there*. Poking her nose in. And you two seem to be such good friends.'

He doesn't bother to respond.

'Oh, Louis,' she says (moving blithely on). 'I just feel so

awful for him. He was just beginning to come into his own. He was joining in . . . He was really starting to look happy. But what can I do? I can't let him stay at the school, not if he's endangering everyone else there. I can't. And I mean, *he needs help*. He's obviously obsessed with setting fire to things . . . and I have a responsibility to *all* the children. Not just to Dane . . . Don't you think, Louis?' Again, she doesn't seem to expect a response. 'I feel like I'm letting him down . . . but I'd be letting the others down if . . . if they're saying he's done it. I mean, if he did it . . . Oh Christ. *He's just got to go.*'

'Mmm-hmm,' Louis says, turning the page. 'It's a difficult call, Fan. It really is.'

Just then Macklan lopes in, eyes fixed to the ground. He's come to fetch a packet of Silk Cut for Tracey, who's too upset to do anything, for the moment, but lie on her bed.

'Macklan!' cries Louis, keen for some fresh company. 'Macklan, over here!'

Fanny smiles. It sounds more like a cry for help. But Macklan doesn't look especially pleased to see them. He nods, makes as if to pass on his way, but as he sweeps by their table Fanny grasps hold of his arm.

'Macklan. Please,' she says. Her voice trembles. 'Please. He's my student. Tell me what's going on.'

'Nothing.' Macklan pulls his arm away, strangely hostile. He sounds uncharacteristically cold. 'They charged him, that's all. They were always going to.'

'I'm so sorry,' Fanny says.

'They found Dane's fingerprints were on the petrol can. Or they say they did.'

'Ahhh,' says Louis ruefully, folding his paper away. 'I guess that kind of decides it then. I'm sorry, Mack.'

Fanny says nothing for a moment. The news has sent a chill through her heart. Without the fingerprints there might have been a spark of hope that it had been someone else, some passing stranger. But the fingerprints are conclusive. 'Poor Dane,' she mutters. 'Poor little Dane. He was doing so well . . . I should have known.' She sighs. 'I should have *known*. I mean, I *did* know . . . I should have got him some help.'

'Did know what?' Macklan snaps. 'He didn't do it.'

Fanny looks at him, amazed. 'Oh, come on, Mack,' she says, almost laughing. 'How can you say that?'

'He couldn't have done it anyway.' Macklan looks at his hands. 'He was having breakfast with me and Trace that morning. If you want to know. So. And last I heard, a person – unless of course he happens to be called Guppy and lives in a village called Fiddleford – a person can't normally be convicted of being in two places at once. It's a ruddy frame-up.'

Louis laughs. 'Is that what you told the fuzz?'

Macklan flushes. He looks very young suddenly. 'In fact, Tracey only remembered when we got back. So we're going in later to tell them. We'll tell them later.'

A silence. Nobody quite dares to look at the other, and Macklan's blatant lie hangs between them, embarrassing them all. Finally Fanny says, very quietly, 'Macklan, I hate to state the obvious, but you know you can get into a hell of a lot of trouble, saying things that aren't strictly – true – to the police . . . Are you sure you want to do that?'

Macklan looks at her, green eyes shining wild. She wonders, briefly, if he'll punch her. So does he. Instead he swallows. Shakes his head.

'Dane was having breakfast with us,' he says again, very quietly, and turns – without the cigarettes – and stalks out of the pub.

Louis gives a low whistle. 'That was very brave.' He smiles at Fanny. 'I sure as hell wasn't going to tell him that.'

'Well, he's lying, isn't he?'

'Of course he is.' Louis leans across, gives Fanny's tense shoulders a friendly squeeze. 'Of course he is. But Fanny—' He can see her, mouth set, eyes glistening. She's about to cry. 'There's nothing you can do about it.' He shrugs. 'People have to do what they have to do . . . People do all sorts of things for love.'

She makes her lips smile. Feeling guilty again. She knows she's being obsessive, overwrought, boring, hysterical. She knows he's trying to be kind. And for some reason, for no good reason at all, she finds that incredibly irritating.

'I love you,' she says.

'Mmm-hmm,' he says, dropping his arm, reaching for his cigarettes. 'Thanks.'

48

Monday morning is, of course, one of Geraldine's mornings at the primary school. She is still so angry with Clive for humiliating her in front of Kitty, that she left the house before he or Ollie had even come down for breakfast.

She arrives at the school over an hour early, expecting to find the place locked. But she finds Fanny, alone in the staff room with Brute.

'Good morning!' Geraldine says breezily. 'You're up with the lark!'

'Morning, Geraldine.' Fanny looks exhausted. 'I hear you had a busy day yesterday. Tracey must be very grateful.'

'I should hope she is. I mean,' Geraldine corrects herself, 'we were only doing what we—'

'Actually, I'm glad you're here. I could do with some advice.'

'Oh!' Geraldine chuckles. 'Well, that's a first, Fanny, I must say. How can I help?'

'She's claiming Dane was with her and Macklan when the fire started. She says she "forgot" to mention it at the police station when you were down there with them.'

'She is?' says Geraldine cautiously, mind on Red Alert. 'I wasn't aware of that . . . What does Macklan say?'

Fanny shrugs. 'He's saying the same thing. He's in love with her. But Geraldine,' Fanny leans forward, 'they're lying. I just don't believe it. Do you?'

Geraldine blinks. 'Do I *believe* it?' she repeats. 'Well. It's not just— I mean, clearly, if Macklan says it too . . .'

'Yes, but he's young. He's in love with her. Tracey's trying to protect her brother. Macklan's trying to protect Tracey.'

Geraldine, under such very direct questioning, prefers to divert Fanny's attention towards coffee. 'Would you like a cup, perhaps? Since I'm making some. Or perhaps you'd prefer tea?'

'They're lying,' says Fanny again. 'And I mean, Christ, I don't want the poor boy to be locked away in some horrible juvenile centre, but nor do I want him roaming around the village setting fire to things. I think he's dangerous, Geraldine. And I really do believe it was Dane who set fire to our school.'

'Fanny, there's—' She stops. Starts again. 'I'm sorry, Fanny. But there is absolutely no evidence to substantiate that.'

'Except the fingerprints.'

'Hmm? Really, Fanny, I don't think it's particularly fair or responsible—'

'I think he's a danger to the school. I think he's a danger to himself. I think he's a danger to the whole village, actually . . .'

Geraldine looks down, takes a deep breath. 'Fanny,' she gives a tight, short laugh, 'you said you wanted my advice. But it sounds to me as though you just want me to—'

'You're right. I was just looking for a bit of support, I suppose. Truth is, my mind's made up. I want to exclude him, Geraldine . . . Which is a shame,' she sighs, 'when you think of all the trouble I went to to get him to come back here in the first place.'

'But there's no evidence to substantiate your allegations,'

Geraldine says. Recites. She's sounding like a robot. 'None at all.'

'There are the fingerprints,' Fanny says again. 'And the fact that the last time I went round to his house they had to call out the fire brigade because he'd started a fire in the sitting room. And, judging by the way his mother reacted, it obviously wasn't the first time he'd done it.'

Geraldine, groping for the right response, sits silently shaking her head.

'And finally,' with another sigh Fanny pulls out Louis's photographs, the same images, only larger, that Clive, Geraldine and Kitty had been squinting over yesterday morning, 'there are these. Louis took them. He took them during Kitty Mozely's press conference.'

Geraldine flicks through them – familiar images now, of course, but she makes a good show, emitting little sounds of shock and awe, as if she'd never before set eyes on them. '*Mmmh!*' she says. '*Goodness!*'

'While you guys were all at the back, applauding Kitty's pearls of wit, Dane Guppy was up front – by the girls' cloak-room, as you can see. Attaching fireworks to dead birds and throwing them on a bloody bonfire.' She waits for some other reaction from Geraldine, but Geraldine just keeps flicking through the images, making the little noises and shaking her head. Her brain whirrs for the safest way to deal with the situation.

'I know,' says Fanny, misinterpreting Geraldine's silence, 'I should have said something at the time. But I felt sorry for him. I felt sorry for Tracey. Christ, I don't know what I was thinking. I could just sort of see his life stretching out in front of him and it's as if nothing *good* was ever going to happen. Like he has a thick cloud of bad luck squatting over his head. I wanted to give him another chance.'

'Yesss,' Geraldine says distractedly.

'Like you and Clive did yesterday, I imagine . . . And I know everyone's entitled to a defence. But, Geraldine, I also know he's guilty. And I believe anyone who saw those pictures would be forced to agree. He needs help. And I'm going to get it for him. But first I've got to get him away from the school.'

'Mmm,' says Geraldine. 'Yes, of course . . .' But she isn't listening. She's just flicking through those photographs, faster and faster, and wishing that Clive were there to tell her what to do or say next.

'Anyway,' Fanny continues, 'I'm going to ask Reverend Hodge to call a meeting tonight. A disciplinary hearing. Can you make it? We need all the governors together. We can hear the case and make a vote . . . But as the head teacher I'm telling you – and I know my vote doesn't count any more than anyone else's – I don't want him at school. Or anywhere near it. I want him out.'

'A meeting tonight?' Geraldine finds her voice at last. 'Of course I can make it. Of course.' Seeing those pictures again, and blown up, with all Dane's glee so large and apparent; hearing Fanny's certainty that the school – that Ollie – is at risk, Geraldine feels terrified. She'd like to lock the boy up herself and throw away the key. Of course she would.

On the other hand, everyone knows now that she and Clive represented him at the police station yesterday. He is their client. She plops the photographs on to the coffee table without making any comment at all. 'Could you excuse me a moment, Fanny? I'm just going to make a quick call.'

In the empty playground, behind the oil tank, she calls Clive. He's still at home.

'Hello, love. You left early,' he says, sounding hurt.

'I was angry. Never mind that. We'll talk about it later. Listen, Clive. Minor crisis. Major crisis, actually. Tell me what to do . . .'

*   *   *

324

She returns to the staff room a few minutes later, wreathed in cooperative smiles. '*Sorry*, Fanny. So sorry about that. I was just checking with Clive. Because it seems awfully silly to me, all the governors squeezing into this wreck of a school this evening. Why don't we have the meeting at ours? We can have a few glasses of wine, perhaps. Try to make the whole thing a little less gruesome. A little more civilised. Don't you think? There's so much more room.'

Fanny eyes her warily. 'Well, I suppose that would be nice.'

Geraldine nods. 'Would it be helpful if I were to call the vicar for you? He and I have become quite chummy recently and you've so much else to worry about.'

'Thanks, Geraldine,' Fanny says, wondering if perhaps she's been underestimating Geraldine all this time, 'but I should probably do it myself.'

'I can do a quick ring-round to all the governors. It would only take me a few minutes.'

Fanny shakes her head. 'Not to worry. I'll call the vicar at break and then, since he's chair, he'll probably want to take over arrangements himself.'

'Right . . . Right you are. Well! The offer's there. I'll pack Lenka off to Safeways anyway. She can get some wine and a few bits. Just in case . . . I imagine Dane's parents will need to be hauled in, will they?'

Fanny grimaces. 'But they may refuse to come.'

'And Dane, of course.'

'Of course.'

'Well, it's all very sad. Very sad indeed,' Geraldine sighs. 'Oh! And after all that I still haven't made the coffee!' She tinkles away, clicking, pouring, stirring, and they fall quiet. Fanny returns to the photographs. She didn't ask Geraldine whether she agreed with her decision to expel Dane Guppy. She assumes from Geraldine's hopeful manner that they are both on the same side. Anyone confronted by such photographs couldn't fail to be convinced that Dane was a threat.

'D'you know, Fanny,' Geraldine chirps up, 'would you mind awfully if I missed this morning's reading sessions? I'm not feeling top notch, to be honest with you. And if we're to have this meeting this evening I think I'd be better off resting at home. Besides which, I've so much to do.'

By the time Fanny puts in her call to the aged Reverend Hodge, at a quarter past eleven that morning, he is already well ahead of her. The meeting is to take place at the Old Rectory at eight o'clock.

'Geraldine called you, did she?'

'Oh, absolutely. And I was only saying to her,' he chuckles boringly – he's a dull dog, the vicar – 'I was only saying to the lovely Mrs Adams, how times have changed. A few years ago these sort of occasions tended to begin at six in the evening. And then it was seven. And then – really, never any later than seven. But as Mrs Adams rightly pointed out, people work so hard these days. Ladies, too, of course . . .'

'They do. We do. So shall you be letting the other governors know or would you prefer me to do that?'

'Not to worry, Fanny dear. It's all in hand. Mrs Adams and I have worked our way through the telephone numbers, and Mrs Adams has very kindly agreed to do a little ring-round. There was a bit of confusion because one of the mobile numbers seemed to begin with 04 instead of 07. Which was misleading. Because of course the preliminary digits for these sorts of telephones changed a number of years ago. With all the 04s changing to 07s, if I remember rightly. However, I haven't heard back from Mrs Adams, so I can only assume . . .'

49

Clive and Geraldine's Problem.
They had to sell some of their investments last month just to keep their creamy-coloured lifestyle on the road. There is no work coming in to the Lamsbury practice. None. Clive says he's going to give it another couple of weeks but if nothing changes between now and then he's going to have to hand the secretary her notice. Clive and Geraldine are feeling the pinch, something they're not at all accustomed to, and a week ago, when Geraldine and Kitty returned from a clothes-shopping bonanza in Bath, she and Clive had the first money-related marital of their lives. Really uncivilised. Geraldine heard herself calling him *a sexist pig*. And Clive heard himself calling Geraldine *a silly little girl*. She was so angry she couldn't speak to him for three days.

It should go without saying that Clive and Geraldine don't want an arsonist roaming round their son's school, any more than anyone else would. Geraldine, especially, hates to think of little Ollie being exposed to such danger . . . (And Clive and Geraldine, like everyone else, are in no doubt as to their client's guilt.)

On the other hand, Clive argues, as a responsible parent,

Geraldine needs also to think of little Ollie's *long-term future*. Ollie is due to go away to prep school in September, anyway. (As has ever been the plan.) Except that if his parents can't make their practice pay, they won't be able to afford his far-from-inconsiderable school fees.

Geraldine cannot afford to be sentimental, Clive says. Nor can she afford to turn publicly on a client, let alone be seen to assume him guilty of the very crime she's just been fighting to have him acquitted of. Public perception, as their useless PR woman might tell them, if she could ever tear herself away from her wretched twins, is everything. If Clive and Geraldine are to succeed, they need to be seen as efficient, sympathetic, reliable, consistent and honest.

So. To expel or not to expel? To defend or not to defend? What a dilemma. The very thing to make cerebral Clive's heart sing.

Clive and Geraldine's Solution.

Best-case scenario – for the school governing body to vote for Dane's exclusion without Geraldine having to be involved. She could, of course, abstain from the vote, but Clive (who, as non-governor, has no vote) feels that it might be wrongly interpreted. At all costs, he believes, she needs to be seen to support her client.

Geraldine must vote to keep Dane in the school, while Clive, as Dane's lawyer, does whatever he surreptitiously can to ensure that the exclusion vote wins the day. Not only for the sake of his son but for the sake of the practice. It would allow the Adams Family Practice to launch an appeal against the decision, thereby generating – with the supposed help of their unsatisfactory PR agent, Jo Maxwell McDonald – some direly needed local acclaim.

By the time they win the case (*if* they win the case) the summer term will be over, Dane Guppy will have left the school anyway, and Ollie (though nobody's bothered to mention this to Fanny) will have his trunk packed up ready for his first term at prep school . . .

While Fanny struggles to get the vicar off the telephone, Geraldine is racing ahead with arrangements for the disciplinary meeting tonight. She has sent Lenka to Safeways for alcohol and 'bits', and has her large, creamy house to herself. She sits at her breakfast bar tapping a long sharp pencil against her list of governors' names and telephone numbers and tries to calculate . . . She has contacted all of them now, except for Kitty. She has quizzed them gently about how they intend to vote, given what they know – that Dane has been formally charged with arson, that he has a history of arson, that his fingerprints were found on an empty petrol can in the neighbouring field, and that there are photographs of him building fires at the school on a separate occasion – and she has a clear idea how the vote will result.

There are eleven governors in all:

Fanny Flynn, will vote: FOR EXCLUSION.

Grey McShane: FOR EXCLUSION.

General Maxwell McDonald: FOR EXCLUSION.

Reverend Hodge: FOR EXCLUSION.

Solomon Creasey, away on business in Frankfurt: ABSTAINS.

Tracey Guppy, as a witness to the case, is: DISQUALIFIED.

Mr Trumpton, LEA representative (holding firm to his habit of non-availability): ABSTAINS.

Geraldine Adams must vote: AGAINST.

Maurice Morrison, rigidly on-message New Labour candidate for Lamsbury: AGAINST.

Robert White will vote anything, as long as it's opposing Fanny Flynn: AGAINST.

Making the score (minus non-participants): 4 EXCLU-SIONS, 3 AGAINST.

And Kitty.

Kitty Mozely, Clive and Geraldine agree, will do anything so long as she thinks it's amusing and she will almost certainly, given the Louis situation, think it's amusing to do whatever she can to annoy Fanny. Which, most inconveniently, will mean voting AGAINST.

Geraldine sits there, tapping her pencil for at least a minute and a half. She decides, with a final tap, that with Kitty's reputation, Geraldine could perfectly well get away with not mentioning the meeting at all, and then claiming that Kitty must have forgotten. Kitty wouldn't mind. At least, not much. In fact, she would probably be grateful to get out of it.

Excellent. Geraldine picks up her bag and keys and drives off to Lamsbury, where she and Clive are going to load themselves with flowers, oily bath salts, rich dark chocolates and dry champagne, before calling on Mr and Mrs Guppy, both of whom much prefer hard cash, and who are unlikely to be very grateful.

50

'Mrs Guppy. Hi-ya! He-lloo!' Big smile from Geraldine. Not reciprocated. Geraldine hesitates. She's never seen Mrs Guppy at such close quarters before. She's thinking of her delicate creamy-white sofas, and suddenly regretting the fact that the disciplinary meeting is to take place in her own 'parlour' after all. 'We haven't actually met, Mrs Guppy. My name is Geraldine. And this is my husband, Clive . . .' They're standing beneath the same dilapidated porch Fanny did, being hit with the same stink of frying, and if either of them cared to look down they would see the tiny dent left on the door by Fanny's foot, now with paint peeling off.

'What do you want?' asks Mrs Guppy suspiciously, keeping the door pressed to her side.

'May we come in?' Geraldine gestures to Clive to bring the flowers forward. An enormous cluster of precious, sweet-smelling orchids sweeps towards Mrs Guppy's nose, briefly masking the stench of her hall. Mrs Guppy sneezes.

'Bless you!' cries Geraldine.

Mrs Guppy sneezes again, and with her big hand shunts the orchids roughly away from her, causing several to snap. 'Take 'em away!' she barks, and sneezes again.

'Oh, dear. Is it the flowers? Mrs Guppy, I'm so sorry! How stupid of us. Clive, for heaven's sake, the poor lady's sneezing! Get them away from her! Mrs Guppy . . . ' She waits, but there seems to be no sign of the sneezes abating, or of Mrs Guppy standing back and asking them in. She tries again. 'We've really come to offer our condolences—' Mrs Guppy straightens up from another sneeze, looks very suspicious, throws herself forward and sneezes again. 'To say how *sorry* we are. About Dane.'

'May we come in?' asks Clive. Geraldine nudges him.

'As Dane probably told you, Clive and I— Clive, dearest, do give Mrs Guppy the chocolates. She's standing here in the freezing draught.' Geraldine rolls the eyes skyward, shoots Mrs Guppy a wife-to-wife look, which Mrs Guppy ignores.

'Dark chocolate,' Mrs Guppy says instead. 'Never mind.' She shunts them behind her. And almost smiles. 'What else have you got?'

Mrs Guppy takes the offerings in, one by one, all £243-worth of them; piling them up behind her, grunting with dissatisfaction as each new package is presented, until finally there is nothing left for the Adamses to give. And still Mrs Guppy doesn't invite them in. 'What do you want, anyway?' she asks at last.

'Ah. Yes. Now. As you're probably aware it was Clive and I who came to see your lovely son Dane at the police station last Sunday morning. We're solicitors.'

'I don't know nothing about that.'

'Mmmm. *Boys!*' says Geraldine deftly. Mrs Guppy is lying, but there is nothing to be gained from making a point about it. 'We have one of the same age. In Dane's class. Ollie Adams? Perhaps Dane has mentioned him . . . ?'

No response at all.

'Well, anyway. We – that is, Clive and I – are absolutely

convinced there is insufficient evidence for the case ever to come to court. However, *Miss Flynn*, whom,' a little smile from Geraldine, remembering the incident in the village hall, 'I believe we're all familiar with—'

'Rather too familiar with,' mutters Clive. 'I think we might all have benefited from being familiar with rather less!'

Mrs Guppy glances at him uncertainly. But he is smiling at her. A moment of acute tension. And then suddenly her great big face lights up in a great big ugly grin, and she cackles, and all her chins cackle with her. Mrs Guppy probably hasn't laughed for twenty years, and the facial contortions it entails obviously disconcert her. She glances nervously at her own shuddering cheeks. And the laughter dies as quickly and unexpectedly as it began. 'What about her?'

'She, er—' But Geraldine's been thrown off by the image of Mrs Guppy settling that vast, juddering body on to her beautiful East Coast sofas. 'She, er— Where was I?'

'Fanny Flynn,' rescues Clive, 'has taken it into her head to declare your son Dane guilty of a crime we believe he didn't do, Mrs Guppy. A crime which the courts have yet to try him for. And which, if my wife and I have anything to do with it, the courts will never be permitted to try him for. There's to be a disciplinary meeting – a sort of trial-by-governors. This evening. Miss Flynn wants to expel him from school.'

'Stupid cow,' Mrs Guppy says placidly.

'Mmm,' smiles Clive. 'Well, absolutely.'

'You can tell that cow from me. He didn't do it.'

'Which is why we're here with you now, Mrs Guppy. You and your husband are invited to attend the disciplinary hearing. Geraldine is a school governor, of course, and will certainly be voting against Dane's exclusion.'

'Tell the bitch he didn't do it.'

Clive gives another of his thin, bloodless smiles. 'Mrs

Guppy, you can tell her yourself. If you come to the meeting this evening.'

But she shakes her head. 'I'm not going there. And Ian's not neither.' She shuffles backwards and begins to close the door on them. 'So don't go asking him—'

'Mrs Guppy!' Clive calls after her. But he and Geraldine are a cool-headed pair. They know better than to put a foot in her door. Besides which, their job for that morning is done.

'Good,' says Clive, when the door is properly closed, and they can hear her heavy footsteps thumping back down the hall. 'That's that, then. I think it went as well as we could have hoped.'

'Do you think they won't come?' asks Geraldine hopefully.

He shrugs. 'They may. They may not. Doesn't matter, does it?' Clive and Geraldine turn happily towards their mushroom-coloured Land Rover, settle their bottoms into its soft leather seats. 'Either way, she knows we're on her side. I'd be amazed if she doesn't let us take on the case.' He starts the engine and a Mozart *Minuet for Harpsichord* fills the car from six separate, mushroom-camouflaged speakers. 'Excellent,' mutters Clive. 'Good good good. Right then. Onwards and upwards, eh, Gerry?' He turns to pat her knee. 'D'you know, I'm almost beginning to enjoy myself!'

51

When Solomon Creasey first told Fanny about her husband's death she'd been drunk; and then numb, except to a sudden lightness, a great lifting of fear. She has thought and felt many things about Nick Faraday since that morning – and about her marriage, about his violence, and about all the years she spent needlessly fleeing from his non-existent shadow. For so many years now, her flight from Nick Faraday has been, if not a driving force, then an excuse for the lack of one in her life. Now, at odd moments throughout the day, tides of grief, regret, foolishness, recrimination, bewilderment, come swinging down on her, all of which she feels unable to share with anyone, least of all with Louis.

She was listening to the little boy called Carl (whose mother ran away with the woman from the mobile bank last summer) describe the difference between a pentagon and a hexagon, when the realisation came to her in a horrible, suffocating thump –

'. . . different sides going off in different shapes, especially the pentagon, which has sides going off mostly *this* way,' says Carl, pointing his arms haphazardly.

– the obvious cause of her husband's death, the reason Solomon had been so obtuse about it.

'But you really need a compass,' says Carl.

'Oooh,' she moans, covering her face, dropping her head into her hands, 'I'm stupid. *I'm stupid*. Why didn't I work it out before?'

'No, you're not stupid,' Carl says, looking at her in astonishment. 'I only just worked it out myself, see?'

The news of Nick Faraday's death has not put an end to the telephone calls, of course. In fact, they've been steadily increasing, so that now barely a day passes without Fanny receiving one, sometimes two, either at school or at home. Whoever it is always disguises his number, and although he (or she) never says anything Fanny can recognise him (or her) from the peculiar hiss, so even and steady, of warm air passing through nostrils. It reminds her of a dentist, or a doctor performing minor surgery.

And she is becoming strangely accustomed to it. Nowadays it's almost routine: she picks up the telephone, registers the cloggy silence, the soft hiss, immediately tells the caller to *fuck off*, and hangs up again. Since she realised it couldn't be her husband, for some reason it doesn't worry her so much. Not usually.

But on this occasion the pattern changes. It is twenty minutes before Dane's disciplinary meeting is due to start at the Old Rectory, and Fanny is still deliberating over how to dress. (Conservative – in case Mrs Guppy comes. On the other hand . . . Fanny's not to know that Solomon won't be there this evening. She hasn't seen him since he prowled back out into the rain with his beautiful silk dressing gown and his beautiful painting, but she's found herself wondering about him, guiltily – as if Louis could read her thoughts. She actually caught herself stepping out of her cottage the other day and sniffing the air for a hint of his sandalwood and lavender.)

On this occasion, the telephone rings – and the caller speaks. She goads him into speaking. On this occasion, for some wild reason, she hears him breathing and it makes her laugh.

'You're pathetic. You're pathetic. You're not scaring me. So really what the hell's the point?'

There is a startled pause in the even, hissy breathing and he hangs up. Fanny is triumphant, emboldened enough to put away the sensible linen skirt and to pull out the low-slung fitted jeans again, and a shirt in orange cheesecloth with very few buttons.

Fifteen minutes later, just as she's leaving the house, the telephone rings again.

'Hello?' she says briskly. She'd already forgotten about him.

A thin reedy voice, muffled by something – a cloth, his hand – held between his lips and the mouthpiece. But she knows the voice from somewhere. She's heard it before. 'Running late, are we?'

'What?'

'I left a little prezzie for you, Fanny. On the door.'

'You what?'

A girlish snigger; an hysterical girlish snigger – and the line goes dead.

It takes a moment, after that, for Fanny to brace herself. She picks up her keys and a bread knife from the kitchen, closes her fist around it, slides the fist into her bag. And forces herself to open the door.

Nothing. There's nothing there. She pushes the door closed behind her – and she spots it at once, hanging limp on the latch: a flimsy piece of red material. She peers at it. Picks it up. Damp. Sticky. A tiny pair of gauze-and-lace silky-look scarlet knickers.

'Oh!' She holds them out in front of her, too shocked to let go. '*Fuck! Oh, fuck!*'

Tracey and Macklan, also running late, just then emerge from the cottage next door. They glance across at her. Tracey looks from Fanny to the scarlet fabric held out in her hand, and then looks again, closer. 'Those are mine,' she says. 'What are you waving them round for?'

'What? I'm not. Of course not!'

Before she has a chance to say more, Macklan, in a dextrous flash of chivalry, has stretched across and snatched them from her. He stuffs them into his pocket.

'Give them back!' Fanny cries. 'They were hanging on my—'

'And you should watch your language,' Tracey says. 'Head teachers aren't supposed to talk like that. Come on, Macklan. We're late for Dane. Let's go.'

'Wait! Tracey, stop! I just found them. Someone put them on my door. I think they're— I think someone's just— Oh, please. Can't I come with you? Please, Tracey . . . *I need your help.*'

Tracey turns back. Heavy body. Billowing clothes to try to hide it. Pale, puffy face. (She used to be so pretty, Fanny thinks.) '*You* need help?' she says coldly. 'And what about Dane?'

Fanny doesn't know what to say.

'It's not his fault he's a Guppy, Fanny. And contrary to what you and everyone else seems to think, it doesn't automatically make him a criminal, neither.'

'Oh, come on! All the evidence. *And he's done it before.*'

'You disgust me,' Tracey says, her eyes filling with tears.

'Let's go,' mutters Macklan. They walk away.

'So-oo,' slurs Kitty Mozely, plopping crisps and a round of drinks on to the table, and settling herself back down in her

338

seat, 'on your tod again this evening, Louis? What's Miss Flynn up to then?'

'Oh. Some sort of meeting,' Louis says vaguely, because he's not entirely sure. He's stopped listening recently. All she talks about is school, and he has enough problems of his own. Like the fact that he has exactly no work at the moment. Nothing. Like the fact that he has no money in the bank, because he spent so much in Spain, and Mr Guppy's rent is due any minute. 'Some meeting to do with the school fire, I think. I dunno. She works too hard, Fan does.' He smiles. 'I can't keep up with it.'

'And does she know how worried you are?' purrs Kitty. 'About the work? About the lack of money coming in?'

'I expect so.' He shrugs. 'I don't know. Maybe not. It's not too interesting. I guess I probably haven't told her so much.'

'Hmm . . . You should watch out, angel boy. I hear Solomon Creasey's been dropping in on your Miss Fanny Flynn.'

Louis smiles. 'I was there, too, Kitty.'

'And he's a *pariah*, that man. So legend has it. Though I must admit he's never bloody well pariahed me . . .' A lazy, untroubled sigh. 'Ah, well,' she chuckles, 'plenty of other pariahs in the sea!'

Louis takes a slurp of his cider and says nothing. Quite nice, he thinks, to be thought of as a pariah again. Because Fanny – he loves her and all that, of course. He'll always love her, but he feels she's already beginning to take him for granted. Or maybe he's already taking her for granted? One way or the other . . .

'So,' Kitty's voice breaks in, 'I've spoken to Twiglet Prick. As promised.'

'Oh.' A pause while he tries to remember who she's talking about. The name certainly rings a bell.

'*My agent*, poppet.'

'Sure. I know. About the illustrations.' He waits, but she doesn't add anything else. 'Well? So what did he say?'

She leans forward. 'Tell me, my friend. Have you mentioned any of this to the little lady yet?'

He shifts uncomfortably. 'Don't call her that, Kitty,' he says amiably.

'Because, darling—' She leans a little closer, taking care not to touch him. He catches her musky smell, feels the warmth of her skin, hears all the libidinous, reckless promise in her voice. He glances over the rim of his cider into her eyes – avaricious, devilish eyes. *She's actually pretty damn fuckable*, he thinks. And Kitty reads it – as surely as if he'd shouted it aloud.

'Because, darling,' she says again, 'you're going to have to tell her sooner or later . . .' Kitty's lips curve. She leans closer, and closer still. 'And, Louis,' she murmurs into his ear, her chubby finger finding the wrist, sliding itself smoothly up inside his sleeve, '*I strongly suspect* your adorable little girlfriend doesn't even know we're friends, let alone business associates . . . Well, does she?'

Louis tries to ignore her.

'She doesn't, does she, Louis? You naughty man!'

'Don't you worry about that,' he murmurs. 'I'll worry about Fanny.'

'Well, then, you should,' she says, finger twirling through the hair on his deliciously golden forearm, 'because I have a funny feeling that you and I and old Twiglet Prick may be on to something big.'

'Is that so?' Louis replies lazily.

'It is so, Louis. He's already spoken to my ghastly publisher—'

'He has?'

She nods. 'And they're waiting, with bated breath, for you to send them your portfolio.'

'My portfolio?' Louis frowns slightly, wondering where it is. He's definitely seen it recently. 'That's exciting,' he says. Thinks about it. He'd actually enjoy doing her illustrations, if she's serious about it. Especially now, with no other work coming in. 'That is pretty damn exciting,' he says again.

She nods. 'My publishers are very keen to please me at the moment. For some reason. I have a feeling they'll do almost anything for me,' her hand drops from his arm, to beneath the table, 'if I ask them nicely . . .'

A heady silence. Louis doesn't move her hand or his thigh. He allows her hand to travel further, slowly, further . . .

'*Mmmm*,' she says. Even better than she'd hoped. 'Even better than I'd hoped!'

'Well, Kitty?' he asks, with another of those lazy half-smiles, allowing free rein to the practised hand at work beneath the table, 'and are you going to ask them nicely?'

'That all depends,' she says, undoing the zip, sliding inside, 'how nicely you're going to ask me . . .'

Why not? he thinks. If he thinks anything at all. 'We could go back to yours,' he says. 'But it's a lovely evening. We could just go for a little walk . . .'

'Ahhh, *wwwwalkies!*' gurgles Kitty. '*What fun!*'

52

Geraldine Adams has gone to town with her bits for the governing body. Her parlour, with its First Lady sofas rearranged to lend an element of a courtroom effect, is dappled with soft-but-sombre lighting, and pretty party plates laden with symmetrical arrangements of chicken satay and miniature vol-au-vents.

She decided champagne would be 'inappropriate' under the circumstances, but she's stocked up on wine and spirits – and beer for Mr Guppy, if he decides to come (no sign of him yet). And some Diet Coke for poor, dear little Dane.

The room burbles with the chatter of those governing bodies who were able to make it: Grey McShane and the General are there, muttering together about the presence of the billionaire, New Labour candidate for Lamsbury, Maurice Morrison.

Maurice Morrison, New Labour candidate for Lamsbury, who knows nothing about it and cares even less, is talking passionately to Clive Adams about Britain's need for further legal-aid reform.

Robert White is nodding distractedly at the vicar, who continues to find new ways to make the same point regarding the very late hour of this governors' meeting.

And Geraldine is in her element, tripping from group to group, putting people at their ease.

'Rather ironic,' she chortles to the marvellous Maurice Morrison, after he's admired the perfect proportions of her sofas and then of her house, asked her how many bedrooms it has, and how much land it came with, 'that the only one of us yet to turn up – apart from the Guppy party – is our terrific little head teacher, Fanny Flynn! But then she works so *hard*, Maurice. I worry for her. Have you met Fanny yet?'

'Haven't had the pleasure, Geraldine. Not yet. And I've been longing to meet her. I've heard so many wonderful things,' says Morrison, who's never heard anything about her, never spared her a second's thought. 'May I ask, how much did you pay for this house, Geraldine?'

'Goodness, what a question!' titters Geraldine. She's eyeing the thick, salt-and-pepper hairdo, the broad, worked-out shoulders beneath the light brown summer jacket, the tiny hint of a golden tan at the throat of his crisp, white open-necked shirt. She's thinking how incredibly important he is, and rich; how thrilling it is to have him in her house. She feels a little shiver of lust, which surprises her. It doesn't happen often.

Fanny arrives flushed, out of breath and edgy, closely followed by Tracey, Macklan and Dane. Tracey and Macklan are asked to join the two other witnesses in the television room. Dane Guppy, who looks on in dazed confusion at the swirl of activity all around him, is directed to a kitchen chair at the back of the parlour, facing into the semicircle of sofas.

'Right-o, everyone!' calls Geraldine, smiling broadly, clapping her hands. 'I think we're all here now. Perhaps we should get started.'

Geraldine has organised a seating plan, with the Reverend

in the middle, and herself with her thigh rubbing up against Maurice Morrison's linen trousers. Not only hostess for the night, but Governing Body Secretary, she has arranged a pretty escritoire in front of her own place, so she can take the meeting's minutes.

First a fireman, then a policeman, and finally Fanny, with her set of photographs, come forward to present their damning evidence. After forty-five minutes, Maurice Morrison glances at his watch, pulls a small, apologetic face, leans across and mutters to Geraldine that sadly he's soon going to have to dash. His helicopter is waiting.

'Do you enjoy school, Dane?' asks the Reverend.

Dane, who's been sitting mutely through all this, keeps his eyes to the floor. Sniffs, but doesn't reply. Clive Adams, his supposed advocate, has chosen to sit on a small chair in a far corner of the room, at least seven foot away from him, so Dane's all alone up there. Does he enjoy school? He has no idea. Silence.

'Dane,' comes a dry, clever voice from the Clive corner, 'suffers some difficulty in learning and has, in fact, exhibited some dyslexic behaviours, although these have yet to be formally identified—'

'Excuse me, Clive,' Fanny interrupts, 'I think I already discussed this with Geraldine, but actually Dane is *not* dyslexic.'

'Mmm.' Geraldine smiles at her, lips closed. 'I'm sorry, Fanny. But I believe he is.'

'And I'm sorry, but which of us is the trained teacher around here?'

'And I'm sorry,' Geraldine snaps back, 'but which of us is the mother of an eleven-year-old boy? I think he's dyslexic.'

'*He's not dyslexic.*'

'Could we possibly move on?' interrupts Grey, in a filthy

344

mood because Geraldine, in her ignorance, has sat him next to Maurice Morrison, whom he loathes and it's taking all his self-control not to wheel around and lamp him. 'I don't see what fuckin' difference it makes one way or the fuckin' other. A boy can set fire to a place without having to read the instructions on the fuckin' matchbox.'

'Please, Mr McShane,' says the vicar weakly. 'We have a young person present.'

'Of course it makes no difference,' agrees the dry voice in the corner. 'I mentioned it simply because, for one reason or another, Dane does not find his school life easy. Do you, Dane?'

Dane doesn't find any life particularly easy but his school life is – was – better than most. Nevertheless, obligingly, because he understands Clive is helping him, Dane shakes his head.

'Which isn't to say,' continues Clive, 'that he dislikes it sufficiently to set the place alight. A boy can dislike his school – even a boy with a predisposition to arson.' He laughs, a bloodless clever-clogs titter. 'I don't think we can say, *ipso facto* he is bound to destroy it!'

Chortles of support from the expected quarters: Robert White, nervous, not paying much attention but getting the gist; Maurice Morrison, not really listening either; and a belly laugh from Geraldine.

'Incidentally, I would be grateful,' says Clive, pushing his advantage as the laughter dies, 'if you would allow me to lead Tracey Guppy and Macklan Creasey through their evidence. Only because they're both so very young, and I worry they might feel intimidated . . .'

He calls them separately. Questions them separately, gently, and to each one of their contradictory answers, gives the appearance of believing every word. They claim Dane was eating breakfast with them right up until the moment he called the fire brigade, but they can't even agree on what it was they were all eating.

Mid-questioning Tracey, his second witness, who claims it was fried eggs, mushroom and bacon, Clive turns with a small, wry smile to the eight governors present, raises both hands in mock surrender. 'Eggs, bacon, *beluga caviar* – what does it really matter? I imagine you will all have spotted one or two anomalies in Tracey and Macklan's evidence . . .'

Tracey, standing silently before them, smiles with him. She doesn't recognise the word 'anomaly', but Clive has assured her he is on her side. 'Nevertheless, no one could deny that what these young people lack in accurate memory, they certainly make up for in love. Because Tracey Guppy loves her brother, doesn't she? And Macklan Creasey loves Tracey. And so I simply pose the question, when you were twenty years old – or nineteen, in Tracey's case – how much detail could you remember about your activities of over a fortnight previously? We must allow them both a little leeway, I think. We must allow them the *benefit of the doubt*.'

A silence. Clive turns to Tracey, dismisses her with a nod. She hesitates, as if she wants to say more. 'It's all right,' says Clive. 'You can go now.' She leaves the room, ruffling her brother's greasy head as she goes. 'You too, Dane,' Clive adds curtly.

'*Well*,' says the General to his neighbour Fanny Flynn, in a loud whisper, 'I didn't think that was much of a defence, did you? Thought that Adams chap was supposed to be top notch. I certainly shan't be employing him.'

Clive Adams turns his cold, watery-blue eyes to the General; he is wearing the faintest hint of a smirk. 'Maybe so,' Clive murmurs. 'But it's a difficult case to defend.'

'I say, Fanny, you're being awfully quiet,' says the General, ignoring him. 'Are you all right?'

'Mmm?' Fanny starts. 'Sorry. What's that?'

A little smile from Robert. 'Yes, we are a bit distracted this evening, aren't we, Miss Flynn?'

She pretends not to hear – is surprised, actually, by the surge of revulsion she feels now, just at the sound of his voice. She turns to the General. 'I'm fine,' she says. 'Are we ready to vote?'

'I believe we are,' says the vicar uncertainly. 'Anyone have anything to add?'

Maurice takes another little look at his watch. Clears his throat.

'I was thinking I could teach him at home,' Fanny says, as if the result were a foregone conclusion. 'An hour a day or something. Plus homework. A few hours at the weekends. Geraldine, perhaps you could help?'

Geraldine coughs. 'We shouldn't jump the gun, now, Fanny,' she says, not quite daring to look at her. 'The verdict isn't yet clear. I, for one, will be voting against exclusion.'

Fanny's jaw drops.

'Me, too,' says Robert, smirking.

'You *what*?' cries Fanny. 'Don't be pathetic, Robert. You're only doing it to annoy me.'

The General snorts with laughter.

'I'm sorry you should think it's pathetic,' Robert replies primly, 'to want to protect a kiddie's future. Of course I believe he started the fire. I imagine we all do, Fanny.' He glances quickly around the room, and seems to find enough reassurance there to go on. 'Of course the little lad may have *accidentally* started the blaze. But kiddies make mistakes. We all do. And even kiddies who make mistakes have a right to a future.'

'I'm not taking away his future,' Fanny snaps. 'I'm getting him out of a school he wants to set fire to, and I'm going to give him one-on-one bloody tutorage until the end of term. Or until he starts at secondary school, if he lets me. I'm not *taking* his future, Robert. I'm giving it back to him.'

'I'm terribly sorry, everyone, but I'm going to have to cast my vote and dash.' Maurice Morrison's handsome brow is slanted into an apologetic frown. He clears his throat, waits until he has everyone's attention. 'Well, now. As you may be aware,' he says, lowering his eyelashes, 'as you may be aware, I am *en principe* very much averse to school exclusions. I believe passionately, as I have said on numerous occasions, both publicly and privately, in the school-as-melting-pot,' (this, incidentally, in spite of having sent his own children, now adult, to a marvellous little melting pot in Switzerland, which cost £25,000 a term), 'as a place where youngsters learn to mix with one another, regardless of their difficulties and differences . . .'

'Just tell us how you're voting and fuck off,' snaps Grey McShane. 'You're not on the fuckin' telly.'

Morrison pays not the slightest attention. 'I've listened to the details of this unfortunate – tragic – case, and the principle remains the same. Whatever that young lad may have done,' Morrison stands up, slides himself into his lightweight linen jacket, 'it's important for him to feel *incorporated*. I believe it's our job as school governors to *care* for Dane, to nurture him. Not to throw him out with the rubbish—'

'Nobody's throwing him out with the rubbish,' interrupts Fanny, exasperated. 'I told you. We're offering him private bloody lessons. For free.'

A smile for Fanny. 'And yet I feel it is our responsibility not to "offer him private lessons". Not to treat him as an outcast, but to *guide* him *gently* back into the fold.'

'Aye. *And yet* – it's not your fuckin' fold that's going to go up in flames, is it?' breaks in Grey.

'Grey, really!' Geraldine frowns. 'It's so generous and kind of Mr Morrison to offer his precious time to our little village problems; to lend us a little wisdom from the front line, so to speak.' She beams at Morrison, who is tapping his pockets, checking for his mobile phones. 'I do think we might all show him a little more respect.'

'One day, my dear lady,' chuckles the General, 'I might tell you a story or two about this kind and generous gentleman.'

Maurice cocks his head, genial as ever, looks down at the General. 'And I assure you, General, my lawyers will always be listening. Incidentally,' he turns towards Geraldine, blinds her with his marvellous smile, 'did I take your card, Mrs Adams?'

'No. I don't believe you did. Clive!' He's already crossed the room, is already sliding a card into Maurice's hand. Maurice takes it casually, slips it into his pocket without even glancing at it. 'But come, General. Let's not fight. We're here for the youngster this evening, not for ourselves. I believe I've cast my vote. What about the rest of you?'

The voting process very quickly degenerates into a row, with the Pro-Excluders (Fanny, Grey, Reverend Hodge and the General) all offering to tutor Dane in their spare time, and the Anti-Excluders (Geraldine, Robert and Maurice) offering nothing, and still managing to maintain the moral high ground. Somehow, between all the arguments, the votes are cast; Morrison makes his excuses and slithers away; and Fanny takes Dane into a quiet corner to deliver the unhappy verdict.

'But I never *done* it!' he says, as the tears slither down his face. 'I never even bloody well *done* it!'

53

By the time Fanny returns to the Adamses' parlour, only her foes are left. The White House sofas are back where they're meant to be and Clive, Geraldine and Robert are sitting on them, muttering to one another. Their heads spring apart as Fanny opens the door.

'Fanny!' cry the Adamses. 'No hard feelings, I hope?'

'No. Not at all. I mean, I won – in a way. I'm just very sorry. He's still adamant he didn't do it, you know, and he sounds so convincing. In spite of all the evidence, there's a part of me which almost believes him.'

Robert smiles. A smile that makes his eyes smart. 'It's painful for all of us, Fanny. Nevertheless we should try not to be too naive.'

'I wasn't being naive—'

'Anyway,' interrupts Clive, 'can I get you a drink?'

'No. No, thank you. Very kind . . .' She's tried Louis's mobile but he's not picking up. She's going to have to make the walk home alone, which she doesn't relish after all that happened earlier, even with the knife still in her handbag. She wants to make the journey home while it's still light outside.

'Nonsense!' Robert shuffles his bony arse along the sofa, pats the seat beside him. 'Come on, head teacher,' he insists. 'Prove there are no hard feelings!'

'There are no hard feelings.'

'Well, come and sit down then!' he says.

'Yes, do,' says Geraldine. 'You must.'

'Rebuild a few of those unbroken bridges,' says Clive.

She sighs.

'Are you all right, Fanny?' Robert half-frowns, half-smiles. 'You look ever so worried. Has something happened this evening?'

It is Tracey, walking home arm in arm with Macklan, who appears to be the most unhappy about the governors' verdict. Her brother Dane trails along behind them plucking at cow parsley along the verge, wearing a goofy, private smile. He has a Safeways overnight bag crammed with dirty laundry slung over one arm because Tracey's letting him stay on the sofa at Macklan's tonight, as a treat, and she's agreed to help him with a wash.

Not only that, Miss Fanny Flynn just told him he was 'smart' or at any rate that he could be. With a little effort. ('We've got six weeks, Dane. In six weeks you could be as smart as any of them,' is what Fanny had said. 'Well. Not as smart as Scarlett. Obviously.' It had made him laugh.) Dane cannot remember a lesson, not ever, when he hasn't felt pissed off and inferior. The way his teacher talked tonight it seemed, after all, that this could change. It makes him grin.

'I didn't do it, you know,' he says cheerfully, tapping Tracey on the shoulder. 'Don't worry, Trace. Because I didn't.'

'I didn't ask, did I?' she says. 'If you want to ruin your life that's your business, Dane Guppy.'

'But maybe he didn't do it, Trace,' suggests Macklan tentatively. 'Nobody saw him.'

'Don't be so damn stupid.'

Just then, from behind a large, oblong tombstone on the other side of the churchyard wall they hear someone laugh; it's a distinctive, throaty laugh, spangled with mischief and sex, and recognisable to anyone who's spent any evening in the Fiddleford Arms recently. 'Kitty?' Tracey calls.

Muffled snorts.

Tracey and Macklan sniff the air. A tail of smoke is rising from behind the tombstone, and with it a sweet, unmistakable aroma.

'Louis?' calls out Macklan. 'Is that you?'

'*Shhh*!' (More muffled snorts.) 'Shh. Shut *up*!'

'Kitty? . . . Are you all right?' Tracey pushes back the churchyard gate. The three of them, Tracey, Mack and Dane, trek inside.

'What's going on?' Macklan demands.

Cautiously, they peer round the edge of the tombstone. They find Louis lying on his side and close by, Kitty, her skirt hitched up, shirt undone, a bottle of wine between her knees and a burning spliff in her fingers. She looks from one to the other, and then to Louis, and melts into a puddle of giggles.

'Tracey! Macklan! Hey! What a surprise,' says Louis, clambering to his feet, grabbing the joint from Kitty's fingers and treading on it. 'We were just talking about illustrations. And stuff. Weren't we, Kitty?'

'I'll bet,' Tracey says.

'Kitty's asked me to do her illustrations. For the book. Haven't you, Kitty?'

'Yyyyup!'

He gives up on her, turns back to Tracey. 'You remember? The book!' He smiles, a wobbly smile, very sweet. 'It's actually important that you believe me. Because nothing— Really, *nothing*—'

'Whatever,' Tracey mutters. 'None of my business anyway. Dane? Macklan? Are you coming?' They're standing side by side, mouths drooping in amazement. Tracey laughs. 'Get it together, lads! You never seen a couple of stoners before now?'

'"Stoners"?' repeats Kitty delightedly. '"Stoners"! . . . Stoners! A couple of stupid — crc . . . crr . . . crrrr . . . crrrr!'

Louis jabs her with his foot. 'Shut up, Kitty.'

'CRRRRRRRRRRR!' Kitty loses her balance, slides on to her side.

Tracey turns away. 'I don't know about you two,' she says to Macklan and Dane, 'but I've had enough of these jokers. I could do with a cup of tea.'

Back at the Old Rectory, Fanny sits on the farthest end of Robert's sofa and gulps back the Adamses' glass of wine as fast as politely possible. It's a large sofa and Robert's body is at least a metre away, and yet his almost-nearness is still burning her skin.

Clive and Geraldine, feeling more alive than they ever have since the Fiddleford downsize, pop up and down, offering nibbles and chattering happily about nothing – as if the conversation meant anything to anyone. No one is listening to a word.

Geraldine suddenly says, 'Fanny, sweetheart, I feel terrible. I'd love to invite you to supper but unfortunately we only have three sole, and I must admit I've promised the third one to Robert. Do you mind?'

'What?' Fanny's on her feet at once. 'God, no! Thank you, no! Actually, I must go!'

Geraldine stands up. 'Well, it was lovely to see you, Fanny. And no doubt we'll see each other very soon.'

'Absolutely. Of course we will.'

'So if it's not rude I'll nip into the kitchen and get the

grill on. And Clive, could you be sweet and fetch some white from the cellar?'

It is left to Robert to see Fanny out. When they're all alone in the dusk-lit hall he leans down from his bony height, places his soft lips very close to her ear. 'I returned a little something to your front door this evening,' he whispers. 'Did you see? I thought you might have been missing them.'

She veers away. Stares at him. 'But they weren't mine,' she hears herself saying, as if it mattered. As if it were faintly relevant. 'They were Tracey's.'

Something in his face changes. He looks stunned, thwarted. He looks revolted. Somehow he manages to smile. He gives a little shrug. 'Well, well,' he says lightly. 'I found them in the street, just outside your cottage. Nice little panties, too.' He winks at her. 'They'd suit *you* better, Fanny. Why don't you keep them? *I promise I won't tell!*'

54

'You tell her, Dane,' Macklan says, bringing in three mugs of tea. 'She won't listen to me. She'd be much better living here with me than living with that miserable old sod, wouldn't she? And you could live with us too, if you wanted,' he adds quickly. 'So long as you don't set fire to the place.'

Dane shakes his head. 'I didn't do it, Mack,' he says calmly. 'I never done it.'

'There's plenty of room for the both of you here. Isn't there, Trace?'

She smiles. 'There's not room, Mack.'

'Any case,' says Dane, 'it's not me what's stopping her, Macklan. It's Uncle Russell. She says he can't look after himself.'

'So better forget it, Mack,' she says before he has time to respond. 'You know I can't live here. Much as I'd like to . . .' She glances up, sees Macklan gazing on her, clearly unsatisfied, and gives him a kiss on the cheek. 'But thanks for asking. I'll come one day, I will. If you'll wait for me . . .'

'Anyhow,' Dane adds sullenly, 'I don't see why you suddenly care so much about Uncle Russell. It's not like he gives a fuck about you.'

She shoots him a warning look.

'He could drop dead for all I care,' continues Dane stubbornly.

'Yeah, well. He's not going to drop dead, is he? So shut your face.'

'He's a twazzock, an' I hate him,' says Dane. 'And a dirty old perv. He spies on people. Everyone knows that. I'll bet he spies on you.'

Her response, which would have been sharp, is blocked by a tremendous hammering at the door. All three of them jump.

'Tracey? . . . Tracey, are you there?' Fanny has run all the way from the Adamses', through the village, past Louis and Kitty in the churchyard, straight to Macklan's cottage. 'It's about the . . .' She stops to catch her breath. 'Tracey, *the red knickers*. Which you took from me this evening. I tried to tell you. Someone had—'

'Get *lost*, Fanny!' shouts Tracey, over her mug of tea.

'Don't, Trace,' mutters Dane. 'She's all right, Miss Flynn is. Don't be like that.'

'Look, I don't want to shout about this in the street, but I will if I have to.'

'Get lost, Fanny. Leave us alone,' Tracey shouts again.

'I think they were covered in *spunk*!'

'What did she say?' asks Dane.

'And you have to give them back so I can take them to the police. Robert White just told me. He just told me he put them there and Tracey, they were covered in . . . I think he . . .'

Tracey springs up. Spills her tea. Mutters under her breath.

'Leave her, Trace,' says Macklan. 'I can talk to her.'

But Tracey has already flung open the front door.

Fanny reels back in the face of her anger, steps away to lean against the garden wall. 'I'm so sorry, Tracey. About

Dane. I didn't want to do it. I had to. I think he needs help.'

Tracey blinks. Looks at her blankly.

'Tell me, Tracey,' insists Fanny, 'what would *you* have done? I want to help him. But I had to think about the other children.'

Tracey shakes her head. 'You said something about Robert White.'

'Yes,' Fanny says in relief. 'I did.' She takes one long, garbled, breathless sentence to explain herself. In the middle of it Tracey breaks away, whirls back into the sitting room, leaving the door open for Fanny to follow her in. 'I put them in the wash,' she says simply. 'With Dane's dirty stuff. We'll have to open the door.'

'How long ago?' asks Fanny. 'How *long*?'

'It was when the hospital show was on, wasn't it?' pipes up Dane. He indicates the silent, flickering television. 'And there's been the other one since then.'

'He's right,' says Macklan. 'It must be half an hour. What the bloody hell's going on?'

'Half an hour,' mutters Fanny. She and Tracey sink, side by side, on to the sofa. Dane and Macklan regard them curiously. A heavy silence falls.

'Well, come on!' yells Macklan. 'Don't just flop!' Tracey glances up at him, offers him a wan smile, but there are tears in her eyes and Tracey never cries. He crouches down beside her, runs a hand over her cheek. 'Maybe,' he says tenderly, 'when you've finished flooding my house and smashing up my clothes washer, you'll tell me what the hell's going on. In the mean time, I don't truly care. Anything, Trace, to get that miserable look off your face. I'll saw it open. I'll blow the bloody thing up.'

But he didn't need to bother. She'd set the machine on to a fast wash and as the four of them draw up in front of it,

357

it emits a subdued little click. The wash is finished. They can see the pants through the glass, resting on top of Dane's tracksuit, innocent, clean – and useless to them. Tracey shudders. She won't be wearing them again.

55

Clive Adams presents his case well when he telephones Jo Maxwell McDonald early the following morning. He lays a heavy emphasis, not on the needs of his ailing practice, not on the sad state of his numerous bank accounts, but on justice, and the powerlessness of the young. Jo's only half-listening. She's more concerned with the whereabouts of her twins, and the worrying silence emanating from the play-room next door, but she nods along.

Speaking in his fluent, glamorously technical, mostly incomprehensible monotone, Clive explains what it is that he and Geraldine intend to do. He says Dane's case could be a ground breaker, a precedent setter, one for the legal history books. In his legal opinion, he says, Dane Guppy's recent treatment had been in violation of Article 14, Article 5–1, Article 5–5 and Article 8 of the Convention for the Protection of Human Rights and Fundamental Freedoms . . . She doesn't entirely grasp what he's going on about but it sounds so impressively significant, and such a change from the usual Manor Retreat PR work, she feels herself gradually being pulled in.

Apart from which she has a contract with the Adams

Family Practice. It pays her a monthly fee, and she is aware that so far she hasn't exactly provided value for money. She disregards her reservations: that Fanny Flynn is a woman with her pupils' best interests carried close to her heart; that Clive Adams is a man who carries his own interests in place of a heart; that a boy who repeatedly sets fire to his school ought not to be allowed to spend too much time there. She smothers all her reservations and offers Clive the professional advice he pays her for. 'Make it a local issue. Make it *emotional*,' she says. 'You need local people to climb on the bandwagon with you.'

'Mmm,' he says carefully. 'That may not be easy.'

'Well, it's a child-friendly cause, and she's a local children's author. I'll put in a call to Kitty Mozely. You'd be doing each other a favour.'

'Excellent,' Clive says, pleasantly surprised. He'd been expecting more of a battle from her. He feeds a thin smile over the line. 'I thought maybe, with your father-in-law being somewhat antagonistic to the action—'

'Thank you, Clive. I'm extremely fond of my father-in-law. And Grey. And Fanny Flynn . . .' She hesitates; wavers a millisecond. 'But I do have a mind of my own.'

'Of course. Oh. And by the way. *Re* La Mozely. There's a small complication.' His line is bleeping. Someone's trying to get through. 'Kitty wasn't actually present at the meeting last night. For some reason. So perhaps you might allow Geraldine to call her first. Give it half an hour, would you?'

Through the window above her desk Jo spots the twins toddling off with their father down the drive. The twins won't toddle anywhere unless someone has bribed them; they prefer to lie on the floor and scream until somebody picks them up. But they're walking towards the village with a positive spring in their step. Bloody Charlie, she thinks. He's sneaking them out to the sweetshop.

'Fine,' she says briskly. 'I'll give it half an hour. Got to go now, though. Sorry. Something's come up.'

She's rapping frantically on the window before she's ended the call. Charlie strides on, pretending not to hear, which only confirms her suspicions. The twins aren't so sharp. They turn to wave. 'Getting Smarties,' they call out ecstatically. Fools. They aren't any more.

It was Kitty doing the bleeping. 'Oh, hello, Clive,' she says. 'It's you. What are you doing at home, clogging up the line?'

'Hello, Kitty!'

She's surprised. He sounds unusually lively. 'Aren't you supposed to be at work, Clive?'

'How are *you* this morning, anyway? Up with the lark! I'd have thought the world's most successful author could afford to get a bit of beauty sleep.'

'Yes, yes, yes.' She's not interested in Clive-bald-as-a-coot's feeble attempts at flirting. Besides which, she remembers distantly that he's been bloody rude to her of late. 'Anyway, Clive, is Geraldine there? I need to talk to her. Urgently.'

'Oh, by the way,' Clive says, 'guess what we've got winging its way to us, courtesy of a certain publishing company in the great city of Londinium?'

'What? Clive—'

'Should be arriving any minute, Kitty. Geraldine rang them up pretending she was a journalist.'

'Honestly. I've no idea what you're talking about. Could I speak to Geraldine, please?'

Clive laughs. 'I just hope you and Scarlett haven't written about us! Friends or no, Kitty old girl, we *will* sue. We could do with the money.'

'Oh, really,' Kitty says impatiently. At that instant, she can hardly remember what's in the book herself. 'Sue away, you silly old sod. Only for Christ's sake, put me on to Geraldine!'

'Oh. Right-o. She's just here . . . Geraldine!' he sing-songs. He's not been in such a good mood for years. Not since moving to Fiddleford. 'It's Kitty. La Mozely. Sounding a bit cross, actually. She says it's urgent.'

'Of course I'm not cross.' Kitty's already halfway through her second sentence before Geraldine's managed to put the receiver to her ear. 'Only I'm gagging to tell you my news, and he wouldn't stop talking to me. GUESS WHAT?' A slightly mad and lecherous gurgle. 'Ahhh. Geraldine! . . . Anyway, *buck up*! I said GUESS WHAT!'

'I'm glad you called actually, Kitty,' says Geraldine, squinting to read the scribbled note Clive has just placed in front of her:

Jo's calling Kitty in half an hour.
We want K to do publicity for us. Please prepare ground?

'You had us a bit worried. What were you up to last night? We were all waiting. In the end we had to go ahead without you.'

'What?'

'Didn't the vicar call you? He said he would.'

'Geraldine, I've no idea what you're talking about. So come on! GUESS!'

'Guess what? What you did?'

'Who I was with, of course! Who was bloody well *rutting me* like a *prize stallion* while you were waiting-for-me to do whatever-it-was last night. Who do you think? *Who?*'

'Kitty, please.' She laughs, in spite of herself. 'I haven't had breakfast yet. I've no idea. Louis?'

'HA, HAAA!' Kitty's laughing so joyously Geraldine has to hold the telephone away from her ear. '*You see?* And *ohhh, Geraldine,*' the lust in her voice sounds ready to choke her. She has to clear her throat. 'Believe me, I've seen a few in my time. But never have I – NEVER – Geraldine, you know I hate to be vulgar, but *WHAT A COCK!* I tell you, that man is built like a God.'

'Kitty—'

'What are you doing for lunch? And he's circumcised, which I *adore*, don't you? Nothing beats a *big, fat, circumcised*—' She has to pause, once again, to clear her throat. 'I was right, you see. I knew I could trust my instincts. I do seriously believe you can predict the size of a man's prick long before you get his trousers off, simply from the way he moves.'

'Kitty—'

'Perhaps I should do a little how-to-guess book. Save everyone a lot of time and disappointment. And make a fortune while I'm at it.'

'Kitty—'

'But that boy, Geraldine, *is a gift*. He's a gift sent to me from – well, never mind. Who cares?' She pauses, breathes in. 'So anyway. While Louis was *rutting* me like a *well-trained stallion*, in the *graveyard*, if you please, I suppose you were at some deathly-dull meeting with Fanny Flynn, were you? He said she had some school meeting to go to. Was I supposed to be there?'

'Of course you were. Didn't the vicar tell you? It was Dane Guppy's disciplinary hearing. Unfortunately – tragically – he was expelled.'

'Oh. Jolly good. So what do you think? Which reminds me, the worst part was— Geraldine, do listen. There we were rolling merrily around in the churchyard, and who should pop their ugly mugs over the wall, but bloody Dane Guppy, and Macklan Creasey and Tracey! All of them!' She gurgles again. 'I must admit I'd been smoking a teeny bit of pot. Haven't smoked pot for years, have you? They looked awfully disapproving.'

Kitty, it turns out, couldn't be less interested in how the governing body came to meet without her, or what they decided about anything, or why, and in her new ecstatic mood, is more than willing to put her name to anything Geraldine asks of her. And the Dane Guppy Appeal is as good a cause as any – rather better, in fact, since it also happens to antagonise her rival, Fanny Flynn.

'*Excellent*,' says Geraldine, once again redirecting the conversation from Kitty's obsessively detailed description of Louis's genitals. 'That's great. It'll be good publicity for you, too, Kitty. Anyway, Jo's going to call you in a bit, and you can fine-tune things with her. In the mean time, let's hold fire, shall we? Until Clive and I have let Fanny and the other governors know what we're doing.'

'What are you doing?' Kitty asks vaguely, although Geraldine's already explained it half a dozen times at least.

'We're making legal history, Kitty. That's what we're doing,' Geraldine's voice quivers with Kitty-like rapture. 'The press'll want to murder us, Kit, but if we play our cards right, we'll be on the front of every newspaper in the – well, in the EU! Yes. Christ. It's actually very exciting!'

56

Holding fire has never been Kitty's speciality. She hangs up on Geraldine, nestles back in the bed, and prepares to run herself through last night's memories all over again. But is surprised to find that she can't concentrate.

Images of Louis's studliness are being superseded by even more beguiling images – of herself, Kitty Mozely, as a Campaigner for Justice. On the front page of every news-paper. She's dressed in flowing white, of course, but with a sartorial nod to the other great female protesters . . . Kitty Mozely, Campaigner for Justice, with a banner and maybe a corset of some sort. And a little hat. And a bank of admiring press people before her – and Louis, of course, in front of them all, gazing lustfully through the lens of his camera . . .

She sits up, suddenly impatient. Why doesn't Jo Maxwell McDonald call her? She can't wait around all morning.

Kitty rummages among her bedclothes until she finds the telephone again, gets the number for Lamsbury's Atlas Radio and asks to be put through to the news editor, Stephen Knightly. It's a quiet office at the best of times, and a quiet news day even for Lamsbury. His only reporter is sitting beside him, reading yesterday's *Daily Mail*. Mr Knightly leaps on the call, listens to Kitty's story, which has plenty of good ingredients: Mystery Fire/Suspected Arson/Celebrity Author/Village at War etc., and dispatches his duty reporter to Laurel Cottage at once.

Jo telephones fifteen minutes later, having rescued her twins from the Smarties. But by then it's too late. Kitty has regained her mental focus. She doesn't even hear the telephone ring.

'I admit I don't entirely understand the legal *technicalities*,' Kitty beams at the Atlas Radio man. (He's nothing like Louis. Who hasn't called yet, in spite of her own three calls to him. But fit and young. And this morning she's insatiable.) 'Anyway, I don't really want to get into technicalities with you. What I want, from this encounter, is for us to *get the ball rolling*. Do you understand? Because this isn't about technicalities. It's about children and liberty. Liberty for children to do and be as they want to do and be.'

'Excuse me – excuse me for interrupting, Miss Mozely. But you've mentioned liberty a couple of times. I'm just wondering – I can see there are several issues at stake here but I'm not clear exactly what liberty has to do with any of them *specifically*?'

'What's that?' She frowns. (What's he talking about?) 'Don't be ridiculous. Liberty,' she says, 'is integral to everything. You can't talk about justice – you certainly can't talk about children – without talking about liberty in the same breath.'

'Well, perhaps, but I mean surely you're not suggesting the boy should be at liberty to set fire to the school if he wants to?'

Kitty and the young reporter are sitting at her kitchen table among piles of old newspapers and general muck.

Before he arrived, Kitty had hauled mind and body from their contemplation of Louis, to rummage through her musty, crowded wardrobe. Inside she discovered an old Vivienne Westwood stretchy satin bodice, quite similar to a corset. She's wearing it (bursting gloriously out of it) with an open shirt, and a wedding hat, stiff and wide brimmed, which she has balanced at a jaunty angle on her head. Both items, she feels, make a sartorial nod to the noble efforts of her sister suffragettes and they inspire her, as she sits there, to let rip on the subject of liberty, justice and so on.

She's slopped a grubby cup of very strong coffee in front of him, with no milk because there isn't any. He's a good, clean boy, ambitious and serious, and he's never encountered anyone like Kitty before. What with her musky smell and husky voice and occasional cheeky caresses, he's ashamed – alarmed – to find himself feeling aroused, and more than a little out of his depth. He earnestly desires to get to the heart of what it is she's saying. It doesn't cross his mind that there *is* no heart, that she's simply killing time until a better opportunity for jollification comes along.

Kitty's hat and head emerge from her enormous handbag where she's been foraging for a pack of Gitanes cigarettes. She puts her matches on the table and a Gitanes to her lips, and waits for the good, clean boy to light it for her. It takes a second or two for him to understand what's expected of him.

'Oh!' he says, pouncing on the matches, striking one with clammy, shaky hands. 'So sorry!'

'Where were we?' she breathes, looking up at him through the smoke. 'What was the question again?'

'I was just saying,' he repeats patiently, 'surely you're not suggesting the boy should be at liberty to set fire to the school just because he wants to?

'Hmm? Don't be fatuous . . .' A pause while he blushes

and she wonders again why it is that Louis hasn't called. 'Could you be sweet,' she says, squinting at her mobile telephone. 'I don't have my contact lenses in. Is this bloody thing on, or isn't it?'

'Yes, yes,' he says helpfully, 'it's definitely on.'

So why hasn't he called? What's he doing? Her mind wanders.

She imagines him, right now, Louis and his magnificent cock, *sticking it* to Fanny Flynn. She is ten years younger than Kitty, fitter, prettier, nicer – *better*. A *better* human being. Kitty feels a shock of self-disgust; of anger and jealousy. It comes upon her from time to time. Inevitably. And the consequences are never positive. 'What I "*suggest*"—' she snaps suddenly. 'Are you taping this? What I "*suggest*" is really neither here nor there. I'm not a lawyer.' Suddenly she leans forward, drops her voice to a husky murmur so that the nice boy has to lean right in. 'But it's a bit rich, isn't it, dear—' (she's forgotten his name) 'Dear – boy – when Little Miss everyone-in-Fiddleford-adores-me Fanny . . . *Fuck-me-Flynn*—'

'Sorry, could you speak up a teeny bit. I don't think the tape's going to get—'

Kitty stretches across him, pulls the tape recorder closer. 'I said it's a bit rich when Little Miss Perfect Fanny Flynn turns out not to be quite so Miss Perfect as she pretends.'

'Hmm?'

Kitty taps his arm, doesn't notice her cigarette ash tumbling on to the back of his hand, 'When Little Miss Perfect turns out to have been secretly married to a junkie, heroin-addict jailbird.' She leans back suddenly. Very matter of fact, and pauses for a deep, malicious drag on her cigarette. 'Who almost certainly,' she adds, 'died of Aids . . .'

'I'm sorry? I don't understand—'

'I mean really – has anyone given the wretched woman a

drugs test? I doubt it. Let alone an Aids test! . . . Have they?'
Kitty's husky voice is growing louder. 'She's probably
infecting our poor children *as we speak*—'

'Miss Mozely,' he interrupts, his innocent brow creased
in consternation. 'Sorry, but I'm not sure if this is really very
relevant—'

'There ought to be legislation. *Paedophiles* aren't allowed
anywhere near our children. So what about junkies? Disease-
ridden junkies? And I demand, actually *I challenge*, that
young woman to be Aids and drugs tested. Immediately! . . .
And *that*, young man, is your story! Never mind all the rest
of it. Do you understand?'

The reporter scuttles back to Atlas Radio's HQ not long
afterwards. He delivers his tape to the news editor, Stephen
Knightly, declaring he doesn't want anything more to do
with it. 'She's barking mad,' he says. 'Seriously. Dangerously
insane. And the whole story's very nasty and very irresponsible.'

Stephen Knightly throws back his head and roars with
bitter laughter. 'I suggest,' he replies, his fingers already
dialling the number for Fiddleford Primary School, 'that you
have a serious think about your future in journalism, my
boy, if "irresponsibility" and "nastiness",' he pronounces
them with a lisp, 'are going to upset you so much.'

Fanny's in her office being outmanoeuvred by Robert, once
again. She had sent glass-eyed Mrs Haywood to summon
him, and he glided into the room wearing an insufferable
little smile.

'I delivered the – object – you left on my door last night
to the police this morning,' she lies, 'I imagine you know
why,' and waits, in vain, for his little smile to wither. It
grows.

'Why did you do that, Fanny?' Slowly, deliberately, he produces a tissue, folds it neatly – once, twice – holds it to his reddened nose, and blows.

They eye each other then, any pretence at civility between them now quite gone. He leans across her desk, drops the used tissue into the bin beside her feet. 'You must think I'm very stupid . . . By the way, has the LEA been in contact yet?'

She can't speak. She wants to throw up.

'No?' he says. 'Only I must admit, I have mentioned a little incident to them . . .'

There is a tap on the door and Mrs Haywood plops a hand-delivered letter on to her desk. Fanny opens it listlessly, with Robert looking on. Something formal, legal, typed on expensive, headed paper. *Adams Family Practice*, it said on the top. 'Oh, yes,' Robert says, peering down at it. 'And then there's *that*. Well. Perhaps I should leave you to it. Was there anything else?'

It's just as Robert is leaving, and Fanny has dropped the Adams Family letter back on to her desk to be read later, that the call from Atlas Radio comes through. Stephen Knightly the news editor explains that one of his reporters has just returned from interviewing Kitty Mozely, whom he understands has a daughter at the school.

'That's right,' says Fanny.

'She's very worried. Are you aware of that?'

Fanny suppresses a groan. 'Really. What about?'

She has to ask him to repeat his next question three times, because the single word 'Aids' keeps drowning everything else out.

. . . Aids . . . drug abuse . . . marital relations . . . under-standable concern among parents . . . can you confirm or deny . . .

'I'm sorry. What did you say?'

370

. . . Convicted criminal and heroin addict . . . Aids . . . children in your care . . . infectious nature . . . do you deny . . . ?

'I'm sorry. Could you say that again?'

She thinks of Nick wasting away, of how lonely and frightened he must have been; she thinks of all his unimaginable suffering, and of how it has been reduced to nothing more than this. For a moment she forgets to hate him, or to hate herself for ever having loved him. Fat, hot tears roll down both cheeks, and all she can say is, 'I've already had an Aids test. Like a lot of women my age.'

An astonished silence from Stephen Knightly. Then, 'So you don't deny it?'

'I've already had an Aids test,' she says again. 'I've had two, actually, since Nick left. Like a lot of women my age. That's all I have to say. You can tell Kitty Mozely she has nothing to worry about. Thank you. Goodbye.'

Stephen Knightly looks down at his notes. He thinks he can certainly make a package out of the story. And why not? A bit of midsummer fun. A mini-scoop. Might brighten up someone's day.

Fanny looks down at her notes, at the hand-delivered letter, on the very thick, headed paper . . . It's from Clive and Geraldine, or rather, from the Adams Family Practice. *Good name*, she thinks. She reads it and rereads it. *Posh paper*, she thinks. *They're taking me to court*, she thinks. *Perhaps*. But the words keep swimming off the page.

Stephen Knightly didn't tell Fanny where Kitty Mozely got her information from and Fanny didn't ask because she immediately assumed it was Solomon. And as she sits there, pretending to make sense of the Adamses' impossibly-worded letter, she finds it's that – Solomon's betrayal – which she minds about most.

She glances at her watch. Outside she sees Robert, back

on playground duty. He's out there in the blazing sunshine, all hunched up in his lightweight polo-neck, blowing into his tissue again. He must feel her eyes burning into his back because he turns, with the tissue still to his nose, and gives her a little wave. She looks away. Picks up the telephone and dials.

'Solomon. It's me. Fanny.'

'Fanny!' He sounds pleased. She pictures his lean, hawk-like face creaking into a smile – his first all day, though she wouldn't have known it. She hears him stretching back in his chair, settling down to gossip. 'I was wondering when you'd resurface! I've been worried about you. How's it going? Are you OK?'

She wavers. The temptation to sink into the warmth of his apparent concern briefly prevents her from answering. She clears her throat, reminds herself why she's telephoned.

'Fanny?' He misinterprets her silence. 'Nothing's happened? Are the children—'

'No, no. The children are fine. *The children are fine.*' She bites her lip. Realises, to her horror, that if she says another word she's going to cry.

He waits.

'Well . . . that's good.' He waits patiently. 'Changed your mind about that painting yet? It's still here, you know. You can come and get it any time. It's just sitting there, and will be until the moment you see sense and agree to take the bloody thing away.'

'I've just had a call from Atlas Radio. If that means anything to you.'

He thinks about it. 'Can't say it does, Fanny. Is it meant to? What did they want?'

'They'd been interviewing Kitty Mozely. And they were asking me about Nick.'

'Oh. I'm sorry.'

'About him and Aids. About me and Aids, actually. They wanted to know how it was that their primary school head-mistress could be "secretly" married to a junkie convict who died of—' She can't say it again. Somehow. She knows if she says it again she'll start crying. 'But what *I* want to know is how the fucking hell Kitty fucking Mozely was in a position to tell them anything about it in the first place . . . Solomon? . . .'

'I'm sorry, Fanny. I'm sorry this has happened. But I don't quite see—'

'*You* drink with her, don't you? *You* said you thought she was funny! Who the hell else would have told her?'

A pause, while Solomon swallows his anger. He deliberates between giving her the obvious reply or simply hanging up.

'Solomon? Tell me. *How did she find out?*'

'I think,' he says gently, 'you should be asking the question a little closer to home . . . Call me again, if you want to, when you've worked it out.' And the line goes dead.

57

Kitty wants Louis. Since the little man from Atlas Radio scuttled away, several hours ago now, she has checked her land line, ensured it's still on the hook. She's called her land line from her mobile and her mobile from her land line. Both in perfect order. She's called his mobile and his land line from her mobile and her land line. She's disguised her number and done it all again. Nothing. Nothing. Nothing.

She's tempted to go to the pub, see if he's there, and yet is unwilling to leave the house just in case he comes to visit. Which he might.

Ooooh. He might. She's pretty sure he said he might.

Finally, at her wits' end, she has a brainwave. She tries him at Fanny's.

He's upstairs on the bed, smoking a spliff, pretending to think of things to photograph but actually feeling too depressed with himself and what he did with Kitty – in fact, with the all-round state of his life affairs – to do anything except stare out of the window, occasionally flicking ash into his trainer.

He's been ducking Kitty's calls all morning, but when she starts leaving a message for him on Fanny's answer machine

– all throaty chuckles and admiring references to his genitals – he realises he's going to have to confront her. He picks up.

'AHHHH!' she cries triumphantly.

'Hey, Kitty,' he says (polite, as ever). 'How's it going?'

'Angel, it would be going a lot better if you could bloody well answer one of my telephone messages. What are you doing?'

'*Working*, Kitty!' he says, as if it were obvious. 'I'm supposed to be in Torquay this evening. Photographing a bunch of guys . . . with metal detectors.'

'Really?' No. Not really. Louis lies very well. 'That's a shame. Because I've just this minute got off the telephone to Twiglet Prick—'

'Really?' No. Not really.

'Of course, "really"! And I've got excellent news. I was thinking you might like to celebrate with a late lunch at the pub.'

She's tickled his interest now. Because just now, when he was lying on the bed without an ashtray or any commissions, he was thinking what a shame it was that he hadn't made a career out of his illustrating instead. And he was wondering, a little wistfully (because at that stage, five minutes ago, he was planning never to speak to Kitty again), whether her offer to him to illustrate the £650,000 children's book had been a genuine one.

'So what's the news?' He smiles.

'Ah-ha! You'll have to buy me lunch to discover that. What time do you have to be in Torquay?'

She wonders, after she's hung up, what news she's going to be able to come up with. Because she has never mentioned Louis's name to her agent or publisher and, until this instant, has never consciously had the slightest intention of doing so.

Nevertheless, she clearly understands that behind her merriness and his pleasantness a tacit deal has been struck. She understands that if she's to have him again she must tempt him with something more than her insatiable, middle-aged body.

She hesitates. The book, she remembers, isn't meant to be carrying illustrations at all. She, Scarlett, Twiglet and the publisher have already discussed it. Her hand hovers over the telephone. She imagines – she *remembers* – Louis's *thick, hot, rigid, throbbing*— Clears her throat. And makes the call.

'Ah. Twiglet,' she begins.

'Twiglet speaking,' he smiles. 'Hello, Kitty, dearest.' He's never asked her why she's taken to calling him that, but he assumes it's affectionate, after all he's done for her recently. He listens while she tells him what she wants.

'But Kitty, we already established, the book's not having illustrations.'

'What? Of course it's having bloody illustrations! Don't be mad. Tell them Louis is doing them. And ring me back when you know how much money you can get. I need some sort of figure by lunch. In about half an hour.'

'Come on, Kitty,' he says. 'You know it's not as simple as that. They don't want illustrations. We did discuss it, if you remember.'

'We did not. I have no memory of it.'

'That's strange. I distinctly remember—'

'It's bloody outrageous!'

'It is, Kitty. And I'm sorry. I'm sure Louis's a fabulous illustrator. However, if you read the contract it is fairly clear—'

'Oh, don't be boring, Twiglet,' she says and plonks down the receiver.

*   *   *

Kitty thinks about that. She turns it over and over, and in the pub later that afternoon she runs her gleeful hand up Louis's perfect thigh . . .

'Good news,' she murmurs, 'they've agreed to give you £10,000, Louis.' She burrows inside the zip of his jeans. '£10,000 for ten little watercolours. Think you can manage that?'

He twists in his seat to look at her, inadvertently pinching her hand in the fold of his jeans.

'They don't want to discuss it with me first? They don't want to look at my work?'

'Nope. They trust my judgement entirely. As they should, of course.'

'Just like that?' He's not convinced, she can tell.

'Our good friend Twiglet Prick is working out the details as we speak. I could even give you an advance, if you like . . . Would you like that, Louis? Would it help?'

Louis doesn't quite meet her eye. He shrugs. 'I, er . . .'

'I only suggest it because you mentioned you were feeling very broke. And God knows, we've all been there. Darling, sorry. Could you budge a bit? Your zip is pinching my . . .'

He looks down. 'Oh! I'm sorry, Kitty.'

'That's better.' She nuzzles his earlobe. 'Let's go home. I think a *bed*, this time, don't you? Scarlett's at school.'

'Actually, Kitty, y'know I'm not really—'

She puts a finger to his lips. 'Let's talk about it when we get there, shall we . . .'

'ARE YOU LISTENING?' Jo's voice, booming out of Kitty's answering machine, sounds angry: controlled but very angry. She's had a horrible call from Solomon Creasey, whom she finds alarming at the best of times. Solomon had telephoned Atlas Radio and in one terse conversation with the news editor, been brought quickly up to speed with everything that was going on. Solomon was furious: peculiarly furious, it occurred to Jo, since none of it especially concerned him.

Jo had insisted she knew nothing about Kitty's Atlas interview, which was true in a way. 'Why the hell not?' he yelled. 'You represent her. And you represent the school. You should bloody well know when it's under attack. Apart from which—'

'OK, OK, OK,' she interrupted. Feeling guilty, and more than a little nervous. (She'd been regretting her secret conversation with Clive Adams all morning, wondering how to prevent herself from getting any more involved. And now this.) 'Shut up, Solomon. I get the message.'

'Good. So I take it you'll be telling the Adamses and Kitty Mozely to organise their own loathsome little self-promotion exercises in future?'

'I don't know,' Jo said stubbornly. 'I'll think about it. What did Kitty say, exactly, anyway?' she asked – again. For the fourth time, in fact. 'Is her first husband dead? I didn't even know she'd been married.'

'And maybe you should call Fanny,' Solomon says. 'Tell her the interview's not going out, will you?'

'It isn't? . . . How come? How do you know?'

'And you can clarify whose bloody side you're on while you're at it. The poor girl's going mad. She thinks she's surrounded by enemies . . .'

'ARE YOU LISTENING? Kitty? Are you there?' Jo's voice continues to blast out from the answer machine on the cluttered kitchen counter. Beneath it Louis, the stallion, pauses between ruts, offers a questioning look to his mount. Who shakes her mane impatiently, and bucks him on.

They hear Jo click her tongue. 'I've just been brought up to date about your interview with Atlas Radio this morning, during which I understand you made some extremely unhelpful comments.' Jo breathes deeply, annoyed that she

378

still doesn't know exactly what they were. 'Which comments, for your information, will never be broadcast. Anyway, I wonder if you could call me. Please.' Another pause, as if she can't decide whether to hang up or to say more. 'In fact, no. Don't call me back. I don't want anything more to do with this mess. I don't want anything to do with any of you any more. Not you or Clive or Geraldine. I don't like what you're up to, frankly, and I'm sorry I was ever involved. You're all bloody well fired.'

'Oops,' murmurs Louis with a distracted smirk, running his hands from stifle to flank, plunging himself deep inside her. 'She sounds a bit upset . . . What was all that about?'

But Kitty doesn't want to tell him and he's not that interested in the answer anyway.

58

Fanny's just winding up a call to her mother (feeling much better; turds good and solid again) and catching the late-afternoon sun on her front porch, when she spots Louis trying to skulk back into his cottage. She hasn't seen him all day.

'Hey, Mum, got to go . . . *Louis!*' He pretends not to notice her. Fanny blows a kiss to her mother and leaps up to catch him. 'Where've you been all afternoon? I've been looking for you. I've got so much I want to tell you,' she gabbles at him. 'It's been such a horrible day. What are you doing now? Shall we go for a drink?'

'Fan!' he says, edging away from her. He tells her he's been at Kitty's, because like all good liars he knows it's always safer to stick with as much of the truth as possible. 'I've been having a drink with your old friend Deadly Nightshade,' he says lightly, hoping Fanny will smile. He explains that Kitty's publisher has commissioned him to do ten little watercolours for her book. 'Good news, hey? Looks like Deadly's come up trumps.' He doesn't mention that Kitty's publisher hasn't yet laid eyes on his portfolio, has no idea what his work is like. He doesn't mention, either, that

Kitty has offered to advance him the £10,000 fee. Fanny might suspect the commission wasn't for real. 'Anyway, I thought I'd just go take a shower, but then maybe we could celebrate . . . Maybe even venture out of Fiddleford for the night,' he adds. Not wanting to bump into Kitty. 'How about that! Life beyond Fiddleford. Imagine it!'

But Fanny doesn't smile. 'You were at Kitty Mozely's?' she says, looking at him strangely. 'I didn't realise—'

'What? What didn't you realise?'

She shrugs. 'I don't know. I suppose I didn't realise you were still such good friends.'

'Well, I'm not,' he says tetchily, '"such good friends".' He backs away from her, slides the key into his lock. 'Anyway, I'll catch you later, OK? Give me ten.'

'Only – because, Louis listen, Kitty gave an interview to the local radio this morning. Did she not mention it?'

But Louis has already slipped inside and shut the door behind him.

Fanny knows Louis. She knows he would never have meant any harm by it. It's just that he's friendly. He loves to talk. But still, when she pictures the moment of his actually mouthing the words, his telling Kitty the long, involved, unhappy story, she feels a stab of pain. She can see the expression of prurience on Kitty's face, of pleasant, conversational detachment on Louis's. She can see their heads bent together somewhere, in some quiet corner – at the Fiddleford Arms, perhaps. Or maybe in Louis's Arms . . .

'Louis!' Fanny shouts through the door at him. 'I think you and I need to talk.' But Louis doesn't reply. And they don't go out that night, after all. Louis telephones her ten minutes later claiming he's just been sick.

'Too much excitement, I guess,' he murmurs, 'or something. I feel like shit, Fan. I'm going to go to bed.'

'All right then,' says Fanny. She doesn't try to argue. She

certainly doesn't offer to come round and help. In fact, as she wishes him goodnight and hangs up the telephone she feels nothing more than a sad flutter of relief.

Next door, Tracey Guppy has locked herself into Macklan's bathroom and is refusing to come out. Half an hour earlier, as they were lying side by side in bed, he'd run a hand over her hard, round belly and tentatively suggested she should go to see a doctor about it.

'Because that's not *fat*, is it?' he said, giving it a tap. 'It's not blubbery like fat. Maybe there's something wrong with you. And if there is, Trace, you're better off finding out sooner than later. I don't need to tell you that.'

'It is *fat*,' she said, trying to wriggle away from him.

'No, it's not,' he said, holding her firm and tapping again. 'Listen!'

Tap-tap.

She elbowed him in the stomach and scrambled wildly out of the bed.

Now he's tapping not on her belly but the bathroom door. 'Tracey?' he shouts through the keyhole. 'I'm sorry. I'm sorry, Trace. I don't care what kind of fat it is. I mean, you're not fat, anyway. *I love you! . . .*'

Silence.

'Baby, I'm on my knees here . . . Tracey? . . . I'm – I'm *proposing* to you . . .'

Silence.

'Tracey? Can you hear me? You're not fat, you're beautiful. I love you. Will you marry me? Please? . . . *Please*, Trace. I didn't mean to upset you. Never. I never want to upset you. *Please*, unlock the—'

Her head pops round the bathroom door. Her eyes are bloodshot, her thick make-up smudged down her cheeks. She's smiling at him. 'Of course I'll marry you!' she says.

But when his face lights up and he opens his arms, something inside her seems to buckle. She drops her head on to his chest and sobs, racking sobs that shake her whole body.

'Trace,' he pleads. 'What is it? What's wrong? We can't be married if we're going to have secrets. You've got to tell me what's wrong.'

But she offers no explanation.

'Is it because you don't want to marry me? That's OK! We don't have to marry, Trace. Not if you don't want. It was just a suggestion. We can do whatever we want.'

'No, I want to marry you. I love you, Mack.'

She sobs for some time, until finally she vomits in the bathroom sink.

They don't mention the swollen belly again, but unlike Fanny and Louis, alone in their separate beds, Tracey and Macklan make love to each other with great tenderness that night. And afterwards Tracey finally agrees that in the morning she will talk to Uncle Russell about moving out.

59

Clive and Geraldine have distanced themselves very smoothly from what they refer to now as 'the Kitty Incident'; they have rung Atlas Radio, thanked them for not broadcasting the dreaded interview, and apologised fulsomely on Kitty's behalf. (Stephen Knightly the news editor had sounded shifty. Having that morning taken delivery of Solomon Creasey's thick brown envelope of fifties, he couldn't wait to get Geraldine Adams off the telephone.) The Adamses have also, in spite of all Jo's initial anger, succeeded in parting company with Maxwell McDonald PR on the most civilised terms, sending Jo a magnum of Bollinger as a peace token.

'Now. We're *absolutely* clear on this, aren't we?' says Clive slowly, having handed over their entire new batch of presents. 'This is not going to cost you a penny, Mrs Guppy. Not a halfpenny! OK?'

Mr and Mrs Adams are back beneath the crumbling porch at Mrs Guppy's house, and though she has melted sufficiently to release her tight hold of the front door, she is still a long way from inviting them inside. She stands before them, a wall of suspicion and inhospitality, with a bank of cuddly toys, flower paintings, milk chocolates, earthenware crockery and TV theme books behind her. (Mr and Mrs Adams have learnt from their mistakes.)

'Not even a quarter of a penny,' Clive reiterates, one more time. 'All our – considerable – expertise, and absolutely, one hundred per cent FREE!'

Mrs Guppy nods, her beady eyes fixed on him. 'That's right,' she agrees.

'That's right . . .' Clive eyes her nervously.

'And so what we need now, Mrs Guppy,' picks up Geraldine – she laughs, as if it were quite the silliest-bittiest thing in the world – 'is a *signature*.'

Mrs Guppy shakes her head. 'You're not getting that.'

'Yes. That is, yes and no,' chuckles Clive. '*Yes*, I can understand your concern. *Of course*. And no, we—'

'You're not getting that.'

The Adamses finally agree to pay the Guppys cash. In exchange for which the Guppys will allow them to defend their son against the school free of charge, and for as long as it takes, and they will also give an interview to a local TV station, expressing their outrage at his treatment.

'Oh, my crumbling Mondays,' says Mrs Guppy, holding a fat hand to her mouth.

'Don't you worry, Mrs Guppy,' assures Geraldine. 'I'm going to coach you! We won't let those TV cameras anywhere near you, not until you're good and ready!'

It takes every molecule of her ambition and courage, but at the end of the meeting Geraldine leans forward, her head crossing the threshold of the Guppy home for the first time, and she pecks Mrs Guppy on her cheek.

It makes Mrs Guppy blush.

'And when all this is over,' says Geraldine, barely missing a beat, 'you must come and have dinner with us at the Rectory. Maybe a little barbecue or something. Wouldn't that be fun? Come early. So the boys can have a little splash. Or maybe all of us—' But then the image of Mrs Guppy in her bathers, having a splash, comes to her unbidden, and strikes Geraldine dumb. Dumb. It is left to Clive to finish the sentence.

60

Uncle Russell is in his wheelchair in front of the television when Tracey and Macklan come to call. There's an advertisement playing, very loud, for a 'lift-firming' face cream, rich in antioxidants.

'TV's mended, then!' shouts Tracey, smiling nervously over the volume. 'That's good! I called the electrician again yesterday. He said he'd drop by, but you know what they're like!'

Uncle Russell's eyes remain bonded to the screen.

'How are you, then?' she shouts, putting her bag down on the cellophane-covered sofa. She knows better than to wait for a reply. 'I brought you some Pot Noodles,' she continues. 'And I put a chicken in the fridge. I'll cook it Sunday.'

Still, he doesn't bother to acknowledge her.

'This is *Macklan*,' she continues. 'Uncle Russell? I've brought my boyfriend to see you. Do you want to say hello?'

He gives Macklan a quick up and down and turns back to the screen, moved on from skin-care products now to the local news.

'Solomon Creasey's boy, you are,' Uncle Russell informs him.

'That's right, Mr Guppy,' agrees Macklan warmly (keen for the meeting to go well). 'Solomon's eldest. Not much younger than he is, in fact! More like a brother, really. Though don't tell him I told you that!'

'Must be wealthy, then.'

Macklan flushes, opens his mouth, but Tracey quickly shakes her head, nudges him not to rise.

Uncle Russell sees it, as he sees everything. He smiles slyly to himself.

'Must be very wealthy,' he says again, for the hell of it, and quickly dissolves into one of his coughing fits.

. . . *Angry parents Marian and Ian Guppy* . . . They hear the names belching out of the television over Russell Guppy's rasping. They glance up at the screen simultaneously, all of them, to see Tracey's mother and father, barely recognisable in their grimacing, smiling Sunday best, wedged together on a sofa.

'That's Mum's sofa!' Tracey cries.

Uncle Russell stops mid-cough, something he hasn't managed to do for a long time.

'Look, Macklan!' she exclaims. 'Mum's got lipstick on! See? Doesn't she look gorgeous!'

'*It's hard enough for youngsters these days, what with all the crime and drugs on the streets,*' recites Mrs Guppy, her oddly coloured lips stretched into a disconcerting smile.

Tracey giggles. 'Don't sound like her!'

'Shut your face, Tracey,' snaps Uncle Russell. 'I can't hear what she's saying.'

'*They deserve nurture-to-go, and also support from the educational arena, not ostracisation . . .*' Mrs Guppy pitches from one unfeasible sound bite to another, until finally, lost in a maze of meaninglessness, she grinds to a random halt.

Ian pitches in. He is small beside her, and throttled in the jersey. '*We're totally disgusted,*' he says. '*It makes us physically sick.*'

'*But Dane's a good boy,*' his wife adds suddenly. '*He's a good boy.*' A pause. The camera turns. Suddenly she drops her head, so that a full two-thirds of the screen is taken with nothing but the grey roots and thick, black strands of her talcum-powdered hair. A snuffle, and then another. Beside her, tiny, wiry Mr Guppy, rigid with embarrassment, stares straight ahead, and the camera continues to turn. '*I love my little boy,*' Mrs Guppy mutters, not looking up. '*Just like I loved all of 'em.*' Ian Guppy glances at her, eyes wide in alarm. '*And I know I haven't always done the best for them, and that's what people are going to say . . .*' Ian looks at her in shock, undisguised. She's off script. Never mind that; in forty years of marriage he's never heard her speak like this. '*And now it's Dane they're going after,*' Mrs Guppy continues, '*and it's not his fault. I reckon it's a witch-hunt. It's a Guppy witch-hunt.*' She swallows, shakes the head, finally looks up. '*And – no,*' she declares, tears streaming, '*say what you want about us. But I'm not having it. Not with the youngest one. It's just not fair.*'

The piece is followed by a brief interview with Fanny, looking spaced out and unnaturally scruffy, but sounding nice; not too trenchant, agreeing that she will do all she can to avoid the expense of a court case, or in any way risk the future of the school, but emphasising that the other pupils' safety has to be considered too. The interviewer finishes with a cheeky reference to Fanny's limbo striptease, which leaves Fanny scowling and without the opportunity to respond.

Next comes a statement from Clive Adams, unnaturally neat. He lays out the Dane Guppy case with a succinctness and elegance which complements Mrs Guppy's emotional explosion and contrasts very well, very professionally, with Fanny's woolliness.

'*Well*,' exclaims Macklan, breaking the stunned silence, putting an arm round Tracey. 'Well, I never! She's either a bloody good actress,' he says, 'or she's nicer than she likes to let on. That was sweet . . . wasn't it, Trace?'

Uncle Russell switches off the television with an angry grunt which quickly turns into a cough. But Tracey says nothing. She shakes her head, unable to respond. Like her mother, she has tears streaming down her cheeks.

'You see?' she mutters, more to herself. '*You see?* She's not all bad.'

Uncle Russell doesn't see. Doesn't want to see. He pushes the electronic lever on the arm of his wheelchair and begins to reverse away.

'Wait there, Mr Guppy! Wait!' cries Macklan. 'Trace and I came to see you. We've got something to tell you, haven't we, Trace?'

Uncle Russell continues as if Macklan hadn't spoken, spinning beadily across the shiny carpet towards the next room.

'Hey!' says Macklan, letting go of Tracey, striding across the floor to catch up with him. He puts himself between Uncle Russell and the door to Uncle Russell's bedroom, blocking his exit. 'Mr Guppy,' he says sternly, 'didn't your mum ever tell you it's rude to disappear in your bedroom when visitors come round?'

'No one told me anything,' says Uncle Russell bitterly.

'Well. It is.'

Uncle Russell pushes his lever and the chair lurches. Macklan stays put, preventing it from moving forward, and the room is filled with an angry electric whirring until Uncle Russell releases the lever, and the noise stops.

'Thank you,' says Macklan. 'Tracey?' He glances across at her standing there hugging her belly, lost in a world of her own. 'Come on, angel. Over here. Do you want to tell him or shall I?'

'Mmm?' she says, blinking. 'Oh. No, Macklan. I'll tell him.' She crosses the room to stand beside Macklan. 'Uncle Russell,' she says boldly, with a brave smile as if she believes he'll be pleased for her, 'Macklan and I have decided to get married . . .'

Russell Guppy stares at her, waiting.

'So I'll be moving in to live with him at the cottage. But I'll be up visiting. All the time. OK? Checking up on you! Honestly, you won't be able to get rid of me!'

'Getting married?' he says at last.

'That's right!' she says brightly, much too brightly. 'He asked me yesterday. We're ever so happy. Aren't we, Macklan?'

Uncle Russell lowers his gaze to her belly. And keeps it there. 'Anything else?' he asks pointedly.

'What?' Tracey blushes.

'Anything else you got to tell me, Tracey?'

'What? No!' She steps away from him.

Macklan laughs. 'Isn't that enough?'

'*That*,' says Uncle Russell with a crafty smile, 'is something *you'll* have to decide, Creasey boy. When she lets you. Eh, Tracey? Something the Creasey boy will have to decide for hisself. When he gets the chance to . . . When you're kind enough to tell him.' He chuckles and immediately creases into another series of body-contorting coughs. 'So,' he gasps impatiently, still coughing, but unwilling to take the time to recover, 'you haven't told him then? 'Course not. Don't blame you. It's not a very nice thing to tell.'

'Tracey?' Macklan turns to her. 'Told me what?'

'Nothing.'

'Told me *what*?'

'Want me to tell him?' asks Uncle Russell, smiling.

'*Tell me WHAT?*'

'Nothing. It's none of your damn business.' She backs

391

away from them. When Macklan moves towards her, she jumps. 'LEAVE ME!' she yells, and runs out of the sitting room, through the kitchen, slamming the back door behind her.

Macklan turns to the old man, sitting there watching it all from his wheelchair, a look of sour contemplation on his face.

'What just happened there? What did you just do?'

Russell Guppy doesn't reply. He tips his head to one side and smiles. 'I want you to get something for me from the shed, Creasey boy,' he says. 'And then you can push me down the hill. I need to pay someone a visit. All right?'

Macklan laughs. 'No. Not all right.'

'Don't you want to know what's up with Tracey?' he wheedles. 'If you help me—'

'I'll ask Tracey, thank you very much.'

Uncle Russell cocks his head. 'And if she don't tell you?'

'She will.' Macklan turns his back, heading for the door Tracey just left by. 'She will if I ask her.'

'*Mr Creasey . . . Please!*'

The words make Macklan stop. Uncle Russell looks back at him, his frail chest rising-falling, rising-falling, his fragile, legless body dwarfed by the state-of-the-art wheelchair. He is begging. 'Just let me down to the road,' he says. 'If you please. There's a little green sweater . . . in the shed. On the ground. Only the ruddy chair won't go over the grass . . .'

Macklan finds the little green sweater, bumps Russell Guppy ungraciously down the garden path to the village road and prepares to leave him there. He hesitates. 'How'll you get yourself back again?' he finds himself asking.

'Ahh . . .' Pride somehow recovered, now that he's on the move, Russell Guppy's relish sounds out through the usual wheezes. 'You tell young Tracey I knows what I knows – as she very well knows.'

'Huh? I said how will you—'

'You tell her I want her here at ten o'clock.' He presses the lever and lurches forward. 'She knows what I knows . . . She knows where she's needed.'

61

Fanny spent the first half of the evening at the LEA offices in Lamsbury, discussing possible legal concerns regarding Dane Guppy. This was before Mr and Mrs Guppy appeared on television but even so, there had been several veiled remarks, so that Fanny came away with the clear understanding, as she was meant to do, that a court case would be out of the question. Fiddleford Primary School, whether it was improving or not, was on the cusp of extinction. After all the trouble of the fire, anything, the slightest added cost or disturbance, might push it over the edge.

Nevertheless, when Louis calls she is at her kitchen table planning next week's lessons. She and Louis haven't spent an evening together since his churchyard escapade and it's becoming pretty obvious now that he's avoiding her. Even so, when she hears his voice talking into her answer machine, she doesn't jump to take the call. Actually, she feels a little thud of guilt and misery, and stays exactly where she is.

'Hey, Fan,' she hears him saying. She knows him so well. She can hear, even in those two syllables, that he's hedging, that the next thing he says is unlikely to involve much truth. 'I'm – ah. I'm in a place called Bishops Lydeard. In Somerset.

Don't ask me why. There's a nurse who's been given some kind of frigging award . . .' He laughs. 'Hold the front page, huh? Still. It's a job . . . Anyway, so I'm not going to make it back tonight. At least not till late . . . And I guess once I'm done I'll head straight back to mine. I know you've got a lot going on . . . So . . . I'll catch you tomorrow . . . OK . . . ? Goodnight, Fan.' It sounds sad. Fanny almost picks up then. 'Goodnight, sweetheart. I love you . . . I do.' And he does. And she loves him. It's nobody's fault, she thinks despondently. Or maybe it is. Maybe it's just that she and Louis are the kind of people who are better off alone . . .

She looks at the telephone, silent now, and it reminds her, as telephones tend to at the moment, about calling Solomon. She should call him. She should apologise. Now she knows it was Louis and not Solomon who told Kitty about her dead marriage. She should call Solomon and apologise.

She should.

She lights a cigarette.

Why, she asks herself, almost as if she hasn't guessed, why is she making such heavy weather of this? She should pick up the telephone . . . *and dial.* Hello, Solomon. Hi! Hi, it's Fanny here. Fanny Flynn . . .

She pours herself a glass of wine, paces around the small table . . . Hello, Solomon. Hi! Hi, it's Fanny here. Fanny Flynn . . . Yeah-but-no-but-yeah-but . . . *sorry* . . . It would be so much simpler – it would seem so much more natural – if she could just say it when she bumped into him. In the pub, for example. Or at his croquet and darts party next weekend. Or in the village street. Fanny returns to the pile of unmarked exercise books.

Fuck it. She can't face it. She'll call him later or something.

62

The uncorrected proof for Scarlett and Kitty's novel arrived at the Adamses' this morning. Geraldine thinks it would make a picturesque and maternal moment if she could persuade Ollie to come into the parlour with her, now that they have a quiet moment. They could sit side by side, mother and son, and Geraldine could read the story aloud to him. Like she used to in the olden days. Or like she would have done in the olden days, if only she'd found the time.

'Ollie, darling, are you busy?' From the hall, she hears the distant, familiar sound of Ollie's blip-blip-bleeping. 'Ollie, darling, switch off the computer game, would you, sweetheart? I want to show you something.'

Blip. Crrr. Beep-blip.

'Ollie? . . . Ollie! . . . Ollie?' She follows the bleeps to the television room, where Ollie slumps, small thighs flopped apart, small shoulders already rounded, eyes fixed on the little screen above his thumbs. Dead to the world.

Poor baby, she thinks. And it pulls at her; a wave of guilt and love for her ten-year-old son. She adores him. Why is it, she wonders, that there's never enough time in the day just to be with him? 'Baby?' she says softly, squashing up on the sofa beside him. 'Ollie, darling. Switch off the machine. Please. Just this once.'

He ignores her.

'Come on,' she says, gently easing the thing from his hands.

'MU-UU-UM!'

'Come on, baby. Be good.'

'MUM! GEDDOFF! GEDDOFF, MUM! Give it back!'

She switches it off, slips it out of reach, under her seat cushion. 'Kitty and Scarlett's book arrived this morning! We've got a special early copy. How about that!'

'How about what?'

'So I thought it might be fun for us to read it together.'

He rolls his eyes. As if he's about to be sick. 'Fun? Yeah, right.'

'Yes. "Right". That's right, Oliver Adams. So be quiet and listen . . .' He looks on the point of telling her to fuck off, which is what he generally does when she attempts to impose her will on him these days. 'No, Ollie,' she says quickly, holding up a hand. 'I don't want to hear it. Not today. Just be good. OK? Just for a couple of minutes . . . And if you sit nicely for ten minutes, I'll give you a tenner. Sound fair?'

He looks quite pleased about that.

'And I'll give you a pound for every minute thereafter.' She smiles, encouraged by his improved expression. 'Think about it, Ollie. If you sit still for half an hour, you get £30!'

'Cool!' he says. 'I'm going to sit here for about ten hours, Mum. Or even longer. I'm going to sit here until I die.'

'Hmm. Right then!' She nods to herself, pleased with her negotiating skills, and opens up the book. '"*A Revolting Boy*",' she reads. '"*By Scarlett and Kitty Mozely.*" . . . Funny name,' she adds, sneaking an arm around his shoulders. 'Hope it's not about you, Ollie!'

He smiles. Allows her arm to stay where it is, just this

once. 'They wouldn't dare, Mum. Not those two. Otherwise they'd have no one to scrounge off.'

Another 'Hmm'. A little frown. Not very kind, Geraldine thinks. But he has a point. Besides, with the one arm around her precious boy, this is a special moment. She doesn't want to contradict him. 'Are you ready?'

Nobody's looking. Ollie allows his head to rest against the crook of his mother's arm. He nods. 'Ready as I'm ever going to be,' he says with a sigh. 'It's seven minutes past. OK? Time starting . . . now. Go!'

'"Mr and Mrs Oliver used to be very important London lawyers",' Geraldine begins, '"but when their revolting son, Adam, was nine years old they worried that being quite so important all the time meant they never had time to have fun. So they moved to live in the country. They bought a large house in the middle of a quiet village called Pigsbury." . . . Oh,' says Mrs Geraldine Adams. 'Oh.'

'What? Go on, Mum. It's going to be even more boring if you keep stopping.' He digs a pointy elbow into her ribs. 'Go on!'

'Hmm,' she says, 'I'm not sure I like the sound of this . . .'

63

He has never, in sixty-three years of living in the village of Fiddleford, ventured to the other end of the Old Rectory's drive. Today, clutching the little green jersey, muttering and coughing as he whirrs along the smooth, shiny-new tarmac, Russell Guppy does so for the first time. He hasn't the slightest interest in what he might find down here, so long as there is a door. And a Mr and Mrs Adams on the other side of it.

Mrs Adams is still in the television room. She has read the first twenty pages of Scarlett and Kitty's book and Oliver Adams has at last spotted some of the many insulting similarities between himself and the Adam Oliver in the story. He is puffed up with rage; Geraldine has called for Clive but had no response and they seriously need to bring him in on this. Action will have to be taken.

'I've always hated Kitty Mozely,' Ollie spits. 'And I hate her spazzer-fatso-gay daughter.'

Geraldine is saved from reprimanding him for that by the sound of the doorbell. She leaps to her feet.

'Oi! Mother,' he shouts after her. 'I'm still sitting here, you know. So it still counts. As long as I'm sitting here I'm still counting minutes. So you'd better cough up!'

She strides out through the hall, finger still marking page twenty-one in the book, legal mind churning. After all the help she's given Kitty over the years, it seems incredible. It does. And they'll sue, of course. They'll sue her for every penny. They'll ban publication. Nobody makes a public mockery of her baby boy. Nobody. She'll make Kitty Mozely pay for this . . .

Geraldine peers through the frosted glass at the figure on the porch, glimpses Russell Guppy muttering and coughing, and feels sure she ought to recognise him. He looks familiar and yet not; she is distracted, of course, not just by her plans for Kitty, but by his enormous, state-of-the-art wheelchair.

'*Hello!*' she says, hysterically warm (because of the wheelchair). It's actually a funny time for a wheelchair to call, it occurs to her. Past dusk on a weekday evening. Perhaps it – *he* – perhaps *he* saw Clive on the television. Perhaps he's in urgent need of some Adams Family Practice legal advice. Geraldine is not, she reminds herself, one to make assumptions about disabled people. They aren't necessarily all broke.

'Well, *come in*! Come-in-come-in!' she cries. 'What can I do for you? Can I get you some . . .' She stands back to allow him in. He looks grey . . . blue-grey . . . *yellow-green-grey* when the hall light falls on him fully. She's never seen anyone so frail, so lacking in legs, so— 'Maybe some hot milk?'

'Hot milk?'

'Sorry. *Medicine*. Oh, fuck. Excuse my French. *Medicine!* What am I talking about?' She laughs, casts around for help. Fails to find any. 'A drink! Would you like a drink? I'm afraid Clive's on the phone.' She wrinkles her nose. 'Bit of a busy time! Perhaps you saw him on the news this evening?'

'That,' says Russell Guppy, 'is what I come to see you about.'

400

She smiles. She arches one of her fine eyebrows. 'Oh, yes?' she says. 'Tell me more!'

'My name,' he pauses to cough, 'is Russell Guppy.'

'*Russell Guppy!* Well, of course it is! I know that! How lovely to meet you at last. I've heard so much about you.' He's eyeing her drily, apparently untroubled by the need to blink, and clearly unmoved by the warmth of her welcome. She finds it a little disconcerting. 'Ollie, baby,' she calls. 'Ollie, dear? Come and say hello to this nice gentleman.' But Ollie has already returned to his Nintendo. He ignores her – as she assumed he would. 'Well, anyway. Come on in. We'll go into the parlour, shall we? I'm sure Clive will join us in a minute . . . Can you manage?'

It's not until they are both settled opposite one another, and Geraldine has adjusted the White House furniture to accommodate his wheelchair, and has handed him the requested tumbler of whisky and ice, that she notices the little green pullover on his lap, with the familiar-looking label peeping out at the neckline.

'Oh!' she says, staring at it. 'Isn't that— Good Lord!'

'That's what I come about, Geraldine. That and the telly.'

Geraldine? A bit fresh, she thinks. Nevertheless. Big smile. Moving on. 'Russell – may I call you Russell?'

'You may,' he says solemnly, taking a gulp of whisky. Nothing like a free drink. Russell Guppy doesn't get out more than once a year these days and just now, before the business begins, the parlour's soft white light and the smell of flowers and the chinkety-clink of ice in the heavy crystal tumbler . . . Makes him wonder if he's finally made it to heaven. He smiles, an unusually happy smile. But the smile makes him cough, which brings him quickly back down to earth. It is a few moments before he recovers.

Geraldine asks if she can get him water but doesn't quite move to fetch it. She's more intrigued by the question of the small green jersey (Brora, cashmere) and how it found its way on to Russell Guppy's lap. She bought it for Ollie the last time she was in London, and at vast expense: Brora cashmere does not come cheap. Seeing it there, in its raggedy heap, she realises he hasn't worn it for weeks. Not surprisingly perhaps, since it is midsummer. She'd forgotten all about it.

'Do you mind my asking,' she says, as soon as Russell Guppy has recovered, 'only I think that little jersey belongs to my son. Could I—'

Uncle Russell hands it to her. It is damp and dirty, and as it passes between them they are both hit with the unmistakable stench of petrol.

'Goodness!' she says, delicately holding it out, taking care not to let it touch the sofa. 'Well, it is Ollie's. Certainly. We've been missing it . . . He'll be delighted.' She folds it neatly on to her lap, pats it, and beams at Russell Guppy. What a lonely man he must be, she thinks, to come all this way for the sake of a child's dirty jersey. Just because he's seen Clive on the telly. 'Thank you. Really kind of you.' She peers at him curiously, and for a moment her heart swells with honest pity. 'Russell,' she says warmly. 'You've come all this way. Would you like to stay for supper?'

Just then they hear Clive striding across the hall towards them. 'That was the rector, Geraldine,' he's saying. 'Of course he's mad keen to cool this thing down. He says the Diocesan Council are coming down on him and he wants to bring about some sort of concord *sans* resorting to the courts, ho-hum. Needless to say I told him— Oh.' He stops. 'Who are you?'

'Clive, darling,' she says, standing up like a nervous bird, stepping towards him. 'I was calling you. Where've you been? We desperately need to talk.' She leans across, murmurs into his ear. 'Seriously. You're not going to like it. Kitty's gone too far this time.'

'What's that?' Clive stares absently past his wife, directly at the wheelchair. At his leg stumps. 'Sorry,' he says to them. 'Have we met?'

'Oh! And this is Russell Guppy,' says Geraldine, quickly remembering herself. 'Sorry! *Dane's* uncle. He's terribly kind. He's actually brought Ollie's jumper back. The lovely green cashmere from Brora. Do you remember it?'

'What?'

'Well, anyway. You can't imagine how grateful I am. I've, er, actually I've just asked him to supper.' She sounds a little surprised by the fact.

'Oh,' Clive says, and immediately starts backing out of the room. 'Well, I've got a hell of a lot of calls I need to make. Pleasure to meet you, Mr Guppy. Geraldine,' he nods at her. 'Catch you later.'

'But wouldn't you care to know, Mr Adams,' demands Russell Guppy, eyeing his host, 'exactly where I found it?'

'Found what?'

'The lovely green . . . cashmere from Bro . . . ra, Mr Adams.'

Clive pauses, shrugs, flashes one of his lawyerly smiles. 'Well, certainly. If you would like to tell me, Mr Guppy. Of course.'

Russell Guppy leans forward in his enormous chair. There is an unmistakable gleam in his eye as he does so – and for the first time, the Adams Family Practice senses danger. 'I found it,' he says, and begins to cough . . .

Clive and Geraldine flick a glance at one another. They wait.

He continues to cough. Pauses. Takes a slurp of whisky, looks for a moment as if he's about to disintegrate into yet further paroxysms, but manages somehow to control himself.

'I found it in my shed . . .' He looks from one to the other, but neither reacts. '*I found it*,' he says again, '*in my garden shed* . . . Right there where I keeps my petrol cans . . .'

'Ahhh!' says Geraldine. Her tinkly laugh sounds shrill. 'Well, that explains the smell of petrol, then, doesn't it? How curious!'

'Not really,' says Russell Guppy.

But Geraldine doesn't seem to hear him. 'Extraordinary! I wonder how it found its way there?'

Clive says nothing. He has his eyes fixed on Russell Guppy, and there is a small muscle pumping away at the emaciated jaw.

Russell Guppy watches them, back and forth, back and forth. Silence. Slowly he raises his hand. He points at Clive. 'And you know when your lad put it there, don't you?'

'I think not,' says Clive with a cool, cold smile. 'Really, Mr Guppy. You're talking Latvian, as far as I'm concerned. How could I possibly know?'

'Because that's about the time he came back here, isn't it? All scruffy and no sweater, and all stinky with smoke and petrol. What did he do, I wonder . . . Run upstairs and . . . bathe 'imself?' He smiles. 'A strange thing . . . for a young lad to do. Wouldn't . . . you say?'

'Really, Russell.' Geraldine laughs; the same neurotic tinkle, only shriller. 'Really, Russell . . . *Clive*?'

He ignores her. 'I'm not sure, Mr Guppy, that I understand what you're getting at.'

''Cause I was watching the little bugger . . . Worse luck on you. Telly was broken.'

'Was it? Well, now, that's fascinating,' Clive says rudely. '*The telly was broken!*'

But the sarcasm is lost on Russell Guppy. Or he doesn't react to it. 'That petrol can was too heavy for him. So he tipped half on 'em out in the ground in my shed . . . see? He leaves his sweater where he drops it . . . The way . . . lads will, eh, Geraldine? . . . And in all the . . . excitement . . . he forgot all about coming back for 'im after. But I didn't.' He laughs. The laugh becomes a choke. Clive and Geraldine watch him, the same wicked thought flitting through both their minds.

But he doesn't choke to death right there in front of them. He straightens up and continues. He says, 'I watched him . . . lugging the thing over the road, watched him pouring it this way and that and . . . this way and . . . that.' Once again he leans forward in his chair. 'Geraldine. Mr Adams. *I watched your boy striking the match* . . . And there ain't no way round that fact. So you'd better get yourselves accustomised to it.'

'Liar!' It's Geraldine, sprung forward. 'How dare you come to my house in your fucking *wheelchair*, you – legless little shit—'

Clive steps across, taps her gently on the arm. 'You're being hysterical, Geraldine,' he murmurs. Very cold. Very controlled.

'But we all know—' She laughs, wild laughter (no tension in it now). 'Tell him, Clive. *Everyone* knows! *Ollie* has nothing to do with the fucking fire! It was Dane!'

'Of course it was,' Clive mutters soothingly, his thin hand gripping her arm. 'Of course it was. Shhhh.'

'Dane, was it?' says Uncle Russell. 'So why are you defending him?' he asks. 'If you're so sure he done it? Which he didn't, by the way, as I knows.'

'We're defending his right to an education.'

'Except he's getting one, isn't he? The Flynn girl's teaching him. She's been having him round every evening.'

They didn't know that. Aren't pleased to hear it, either. 'We're defending his right to an education,' amends Clive, 'without enforced segregation or isolation from his peers.

Guilty or not, Dane Guppy has a basic and inalienable human right to be taught alongside children of his own age. Not at some – *idealistic young woman's kitchen table*, but in a classroom. At a school. And I intend to prove that. I intend to *make history* proving that.'

Uncle Russell chuckles. 'Except he can't go in a classroom, can 'e? 'Cause your son went an' burnt it down.'

'*He did not!*' yells Geraldine. Clive tightens his grip on her arm and she winces distractedly, barely noticing it.

'That sweater's been in my shed ever since the morning of the fire. And frankly, Mr Adams, I wouldn't have done nothing about it . . . It's only when I see them . . .' His face contorts so much it triggers another coughing fit. 'It's when I see them *pricks* being saintified on my television set – sitting on their sofa like they own the fucking world. That's when I says to myself, *That's enough . . . Enough's Enough!* I'm not having no more of that!'

A silence falls. Clive and Geraldine are struggling. They can't quite bring themselves to look at each other – because inside them both there have always been tiny, secret whispers of suspicion, unacknowledged, never mentioned, not to themselves – certainly not to one another. Ollie had emerged after the vicar's drinks party that day, with a clean set of clothes and wet hair and no explanation as to where he'd been all morning. It was Ollie and his little pack of friends who, days later, had made the great discovery of the petrol can, half-buried under brambles in the neighbouring field. It had been Ollie who rolled the can triumphantly back into the playground.

Clive says, quietly, 'Mr Guppy. What is it, exactly, that you want from us?'

'I already told you what I want. I want them ugly pricks taken off my TV.'

Clive releases his wife. 'I'm not certain I understand. You want—' A gurgle of laughter escapes him. 'Excuse me—'

'I'm not being funny, Mr Adams.'

'No, of course not. I'm just – I'm sorry, I'm just struggling to understand. You've come all this way not because your nephew Dane may have been the victim of some miscarriage of justice, but because you want—'

'I want them ugly pricks off of my TV! And if I so much as peep 'em there,' another bout of hacking, angry coughs, 'I'm taking that sweater and I'm going to the police.'

64

Mr and Mrs Ian Guppy had gone next door to Ian's brother's place to watch themselves on the telly that night, so they could be certain to get it all on tape at home. With Dane gone, they weren't sure how to watch something and video it at the same time, and they didn't want to take any risks.

So they all squidged in together, cups of tea and ashtrays on the Mrs Guppys' laps as per usual, and cans of cider for the men. At the end, after Mrs Guppy's tearful bit, and the clever topping-and-tailing from Clive, there was a stunned, embarrassed silence. Nobody knew quite what to say. And so, to avoid having to say anything at all, the Guppy brother, who knew better how to work his video player, leant forward, rewound, and played the whole thing again.

They do this several times, maybe four or five, without anyone advancing any kind of comment. The brother is leaning forward to rewind yet again when his wife turns to Mrs Ian Guppy, wedged beside her on the leather sofa. She lays a hand on her thigh.

'Marian!' she says softly. 'That were beautiful.' Which

three words are probably the most beautiful, gentle, honest words Marian Guppy has had addressed to her in her life.

Marian, startled, and – extraordinarily – on the brink of tears yet again, can feel a sweat of shame rising. She can feel it on her forehead, on her cheeks, on her tremendous thighs. She can feel it itching as it mingles with the talcum powder in her hair. 'Well,' she growls, with a whisper of a smile, and staring through burning eyes at her fat, fat hands, 'we had to give them cameras somethin' showy, didn'um?'

'That's right,' says her husband with a shifty laugh. But he, too, is looking at his Marian a little differently. 'Mum's the werrd,' he declares brightly. 'Everyone needs a mum like Marian!'

'Mum! Mum! . . . MOTHER! It's . . . Tracey!' Nobody moves. 'Mother, please . . . *I need you.*' Nobody speaks. 'I saw you talking . . . on the telly . . .' They all hear her slumping on to her parents' porch. And then nothing . . . A soft sound, animal-like, some cross between a sigh and a moan, something filled with despair.

Mrs Ian Guppy looks at none of them. She flushes with emotion: with anger, possibly, embarrassment, almost certainly, but most of all, with hope.

She hauls herself up from the sofa. ''Scuse me,' she says.

The three Guppys left behind sit quite still, listening. They hear Mrs Ian Guppy thumping over the tarmac. They hear Tracey's sudden silence and then nothing . . . Crying again – but it's quieter, more subdued – and then voices, also subdued, and the opening and closing of the other front door. Ian Guppy tiptoes to the window. His wife has taken Tracey back into the house.

65

Macklan has searched the village for Tracey; he has searched everywhere he thinks she might feasibly be hiding. Tracey doesn't drive, and the bus doesn't come to Lamsbury after seven o'clock. Nobody's seen her anywhere. He's beginning to worry.

At ten o'clock he finds himself lingering at the bottom of the path leading to Russell Guppy's bungalow, leaning against a tree and smoking a cigarette – hidden from view. He hears the whirring of the Guppy wheelchair and listens out for voices. But there are no voices. It's only as the chair draws up in front of him that he notices the light-footed, tight-lipped Clive Adams walking alongside it.

'Tracey's not here yet, Mr Adams. So you better push me up the path yourself,' Russell Guppy wheezes. 'Chair can't do it on 'is own.'

Mutely – oddly submissively, Macklan thinks – Clive Adams pulls his hands from his suit-trouser pockets and prepares to take hold of the wheelchair. Macklan flicks his cigarette to the ground and steps out towards them. His silhouette looms in the darkness – tall and powerful, just like his father.

Clive screams.

'Not to worry,' Macklan says. 'It's all right, Clive. Only me.'

'*You!*' says Uncle Russell. 'Where's Tracey?'

Macklan ignores him. 'I'll take over from here,' he says, gently shunting Clive Adams aside. 'You go home, Clive. Mr Guppy and I have a few things to talk about.'

Clive hesitates, glances nervously at Russell as if seeking permission. Russell nods.

'Right you are, then,' says Clive. 'Goodbye.'

He sounds miserable. Macklan glances at him, briefly distracted by it. 'You all right, Clive?'

'Me? Fine! I'm *fine*. Never been better!'

Between them, in the darkness, they hear Russell Guppy laugh.

66

Jack and Jill went up the hill to fetch a pail of water.
Don't know what they did up there
But now they've got a daughter.

Uncle Russell saw Robert White take Tracey up the hill, or at any rate follow her into the sports hut on the near side of the school playing field. That was twenty-one weeks ago, a good two months before Macklan appeared on the scene. Uncle Russell doesn't know what they did in there either, but he saw Robert walking out of the hut not very long afterwards, doing up his flies, and looking mighty pleased with himself. So he has a pretty shrewd idea.

Then he found Tracey's pregnancy test tucked under the mattress in her bedroom, stuffed back in its box, but obviously used, with the blue lines clearly showing. And Uncle Russell had nothing better to do. He put two and two together.

By the time Macklan gets Uncle Russell into the empty bungalow Uncle Russell is quite ready to tell him just about anything. Everything. If needs be, he'll make something up. What does he care? He's actually more than a little frightened.

And quite rightly, too: Macklan, unbalanced by love, and with the door closed behind him, is a force not to be fooled with that night. Uncle Russell senses it.

Macklan Creasey looms down on him and the russet hair falls forward over his face, briefly shielding Uncle Russell from his wild green stare. He sweeps the hair away, places a hand on both arms of the wheelchair. '*Mr Guppy*—' he begins.

'OK, OK. She's *pregnant*.'

He steps back as if he's been slapped. 'She's – what?'

'And has been,' he adds quickly, 'a good time before *you* came along . . . Satisfied now?'

Macklan is not. 'How do you know?' he says. Stupidly. Just words.

'Pretty bloody obvious, isn't it?'

'But who— So who— Who's the—' Macklan stops. He's not sure he wants to hear it. Not from Russell Guppy.

Russell Guppy grins. 'Who's the daddy? Is that what you're asking me, rich-as-Creasey boy?' He bends, begins to cough. He fumbles this way and that for his oxygen, finds it at last, presses it to his mouth, breathes in, breathes out, and in, and out. By the time he's recovered, Macklan is nowhere to be seen.

'And good riddance,' he snarls to the empty room.

It gives him time to think.

What next? he asks himself, looking down at the precious green Brora sweater. *What now?* He's tired. Very tired. It's been a long, hard, exhilarating day . . .

Clive and Geraldine had offered to buy the sweater from him. He might have sold it, too, but they insulted him by only offering £150. And Russell Guppy had seen the look in Clive Adams's eye when he'd turned them down: clocking the tubes going in and out of him, the crêpey yellow skin, the helpless knee stumps. Clive had been calculating the risks

413

of simply snatching at the thing, taking the jersey and setting light to it there and then. Uncle Russell had smiled. 'Macklan Creasey's seen this sweater, Mr Adams. He knows where I'm gone even if he don't know why . . . And the sweater's not for sale. So you needn't think no more about that.'

Russell Guppy smiles to himself. He can't remember a more eventful evening. Not in sixty-three years. So . . .

What next then?

67

It was Monday, mid-February, a quarter past four on an icy afternoon and already beginning to grow dark. Small residues of the previous week's snow lay in muddy patches over the empty playing field and Robert White was gazing out from the staff-room window, a pile of unmarked books behind him and a mug of blackcurrant Lemsip cupped between his wind-chapped hands. He was paid extra, back then, when Mrs Thomas was still in charge, to organise a Monday-night football club. Somehow he managed to arrange things so that it never actually took place. Each week he used to find a reason to cancel. Either it was raining or it was going to rain, or he was sick, or he was going to be sick. There was never a shortage of excuses, not for Robert, who always knew where to look. This week, of course, there were the patches of dirty snow.

So the footballers, like everyone else, had been sent home at a quarter past three and the school was deserted. Only Robert remained. That Monday his Fiat Panda was being serviced and he was waiting for a lift home. Girlfriend Julie, who worked in the environmental health department at Lamsbury Council, wasn't free to pick him up until six.

Julie. Is still the only woman Robert ever dared to call his girlfriend. Julie was thirty-nine years old, and no beauty. Julie wanted to start a family. She desperately wanted to start a family, and at that stage she would have done anything for Robert, as long as he offered her hope. Robert did that. He allowed her to dream. Because she was (though he always knew he could do better) what he called 'a super girl', helpful to him in lots of little ways. She cooked for him, shopped for him, ironed his shirts.

Sometimes she said 'Thank you' when he screwed her, which he found disgusting. But she was a super girl on the whole. Just not quite super enough for him.

No, the girl he had his eye on – not to marry, of course (Robert would never marry someone like Tracey) – was young and shy and innocent and sweet; and just then making her way across the playground towards him.

Tracey liked him, so Robert believed. She blushed when he dropped in on her at the pub. Which he had taken to doing a lot recently. He liked to lean nonchalantly against the bar where she was working when she wasn't cleaning the school, buy himself a drink and then ask her, 'Can I get one for yourself, Tracey?'

Tracey would take the money and plop it in the tip glass by the till. 'I'll drink it later,' she always said. 'When it's not so busy . . .' Robert believed her. He dreamt of being there with her one day. When it wasn't so busy.

And now he was. There were just the two of them, all alone and not so busy. He was meant to be marking books, and she was meant to be cleaning. But not so busy. Her top half, he noticed, was bundled up in a thick, hooded anorak which rubbed unattractively at her cheeks, made her look like an Eskimo. Horrible. But the bottom half told him a different story. She was wearing the tartan woollen mini-skirt he knew so well, and the calf-length black suede pixie boots. And between them – nothing. Her smooth young legs were mottled with cold, and naked.

Naked. Robert tapped distractedly at his Lemsip. Mrs Thomas kept a bottle of wine in the staff-room cupboard for emergencies – exactly such as this. And there were plastic cups somewhere. Perhaps they could crack open a bottle of wine together? Perhaps they could do that. On this cold February afternoon. Why the hell not?

Tracey must have felt his presence because she glanced across at the window. He waved at her. Very cheery. She couldn't have guessed, he thought, that while his eye had lingered on the exposed flesh, young, smooth and cold, his mind had travelled further, to where the flesh was warmer, to where the flesh was always warm. She couldn't have guessed that beneath the cheery wave, the steaming mug of blackcurrant Lemsip, Robert's erection was prodding rapaciously against the staff-room window sill.

Tracey hadn't been especially pleased when she saw him at the window, but she smiled anyway; a quick non-committal smile. She didn't like him much. For the first term that she worked at the school he had barely deigned to learn her name. But then she did something – she didn't know or much care what; cut her hair, flashed a bit of cleavage – she did something, anyway, which made him notice her, and since then he'd not left her alone.

He was always on his own when he came to the pub. No one ever spoke to him, except her – when she had to; when she was taking the tip money and plopping it into the glass by the till. She didn't think he had any friends, and she couldn't help feeling sorry for him.

Which was why, when he popped his straw-coloured head out of the staff-room door, tiptoed up behind her, grasped her softly by either hip, and whispered 'BOO!' she didn't push him away, as she wanted to. She forced herself to smile.

'Hello, Robert,' she said, twisting subtly away from him. 'You're working late today.'

She felt sorry for him. That was her only mistake.

'I've got a little surprise for you,' he said, still with his hands on her hips. 'Got a bottle of vino in there. And a couple of glasses. What do you say? Fancy having a drink with me, Tracey?'

'Not really. Thanks, Robert. I'm in a bit of a rush today.'

She smiled at him kindly, saw his face drop, felt his hands drop. 'I'm sorry,' she said.

'Just a quick one?' he said. 'Won't take a minute. I've laid it all out ready . . . It'd be nice . . . just to have a little chat.' He smiled – a lonely, pathetic smile, she thought. 'I feel like I hardly know you, Tracey. Here we are, working together. It seems ridiculous. I'd love to get to know you a little better.'

Tracey, only nineteen, and not especially used to alcohol, very quickly became drunk. Robert refilled her glass at twice the speed he filled his own. By a quarter past five that afternoon the bottle was finished, most of it by Tracey. They were sitting side by side in the staff room in almost total darkness. Tracey had been chattering away, giggling, and Robert had been watching her, watching the moonlight on her bare white thighs, murmuring little encouragements, not listening to a word. She had asked him a question and at some point he became aware of silence, aware of her expectation. He leant over as if to kiss her. She froze, horrified, but then his head dipped and his lips fell not on her mouth but there, where the skirt ended and the pale flesh of her legs began, where the legs were pressed together. And he didn't kiss. He licked.

Tracey leapt to her feet. Managed not to scream. Because even after that, she felt she couldn't be rude. She felt she oughtn't to hurt his feelings. She stood in front of him and he watched her straightening her skirt. When she fumbled and finally flicked on the light he was still watching, eyes slightly glazed. He was smiling at her.

'Right then,' she said busily. But standing up had made her realise how drunk she was. 'I'd better get on. Thanks ... thanks very much for the drink.' She lost her balance, stumbled against the door frame as she made her way back out into the hall.

She headed outside, not wanting to stay alone with him in the empty building. She thought the icy cold air might clear her head. She staggered out on to the playing field. Light from the school building flooded over it, but it was freezing out there without her anorak, and she felt exposed. She didn't want Robert to see her, to feel he could come out and join her, which was when her eyes fell upon the sports hut and she hurried towards it. If she could hide away in there for a moment or two, try to stay warm, gather her thoughts ...

'Tracey?' A little tap on the sports-hut door. 'Are you OK in there?'

She jumped. 'Fine. I'm fine, thank you.'

In the darkness she heard the door creak open, and saw Robert's silhouette framed by the light from the school.

'Are you sure?'

'I'm fine.'

'You don't sound fine.' He moved slightly, took a step into the small hut and the light fell on her: her enormous, terrified eyes; her breasts rising and falling beneath the too-tight T-shirt. It had 'You Couldn't Afford Me!' written in crazy letters across the chest. But of course he could.

She's frightened, poor little thing. She's terrified.

And he found he can't resist.

68

He's been the rector of Fiddleford and chair of governors at the village school for over twenty-five years, but never has the Reverend Hodge had to witness squabbles in his own parish being broadcast on the public airwaves before. When he saw Mrs Guppy's emotional outburst on the local news his heart bled, not only for her and Dane but for the whole of Fiddleford.

He tucked himself into bed last night feeling heavy with sadness, and the sense of personal failure. Reverend Hodge loves Fiddleford; more than he had realised, perhaps. It is his village, his home, and as its rector he feels responsible, at least in part, for its harmony. Now the airwaves are buzzing with acrimony and all the vultures are looming. The governors are at loggerheads, the Diocesan Council's chief communications officer is hinting that he should consider retirement and the LEA is overtly threatening to close the school. Reverend Hodge feels he has let everybody down.

He lies awake all night trying to think of a solution. As the morning light begins to creep through his bedroom curtains, he still hasn't found one. But he has prayed for guidance. And he has decided to call the governors back together again this evening and beg them to help him in his search.

This meeting, he decides, is to be held not at eight at the Old Rectory, where they had all (he thinks in retrospect) been so distracted by the hour, the alcohol and the luxuriant surroundings, but at six o'clock in the village hall. With tea.

He sets about telephoning his fellow governors immediately after breakfast. He calls the school first. Fanny is taking assembly so he speaks to Robert. 'Sounds like a very good idea, vicar,' Robert says, blowing his nose. 'As a matter of fact, there was something else I've been wanting to bring up with the governors for some time now. Perhaps we can take a moment—'

'Certainly, Robert. I'm sure we can,' Reverend Hodge sounds distracted. 'And you shan't forget to mention it to Fanny?'

By noon he's received confirmation from Fanny but still hasn't managed to track down Geraldine: no answer at work or at home, and the mobile isn't taking messages. Maurice Morrison can't make it. Ditto, of course, the LEA's Councillor Trumpton, who lives in Exeter. And ditto Grey McShane, who has a very full restaurant tonight, and no Messy, who's taken the baby Jason to stay with her parents. But the General is available, and so is Kitty.

Kitty is reclining naked on her bed when the vicar calls, being sketched by Louis, goofy with spliff. She tells Reverend Hodge she's heard not a squeak from Geraldine for a couple of days. 'However,' she says, because there is something very erotic about talking to a Reverend under the circumstances, and it puts her in mind to be friendly, 'I, on the other hand, would be delighted to attend your meeting this evening, Reverend.' She winks at Louis. 'I'm positively looking forward to it!'

'Excellent,' says the Reverend, somewhat taken aback. 'And I shall see you on Saturday, no doubt, at Mr Creasey's darts and croquet.'

'Oh, goodie, are you coming?' cries Kitty. 'What fun! It's going to be the Event of the Summer, I think. Don't you think?'

Which leaves him with only one more call. To the host of that Event, no less. Reverend Hodge tracks down his final governor *en route* to a convention at the Tate in St Ives. 'Ah, Mr Creasey. Reverend Hodge here. School governors' meeting this evening. Six o'clock. Can you make it?'

Solomon's heart lifts. He's not sure why, but he feels it. 'Certainly!' he says. 'Oh, bugger! Six o'clock? You can't make it any later?'

'I fear not,' says the Reverend smartly. Though he, like Kitty – like most of the village – anticipates enjoying himself enormously at Mr Creasey's darts and croquet event this Saturday (Reverend Hodge is quite a killer on the croquet lawn), it doesn't alter the fact that he can't quite bring himself to like the man. He is, in fact, with all the best will in the world, offended and bewildered by almost every aspect of him, from the smell of his aftershave to the rumble of his vulgar cars as they purr up and down the village street; from the glamorous, silent girlfriends to the bellowing, boisterous laugh; to the wholly unapologetic, inappropriate *unEnglishness* of him. 'What a shame,' the Reverend says. 'Never mind. I shall see you on Saturday, no doubt. At the party. I must admit, I'm looking forward to it, Mr Creasey. Very much indeed.'

69

So. No Solomon, no Grey, no Tracey, no Geraldine, and no one from the LEA; for the first half-hour not even Fanny Flynn. It's a diminished collection of governors in the village hall that evening: only the Reverend, Robert White, Kitty Mozely and the General. They sit in a crooked circle on four ancient metal chairs and listen with varying degrees of politeness while Reverend Hodge describes his dismay at the recent publicity, and his determination that they should work towards a peaceful and private resolution.

'As I say I've had very strong, not to say overt intimations from the LEA that they're simply not willing to underwrite the cost of a protracted legal dispute. Or of any legal dispute at all, if they can help it. On the contrary. I received the clear impression that, with the tragic fire adding further to their irritation, they are really itching for a pretext to surrender altogether; to close our little school down for good.' He glances around the group. 'And it occurs to me that this dreadful dispute is playing right into their hands.' A gentle, bewildered sigh. 'Which is why the four of us – and Fanny, if she's ever good enough to appear – *must* find a way to sort this out . . .'

He had taken the precaution of arriving at the hall ten minutes earlier than everyone else in order to set out the teacups and, because he always suffers from the cold, to light the enormous Calor heater which now hisses soporifically beside him, and makes the whole drab room stink of gas. By half past six, with the sun still beating down on the corrugated roof above them and all the windows nailed closed, everyone but the vicar is sweltering.

Kitty wriggles in her chair, furious to find herself sitting in it at all; how, she keeps asking herself, had the bloody vicar cajoled her into attending this ridiculous meeting in the first place? *And where the fuck was Fanny?* FUCK, of course, being the operative word, since Louis, who'd pretended he had a job to go to, was obviously with her . . . *now* . . . undressing her . . . caressing her, brushing his glorious lips against her firm, pert, *youthful*—

'Well, Miss Mozely?' says the vicar. She jumps. 'If I may begin with you?' She gazes back at him blankly. 'In summary,' he prompts, 'do you believe, as I now do, that young Dane should be allowed another chance, that – with some supervision, that is to say *full-time* supervision, of course – he should be reintegrated into the school as soon as possible, in order to continue his studies. Until such a time, that is, as the courts have actually tried him?' Reverend Hodge offers a small, dreary chuckle. 'I'm sure I don't need to tell you, Ms Mozely, were you to make such a choice it would, without doubt, bring a swift ending to our current legal difficulties, thereby, I imagine, allaying what I believe to be a genuine threat to the life of our beloved school.'

'Hmm,' says Kitty. Louis had said he was on his way to a job in the village of Kidstead-St-Vincent to photograph – she can't quite remember what. He'd left her bed earlier that afternoon with a kiss on the end of her nose (which had infuriated her) and a regretful smile on *those lips*. He'd looked into her eyes and muttered something about 'never wanting to hurt Fanny', about 'maybe putting a check on all this', which Kitty had carefully pretended not to hear. 'Because, Kit – you're such fun,' he'd said. 'Honest to God. You're wicked. You're just adorable . . . But Fanny . . .' And these were the words he had left her with, and they had ripped at her pickled old insides: 'Well, I love her, you see. Fan's my best friend in the world.'

'Miss Mozely?' the vicar asks again.

'What? It's awfully bloody hot in here,' says Kitty irritably, fanning herself ineffectually with a puffy hand. 'Do we have to have that heater on?' The Reverend Hodge inclines his head; a polite but stubborn *yes*. She glances across at the General, who appears to have fallen asleep, and then at Robert, sweltering happily in his polo-neck.

'What *I* don't understand is why the little shit was ever granted bail,' she snarls.

'Ahh,' smiles Reverend Hodge. 'Yes. If only. But he has two very skilled advocates on his side.'

'You know,' Robert White interrupts peevishly, 'Fanny is actually over thirty-five minutes late at this point. I do think it's a little inconsiderate. Perhaps we should telephone. Find out what the problem is exactly.'

Just then they hear footsteps pelting up the street towards them. 'Everyone! Everyone!' she yells out. 'I was wrong! I got it all *wrong*! We *all* did! We just assumed. *But he didn't do it*! The police have dumped the charges. Everyone, DANE GUPPY IS INNOCENT!' The hall doors burst open and Fanny tumbles in, grinning from ear to ear. 'He didn't . . . *do it!*' she says again.

'He didn't?' says the vicar incredulously. 'But how do you know?'

She stands a moment, recovering her breath. 'Russell

Guppy just signed a statement – I've just come from his place. And he's told the police. He says the fire was already roaring by the time Dane noticed it and he rushed out straight away to take a better look, and then . . .' Fanny shrugs. 'Well, Dane obviously realised what a selfish b— man his uncle was. Russell Guppy obviously hadn't called the fire brigade, so he went to the call-box in the village and called them himself . . .'

'Slow down,' demands Robert irritably. 'What makes you think Russell Guppy's suddenly telling the truth? It all sounds very convenient, Fanny.'

'Because he is,' Fanny says. 'Because Russell Guppy—' She stops, glances cautiously around the room. 'Where's Geraldine Adams? Not here?'

'Unfortunately not,' says the vicar. 'But Fanny, dear. This is marvellous news! And we're certain, are we, that Dane had nothing to do with it?'

'Russell Guppy's not named anyone, though I get the impression he knows. He's known all along . . . But he's come up with a whole load of evidence which for reasons best known to himself he hasn't wanted to share until now. So—'

'So who was it?' asks Kitty. 'Do we know?'

Fanny shakes her head. 'Not at the moment. I spoke to the police. They say they're "following new leads", whatever that means.' She shrugs. 'They sounded pretty confident they know who it is, I thought. But they wouldn't tell me . . . And that's all I know. I feel terrible. Poor little Dane . . .'

'*Intriguing*,' mutters the General, arms folded across his chest, still in sleep mode, eyes still mostly closed. 'I imagine what stirred Russell Guppy's stumps was seeing his dreadful brother and that fat wife being lionised on the box last night. Did you see it? Infuriating. Must have driven him wild.' He chuckles. Sits up. 'Well. That's excellent news. Good for Dane. We all owe him an almighty apology.'

'*Don't we,*' agrees Fanny, rolling her eyes. 'God. Don't we just.'

'Speak for yourself,' Robert says pettishly. 'I wasn't the one trying to kick him out of school.'

'Not because you thought he was innocent,' retorts Fanny. 'God knows what your reasoning was, Robert. But you certainly weren't doing it for Dane.'

'No doubt,' interrupts the General before Robert has a chance to respond, 'we shall discover the genuine culprit in the fullness of time. In the mean time, can we go? It's awfully hot in here.'

'We certainly can!' shouts Fanny, laughing, throwing her arms open. Kitty notices the easy, fluid way she moves, the wonderful haphazard way she tosses her head back when she laughs. It reminds her of Louis. Of Fanny and Louis. Kitty notices the whiteness of her teeth, the wonderful pertness of her flesh. 'And of course, it goes without saying, Dane's welcome back to school any time. As I've already told him.' She laughs again. 'I told him I owed him more than an apology. I owe him a—'

'By the way, Fanny,' Kitty says suddenly, 'did Louis tell you what he was doing in Kidstead this evening? *He told me* – barely an hour ago. And I feel such a fool because I simply can't remember . . .'

Fanny double-takes. *Louis*, she remembers guiltily, had called her mobile during lunch and she hadn't picked up. Hadn't even, what with all that was happening, got around to listening to his message. 'You saw him this afternoon, did you?' she says stupidly.

Kitty beams. 'Certainly did!'

'Certainly did,' repeats Fanny. 'Well . . . Great. Did he say when he'd be back?'

Suddenly, Kitty turns to the vicar. 'Reverend Hodge,' she says, 'I was wondering earlier this afternoon – what is the Anglican line on circumcision?'

'What's that?' snorts the General.

'I was asking the vicar – since he was here, and the question just sprang to mind – but he's looking blank. Perhaps you can help me, General. Are you circumcised?'

'*What?*'

'I was wondering what was the Anglican line on circumcision. Is there one? Because I think there should be. I think it should be compulsory for everyone. Robert, what about you? Are you—' She breaks off, gazes at him. Robert's thin body is crunched in mortification, his thin, white face folded in, hidden somewhere between chest and thighs. 'Oh. He's embarrassed,' she says blandly. 'Silly billy.' And turns back to the General. 'Only, I recently came to the conclusion that there is probably nothing on God's earth,' she gives a nod to the vicar, noting the religious reference, 'more beautiful than a nicely proportioned and circumcised penis. Don't you think, Fanny?'

'Has she gone mad?' asks the General.

'Perhaps we could move on?' murmurs a weary Reverend Hodge. 'I don't really see what this has to do with anything. In fact, I'm not certain we have anything further to discuss. So! Many thanks, everyone, for turning up at short notice. And perhaps,' he turns to send a small, scolding look towards Kitty, 'we all might take a moment to remind ourselves of how blessed we are in having such a wonderful, dedicated head teacher. Who cares so much for her students, who gives so freely of her time, who has done so much for the school and over such a short period. Fanny. *Thank you*, my dear. From all of us. Not least for being the messenger of such felicitous news—'

'Oh, but wait one moment,' says Robert, quietly uncoiling

428

himself. 'Before we get too carried away. As I mentioned to Reverend Hodge earlier, there is just one other thing I would like to discuss . . .'

70

An inaudible, resentful sigh passes over the stifling room. Robert feels it; feels a pop of glee; can't prevent those lips from curling slightly as he waits, patiently, for all eyes to be turned towards him. 'It's a worry which I've had for some time now, and which one or two parents have also voiced concerns about. I feel, as deputy head of the school, it's my responsibility to draw it to all the governors' attention—'

'Well, get on with it,' snaps the General.

'It's about Fanny's conduct. There have been one or two incidents involving – I feel – highly inappropriate behaviours towards the kiddies.'

The General thuds himself back against his chair, rolls his eyes. 'Oh, bilge!' he mutters. 'Here we go.'

Robert turns to Fanny. 'On 4 May, Fanny, I believe you kept Scarlett Mozely back from school – without any advance warning to her or to her parent/guardian. Am I right?'

'What? . . .' She thinks about it; remembers the occasion. 'Well, yes, I did, but—'

'As guidelines require us so to do.'

'They do, but—'

'But of course guidelines aren't for the likes of you, Fanny, are they? At one point I believe you pulled the young lady towards you, entirely against her will. You pressed her head to your – breasts, and held her there . . . bore down on her with open lips, while she struggled as best she could to get away. I believe she very nearly lost her balance.'

Fanny laughs. 'Robert, what are you trying to imply? I gave her a kiss! A tiny little kiss! She'd never shown me any work before, and— But I would never want to upset her. Has Scarlett complained about this?'

'I saw you,' says Robert; whispers Robert. '*I saw you!*'

'You were spying on me!'

'And on 22 May, can you deny that you physically and verbally abused and humiliated young Oliver Adams on the stairs outside your office?'

'What? No!'

'Didn't you, as punishment for bringing an unsuitable object into the playground, point a finger between his eyes and prod him, hard, on the forehead, inflicting damage to his ocular, auditory and cognitive facilities?'

'What damage did I inflict? It was harmless.'

Robert nods at her. 'His mother has lodged a complaint, you know.'

'Has she? Who to? . . . Not to me, she hasn't.'

He hesitates. He also has been unable to reach Geraldine since yesterday. Since she knows nothing about the prodding incident (so far as he knows) she hasn't had a chance, yet, to lodge a complaint. But she will. When he tells her. He feels confident. '*Wild flowers* we may be, Miss Flynn. Out here in the back of beyond. Or rare flowers. Or garden weeds. Whatever you and your little friend so patronisingly choose to call us. But we still have to abide by the law. *And I saw you!*'

'Because you've been spying on me!'

He tilts his head. Doesn't deny it. 'I felt I needed to,' he says simply.

431

'Well, fuck you, Robert.'

'Incidentally,' he says, 'I've been wondering – you said Scarlett was the rare orchid, didn't you, and her mother was the Deadly Nightshade. Isn't that right?' He smiles, enjoying the shock on her face. 'So what does that make the rest of us, Fanny? What does that make me?'

'Nothing,' she says, too stunned to come up with anything clever. 'You've been spying on me,' she says again.

'As I said—'

'*Fuck you!*'

'Really, Fanny,' clucks the vicar. 'That's not quite . . . I must say, Robert, I'm certainly unaware of any complaints being lodged. However, these are serious allegations, Fanny . . . Really, physical—'

'*Sexual* abuse,' spits out Robert. '*Sexual abuse* of a defenceless little kid, of a physically challenged little kiddie . . . whose only crime was being in the wrong place at the wrong time . . . Don't, Reverend, whatever you do, attempt to trivialise this . . .'

The vicar licks his lips. He glances nervously at Kitty who sits there relishing every minute of it. His mind spins, imagining the telephone calls from the diocese, the LEA . . . 'I presume you deny it?' he asks Fanny hopefully.

'What? Of course I deny it!'

'Well. That's all right, then.'

'How can she deny it?' demands Robert, pointing at Fanny. 'She's already admitted to it! We heard her!'

Fanny glances from one to the other. 'No,' she says. 'I mean – *no*. I deny what he's *calling* it. I don't deny I gave Scarlett a hug. And, yes, as for Oliver Adams . . . I mean, *no*. Maybe I prodded him. Maybe I shouldn't have. But I certainly didn't do him any harm . . . I just . . . Christ, he hardly even noticed.' Mistake. She sees the look of victory on Robert's face and falls silent.

432

The vicar gives a deep sigh. 'But Fanny, there are *rules*,' he says sadly, shaking his head. 'You know it as well as I do.'

'I know, but—'

'There are *systems, processes, guidelines, regulations* . . . All of which have to be put in place for allegations such as these.'

'*Really*,' crows Kitty, 'little did I know when I entrusted my daughter's care to you—'

'Oh, shut up!' snaps the General.

'And I must say,' continues Kitty, 'I'm extremely grateful for your vigilance, Robert. I shall certainly be pressing charges, or whatever one does. At this stage. Vicar, what does one do? Scarlett has already complained about the incident. I've been meaning to mention it. Actually she's been complaining about it for weeks.'

Fanny struggles, for a moment, to control herself. 'I don't believe you, Kitty,' she says at last. 'I don't believe you.'

Kitty shrugs.

'And furthermore, I don't believe *you* believe it either.'

Kitty guffaws. 'What?'

'I haven't done anything wrong.' Fanny's voice wobbles. She swallows.

'Of course you haven't!' says the General.

'I'm sure you haven't,' soothes the vicar. 'There's not a doubt in my mind. However, *protocol* . . .'

Fanny shakes her head. 'I'm doing a good job. Reverend, you said so yourself. The school's come alive. The children are happy. *Ask them*. Ask them! And I can't understand. *Why would you all want to ruin that?*'

'I don't!' cries the General. 'Fanny Flynn, if I may say so, you're the best thing to have happened to this village in years.'

She smiles at him gratefully, then looks around the room;

433

at Kitty and Robert, staring back at her, their gloating faces brimming with hostility; and at the vicar, staring at his hands, unhappy, annoyed, disappointed, maybe even a little suspicious . . . 'If you don't believe me, read the inspectors' report. They've never— It says in there that they've never—' She frowns, to pull back the tears. But she can't remember the exact words. '*I've done a good job!* I've done a bloody good job!'

'Nevertheless, Fanny,' says the vicar kindly, 'if you really won't deny it—'

'How can she?' asks Robert smugly. 'When she's already admitted it? Not once but twice, now. In front of all of us! She can't deny it.'

'Well then, I'm forced to admit that under the circumstances—'

'This is absurd,' splutters the General. 'This is appalling!'

Robert raises an eyebrow, says nothing. Doesn't need to.

'As I say,' perseveres the vicar, 'these are – will be – considered serious allegations. Made,' he glances at the General, 'by the school's *deputy head*, and substantiated, or so it appears, by one of the victims' parents. They are unfortunately allegations which we're simply not permitted to ignore. And I'm sorry, Fanny, I have no choice. As you know. Pending further inquiries, a move will have to be made for temporary—'

'Suspension?' Fanny laughs in disbelief. 'After all this? You can't do it!'

'Unfortunately, I must,' says the vicar, not daring to look at her. 'I believe these things can take several months. After which, of course, there are various appeals procedures—'

'Reverend Hodge, you know as well as I do,' interrupts the General, 'the school won't stay open for appeals. They'll close it down. And the only person to benefit will be,' he leans forward, jabs a finger at Robert, '*that gentleman over there*. To whom the public purse will no doubt have to fork out some phenomenal sum. For doing nothing. Except single-handedly wrecking a perfectly charming 150-year-old village school. Actually, thanks to Fanny, a bloody *good* 150-year-old village school.'

'Steady,' mutters the vicar, agreeing with every word. 'Steady on, General. I don't think we can quite say that.'

'*He's* the winner, Reverend! No one else!' The General's face is very red. Fanny puts a hand on his shoulder. 'General. It doesn't matter,' she says.

'Yes, it bloody well does! If that bugger persists with his repulsive allegations, they'll close the school down. Mark my words. Within a month they'll find some excuse, and they'll—'

'Please, General,' she says quietly. 'You're going to hurt yourself. Nothing's going to go to court. I'm resigning, that's all.'

'Certainly not!'

Fanny looks at him, sends him a crooked smile. 'You know my track record. I'm a very restless person . . .'

'Absolutely not!'

'We-ell, General,' says the Reverend, 'given the circumstances, I think it might be the best option. If we can just make a smooth transition . . .'

'In that case, I would like to put my name forward to be the new head,' says Robert. A glimmer of a smile at the vicar, at Fanny, at the General. They all hear the implied threat. 'I hope that's acceptable?'

'Over my dead body!' cries the General.

Fanny ignores him. She nods to herself, turns to the vicar. Silence. She clears her throat. 'Reverend Hodge, I resign.'

'Nonsense!' the General shouts.

'Too bloody right, it's nonsense. You're not "*resigning*", Fanny Flynn,' shouts Kitty as Fanny walks away, towards

435

the door she'd burst through so happily only a few moments earlier. 'You're *fired*! Isn't that right, vicar? Eh, Robert? We're voting you off the board, baby. And it's good riddance –'

Bang! The door closes.

'– to bad rubbish!' A silence. Kitty clears her throat, rolls back her head and begins to laugh. 'Good work, Robert. Well done! Didn't think you had it in you.'

71

Fanny walks for miles after that, saying her goodbyes to the landscape; she and Brute walk until it's dark. Perhaps, she thinks, they will move to America now. Or maybe to Spain; spend some time with her mother and the retired tax inspector. Or maybe to Edinburgh . . . Or Australia. Australia sounded good. It was miles away.

She sighs. 'That's what we need, isn't it, Brute? You and me. And Louis. If he wants to come. We can go anywhere. Anywhere in the world! We'll have a new beginning.' But even thick Brute fails to be fooled by her optimism. 'Eh, Brute? What do you reckon? How about a new beginning?'

He ignores her.

She returns to the cottage – where there is still no sign of Louis. She should pack, she thinks. That's what she normally does at this stage in the cycle. *Get busy. Move on. Start the packing.*

Instead, she takes a packet of Marlboro Lights and a bottle of whisky, and wanders out into the garden . . . *Lavender and sandalwood.* Solomon must be home. She breathes in. Must be out in his garden . . . She finds herself wishing she could go over and join him. Tell him all her problems, while his three sweet little daughters sleep upstairs. Lie under the stars drinking wine, putting the universe to rights with him. And his new girlfriend, if he has one yet. She feels a sharp internal shrivelling. *Jealousy*, for crying out loud. Where had *that* come from? As if she doesn't already have enough to worry about.

She spots Macklan at the far end of their own, shared garden, sitting under the peach tree, in the very place she'd been planning to sit herself. The moonlight on his handsome face makes him look pale and drawn. She smiles – an exhausted smile – and plops herself down beside him. 'You and Grey McShane look just like vampires,' she says. 'After dark. Budge up.'

He budges up. She offers him a cigarette, which he takes. She lights his and her own, and they sit in silence, listening to the quiet breeze and to the Maxwell McDonald lambs, chattering away in the field behind them.

'Good day?' she enquires eventually.

He smiles. 'Shitty day . . . What about you?'

'Yeah, well.' She shrugs. 'I suppose it could have been better . . . Tracey working tonight? Why aren't you at the pub?'

'Her Uncle Russell told me yesterday. She's pregnant.'

'She's pregnant?'

'I suppose you knew all along, did you?'

'No. Of course not. I noticed she'd been putting on weight. But I thought, you know, looking at her mother . . .'

He laughs. 'So did I, if you want the honest truth. But it's pretty bloody obvious, isn't it? When you know. I feel such an idiot.'

Fanny doesn't reply. Doesn't know what to say, where to start. Tracey's Uncle Russell had been making himself very busy recently.

'She's staying at her mum's. She won't speak to me. Won't tell me anything.'

'At her *mum's?*' says Fanny. 'Bloody hell. Things must be bad.'

'I don't even know who the father is.'

'Oh! I assumed— Macklan, I'm sorry.'

He shakes his head. 'The stupid thing is I don't even care. If she came to me with a Martian in her belly, I wouldn't care. I'd love it. I would – if she wanted me to. I mean,' he laughs, 'it's not like *I* was the most carefully planned baby of all time . . . I'd do anything for her, Fanny. I love her.'

'I know you do,' says Fanny, taking a swig from the whisky and passing it to him. 'It's very obvious.'

'So why won't she trust me, then? Why won't she talk to me about it? *Why?*'

Fanny doesn't have an answer to that. She takes the bottle back, swigs it down again, takes another pull from the cigarette. 'Got fired this evening, Macklan. Can you believe it? Incidentally,' she adds, after a pause, 'have you seen Louis today?'

'He went to Kidstead, I think. Or somewhere. One of the newspapers sent him. He was very pleased about it. Fanny,' he adds suddenly, 'maybe now's not the time to mention this but there's something you should probably know about Louis . . . Louis and Kitty Mozely . . .'

'Ahhh yes,' she says quietly. 'Of course. Kitty and Louis. Kitty more or less told me this evening.' She smiles, and feels a wave of unmistakable relief wash through her. And sadness. And no surprise, not even a flicker. So it's over. Over. They are free to stop pretending. She is free to go. 'Well . . .' She sighs. 'We had to give it a try, didn't we, Mack? I don't think Louis and I were ever honestly cut out to be anything more than friends. Not like you and Tracey . . .'

He shakes his head. 'Sorry, Fanny.'

'Doesn't matter,' she says, more to herself than to

439

Macklan. 'It doesn't matter.' She's not going to cry. 'At least not very much.' She won't cry. 'And we'll still be friends. Eventually. Definitely, we will.'

A pause, broken by Macklan, unable, in spite of Fanny's troubles, to stay off the topic closest to his heart for very long. 'But do you seriously thinks she loves me, Fanny?'

Fanny laughs. He'd not even remembered to commiserate about the job – not that she cared. 'I'd lay my last 20p on it, Mack. When you two are together there's something . . .' she searches for the right word, '*luminous* about you, a sort of luminous happiness that makes other couples look a bit pathetic, makes us feel like we're trying too hard. I think you two were born to be together. Seriously. I do.'

He beams at her.

She gives him a wan smile. 'Anyway, I don't really know what you're doing talking to me about it. You should get yourself down to the pub. Talk to her. She's working tonight, isn't she?'

'Of course she is.'

'Well, go on then!'

'She won't speak to me.' But he's leaning forward, hopeful again. 'I'm standing there on the side of the bar calling her name and she acts like she's deaf. She won't bloody well answer.'

'But she can't stop you talking to her, can she? Does she know how you feel – about the baby? That you'll love it like your own? Have you told her what you just told me? Because if you haven't—' Fanny laughs. 'I mean, Christ, Mack. There aren't many men— She certainly won't be assuming it.'

'She won't?' He sounds surprised.

Again Fanny laughs. 'Erm – no, Mack.'

'I'm going to tell her.' He springs up, stops, glances back

down at Fanny. 'You'll be all right, though, won't you, Fanny?'

'I'll be fine. Go on, Macklan, GO!'

He's already halfway across the garden.

72

She's still sitting there, alone under the peach tree two hours later, when Louis finally returns from Kidstead. He'd assumed Fanny would be working, since she usually was, and had stopped off at the pub on the way home, vaguely hoping to bump into Kitty. He found an edgy-looking Macklan Creasey instead, perched on a stool at the corner of the bar, being ignored by Tracey.

Macklan didn't greet Louis warmly. Didn't feel like it. 'Fanny knows,' he said, without even a hello. 'She knows about you and Kitty. Plus she got fired today. She's on her own in the garden, drinking whisky.'

'She knows— Did you tell her?'

'I was about to, Louis. Didn't think you were being very fair, keeping secrets from her, since you were *supposed to be together* . . .' He sent a pointed look towards Tracey, busy polishing glasses. 'But she already knew.'

'The whole ruddy village knows,' snapped Tracey. It was the first time Macklan had heard her speak since she ran out of her uncle's bungalow the previous evening.

'That's true, Tracey,' he said enthusiastically. 'I agree with you! That is very, very true.'

She slid him a furtive glance, caught his eye, quickly looked away. 'I reckon Fanny could do with some company, Louis,' she said.

'Ohhh,' Louis groaned, 'fuck and *damn*,' pocketing his wallet, forgetting the drink. 'I'm a jerk . . . I'm a stupid fucking *jerk*.'

So Louis found her, propped up against the trunk of the peach tree, whisky bottle in one hand, burning cigarette in the other. As he stalks across the grass towards her he can hear her muttering to herself; banging on about new beginnings again. He halts in front of her, slides gracefully to his knees.

'Fan?'

She looks back at him. Smiles. 'Cheater,' she says. 'God, you're a waste of time.'

'I know.'

'Kitty thinks all men should be circumcised. She says there is probably nothing on God's earth more beautiful than a nicely proportioned dick. When it's been circumcised.'

He smiles; that lazy smile. 'So she keeps telling me.'

'Oh, Louis.' At last, the tears that have been waiting to spill all this time, begin slowly to run down her cheeks. He puts his arms around her.

'I'm so sorry,' he says. 'I'm so, so sorry.'

'We really believed we had something though, didn't we? I mean, for a little while. When we were in Spain. We did, didn't we?'

'Yeah. We did.'

'We thought we'd cracked it. We were so smug. We'd found the holy fucking grail.'

'I'm seriously beginning to wonder if it exists.'

'Oh, it exists,' says Fanny bleakly. 'It's just it comes along when you're standing in a bar, minding your own business, in *Buxton*, and then it turns out to be—'

'Crap,' Louis finishes for her.

'Horrible. Maybe it wasn't the real thing, anyway. Maybe it wasn't. Maybe—'

'It was crap, Fan. Come on,' he nudges her. 'We were better than that.'

She chuckles limply, more than a little drunk. 'Maybe the harder you look the better it hides. Maybe that's it . . . I got fired, by the way.'

'Mack told me.'

'Robert White says I've been molesting the children.' She giggles – it turns into a tiny, feeble retch – and falls silent again.

They hold each other for a while, hearts aching with their own failure, with the endless, exhausting loneliness of their free-floating lives. Finally she disentangles herself. 'Got a call from Ian Guppy, too,' she says. 'Don't know what took him so long, except of course I've just paid him the rent. He says he wants me out by the weekend.'

'He can't do that!'

She shrugs. 'I'm leaving tomorrow, anyway. Tomorrow morning, preferably. Pack up tonight. Write a letter to the children. Can't see much point in hanging around.'

'Do you want a hand? Can I help you?'

'No. Thanks.' She hauls herself up from the grass. 'Thanks, Louis.' She smiles at him, and he at her. 'What are *you* going to do?'

He glances away. 'Oh, you know,' he says evasively. 'Maybe stick around here a while. Maybe, gosh, I dunno. But the work's picking up again, so I guess I'll hang around a couple more months.'

Fanny smiles. 'Of course you will. Well – goodbye, Louis. See you later.'

And with that she turns and walks unsteadily back into the house.

*   *   *

She spends most of the night struggling to write a separate farewell letter to each of her pupils, which she intends to post (since Robert would be unlikely to distribute them) through Grey and Messy's door as she leaves.

Finally, as the dawn seeps in beneath her hand-made curtains, she climbs up to the loft and pulls out the giant red New Beginnings trunk she'd been hoping not to use again. She throws it open in the middle of the sitting room and stops; gazes at her small house, at all the little artefacts arranged so lovingly around the place – those sari curtains, the Iranian embroidered wall hangings, the Peruvian llama rug, the broken Mexican silver lamp, the African animal carvings, the wretched dressing table left her by her grand-mother . . . She looks at all the random tat she's been amassing through life, lugging from one New Beginning to the next, and she thinks, *What's the point?*

Minutes later she stands with Brute and a small suitcase and two Safeways plastic bags full of chosen belongings: clothes, make-up, CVs, a couple of unread novels. The front door is open and she's ready to leave. She takes a last look around her: at the bright red trunk, open and empty, and everything else still in place. As if she were only nipping to the pub. She falters. The room glimmers slightly with all the hope she invested in it once, and it makes her wish she could stick around and fight. She would *like* to stick around and fight . . .

She picks up her bag, 'Come on, Brute. Let's go.' She steps out into the cold, clear, early morning, slams the door behind her, and quickly, before she can change her mind, posts the key inside.

73

Solomon has a ten a.m. meeting at his London gallery with an exciting new Russian client, a man with two bodyguards and a feverish gleam which reminds Solomon of some of his old prison associates. Not a man who would appreciate being kept waiting.

He ought to have travelled up to London last night, but it had been a beautiful evening in Fiddleford and he'd spent all day in the car going to St Ives and back. Apart from which his darts and croquet party was on Saturday, and Macklan had vaguely mentioned he might come round for dinner to drop off his trophy stand. (Macklan didn't show, of course, but true to form where his father is concerned, he forgot to call or to cancel.) Which is why, at five thirty-five that Friday morning, just as Fanny is listening to her front-door key drop on to the inside mat, she hears Solomon's new Bentley purring elegantly up the village street behind her.

She listens, panic-stricken, frozen to the spot. But to her surprise the car makes its way on and past her.

'Lucky!' she says to Brute, as the engine sound fades. '*Lucky!*' again, to cover the sharp pang of disappointment. 'Come on. Let's go. It's time to go.'

But then, distantly, she hears the car brake. Stop. And slowly start reversing.

'Oh, shit!' She turns back towards the cottage again, squeezing her hand through the letter-box, in the wild hope of somehow retrieving the keys. She can hear his car drawing nearer. 'Shit . . . *fuck! Shit!*' She doesn't need this. Not now. She can't face this. Desperately, she drops into a crouching position beside the garden gate, shunts the suitcase behind her and pretends to be searching for something on the ground.

He stops. Winds down the window.

'Fanny?' Wonderful deep voice, she thinks: authoritative, confident. Bloody sexy, actually.

'Hmm?' She glances up. 'Oh! Goodness! Hello, Solomon! I didn't see you there!'

He frowns. 'What are you doing?'

'What am I doing? . . . Nothing!'

'Where are you going, at this time in the morning?'

'Nowhere!'

'Nowhere? What are you doing with those bags?'

'What bags? Oh. Well, that's because I was on my way—' She stops. Tries again. 'I seem to have lost my keys. I'm sort of locked out. Actually. Gone and posted my house keys through my own postbox!' She rolls her eyes. '*That's* the problem.'

He eyes her suspiciously. 'Are you all right?' he says. 'How did the meeting go last night? Sorry I couldn't come along and support you.'

'Ah. *The meeting*. Didn't miss much. No. I was fired, actually.' A breathless, dry-throated laugh. 'Well – suspended. I mean, I resigned. Robert White said I'd been molesting the children. Which I haven't,' she feels compelled to add, 'by the way.'

'Well, I'd be very surprised.'

'So – when I said I wasn't going anywhere it wasn't *strictly* true. I was actually on my way, Solomon.' She gives a little shrug. 'I mean, I'm off. So,' she continues quickly, not giving him a chance to speak, 'well. Thank you for everything. For being my friend. And – telling me about Nick. And I'm sorry, actually I'm *really* sorry, about that time I called you . . . It was Louis, of course, who'd been jabbering my business around the place. *Louis.*' She glances resentfully up at his window. (He's not there. He's over at Kitty's, snoring peacefully.) 'Who's having it off with Kitty Mozely, it turns out. Probably as we speak. Anyway, sorry. More than you needed to know.' She realises, distantly, that she needs to shut up. 'So. What with this and that and the other, and bloody Ian Guppy's chucking me out of the cottage, there's not a great deal to keep me here any more. Not really—'

'Bollocks,' he interrupts. 'Only a school full of children, all of whom seem to worship the ground you walk on. And, with the exception of four or five idiots, a bloody village full of supporters. Supporters and *friends*, Fanny. Christ. What more do you want?'

'Well,' she says pertly, fighting back tears yet again, eyes already stinging, 'a job might come in handy.'

'You've got a fucking job!' The words explode from him. They roar down the empty street. Silence. 'Apart from Robert White,' he adds more quietly, 'and Kitty, I presume, have any other governors accepted your resignation? I know I haven't.'

'Solomon,' she laughs, 'you can't force me to stay.'

'Probably not.' He sighs. 'But I thought you might want to. After all the effort you've put in. I thought you were a fighter, Fanny Flynn. I thought you and I were fighters . . . Shame.' He sounds disproportionately cast down. 'I was obviously wrong.'

'*Obviously*,' Fanny says. She looks at the ground, mortified.

She knows, if she moves her eyeballs, her tears will spill over, and he'll see. 'I'm sorry.'

'Oh, God. Don't *apologise*,' he says, suddenly light again. He switches off the engine, opens the driver's door and climbs out on to the road. 'Not to me, anyway. So where are you headed?'

He's wearing a loose-fitting cream linen shirt, no tie and a pale grey suit. She's never seen him in a suit before; never seen him fully dressed, now she thinks about it. Either way he is disturbingly good-looking. 'Where am I headed?' she repeats. She looks baffled.

'That's right.'

'Erm – must admit I'm not quite sure yet,' she laughs self-consciously, aware of how pathetic it must sound. 'Sort of thought I'd think about that once I'd loaded the car. But maybe London?' He's standing beside her. Close. The smell of him catches the breeze. Lavender and sandalwood. And the warmth of him. She looks up. 'Or Australia. I dunno.' He's looking at her thoughtfully, hands in trouser pockets. Dark eyes, she thinks: impossible to read. Impossibly bloody sexy. Why hadn't she noticed it before? Perhaps she had. She tries to pull herself together. 'Anyway, goodbye, Solomon,' she says, stepping gracelessly back from him, shoving out a hand for him to shake.

He keeps his own in his pockets. And then a flash of humour at some private joke seems to light across his face.

'What?' says Fanny, dropping the hand. 'What's funny?'

'Nothing,' he says briskly. 'Give me your car keys. I'll help you load.'

Perhaps it strikes her, distantly, as an odd request, as a peculiarly fast *volte-face* for a man who's just called himself a fighter, but he's delivered the line with such total assurance, with so little doubt she will go along with it. And she is, anyway, feeling very muddled: half relieved that he isn't trying to argue with her, half – more than half – disappointed. And above all, distracted. He is standing very close to her.

So she passes him the keys. He says 'Thank you' and puts them in his pocket. 'Right,' he says. Change of tone now, as he climbs back into his own car. 'I've got to be in London this morning, but I'll be home about six. I'll call Sabine, let her know what's happening, but she'll leave you in peace if you want her to. So make yourself comfortable. Feel completely at home. And I'll see you later.'

'What are you talking about?'

The Bentley engine hums back into life. 'And tell Sabine to make you a decent breakfast,' he says, eyeing her critically. 'You're wasting away, Fanny.' He grins at her, slowly begins to edge the car forward. 'Must be all the stress.'

'Hey!' yells Fanny, grabbing at the car door. 'Where are you— What the— Give me my keys! . . . Stop! WAIT! This is illegal! *You can't do this!*'

Solomon stops. 'You've got nowhere to go, Fanny. You said so yourself. Nowhere to go. No one to see. And nothing to do. What's the big hurry?'

'It's none of your business what the hurry is.' But he has a point. 'Anyway, screw you!'

He clicks his tongue. Laughs. 'Seriously,' he says. 'What's wrong with spending a day cooling off? And then when I get back, maybe I can help you drum up some kind of—' He stops. His mouth twitches. 'Well, shall we call it a plan?'

'Give me my fucking keys!'

He looks at her curiously. 'Did you even say goodbye to *anyone*?'

Fanny glances away. She doesn't reply. Grey, Messy, the General, Charlie and Jo, Macklan, Tracey, Dane, Scarlett – Solomon. She's leaving them without a word, without a forwarding address; without any intention of seeing any of them again.

450

'You do this all the time, don't you? I bet you do. Drop everyone. Dump everything. Run away – as soon as people start getting used to having you around.'

'*No* . . . No. *No*, of course I don't. Anyway, it's nothing to do with that. I've just been bloody well *fired*.'

He sighs, apparently unconvinced. 'Just this once, Fanny, before disappearing in a great puff of self-righteous smoke, spend the day thinking about it first . . . Please? What have you got to lose? You won't have to talk to a soul. There are books and newspapers and videos. The children are asleep, and then they'll be at school. Nobody's there except Sabine. And I'll tell her to look after you – or to ignore you. Whatever you prefer . . .'

She's torn. She knows she ought to be angry. She tries to feel angry but actually what she feels is touched. More than touched: relieved, happy – exhilarated – that for once in her exhausting life, someone else is offering to take control.

'Give me back my keys,' she mumbles doggedly. It sounds very half-hearted.

Solomon chuckles, shakes his head and accelerates away.

74

No answer. Not even a machine. And he's been trying all morning. With a bitter sigh, Robert White replaces the telephone receiver on Fanny's desk – *his* desk – and gazes disconsolately down at the mountain of papers she left behind her. His victory, it occurs to him belatedly, has come at a cost. There is an absurd amount of work to do. He had no idea . . .

It is ten o'clock on the morning of Fanny's attempted dawn flit. Robert is a mere hour into his honorary headmastership and although assembly was fun, when he sat on the stage where Fanny had sat and grandly proclaimed himself leader (to a deafening silence from the children), the novelty is already beginning to wear thin.

His class has once again been put in front of a video (*Are We Being Served?* since it was at the top of the pile) and Linda Tardy is sitting at the back of the room, reading *House Beautiful* and eating a tuna sandwich.

In the mean time, he has forms to fill in, allegations to substantiate and a meeting with the vicar in an hour, who is extremely unhappy at the loss of Fanny, and demanding immediate corroboration for the charges against her. Which corroboration, of course, Robert can't provide until either Kitty and or Clive or Geraldine deign to answer their fucking telephones.

Kitty waddled off out of the village hall last night, promising to get a written statement from her daughter. Scarlett was meant to bring it in with her this morning, but so far she hasn't even turned up. Ditto Oliver Adams. In fact, Robert's not heard a squeak out of Ollie's parents for two days.

Robert feels a blast of pleasure, however, as he buzzes through to Mrs Haywood the glass-eyed secretary – *his* glass-eyed secretary. 'Mrs Haywood?' he yells, buzzing away. 'Mrs *Haywood*!'

But she doesn't answer at once.

He buzzes and yells, intermittently, for longer than it takes, he thinks, for an old woman with one eye to go to the toilet and back; for longer than it would take her to make a cup of coffee and go to the toilet and back. Finally, he gets up from behind his own desk and makes his way into her room.

Her desk is bare. Her coat and bag are gone. Mrs Haywood has disappeared. *The bitch*. Without so much as a—

'Ahem . . . Excuse me, Mr White?'

A child's voice. Robert spins around. '*What?*'

Eight-year-old Chloe Monroe is standing shyly behind him. 'The video's ended.'

'Well? Watch it again.'

She sighs. 'We've already watched it a lot of times.'

'And I suppose you think you know all there is to know, do you, about the service industry in the Midlands? I doubt that very much, madam. Indeed, I do.'

'Also, Mrs Tardy's fast asleep.' Chloe's pretty face breaks into a grin. 'Her shirt's popped open and you can see her –

you know – boobies. And also, I think she's about to fall off her chair.'

He sighs. 'Well, wake her up then, for crying out loud! And put the video on again . . . And Chloe, when she wakes up, tell her I'm going out for a second. OK? I'll be back in half an hour.'

It's a three-minute walk from the school to the Old Rectory, and another beautiful morning in Fiddleford. But Robert shivers as the warm, fresh air touches his face, and heads for his Fiat Panda. He drives through the village, mind humming with worry, and oblivious, as ever, to its unassuming loveliness. Unaware of the soft morning sun, the bluebells, the stitchwort and periwinkles bursting from green banks by the side of the road, deaf to the peal of the Fiddleford church bells striking the hour – and profoundly irritated when his path is blocked only metres from the top of the Old Rectory drive, by the slow progress of Charlie Maxwell McDonald and his herd of heifers as they move from one field to another.

Nothing seems amiss to his unobservant eyes as he finally turns in towards the house. He steers down the winding drive, rehearsing what he will say to Geraldine when he finds her. He is angry with her. Angry and hurt. And he intends to use both of those words – before she gets a chance to reprimand him for having laid his pupil-abuse allegations against Fanny without first consulting her.

'Angry-and-hurt. Angry and *hurt*.' She was supposed to be on his side. They were supposed to be working together and yet for two days he's heard nothing but silence. He feels nervous as he slams the car door. 'Angry *and* hurt . . . And let down and disappointed.'

He rings on the doorbell. It resonates shrilly through the silence . . . The absolute silence.

The front door is closed. Robert glances behind him. But

the cars, he thinks, might be parked at the back. He looks up. The shutters, put on by the Adamses at such vast expense, are all closed tight. He peers through the letter-box. There is no sign of life in the hall. Nor any furniture, come to that. Did there used to be furniture in the hall? He can't remember.

He steps away and his feet crunch noisily on the Adamses' crispy new French-imported gravel. The house is empty, closed up, *deserted*. They have taken a holiday, perhaps. Odd. In the middle of all that's been going on. It's only when he turns out of the drive, back towards the school, that he notices the 'FOR SALE' sign attached to the gatepost.

Impossible, he thinks, slamming on the brakes. Without the Adamses he is lost. He feels a flurry of fear. Why hadn't they called him? How could they desert him at a time like this, just when everything was going so well?

Robert parks the car and crosses the road to the post office. Mrs Hooper always knows what's going on.

'That's right, Mr White,' says Mrs Hooper, coldly. She's just had the General in, bringing her up to date. She knows what happened at yesterday's governors' meeting, and she's a supporter of Fanny. Even so, she can never resist the oppor-tunity for a gossip. 'The Adamses upped and offed, day before yesterday. Middle of the night. And frankly I don't know of anyone who'll miss them.'

'I will!' Robert cries.

'Oh, well. Yes, I dare say *you* will.' Mrs Hooper glances through the shop window behind Robert, gives a wave to Macklan Creasey, walking past with his arm wrapped tightly around his new fiancée, Tracey Guppy. They look so happy together, she thinks, and so happy when they came in earlier to tell her the news. Like they were made for each other. Just looking at them makes her smile.

'But are you certain they've gone? . . . Mrs Hooper? . . . Are you absolutely *certain*?'

She looks back at Robert. It wipes the smile off her face. 'Of course I'm certain,' she retorts. 'I wouldn't tell you if I wasn't. Have you come here to buy something, Mr White?'

'But why?' he wails. '*Why would they suddenly leave like that?*'

She shrugs. 'He's got the law after him, apparently.'

'No!'

'Evidently, Mr Adams was into some insurance-fraud thingummy. So I'm told.'

'*No!*'

'Of course, everyone knew the business down in Lamsbury was doing badly . . .'

'Yes.' (Robert hadn't.)

'And these high flyers,' continues Mrs Hooper, 'they don't like it when things don't go their way . . . So, yes. Done a moonlight flit. And I don't suppose we shall ever see them again.'

'But that's so . . . extraordinary,' says Robert. 'I'm shocked.'

Mrs Hooper shakes her head. 'I never liked them myself. They were snobs. Especially him.' She shivers. 'He was a cold fish.'

'Oh, but it's awful, Mrs Hooper. It's awful. It's just awful . . . I just don't know what to say . . .'

'Right,' she says, briskly. 'Are you buying, then?'

'Mmm?'

She stares at him. 'What can I get you, Mr White?'

'Oh! Yes. Sorry.' He dithers. Casts about for the cheapest thing.

'Enjoying ourselves, are we, now we've booted poor Fanny Flynn out of the job?' She folds her arms. 'I don't believe a word of it, by the way. All this nonsense about abusing the kids. You should be ashamed of yourself.'

'How much are the Tunes?'

She folds her arms. 'I expect you'll have your work cut out now, won't you, following a lady like Miss Flynn. She was doing a super job. All the parents liked her.'

'I suppose Lockets are more expensive, are they? Because of the honey.'

'The children must be ever so upset.'

'Oh! You've got Fisherman's Friends. I'll take them.'

'I don't suppose you'll be showing your mug at the darts and croquet tomorrow? I wouldn't if I were you.'

They finish the transaction in silence, and Robert trips hurriedly out on to the street again.

'Robert,' says Macklan pleasantly. He'd been waiting for him, leaning against the wall to the side of the post office door, just out of sight.

Robert jumps. Spins around. 'Oh. Hello, Macklan,' he says uncertainly. 'Nice day.'

Macklan straightens up, takes what might appear to be a friendly hold of Robert's arm, just above the elbow. 'Where are you headed, then?'

Robert glances at the hand, callused from the years of carpentry; alarmingly strong. 'Ow,' says Robert.

'Come,' says Macklan lightly, giving the arm a pull.

'What – what are you doing? Ow, Macklan, you're hurting me!' Robert glances at Macklan's face. It is barely recognisable, warped with hatred. 'Come on. This way. I want to tell you a little secret, OK? A little secret between you, me and Tracey.'

'*What secret?*' Robert tries to ask. But his voice fails him. 'What—' It sounds like a mouse squeak.

'*What secret?*' Macklan finishes for him. 'Tracey and me just want to have a little chat with you,' he says.

But where Macklan takes him, back down the drive of

the deserted Old Rectory, and to the woodland beyond, Tracey is nowhere to be seen. Tracey has gone home, to her new home. She wants to concentrate on babies' names and wedding dresses and *happy things*, and she knows exactly what is going on.

By the time Robert is strong enough to drag his bruised and bloodied body back to his car it is early evening, and the vicar and the two men from the Diocesan Council with whom he had arranged meetings, have long since been and gone. There are (though he doesn't know it) seven messages from the LEA on the school answer machine, six from angry and worried parents, nine from the Diocesan Council, five from the vicar, five from Atlas Radio, six from the *Western Weekly Gazette*, one from the *Daily Telegraph*, and one from Mrs Haywood the glass-eyed secretary, resigning.

It is Friday. He has, he thinks, as with shaking hands he starts up his faithful Fiat Panda, at least the weekend to recover.

But when he gets back to his house he finds Mrs Guppy lurking: Mrs Guppy and a rusting metal stick, waiting to make him feel at home.

And at some stage in her barbaric welcoming ceremony she happens to whack him, with her metal rod, right there where he always aches the most. And she whacks him in such a way that it would be a miracle if he ever felt erotic pleasure again.

But really, given Mrs Guppy's track record, and her general hatred of men, he is very lucky to have been left alive at all.

75

Much earlier that same morning Fanny had not taken long to realise that, since she was anyway stuck in Fiddleford until Solomon returned with her keys, and since she was keen not to bump into anyone while she waited, she might just as well take up his annoying invitation, and spend the day hiding out in his house.

Solomon's house, invisible from the street, can be approached by car only via a longish detour; its short drive forks off from a lane behind the village which loops up behind the Manor and on towards Kidstead-St-Vincent. It is more easily approached by foot. From her car, parked outside number 2 Old Alms Cottages, Fanny and Brute needed only to cross the road, walk forty yards to the old stone wall separating Solomon's garden from the village street, find the small weather-beaten door, half-hidden behind ivy, and push it open. Fanny had walked past the high wall often enough – and often found herself wondering what lay beyond it. She had imagined something plush and vulgar – something, perhaps, to match Solomon's cars and laugh – but she misjudged him.

Hawthorne Place, long and low, was more of a large

cottage than a house. Painted a warm pinkish orange to complement the dark red soil, it stood in a sweeping private garden enclosed on each side by old stone walls. Walls which looked, to Fanny, as though they were emerging not from the earth but from dense clouds of wild flowers: foxgloves and cow parsley, forget-me-nots and meadowsweet. To one side, water trickled gently from an ancient russet-stoned church font (rescued by Solomon many years ago from a junk shop in Barnstable); to the other was a terrace surrounded by giant pots of wild geranium. And around the terrace lay a vast, sweet-smelling lawn, long-grassed, daisy-speckled and dotted with fruit trees.

Fanny stood quite still, drinking it all in, enchanted. She might have lingered longer, only fear of Solomon's children spotting her there, roaming about at five in the morning, drove her, eventually, to continue on to the front door and ring the bell.

Sabine, the Creasey children's Filipina nanny, is usually quite detached from activity in the Creasey household. But when she opened her employer's front door and glimpsed first Brute, and then Fanny's angry, messy, defensive early-morning face, she began to laugh.

'What's so funny?'

'Nothing funny. Nothing funny,' she said, pushing back the door to let in Fanny and her dog. 'Mr Creasey already say you're coming. I got you breakfast.' At which point she started laughing again, and continued to laugh as she ushered Fanny and Brute through the hall, which smelt of ancient, polished wood and wild flowers, to the breakfast room.

It was a lovely room, small and square, with a large, east-facing window, through which the early-morning sun streamed in. The walls, painted yellow, were crowded with artwork from different centuries and different corners of the globe. An old Tabriz rug covered most of the wooden floor, and in the middle of the room was a round oak table on which Sabine had laid newspapers and food. Fanny was hungry, she realised; actually, she was famished. She hadn't eaten properly since the day before yesterday. Now, freshly sliced mango, lime and papaya gleamed at her enticingly beside a basket of giant croissants. There were saucers of strawberry jam and marmalade, and a jug of steaming coffee.

'Wow!' she said, staring at it. 'Is that for me?'

Sabine laughed again. She said the children weren't due to get up for at least another hour, and that anyway they only ate Coco Pops. 'Solomon said you're skinny. But all his ladies are skinny!'

'Actually, Sabine, I'm not—'

She ordered Fanny to sit down, and disappeared into the kitchen to fetch bacon, sausage, mushrooms and scrambled egg.

Between them, Fanny and Brute ate everything, making Sabine, when she came in a little later, rock with laughter yet again. 'Nothing funny,' she said again, wiping her eyes. 'No no. Nothing funny! All the other ladies just pushing it here, pushing it there. But you – not like the others. You more like a boy, I think.'

'I'm *not*,' snapped Fanny. 'Actually, Sabine, I am not one of Solomon's "other" ladies. I'm not . . . And I'm not like a boy, either. I'm just a – person.'

'OK, OK. Whatever you like. Person.'

'Anyway, I shared it with Brute.' She glanced at her watch; still only six o'clock. 'So – anyway. Anyway . . .' She felt a fool for having reacted so strongly. 'Thanks for a lovely breakfast . . . D'you want a hand with the washing-up?'

Sabine said no, but Fanny felt uncomfortable leaving her with it, so they went together to the kitchen and stood side

461

by side at the sink, washing and drying in an oddly companionable silence, interrupted only by the occasional guffaw from Sabine.

Fanny couldn't quite face the children, so at the sound of their rising she left Sabine on her own, and went to hide out in the spare bathroom. She was lying back in a richly scented bubble bath, revelling in a first-of-the-day cigarette, when Sabine yelled at her through the bathroom door to pick up the telephone, attached to the wall beside her.

It was Solomon, calling from the motorway.

'It's beautiful, this place,' she said. Relaxed and warm and well fed; much too comfortable to remember to be angry, or even miserable. The world and her troubles all seemed a very long way away. 'I'm having a cigarette in the bath.'

At the other end of the telephone, Solomon nodded. Smiled to himself. 'Glad you like it. Sabine tells me you enjoyed breakfast.'

'Yes.' Fanny exhaled, watched the smoke from her cigarette mingle with the rising steam. 'Don't know why, she thought it was hilarious.'

'So. Have you done any thinking?'

'What? Oh.' It brought her back down to earth. She sat up.

He heard the water dripping from her; put the image aside. 'Have you done any thinking yet?' he said again.

'Er, no. Sort of been eating breakfast and things,' and feeling weirdly, eerily disconnected. Exhaustion, perhaps. But she couldn't remember having felt so mellow in years. What was the matter with her? 'So I've not quite— *Shit!*'

'Ah-ha!' said Solomon, who knew only too well. 'That's what comes of smoking in the bath.'

She laughed.

'So,' he said yet again. (Always keen for a plan, Solomon is. Action Man. Doesn't believe in – is incapable, actually –

of allowing situations to fester.) 'Have you thought about what you're going to do?'

'By the way,' she said, 'it may not sound like it at the moment, because I'm in the bath, but I am extremely – *incredibly* – angry with you. You had absolutely no right to—'

'Obviously. If it weren't for me you'd be sitting in a motorway café somewhere between here and Bridgwater, I imagine, crying your heart out and wondering why the bloody hell, at the age of thirty-three, or whatever you are—'

'Thirty-four.'

'—your life is still in such a total fucking mess.'

He was right, of course. If she weren't so exhausted, and so well fed and so damn comfortable, she'd be sobbing now. In fact, she didn't understand why she wasn't. Lying there talking to Solomon, hearing his voice, making herself at home in his bathroom, she felt as though nothing much about her life needed improving. She wished she could be motivated to pull herself together.

'I woke up the General, by the way,' Solomon continued, 'and he's filled me in on what happened yesterday. He says Robert White doesn't have a leg to stand on.'

'The General said that?' Fanny was flattered by the General's unconditional support, and touched by it. 'Very kind of him. But he's wrong. You're not allowed to kiss the children. Or poke them on the forehead. I shouldn't have—'

'Oh, nonsense,' said Solomon dismissively. 'There's a "For Sale" sign up outside the Old Rectory. Have you seen it?'

'Is there?' she sighed. 'Beautiful house, isn't it? Wasted on them . . . I wonder who'll buy it.'

'The Adamses have gone. Done a runner, apparently. Lots of rumours as to why. But anyway it means— Oh, bugger. Police car. Wait there. Incidentally, I think you should get out of that bath. Or add some cold water, maybe. You're sounding as though you've had a lobotomy.' He dumps the telephone on the passenger seat, waits for the police car to pass and picks it up again. 'Gone. Good. Are you still in the bath?'

'Yes.' But she sounded alert now. 'Solomon, if the Adamses have gone . . .'

'Exactly. It means the boy won't be around to back up Robert White's story.'

'But there's still Scarlett Mozely,' Fanny said quickly, to douse any sparks of hope – her own or Solomon's. 'And I did. I *kissed* her. I saw her work for the first time and I was so excited I kissed her. And she was *mortified*. I had to apologise afterwards.'

'Does Scarlett like you?'

'Well, yes . . . I would have thought so. I mean, *yes*. But Kitty doesn't. Kitty hates me.'

'But if somebody could speak to Scarlett . . .'

'Scarlett's completely under her mother's thumb. Kitty's going to tell her what to say, and she'll say it. She'll do anything Kitty tells her, poor little thing. In any case,' Fanny added irritably, as if suddenly noticing she'd been drawn into the wrong conversation, 'it doesn't matter any more. They've suspended me. Or rather, I've resigned. And I'm gone. So that's it. As soon as you give me back my keys.' She made her voice light, tried to make it sound carefree. 'I'll stop smoking in your bathroom and leave. I'll be out of your life completely.'

A pause. Solomon was thinking hard. 'It's my darts and croquet party tomorrow,' he said, as if suddenly remembering.

'Yes . . . I know. I'll be sorry to miss it.'

'Well, don't, then. Stick around. It's only one more day.'

'*What? No*, Solomon. The last thing I want—'

'At least you could say goodbye to people. Oh, shit. Got to go. The buggers are flashing me. They're pulling me over. Must have been following me all this time. I'll see you later, Fanny. Have a good day. Help yourself to whatever you want. Except the children, of course. I'd like to keep them.' With a satisfied smile, Solomon hung up and sped right on towards London. There were no police anywhere near him this time, and he was making excellent time.

76

Louis. Post-coital. Relaxing, on top of Kitty. Noticing how old her neck looks from this angle, and feeling a twitch of distaste. His preliminary sketches for her book are strewn all over the bed, and so is a cheque for £10,000, written to Louis and signed by Kitty in advance, she says, of the publishers ever getting round to paying him.

Moments earlier, Kitty's noisy enthusiasm for the work he'd done had been jangling on his nerves. So it was he, most unusually, who had initiated the lovemaking. He eased the sketches from her paws, kissed her at the back of her neck, murmured '*Shhhh*' into her ear, and finally, when that failed, placed his lips on top of hers, and kept them there.

He would finish the illustrating job. Of course. For £10,000 he'd be a fool not to, given his current financial situation. But it occurred to him, as he ran his tongue between her voluptuous breasts, and Kitty moaned ecstatically, that he should concentrate his efforts back on photography after that. It was more fun. He was better at it. And now that the commissions were picking up again –

'Mmm, sweetie, angel, oh! *Louis*. Don't stop . . .'

– he was feeling much more positive about everything.

Well, almost everything . . . He'd learnt two important lessons this last month. Firstly, never fuck a friend you really care about. Secondly, never, as a freelance photographer, disappear on holiday without a mobile.

'Sweetie! . . . Ohhh.' She came. He came. Post-coital flop. And then his mobile rings.

'Leave it,' she orders.

He ignores her.

It's the picture editor from one of the Sunday magazines with a big assignment; the biggest of his career so far. They want a series of full-page colour photographs to accompany a piece about a village deep in the south-west, which is on the brink of civil war.

'Sounds like fun. What're they fighting about?'

The picture editor chortles. 'I'm going to email you the paragraph I've got. It's complicated. Basically, it's a piece about the New Village Life, OK? The impact of our new "Urban Refugees" on English country life. So it's a – you know – gone-are-the-days, blah blah blah, when Farmer Higgins did whatever with his cows. God knows,' she adds, from her seventeenth floor in Canary Wharf. 'I don't know what he did with them in the first place . . .'

'The mind boggles,' drawls Louis, stifling a weary sigh, because Kitty's going down on him. Again. Gently, with a friendly smile, he pushes her head away.

'The point is, there's going to be some sort of garden-party *sit-in*, on the Saturday afternoon. Tomorrow, that is. Tomorrow afternoon. Very picture friendly, you can imagine. Old world meets new, etcetera. Organised by a London-based art dealer who has a house down there.' She snorts. 'He's having a croquet and darts party, if you can believe it, for the entire village. Only it's sort of transmuted into a quasi-political rally. Their head teacher's been fired for abusing the pupils. I don't suppose you've heard about it?'

'Mmm. Uh-huh. Certainly sounds familiar,' says Louis, swatting at Kitty. 'I guess you're talking about Fiddleford?'

'That's the one! We've had the woman who runs the Manor Retreat on the telephone most of the afternoon. She's trying to whip up support for the head teacher.'

'Jo Maxwell McDonald?' he asks.

'That's the one. Nightmare. Unbelievably pushy.'

'Not really,' says Louis, feeling a rush of gratitude for her. 'Jo's kind of sweet, actually.'

The conversation takes some time after that. He has to disentangle himself from Kitty to fetch paper and pen, but as he leans against the chest of drawers, balancing the mobile between shoulder and ear to take notes, Kitty's already dragged herself off the bed. She's on her knees, burrowing away, trying to get at him.

Finally he hangs up.

'For Christ's sake, Kitty!' He says it through his teeth. Louis never speaks through his teeth. 'That was *business*. That was an important call. What the fuck is the matter with you?'

'Oh, Louis. Don't be such a baby!' She laughs bravely but she immediately moves away from him. She pads back towards the bed for the cigarettes. Lights one. He notices her hands are trembling.

Downstairs they hear Scarlett, distantly, banging the front door as she comes in.

Louis goes to the bed. He sits, puts an arm around Kitty's shoulders. 'I'm sorry, Kitty. I didn't mean to snap.'

'Besides which,' she exhales, 'it's awfully low rent not to be able to do two things at once. You'd make a rotten President Clinton.'

'And is that such a terrible thing?' He makes himself smile. He looks at Kitty: brittle and still wounded, but determined at all costs to keep her tone light. Witty and bright. He feels a wave of intense claustrophobia. Kitty's old enough to be his mother. Almost. Not really. But old and crazy, and not only that but also an open, unabashed enemy to his only real friend . . . *What the hell was he doing in here?*

'Kitty, honey,' he begins . . .

He's never done this face to face before. Not officially, with an actual, verbal declaration. He takes a deep breath.

'*Kitty*,' he says again. She knows what he's going to say, probably even before he does. She's heard it so many times. 'I swear I've had some of the best fun with you, Kitty. You know I have. But . . .'

On his way out he knocks gently on Scarlett's bedroom door. 'Hey, Scarlett,' he says, 'your mom's in a bit of a state. I'm sorry . . . I'm sorry to drag you into this. But maybe you could go see her?'

He leaves his sketches – and her £10,000 cheque – on the bed.

Later that afternoon, as Robert rests semi-conscious in a pool of blood on his otherwise very clean kitchen floor, and Fanny, Brute and the Creasey girls roam the garden, waiting for Solomon and looking for grass snakes, Kitty stays in her bed and cries.

Scarlett brings her toast and tomato soup, as she always does when Kitty has a break-up. She is kind. (Scarlett is generally kind.) But for once there is a hint of weariness about her, and Kitty senses it.

She says, 'I don't blame you, Scarlett. Of course I don't. It's just that ever since you came along . . .'

Scarlett lets out a sigh. 'Come on, Kitty,' she says. 'Maybe it's time you and I tried to get beyond that.'

Kitty, lying back on the pillows, glances up, startled. Frightened, actually. She changes tack at once. 'So,' she says brightly, giving Scarlett a watery smile. 'How was school? Did you give your little statement to Robert? About the assault. I'm so sorry you didn't feel you could tell me about it earlier. You do realise that, don't you, Scarlett? I feel awful about it. Sometimes I think you forget it . . . perhaps we both forget it a teeny bit.' Another half-smidgen of smile. 'But darling, I am your *mother*.'

Scarlett looks away. 'As a matter of fact, I didn't go to school today.'

'Oh.'

Silence. *Oh.* They both know what it means. When Kitty demanded the statement last night Scarlett hadn't said anything; she'd stood up and hobbled out of the room. Kitty had been irritated, but said nothing. Back then, yesterday, Scarlett always did what Kitty asked her. Always. She shared her book credits with her, cooked her mother chickens, cleaned her mother's dirty clothes. Last night Kitty had assumed that Scarlett would do this for her too, and so did Scarlett. But something happened to Scarlett while she was sleeping. Something shifted. Kitty's last request had been the request too far, and she woke up knowing she wasn't going to agree to it.

'I like Miss Flynn, Kitty,' she says, her voice low but clearly audible as she stands there, holding the soup. She looks Kitty straight in the eye. 'And I don't remember her kissing me. Or hugging me. Or whatever it is Mr White says she did. I don't remember it at all. Miss Flynn has never laid a finger on me. She's the best teacher I ever had.'

'*Oh.*' It is Kitty who looks away. For once she is lost for words.

470

77

Solomon doesn't arrive back from London until almost eight. The Russian with bodyguards had taken up the entire morning, and then insisted on joining him for a long and heavy lunch, before leaving at four without parting with a single rouble. Solomon spent the long drive back to Fiddleford on the telephone, making frantic, last-minute plans for tomorrow's party.

He finds Fanny and the children swinging croquet mallets, heavily involved in a discussion about where on the long-grassed lawn they should hammer in the hoops. He watches them for a while, unwilling to interrupt. She looks happy, he thinks. They all do. He hesitates, unwilling to ruin things, and imagining how her face will cloud when she sees him; she has, after all, every reason to be angry. Finally, he clears his throat and prowls silently across the space towards them.

'We're going to have to cut the grass before we put in the hoops,' he says. They all jump. The children immediately throw themselves into a fresh argument about whose turn it is to operate the mower (a mini tractor variety, and the only one of Solomon's many vehicles he allows his young daughters to drive). He and Fanny look at each other over the children's heads. And Fanny, for no good reason at all, feels herself blushing.

'Have you got a drink?' Solomon asks.

'No. Thank you. I don't want a drink. I ought to go.'

Except somehow he and his daughters manoeuvre her into helping lay out the croquet lawn first. Which takes ages, much longer than Solomon has promised. Then the children insist she sticks around until they're all in bed, and she feels it would be mean to refuse.

'Everyone at school wishes you'd come back, you know,' Dora says, as Fanny kisses her goodnight. 'Mr White's *foul*. Please don't leave, Miss Flynn.'

Fanny doesn't answer; she nods very briskly, straightens up. 'Goodbye, girlies,' she says. 'Have fun. And go to sleep. It's very late.' She leaves them with Solomon.

She's standing in the hall, holding a hand out for the car keys, when he finally comes downstairs. 'Come on, Solomon,' she says. 'I've really got to get going now.'

He stands in front of her as if considering it. He puts a hand in his suit pocket. She hears a jangle of metal and feels her heart miss a beat. *Please don't*, she's thinking; *please, please, please—*

With a grin he pulls the keys out, dangles them in front of her. 'All yours,' he says.

She wavers.

'Ah-ha!' And in one swift movement he snatches them away again and drops them back into his pocket.

'*Solomon!*'

'Why don't you stay the night?' he says. 'Come on. It's nearly ten already. I'll bet you still don't even know where you're going.'

'Darlington.' It's the first town that comes into her head.

He rolls his eyes. 'Have a drink. And stay the night. You

472

look exhausted, Fanny. Get a decent night's sleep and you can be on the road first thing tomorrow morning . . .'

They don't bother with dinner. It's a warm, clear evening. Solomon takes a bottle of wine from the fridge and they wander outside on to the terrace. Sit side by side on the russet stone bench, not touching each other, watching the stars and talking. About this and that. About Robert White, and Louis, and Kitty Mozely. She asks him more about Nick Faraday, about the last few months of his life, and Solomon tells her something of what he remembers, but not everything.

'Did he . . . talk about me?' she asks eventually.

Solomon hesitates. 'Not much. A little bit.' All the time. Incessantly, towards the end. Solomon remembers that Faraday had been trying to track her down. 'I think,' he adds tentatively, 'he wanted to see you.'

One more time – for the last time, perhaps – she feels the tears spilling for him, rolling fat and slow down her cheeks. 'I wouldn't have come, anyway,' she says. 'I hated him. I *hate* him.'

'Well. He's dead now.'

'I know . . . I know.' A silence. *So what next?*

'The question is, Fanny,' Solomon turns to her, 'what do you tell yourself you're running from now?'

She looks down at her glass, takes a long, slow glug, until it's empty. 'Well, Solomon,' she says brightly, 'I think, before we get on to that, we need another bottle, don't you?'

'Fine.'

'And by the way, after we've sorted me out, we're going to move on to you.' She tilts her head, grins at him. 'Because, honestly, I don't know what it is about you, but it strikes me you're even more fucked up than I am.'

He laughs his big booming laugh (it will be heard all over

473

the village). 'Fair enough,' he says, standing up to fetch a new bottle from the kitchen. 'Perfectly fair enough.'

'And have you got any crisps or anything? Or biscuits. I'm starving.'

He blinks. *All the other ladies* . . . just pushing it here, pushing it there . . . In Solomon's world women didn't eat biscuits. 'I'm not sure, Fanny. I'll have a look.'

Solomon disappears into the house, spends several minutes rifling through his kitchen in search of crisps he knows he doesn't have, and returns, finally, with a plateful of cheese-and-pickle sandwiches. He finds Fanny stretched out on the red stone bench, fast asleep.

He looks at her, screws up his eyes. She has a bra strap, grey – a grey bra strap – showing, and the yellow string of her cotton pants has ridden up above the waist of her jeans. She has greasy, messy hair and trainers – *trainers* – which almost definitely stink . . . And she likes eating crisps. He wonders what it is about her, exactly, which moves him so much.

She scowls in her sleep, mutters a word, something, possibly '*fuck*', and follows it with a ripping snore. Quietly, Solomon puts down the sandwiches and carries her indoors.

78

It's always the same after Kitty's been dumped. Scarlett has to coax her out to the first few social engagements before she rediscovers the impetus for herself again. On this occasion, however, Scarlett is noticeably less persuasive than usual. When, at ten past eleven the following morning, she finds her mother still flopping in bed, she sounds positively pleased about it.

'Oh. Are you not coming, then?' she says, not at the bedside, where she normally stands, but at the door, her hand resting on the knob, ready to pull it closed again.

'I can't face it, Scarlett,' Kitty moans, eyes to the wall. 'Truly, I can't.'

'All right, then. Well. It starts in about half an hour, so I'd better get going. If I'm going to walk—'

'*What?*' The head turns to look at her. '*Walk?* No, no, no. I can't let you walk. You poor angel. Have you gone mad?'

'Kitty,' Scarlett laughs, 'I walk to school every single day. And the school's further away.'

'Don't be silly.' Kitty begins to haul her puffy, panda-eyed face from the pillow. She looks dreadful. 'Give me two minutes and we'll go together. We'll go in the car.'

'Seriously. I can walk.'

'No, you can't.'

Scarlett's hands twist on the bars of her crutches. She's frowning. 'Are you sure . . . you're up to it?'

'Of course I am, Scarlett. Thank you for asking. But one has to be brave in life; one has to *face down one's demons*. And so on. Life must go on.'

'Seriously, Kitty. Louis'll be there. You look awful.'

'Try not to be too cruel, Scarlett. I'm coming. And that's that.'

'Well—'

'Apart from anything else, there's sod all else to do in this village . . . And *God knows* where bloody Geraldine's gone.' Kitty glances irritably at her daughter. 'Aren't you hot?' she snaps. 'Why have you got that bloody great jersey on? Just looking at you is making me sweat. Take it off!'

Scarlett ignores her, breathes in. 'Kitty, are you sure you want to come to this party? I don't think you're going to like it.'

'I'm going to adore it. I've always been very good at croquet. Scarlett, could you be very kind and quickly run an iron over that Monsoon skirt? Pretty please? While I have a bath? I'm not certain where it is. It may be in the sitting room . . . Or what about if I wear the new one, with the floaty bottom bit? Which do you think? Perhaps you could have a quick scout around for them both, Scarlett. Could you?'

'We ought to be leaving.'

'Please, Scarlett, don't be horrid. I can't go anywhere until I've had a bath.'

With a sigh, Scarlett sidles off to the telephone. She needs to warn people that she's going to be late.

476

79

Upstairs in Solomon's spare room, Fanny opens her eyes for the first time in twelve and a half hours. She is lying beneath a duvet, fully dressed except for her shoes.

It takes her a moment to work out where she is. She can hear activity outside, the sound of hammering, people carrying things. She can hear children playing.

Of course. Today is the day of the great darts and croquet party. And Solomon Creasey still has her car keys.

Her last memory – or, no, one of her last – is of sitting out on the terrace waiting for him to bring back another bottle of wine, and then of lying back on the hard stone to get a better look at the stars . . . She must have—

She feels her stomach tighten. She imagines Solomon – no, fuck it, she *remembers* Solomon – carrying her up the stairs. She remembers the feeling of his chest against her cheek, and the smell of him . . .

She springs out of bed. Peers through the window. It's a beautiful morning; a perfect morning. The softest of breezes and not a cloud in the sky. And beneath the cloudless sky—

—alarming levels of activity. The tranquil garden she fell asleep in last night is unrecognisable. A small, open-sided marquee has been erected, and trestle tables, and around them people are bustling about with bottles and balloons and boxes of glasses, shouting orders, arranging chairs, hanging bunting from the fruit trees. Macklan's custom-built podium, with the silver trophies arranged on it, stands between the croquet lawn they laid out last night and a row of eight gleaming dartboards. She glances at her watch, swears under her breath. How could she have slept through so much? The party is due to begin in less than half an hour. She had wanted to be well clear of Fiddleford by then.

But she still needs to get her keys off Solomon. Which means talking to him. Which means looking him in the eye and pretending not to remember how last night, as he carried her upstairs, she nestled her cheek against him and breathed in, *and said*: '*Mmmmm.*'

She said that. With her eyes still closed. Still half-asleep, but not really. *Mmmmm.* She remembers feeling him laughing.

Fanny has no fresh clothes to change into. She throws water on her face, runs a hand through her horrible dirty hair, then gives up (it seems pointless anyway – she'll be on the road in a minute) and heads downstairs.

'For Christ's sake, Macklan. I must be allowed to give my own son a fucking wedding present! Tracey – please – will you tell him?' The door to Solomon's study is wide open. Tracey, standing slightly apart and dressed, on this glorious day, in a cotton skirt and a thick, dark jersey, glances out of the room, spies Fanny hesitating on her way down the stairs, and beckons for her to come in. It's the last thing Fanny wants to do but she approaches, dragging her feet.

'Fanny. Good morning,' Solomon says, barely glancing at her; sleek, and still, as he always is; lean of face, economical in movement, and yet exuding energy; exuding anger on this occasion, and impatience, and, as he looks across at Macklan, a sort of desperate, flummoxed devotion. 'Can you talk some sense into this idiot?' Solomon demands. 'Macklan, my beloved, only son, announces he's getting hitched to this wonderful, exceptional woman. Not that I know you well, Tracey. But I've no doubt you're—'

'You reckon I look promising,' Tracey says drily.

'Exactly. Very promising,' he says, with a nod of amusement. 'Aside from which he and Tracey are having a baby together, as you can probably see.'

'You are?' Fanny daren't look at Macklan. 'That's wonderful! Tracey! Congratulations. My God! So . . . you're pregnant!'

'Only just!' say Macklan and Tracey simultaneously. 'She looks big, doesn't she?' He stares at Fanny meaningfully. 'But it's early days, isn't that right, Trace? Only two and a bit months gone.'

'And the stupid bugger,' Solomon continues, the watchful dark eyes observing, but the tone unchanged, 'won't let me buy them the house.'

'Because it's too big,' Macklan says.

'Nonsense.'

'We're perfectly happy where we are. Aren't we, Tracey? Tell him we don't want it.'

Tracey looks at her belly; doesn't quite reply.

'We can survive perfectly well on our own, can't we, Trace?'

'Of course we can,' she mutters. 'But it *is* a lovely house . . .'

'You see? At least your future wife has some sense! It's by far the nicest house in the village.'

Macklan sighs. 'We don't need the nicest house in the village.'

'I didn't say you did, Mack. Nobody mentioned *need*. Don't be such a prig.'

'Anyway, I don't want you thinking, just because you buy us a house—'

'Oh, bollocks! I'm not thinking anything at all. I'm just trying to give you a fucking wedding present. By the way, Fanny,' he says, turning abruptly to her, not quite smiling, 'you conked out last night before I could get you anything to eat. You must be starving.'

'Oh, yes . . . Yes . . . Sorry about that. I don't remember how I got upstairs. You must've had to—'

'Mmmmm,' he says.

Fanny's whole body jolts. *Did he say that? Did he say it? Why?* Impossible to tell. She peers at him. He's wearing a dark pullover, which emphasises the shoulders, the chest . . . and he's leaning back, resting against the desk, hands in pockets, legs stretched out in front of him. He's watching her, with his black eyes. She can't tell if he's laughing.

'Mmmmm,' she says stupidly. As if once hadn't been enough. She can feel his eyes still on her, waiting. She adds, 'Mmm. I mean *yes*. I must have been heavy. So . . . sorry about that.'

'Not at all,' he says, with the flicker of a smile. 'It was lovely, actually . . . Anyway,' he straightens up, 'you must be starving. Have you had breakfast yet?'

'No.' Thud. It reminds her why she's down here. Reminds her of the other people in the room. And everything else. All her troubles. The knot of dread in her stomach at the thought of that open road, and the next beginning. And not even Louis to depend on. Reminds her that it's time to get going. 'I've not really got time for breakfast. I've come for the car keys, Solomon. So please . . .'

Solomon doesn't move at once. He glances at Macklan and Tracey, who glance at him, and then at Fanny, and then at each other, and then back at Fanny again.

'Please,' Fanny says again, sensing some kind of

conspiracy, not liking it at all. '*Please.*' She holds out a hand. 'The party's starting any minute. I really have to go before it begins.'

'But why?' Macklan asks.

Why? She glares at him. Why? A very simple question . . . *Why?* The answer to which has temporarily escaped her. She feels a lump in her throat, and a familiar feeling of panic rising. Why? Because that's what happens next, of course. 'Because . . . I really have to go.'

'Well, I'm sorry,' says Tracey suddenly. 'That doesn't sound like a reason to me. Anyway, you can't. Not now. Everyone's expecting you. We've got the whole damn village coming out for you, Fanny Flynn. You can't leave now!'

Fanny blinks. Doesn't quite hear her. Isn't listening. She looks at Solomon. 'Solomon,' she says, trying to sound calm, 'give me the keys. I *insist* that you give me my car keys.'

Silence, while his and Fanny's eyes lock in private combat, until, with a small shrug, Solomon once again pulls the keys from his trouser pocket. Fanny steps up, hand outstretched. She pauses. 'I'm sorry,' she mutters, 'thank you – for everything,' and lifts her hand to take the keys. In a flash Tracey lunges forward and snatches them.

'You're not going anywhere, Fanny Flynn. I told you, you're staying here. Solomon's been working bloody hard for this. We all have.'

'I don't— Working bloody hard for *what*, anyway?' says Fanny. 'Tracey, this isn't funny.'

'I never said it was funny.'

'Give me the keys.'

'No.' She hands them to Macklan.

'Macklan? Give me the keys!'

With a sheepish grin he puts them behind his back, and shakes his head. 'The party's kicking off in half a minute,' he says. 'You're not leaving Fiddleford now. Sorry, Fanny. But you can't. We're not letting you.'

'Solomon? . . . But this is— This is— Give me the fucking keys!'

'Errr.' He folds his arms across his chest, pretends to think about it. 'Urmmmm.' And grins. 'Nope.'

They hear a bang on the front door. 'Hello? Anyone about?'

'It's open!' Solomon bellows. 'Come on in! We're in here. Perfect timing, if I may say so. Things were just beginning to get a little bit tetchy.'

Fanny sees a flock of familiar faces trudging across the hall towards her. All of them – Grey, Messy and the new baby Jason, Charlie, Jo and the little twins, and finally the General – are wearing identical white, baggy T-shirts.

'What the—' Fanny looks from one to the other. 'I don't—' She turns back to Solomon. He, Tracey and Mack are pulling their own jerseys off to reveal the same T-shirts underneath. Each one bears the same simple message across its chest:

FIDDLEFORD
NEEDS
FANNY FLYNN

'Sorry,' says Jo matter-of-factly, when Fanny remains too flabbergasted to speak. 'We didn't really have time to come up with anything snappier. But I think it gets the message across. Plus,' she spins herself around: 'MISS FLYNN FOR HEAD' is printed on the back, 'we've got that as well.' She turns back to the other three. 'Louis kept coming up with smutty puns, so we finally sent him off with Reverend Hodge as a punishment. They're doing the trailer together.'

'Have the others arrived?' Solomon asks.

'W-what others?' says Fanny. 'What is all this?'

'Scarlett Mozely will be here any minute,' Charlie Maxwell McDonald says. 'She's just called. Unfortunately, Kitty's coming too, but it can't be helped. And the rest are arriving now. The vicar's still attaching things to the trailer, and Louis's trying to get all the children on to it for the photograph.' He laughs. 'We're going to need you, Fanny, at some point.' Charlie smiles at her. 'You seem to be the only one who can control them.'

'Louis? *Louis*? What trailer? What photograph? Control *who*? What's going on? Really, this is— I don't know what it is. But *I've got to go*.' Suddenly she spots the General, standing slightly apart from the group, miserably ill at ease in his T-shirt, the first he's worn in his life – and she stops. She'd been planning to abandon them all without even bothering to say goodbye, and they have done all this, put on these absurd T-shirts . . . A laugh escapes her. 'You all look completely ridiculous! But I'm— Thank you . . . I don't know what to say. I'm—'

'You don't need to say anything,' interrupts Solomon, glancing at his watch. 'From what I understand, the last time you said anything on this subject you incriminated yourself so badly you forced the poor Reverend to suspend you.'

'That's right. And then she bloody well resigned,' says the General. 'Which resignation, incidentally,' he adds, 'in case you aren't aware, can't be accepted since it hasn't yet been delivered in writing.'

'All you have to do, Fanny, is be there for the party,' Grey tells her.

'It's a day in your life,' Solomon says. They wait.

'Just stay for the party, that's all,' agrees Messy.

'Come on, Fanny,' snaps Grey. 'Don't a stupid cow.'

'Fine,' she says. 'I'll stay. Just today. But after that, you know, if it doesn't work – and it won't, because I did *do* what Robert said I did. I did kiss Scarlett Mozely and I did—'

'Oh, shut up!' they all groan at once.

'And after that I've really got to go.'

'Yes, yes, obviously,' says Solomon.

'I'm not joking. I've actually decided to go to Cuba.'

'Cuba, Darlington,' he says vaguely, standing up, and shooing everyone back out towards the hall. 'What's the difference, eh, Fanny? As long as it's full of strangers . . . I get the distinct impression,' he raises his voice to include everyone, 'that Fanny Flynn doesn't like it much when people grow too attached to her. Is that right?'

'That's rubbish!' she says irritably. 'That's completely wrong.'

'Any more,' he adds, 'than she likes *herself* to grow too attached to people.'

'Oh, rubbish!'

'Or to places, come to that.'

'*Rubbish*.'

'Not rubbish.'

'*Fuck off!*'

Everyone laughs, except Fanny.

'Right then,' he says, striding out towards the garden. 'Come on then, everyone. Let's get on with this. Is it too early for alcohol?'

80

'*Now, Kitty,*' Scarlett says. Mother and daughter are sitting in the car directly outside Solomon's house, having parked up exactly where they weren't supposed to, directly opposite the door in the wall leading to Solomon's garden. It's twelve noon. They're half an hour late, and Scarlett still hasn't told her. She takes yet another deep breath. 'Kitty,' she says, '*I'm going to take off my jersey . . .*'

Kitty glances at her. 'I should think so.'

'You may like to know that the reason I've insisted on wearing this jersey all morning . . . is because underneath I'm wearing a T-shirt.'

'Well, good. I should hope so. Ha! Unless you plan on doing a Fanny Flynn – which, Scarlett, I most definitely do not advise. You haven't got the figure. Come on. Let's go.'

'Kitty, my T-shirt has a message on it—'

'Oh, do shut up.'

'Which you're not going to like. So I'm going to show you now, OK? Before we go any further. You have to realise, Kitty, before you go in there, that the majority of people at Solomon's party will be wearing the same thing. Not only that, they're going to give me a microphone, and I'm going to make an announcement denying what Mr White accused her of.' Slowly, clumsily, she peels off her outer layer, turns her chest to her mother. She closes her eyes, wincing in anticipation of the explosion.

'AT LAST!' yells Jo Maxwell McDonald, running across the road and yanking open Scarlett's door. 'Thank God. I was beginning to think you'd never make it. Oh. Hi, Kitty—' She turns back to Scarlett, almost drags her out of the car. 'We're ready to go. Louis and the vicar have got everyone on to the trailer.' She ushers Scarlett back across the village street, puts a hand on the door leading through to the garden – and stops. 'You're sure about this, aren't you?'

'Of course I am.'

'Not too nervous?'

'I don't think so.'

'It's easy. Just stand in front of the trailer, with all the children behind you. And say whatever you like.'

Scarlett nods. 'I'm going to say that Miss Flynn has never gone anywhere near me. She's never touched me—'

'Scarlett, Fanny admits she gave you a kiss. I don't think you should lie. I think you should just say—'

'What, and let Robert White twist all my words around? Not likely. Anyway,' Scarlett regards Jo, 'so far as I remember, it's the truth. I've no memory of Miss Flynn kissing me whatsoever. It's probably just wishful thinking on Miss Flynn's part.'

A cheer erupts as Scarlett and Jo appear side by side. Jo's eyes scan the crowd: a mass of white T-shirts, with the occasional defiant blob of colour; about eighty people in all, if you counted the *Western Weekly Gazette* man, the glamorous girl from the *Telegraph Magazine*, and the boy from Atlas Radio. Not a bad turn-out for a small village . . .

There is Mrs Hooper, cheering like mad, and Macklan and Tracey, and beside Tracey, her mother and father, not cheering, perhaps – certainly not wearing the T-shirts – but present, at least. There's Louis, T-shirt obscured somewhat by his three cameras. He's clapping nonchalantly, muttering something – something delightful, if her rapturous expression is much to go by – into the ear of his glamorous *Telegraph Magazine* colleague. And behind them, Reverend Hodge in T-shirt and dog collar is talking to the marvellous Maurice Morrison (pink shirted) who's brought along his downtrodden, peculiarly hideous wife, Sue Marie. There's young Colin Fairwell, chatting up one of the Guppy cousins, and the General talking to Pru Ashford; Mr and Mrs Cooke from the pub talking to her husband, Charlie; Grey and Messy McShane . . . And there in the corner, in the shade of the cherry tree, Russell Guppy, looking surly in his state-of-the-art wheelchair. (He hadn't wanted to come but Dane, in his misplaced gratitude, had insisted on wheeling him along anyway.)

'Everyone,' says Jo. Nobody bloody well listens. 'Excuse me, everyone. Could we have a bit of— Guys, honestly. Could we have a bit of— *Excuse me*—'

'Quiet, please,' comes Mrs Hooper's voice, from the middle of the crowd. 'MISS SCARLETT MOZELY WOULD LIKE TO SPEAK.'

Cheers all round: from the trailer of children behind her, who've barely acknowledged her existence before now; from her mother, shambling in through the wooden door beside her. 'Good for you, Scarlett,' yells Kitty carelessly. 'And for God's sake, REMEMBER TO PLUG THE BOOK!'

Someone hands Scarlett a microphone. Reporters from Atlas Radio and the *Western Weekly Gazette* edge forward. Louis's camera whirrs.

'Well, everyone,' she begins. 'Sorry to interrupt. I just wanted to say that we all really like having Miss Flynn at our school. She is the best teacher I've ever had. The best

487

teacher I think any of us has ever had. And not only that, everyone, I want to make it clear that I completely and utterly deny—' A hand reaches out from behind her and snatches up the microphone.

'Ladies and gents – sorry about that, Scarlett.' It is Solomon. He sends her a brief smile, but he looks edgy. There is a muscle going in one cheek. 'Sorry to interrupt. But Mr Robert White would like to say a few words.'

Solomon holds out an arm to the house. Heads turn. From around the back of the building three figures emerge and slowly begin making their way towards them. The middle one, long and lanky, his bony arms hugging tightly at its own midriff, appears to be finding it very difficult to walk. He is flanked by two strangers, bull necked, forty-something, hard eyed and shiny suited: both unmistakable villains.

A gasp of ghoulish pleasure sweeps through the crowd as it parts to allow the men through. They come to a stop beneath the bunting-covered trailer, right beside Scarlett, who looks terrified. Kitty, standing behind her, instinctively takes Scarlett's arm and pulls her away.

'Well?' enquires Solomon coldly, of the black-and-purple football which was once Robert's head. 'What have you got to say for yourself today?'

A trembling, wind-chapped hand emerges from the huddle of unhappy body parts. It takes the proffered microphone.

'My name is Robert White.' Robert's familiar, reedy voice breaks off. He clears his throat. Starts again. The rest of his speech is delivered in a slurring, galloping, whispering mono-tone. But it echoes through all fourteen amplifiers across the dumbstruck garden. Not a word is missed:

'the allegations I made recently against Miss Fanny Flynn were a complete invention by myself and I apologise for any incon-venience this may have caused I am a liar and I would therefore like to tender my resignation from the school which resignation I have here put in writing thank you.'

An astonished silence while Solomon takes the microphone from him, and the two ageing thugs step up to escort him away.

'Bloody well ACCEPTED!' yells out Tracey.

'And Good Riddance to Bad Rubbish!' Kitty shouts. For the second time in a week.

It breaks the spell. The children break into a unified whoop of approval, and then so does the village, so loud that the roar of Fiddleford's rejoicing can be heard for miles around. It thunders in Robert's ears as he staggers away down the village street, climbs into his faithful Panda and drives away, never to return again.

81

Solomon roams his own party, not enjoying it very much. He can't walk a centimetre without someone accosting him, mouthing platitudes at him and blocking his progress. He doesn't want to talk to any of them. He already knows they've been lucky with the weather. All he wants to do is to find Fanny.

First Mrs Guppy. 'Macklan seems like a nice boy,' she said.

'Thank you,' Solomon said. 'I've always thought so.'

She nudged up a little closer. He could smell the sweat. 'I suppose you'll be settling a bit of your money on him now, will you? With the baby. Because they shan't be getting anything from us, unfortunately. Unfortunately, we don't have too much spare cash to be handing around . . .'

Then the marvellous Maurice Morrison. 'Solomon Creasey, isn't it?' he said, his handsome, pleasant face fizzing with silent agendas. 'I do so hope you don't mind me barging in. *Wonderful* party. Really *terrific*. Haven't we been lucky with the weather?'

'Yes. Lovely weather. I'm glad you could come. I was actually looking for Fanny Flynn. Have you seen her?'

'*Nooo*. I am *sorry!* Only I've just got off the line to the agent. The chap who's dealing with the Old Rectory sale. There seems to be some sort of confusion.'

'Oh?' says Solomon, as if he couldn't guess.

Morrison's face twists into an agonising, tooth-baring smile. 'Ha! Silly question, when you have such a beautiful home of your own. But – are you by some chance trying to buy it?'

'I've bought it.'

'Well, ha, *no*. That can't be right, you see. I'm actually – rather, my wife and I are actually – *en route* to a special early viewing. The man sweetly *assured* me we were going to get first dibs. So, Solomon— May I call you Solomon? I don't quite see how it's possible—'

'Ah!' says Solomon. 'But it's the nicest house in the village, Mr Morrison.'

'Well, yes. Apart from the Manor, of course.'

'So I bought it.' He spots Kitty Mozely making her way over. 'Excuse me.'

But it's marvellous Maurice she's after. 'Hello, Mr Morrison,' she breathes over him. 'We haven't met. I'm Kitty Mozely. The writer. And a school governor, as well, actually. Just like you.'

'Ah!' says Mr Morrison, unconsciously pinching at the cotton of Solomon's T-shirt, to prevent him from slipping away. 'What a pleasure.'

'I wanted to thank you for your "anonymous" donation to the school library,' Kitty says. 'Since nobody else will actually come out and say it. £50,000, Solomon. Did you hear? We're very very grateful.'

Mr Morrison smiles, albeit a little uncomfortably. 'As a matter of fact, Geraldine's already— Please. I beg of you. Don't mention it again. You embarrass me.'

Solomon, casually unhooking the fingers from his T-shirt, catches Morrison's eye. 'Really, Mr Morrison. *£50,000?* How incredibly generous of you!' Maurice Morrison blushes. 'Well – no – I . . .'

Solomon winks at him, bellows with laughter, and strides away.

'So, anyway, Maurice,' Kitty says blithely, delighted to get him on his own, 'I've just been speaking to your – extraordinary – wife. Isn't she – wonderful?'

'I'm glad you think so,' says Morrison sourly.

Kitty gurgles wickedly, gusting Morrison with alcohol and cigarettes. She loops her arm through his and with light but iron-hard resolve, starts them walking along. 'So tell me, Mr Morrison,' she growls, 'do you play croquet?' She looks up into his eyes, leans forward, pushing her breasts together. Maurice Morrison half-gags in revulsion, but she doesn't seem to spot it. She murmurs into his ear, 'But first, Maurice – May I call you Maurice? Do tell me – it'd save so much time – *are you circumcised?*'

'Splendid party, Mr Creasey! *Great fun!* Aren't we lucky with the weather?'

'Thank you, Reverend. Very lucky. Have you seen Fanny anywhere?'

He has not. Nobody has. Solomon's looked for her all over the garden. He's shouted for her all over the house. Now the vicar's standing in front of him, with apparently no intention of ever moving aside. 'Only, word reaches me, Mr Creasey – and you will forgive me for bringing this up, but it's a small village, and we all tend to get to know each other's business, don't we? . . . Did you, by any chance— Am I right in thinking, Mr Creasey – and once again I do apologise for mentioning it – but what with— I must say I was under the impression that those *extraordinary gentlemen* who escorted poor Mr White seemed to be acquaintances of yours . . .'

Solomon nods. 'One should never forget one's old friends. Isn't that right, vicar? Very important.'

'Oh, yes. Absolutely. *Quite*. But it begs the question, Mr Creasey, it does—'

'Yes?'

'Well, they seemed – how can I put it? – of the *villainous* variety, if you'll forgive me for saying so. And one does hear rumours. Have you at some point in your – manifestly glittering career – spent some small amount of time at – ahh – *Her Majesty's pleasure?*'

Solomon grins devilishly. 'Now who, I wonder, would have told you a thing like that?'

'Oh, you know how it is. Small villages and so on.' He laughs nervously. 'We all have our little secrets!'

'Is that right, Reverend? And what's yours?'

'*Me?*' The vicar gives a high-pitched giggle. WANKING flashes up in capitals in his rusty old head. 'Gosh. Never mind me . . . I only mention it because, well . . .' He flaps his forearms; an incongruously extravagant movement. 'Former convicts, shall we say, are not *strictly speaking* allowed to serve on governing bodies.'

'What about Grey?'

'Mmm? Gosh! Well, exactly. Exactly. No, I suppose I'm just being nosy, Mr Creasey! Never mind. Well,' he says, backing away. 'I suppose I should let you get on. Do let me know if you find Fanny. I mean,' he frowns, 'I *assume* we can expect her back at work on Monday?'

'I'll tell you,' Solomon says heavily, 'as soon as I find her . . . And congratulations, by the way. On the croquet. What a player!'

'Oh! You're too kind. Too kind, Solomon . . . I must say, I've always been very *keen*. But you know, if it were simply a matter of talent I fear the dreaded Miss Mozely might have reigned supreme . . . And haven't we been lucky with the weather? . . .'

*   *   *

He finds her eventually. Having checked every other room in the house. He finds her crouched beneath the basin in the downstairs lavatory, with Brute at her side, panting from the heat. Solomon squeezes in beside them without a word.

'Hey, Solomon,' she says.

'What's up?'

'What? Oh, I dunno . . .'

'But we won!'

She nods. 'I should be happy. I mean, I *am* happy. I'm so *grateful*. I'm so bloody touched . . .' Her head drops. She covers her face with her hands. 'I just . . .'

He puts an arm around her, over the edge of the lavatory, under the bar for the hand-towel rack. It's a tight squeeze, what with Brute as well. 'Hey,' he murmurs. She can feel his breath on her cheek. 'Fanny, you're not duty bound to stay with us, just because we want to keep you . . . That was never the point of the exercise.'

'I know! I mean, I do know— Oh, bloody hell.' She sniffs, wipes her nose on the back of her hand. 'Why does it have to be so complicated?'

'But it isn't.'

'I thought I'd be on the road by now. Everything would all be so simple. Just me and Brute . . . you know, travelling light . . . starting again.'

'And you still can start again. If you want to. Any time you want. *If it's what you want* . . . Where are you thinking of going?'

'*I don't know.*' It sounds terrible.

It makes Solomon snort with laughter. 'So give yourself some time. And you can start again tomorrow when you've thought of somewhere to – start. Or the next day, if you feel like it. *You can always start again* . . . So why don't you wait until the end of term? It's only a couple of weeks. And after that—'

'I've got nowhere to stay.'

'Stay here. If you want.'

A look of panic crosses her face.

'And then in the summer if you feel like pissing off to Cuba . . .'

She looks up at him, smiles. 'Or Darlington . . .'

'Or Darlington. Or Reading . . .' His voice is very low.

'Or the Coral Reef . . .'

'Or Jamaica . . .'

'Or . . .' But he's so damn close, she can't remember anywhere else. Not a place in the world. 'Or maybe I could just stay with you in Fiddleford . . .' she says. She hears herself saying. 'I mean for a while . . .'

He kisses her. 'And we can just take it day by day . . .' And he kisses her again.

'. . . day by day . . .'

'. . . by day . . .'

The door rattles. 'Mr Creasey, sir. Are you in there? You've got to come quick!'

Fanny leans back against the waste pipe and sighs. 'Yes, what is it, Dane?'

'Oh! . . . Miss Flynn . . .'

'What's up?'

'Nothing! I mean— Nothing. Only someone's stuck a load of fireworks under my Uncle Russell's wheelchair and it wasn't me. But I sees them, and I says to myself, oh my crumblin' Mondays, someone's going to get hurt. So I rushes out to find you . . .' His face breaks into a grin. They can hear his grin through the door. 'Scuse me, Miss Flynn, but is Mr Creasey in there, too?'

'None of your business. What're you saying about these fireworks? Have you just left them there?'

''Cause if he is, Miss Flynn, tell him. He's going to miss a big explosion if he doesn't get out here quick. A mighty

495

blow-up, with Uncle Russell blasting off into the sky just like a rocket, I imagine. You'd better tell him.'

Solomon smiles. Kisses her one more time. 'Seriously,' he says, 'we've got to get that boy some help.'

'. . . How about Sri Lanka, Clive? We could open a little hotel. A smart little boutique hotel. And,' she leans across Swindon's Happy Eater dining table, pulls down on her baseball cap and drops her voice even lower, to a whisper, 'I mean, think of the staff, Clive. My God! We'd never have to do another chore the rest of our lives!'

CRRR-Bleepbleep-BRRRR. 'Is there any ketchup?'

'I didn't go to law school for four years,' snarls Clive, 'to wind up running a fucking doss house. Anywhere. Least of all in Sri Lanka. Ollie, I've told you four times already. Switch off that bloody toy. Now.'

CRRR-Bleepbleep-BRRRR. 'Is there any ketchup?'

'Which is why, Geraldine darling,' he continues, 'we must all go back to London and face the music. That way Ollie can learn from his mistakes.'

CRRR-Bleepbleep-BRRRR. 'Mum, I really want some ketchup.'

'Are you insane, Clive? They'll lock him up! They'll lock up our only little boy! How about Jamaica? Jamaica's lovely. We could open a golf club. Just think,' she adds wistfully, 'no more English winters. It'll be terrific. We can get involved with the local community. Do something with the kids, perhaps. Put something back . . .'

'Geraldine . . .' Patiently, Clive Adams lays down his knife and fork, wipes the HP sauce from around his bloodless lips. (Chips, beans and bacon cheeseburger; possibly the most delicious lunch he's eaten since leaving university.) 'Geraldine, it's highly unlikely they'll "lock him up". Don't be so hysterical. And if they do . . .' He smiles, rests a dry hand on his wife's bony shoulder. 'Darling. I know it's horrid, but as responsible parents we have to think of the Big Picture. We have to think of ourselves. Because if we're unhappy what use will we possibly be to our only-little-boy then? I don't want to live in some God-awful colonial outpost for the rest of my life any more than you do.'

'Actually, Clive, yes, I do.'

'I want to put this whole, silly "rural" experiment behind us. Once and for all. And I think it's in Ollie's interests –'

CRRR-Bleepbleep-BRRRR.

'– that we return to London as soon as possible. I've already contacted dear old Vernon and he's assured me the job's there. If I want it. Which, Geraldine, I do.'

Geraldine gasps. 'You . . . bastard!' she says in amazement.

'Not at all. I've thought it through very clearly—'

'You want to turn him in!'

'I want to behave like an adult, Geraldine.'

'You want to turn your own son in!'

'That's not the expression I'd use—'

CrrrBlipBRRRCCRRLRPblpCrrrblipblopSPLASHSHSH SHSH.

Outside the lights are flashing. Clive's pale face is turning alternately blue, white, blue, white. They hear the car doors slamming, the noisy hiss of the walkie-talkies.

'Oh, bollocks,' Ollie says . . . GAME OVER . . . GAME OVER . . . GAME OVER . . . 'Stop jogging the table everyone.'

Ten Steps to Happiness

Daisy Waugh

She's left the rat race behind – but taken her contacts book with her.

Jo Smiley abandons her glamorous London lifestyle to decamp to a draughty manor house with her new husband, the divine Charlie. Happiness awaits: all they need is a plan to make it pay.

Deep in the English countryside, Fiddleford makes an ideal refuge from the media. And as the first few paparazzi-battered guests arrive, Jo allows herself to hope. The house might be crumbling, the chef temperamental, but the Fiddleford magic never fails … apparently.

But while for the guests, happiness might be a warm cow's nose and a ramble in the wild and beautiful gardens, the local council has other ideas. Suddenly Jo and Charlie's rural retreat looks shaky. Can they fend off the officials, save their dream and stay on their own path to happiness?

'Sparkling fun.' *Heat*

'Full of laugh-out-loud funny bits.' *New Woman*

ISBN 0 00 711905 4

The New You Survival Kit

Daisy Waugh

Is it time to break all the rules?

Jo Smiley has got a desperately glamorous job, she's a member of all the right clubs, and her friends are the coolest and cruellest in London.

Ed is a TV producer famous for his gritty and important documentaries. He's also a liar, a cheat and a phoney. In other words, he's Mr Right.

And **Charlie's** a charmingly clueless pub singer in cowboy boots. Until he meets **Jo** who thinks she can make him a social success.

But who is really showing who the way to survive? Will **Charlie** learn to play by the rules? Or is it **Jo's** breathless life that needs the makeover? And is it too late for either of them?

From PR heaven to paparazzi hell, this wickedly funny novel has all the social tactics you need to survive the twenty-first century.

'A hilarious, witty comedy of modern manners.'

ADELE PARKS, author of *Playing Away*

ISBN 0 00 711906 2